THE MURDEROUS AFFAIR AT STONE MANOR

LAURA STEWART

BLOODHOUND
— BOOKS —

Copyright © 2021 Laura Stewart

The right of Laura Stewart to be identified as the Author of the Work has been asserted by her in accordance to the Copyright, Designs and Patents Act 1988.

First published in 2021 by Bloodhound Books.

Apart from any use permitted under UK copyright law, this publication may only be reproduced, stored, or transmitted, in any form, or by any means, with prior permission in writing of the publisher or, in the case of reprographic production, in accordance with the terms of licences issued by the Copyright Licensing Agency.

All characters in this publication are fictitious and any resemblance to real persons, living or dead, is purely coincidental.

www.bloodhoundbooks.com

Print ISBN 978-1-914614-14-9

To Pete, Thalia, Adeline and Oriana

1

Amelia Adams stopped telling people she worked for an advertising agency about a week after starting at Morrison, Gray and Compton. The words 'advertising agency' conjured up visions of power meetings and takeaway coffees littering her desk as she worked into the early hours of the morning on a multi-million-pound project: a far cry from her actual job. Arriving at her desk half an hour late courtesy of some thoughtlessly wet leaves on the railway line, her coat dripping with rain and her feet squelching in her Jimmy Choo rip-offs which pinched just a little too much to be comfortable (they'd never stretched with her feet as the shop assistant assured her they would), Amelia was met by a pile of mail on her desk resembling the leaning tower of Pisa. Amelia moved the date stamp on to Monday 2nd October and picked the first letter off the top.

To anyone visiting, the high-tech offices of Morrison, Gray and Compton looked impressive. The steel- and chrome-edged design matched the chiselled jaws and sharp tailoring of the Young Upwardly Mobile Advertising Executives, the smell of their raw ambition masked by the weekly delivery of lilies artfully arranged in the half-dozen vases dotted around the reception area. Amelia had been working there for almost a year; she'd arrived as a temp and after six weeks, when she hadn't complained about the mind-numbing tedium of the job, they'd bought out her contract.

She now despised the smell of lilies.

Heaping an extra spoonful of coffee into her mug, the one the previous incumbent had left in the top drawer with the 'You don't have to be crazy to work here, but it helps' gag emblazoned around the rim, Amelia reminded herself she was lucky she had a job at all. With depressing headlines of soaring unemployment figures, she knew a crap job was better than no job just as the damp shoebox of a flat she lived in was better than an actual damp box to sleep in. She needed to be grateful for what she had, and Amelia had a little something over and above her secretary's salary to encourage her to turn up to work each morning.

It was the oldest cliché in the book – a boss and his secretary. *She* didn't mind so much if others in the company knew – it might mean she would stop getting the worst jobs handed down to her, but for Jonathan it was different. As head of finance, he had to remain above office gossip and speculation. It didn't seem to bother him that the rest of the typing pool had bets on him shagging Melissa from the director's suite, but evidently a lowly receptionist like Amelia was beneath him.

Quite literally, Mondays, Wednesdays and Fridays.

Five months previously, when they'd had their first, furtive snog in the stationery cupboard, Amelia didn't mind their relationship starting off slowly. And she had to admit, the sneaking about added a certain frisson to their relationship. It also meant she'd stayed far longer in the job than she'd intended. She didn't like the job but she *did* like Jonathan – how could she not? He had romantic-hero good looks. He was tall and whip-slim with a shock of blond hair, dimpled chin, long blond eyelashes framing beautiful blue eyes and he had a knack of smiling and looking like a naughty schoolboy which resulted in her forgiving him anything. But although at first she had welcomed a slow start, as the months rolled on nothing changed in their relationship. Amelia had tried pushing for them to be seen as an item and that was when Jonathan dropped the bombshell that he'd never be open about their relationship while they worked in the same office.

And in the present work climate, finding another job wasn't that easy, even a badly paid job where the office manager treated you like their personal slave.

Amelia's stomach gave a growl of hunger and she rummaged about her bag for breakfast. Unable to locate even a fun-size Mars bar, she did, however, find the latest Denholm Armitage crime thriller she'd bought yesterday, nestled in the folds of her oversized tote. Her fingers danced over the embossed gold writing before she surreptitiously opened the cover, already desperate for lunchtime, when she could immerse herself in a world of murder and intrigue – even if only for forty-five minutes.

She'd just skim-read the opening paragraph, describing a mutilated body washing up on a beach, when an all too real shadow of doom loomed over her desk. Doom, smelling of Youth Dew – an irony obviously lost on Doreen, head administrator, pushing sixty-four and as dehydrated as a Cup a Soup.

'I take it you'll be making up the half hour at the end of the day?'

'Of course,' Amelia said, dropping her bag and deftly kicking it under her desk to hide the book.

Slightly deflated at no argument or offered excuses, Doreen heaved up her right bosom with her forearm. 'Mr Harris wants to see you,' she said frostily. She looked her up and down in distaste. 'You might want to do something with your hair first.'

'Oh, I'm sure he won't mind me being a little... *moist*,' Amelia said saucily, smoothing down her hair. Cut into a gamine style which accentuated her petite heart-shaped face, it was the colour of rich chocolate ganache, which brought out the warm hazel tones of her eyes. What could be an unforgiving haircut on some worked for Amelia as it juxtaposed with her curves, which were pure femininity.

With a disgruntled huff Doreen led the way past the other Stepford secretaries to Jonathan's office, rapped on the door with great efficiency and opened it wide.

'Amelia to see you.'

'Thank you, Doreen. Please make sure we're not disturbed.' Jonathan smiled at the older woman as he smoothed down his tie.

'Of course,' she simpered and Amelia could have sworn Doreen dropped a curtsey as she backed through the door.

Jumping up from his swivel chair, Jonathan twisted the venetian blinds shut and flipped the lock on the door before pulling Amelia towards him, dropping butterfly kisses along her collarbone.

'God, the weekend always seems intolerably long, I can't wait for tonight,' he groaned into her neck as he pulled her towards him and she was engulfed in the familiar scents of toothpaste, hair product and his expensive aftershave.

'Well, you're the one with the hectic extended family of cousins, nieces and nephews you have to visit,' she said, studiously keeping her voice light. From the outset he'd been the one who'd come up with the rule that they didn't see each other over the weekend; that was his family time.

She very gently pushed his head away from her neck. Delicious as the kisses were, she really needed to get back to her desk otherwise she'd have to work through lunchtime to get through the pile of mail. 'You wanted to see me, sir?' she purred, clasping her hands behind her back and swinging her body side to side, playfully.

'I always want to see you. Every last inch of you. Naked...'

'Jonathan!' She laughed in mock outrage.

'I want you to take some things down for me,' he whispered as he fiddled with her belt.

'I forgot my dictation pad.' Amelia laughed, her stomach contracting with lust as he kissed her neck.

'That wasn't what I had in mind,' he murmured as his hands inched up her pencil skirt, stroking the inside of her thigh. He stopped abruptly. 'You never wear stockings anymore,' he said petulantly.

Amelia didn't like to tell him she couldn't afford to keep buying a new pair each day; if only he didn't always want to rip them off with his teeth.

'Let's have a quickie, I've not got a meeting for another half hour,' he coaxed, pulling her over to his large mahogany desk.

'Who said romance was dead!' Amelia said, evading his embrace. She didn't want to act like a killjoy but having sex on his desk didn't hold as much allure since the time she caught her left buttock in the metal jaws of a lever arch file.

'We'll be quiet,' he said, widening his puppy-dog eyes and hooking his finger inside the waistband of her skirt, pulling her towards him again.

'You're too much of a screamer.' She laughed, batting him off.

'Only cause you drive me wild,' he growled into her neck.

She wriggled away from him, playfully slapping his hands away. 'What I really want to do is have you tell me the itinerary of our holiday.' She'd been counting down the days to their weekend in Sweden since Jonathan had first surprised her with the suggestion a month before.

But her excitement evaporated as he tensed up and drew away from her.

'Ahh. Well. There's a bit of a problem with that,' he said.

She watched him walk around his desk and sit back down in his chair.

'What kind of problem?' she asked, keeping her voice light as she smoothed down her skirt.

'I don't think I'll be able to get the time off,' he said, flicking through his signature book.

Eventually, after a couple of minutes when she hadn't said anything, he looked up at her, fiddling with the knot of his tie.

She folded her arms over her chest, drawing herself up to her full height of five foot seven, five inches of which were scarlet patent leather stilettos. 'It's a weekend. From Friday night to Sunday morning, none of which coincides with office hours.' She tried to keep her voice calm, but could feel her eyes start to smart from disappointment.

Jonathan began to click and unclick the top of his rollerball pen.

'You were the one who bloody well suggested it in the first place!'

He winced as she swore. 'Shhhh, someone will hear.'

Now he was concerned with keeping quiet!

'Look, we'll try and get away in a few weeks, maybe after Christmas,' he tried to reason.

But Amelia was in no mood for being reasonable.

'I wanted to go away *this* weekend,' she said, not caring that she sounded like a toddler on the verge of a tantrum.

'Oh, baby, we'll get away soon. Let's face it, it was only going to be to Stockholm, hardly the most exciting place in the world.'

Maybe not to Jonathan, but she'd been ridiculously excited

to be in the country that had produced the crime writers Henning Mankell and Stieg Larsson and couldn't wait to wander the streets and look at the same sights the fictional characters Wallander and Lisbeth Salander had, before her. As the only thing Jonathan ever read was *Men's Health* magazine, he just didn't have a clue what it meant to her.

He flashed her his boyishly charming 'forgive me' smile, though for once it didn't have the same effect on Amelia. He tried to cajole her into a better mood. 'Come on, cheer up, I'll take you out to dinner tonight.'

She bristled. 'Where?'

'There's a charming little out-of-the-way Italian I've been...'

She zoned out, knowing the routine – they never went anywhere trendy or new or local in case someone from work saw them. For a man who took great risks in his professional life, he was a pipe-and-slippers guy when it came to relationships. His office bravura masked his lost and vulnerable side and she knew she shouldn't be so angry with him, but she now wanted more from the relationship than secretive sex and dimly lit restaurants.

'Why can't we go to the new Argentinian place? Or even the Pizza Express on the main road.'

'You know a lot of the girls go there after work...' His phone buzzed and he pounced on it, obviously relieved at the interruption.

'Doreen. Yes, she's still here. One moment.' He held out the phone to Amelia. 'It's for you, a lawyer?' Amelia took the phone from Jonathan, knowing that Doreen would love to know why a lawyer was contacting her, no doubt jumping to lots of wrong, but juicy, conclusions she could spread around the typing pool.

Amelia continued to glare at Jonathan across the desk as she listened to the lawyer. A few seconds later she put down the receiver.

'That was Dotty's lawyer, everything's been settled and I've just to go round there and sign a couple of documents.'

Jonathan nodded encouragingly, his relief at the subject change palpable. 'Ah yes, your aunt. Your mother's sister, wasn't it?'

Amelia refrained from clobbering him over the head with his desktop stapler. She'd told him enough times about Dotty, but he never seemed to take any of it in.

'No, she was my godmother. I used to call her Aunty Dot, but she wasn't my real, flesh-and-blood aunt. She was an old friend of my mother's, they met when she and Dad were posted to France. Dotty had a house there and was their neighbour. Dotty was godmother to my brother Toby and I, then became our guardian and looked after us when Mum and Dad died,' she said, prompting Jonathan to remember, but he just nodded blankly at Amelia. It was difficult for Amelia to put into words just what Dotty meant as she'd been so much more than a godmother to Amelia and Toby.

Her own parents had died when Amelia was very young but apart from eavesdropping on hushed conversations behind closed doors and being passed around a selection of relatives she and her younger brother had never met before, Amelia hadn't really been touched by her parents' death. Being packed off to boarding school from an early age with another load of ex-pat offspring, Amelia had only very hazy memories of them and until Dorothea Campbell-Delaney stepped in to take charge, she and Toby never had any secure base to call home.

She and her brother continued to board at school and Dotty wasn't really meant to do anything other than be there if there was an emergency, but she'd looked after them, picking them up every Friday so they could stay with her each weekend in her crazily chaotic Chelsea flat. It was Dotty who'd started Amelia's passion for mystery and crime novels after giving her a Poirot book and soon Amelia had become charmed with the little Belgian detective as well as the genre. Dotty didn't have any family, just a couple of distant second cousins she never really talked about. She was an eccentric and Amelia loved her for it.

Her death came as a horrendous blow.

Amelia knew full well she wasn't some daft teenager anymore but suddenly, six months ago, she had waved goodbye to her previous carefree life where the worst thing to happen to her was getting dumped by a boyfriend or snapping a heel on a night out. At the age of twenty-six Amelia had to turn into a grown-up who'd had their world shattered.

With Toby off travelling, Amelia had been all on her own. There was no one else to discuss funeral arrangements with or how to word an obituary for the paper. No one else was able to collect Dotty's belongings from the hospital. Amelia had wept as she'd crammed all her godmother's beautiful clothes and jewellery into an oversized Boots carrier bag and dragged it on the underground. She'd sat hugging the bag so tightly the plastic made her lap and torso damp with perspiration but she'd been terrified someone would try and snatch it from her and get away with the emerald-and-gold bracelet she'd stashed in the toe of Dotty's taupe court shoe. Or that someone would guess the furry sleeve poking out the top of the bag wasn't fake but actually real sable and spray-paint it, and her, in disgust. The hospital had tried telling Dotty not to keep anything of value with her but her godmother was adamant she let her standards slip for no one; not for the NHS and especially not the Grim Reaper. And when Dotty was adamant, no one dared stand in her way. Even at the end, with her body shrunken and skin hanging loosely on her frame, Dorothea Campbell-Delaney was an imperious force of nature, one that no staff nurse, senior surgeon or even minister for health dared cross.

Amelia was the executor of the will and also, rather

surprisingly, a benefactor along with her brother. The Chelsea house and French holiday home were to be given, along with some of the money, to the distant members of her family, and the lawyer had confided in her that a huge chunk would be swallowed up by death duties. Amelia had nearly fainted when the lawyer told her she'd inherited a house in a village called Glencarlach, in the Scottish Highlands. Amelia had never even heard of the place. She knew Dotty was born in Scotland and her family hailed from there but since Amelia had known her, Dotty had always lived in Chelsea and she'd had no trace of a Scottish accent. Over the years, Dotty had spent occasional long weekends in Scotland, visiting an old friend, she'd said. But she never hinted that she had a house there. Even stranger, Dotty had made specific arrangements so that the house couldn't be sold on. She'd even put it in Amelia's name over a decade before so it wouldn't be liable for inheritance tax. Amelia had never even seen a photograph of the house and was deeply intrigued to see what it was like. In her mind's eye it was a lovely little whitewashed stone cottage with a real fire and low-beamed ceilings with walls a foot thick, a haven where she could seek solace from London life.

In fact, it would be perfect as a getaway for her and Jonathan.

'You know I'm inheriting the house in Scotland, why don't we go there for a weekend, in two weeks' time?'

Jonathan gave a small laugh. 'Can you really see us schlepping around a but and ben in the middle of nowhere? Darling, please don't get your hopes up, it'll probably be nothing more than an outhouse where livestock have taken up residence for the past twenty years. It's not even as if you can sell the ruddy place.'

The vision of her lovely little cottage started to crumble away from her. Jonathan dealt with facts and figures and practicalities, he didn't do romantic notions or whimsy. He liked functional hotels with power showers and room service and there was just no way he would ever find any sort of charm in a slightly dilapidated house in a windswept glen.

'D'you mind if I take an early lunch so I can go sign the papers?'

'Of course not! Why don't you leave now? I'll smooth it over with Doreen.'

Guilt made Jonathan very magnanimous.

'Oh, and one thing,' he called after her as she was leaving, 'would you also be an angel and pick up my suit from the dry cleaners?'

Steering clear of the railway station and the potential hazards of wet foliage, Amelia caught the bus to the lawyer's offices. Standing at the bus stop huddled under her umbrella, which was little use against the lashing rain, her mobile beeped at her. A text message from Jonathan. With a soaring heart, hoping he'd changed his mind about their weekend away, she opened the text, but he was merely confirming he'd booked dinner for eight o'clock and would be round at hers at seven. With a bottle of champagne.

Amelia seethed. The only bubbles she appreciated were the ones that came courtesy of a Radox bottle in a hot bath. She'd lost count of the times she'd told Jonathan she didn't like champagne; it gave her terrible heartburn. She scrabbled about her bag for her notepad. First page was her 'Top Priority To-Do List', over the page was her 'Secondary Important To-Do List' and under that she wrote 'buy indigestion tablets' before dropping the pad back in her bag.

The dry cleaners was on the way and she hopped off the bus to collect Jonathan's suit. It was the one he'd worn on their last date and she checked to make sure the shirt, tie and suit were free of the garlic oil he'd managed to splatter all over himself in his haste to hide under the table, thinking he'd seen someone from human resources. Paying with her own money, she bundled the suit over her arm and headed to see her lawyer.

Her lawyer's office was a musty time-warped relic where all modern technology was eschewed for old-fashioned pen and paper. A relic himself, James Armstrong was a gentleman who stood when a woman entered a room. He'd been readying himself for retirement by cutting down on all his cases since his firm had merged with a massive corporate behemoth and he'd vowed to leave the moment a computer or printer was foisted upon him. Judging by the state of his room, Amelia noted he'd still managed to avoid anything that needed electricity to function.

After the usual offer of tea (always loose and served in bone china cups and saucers, with two rich tea biscuits on the side) and small talk of how awful the weather was, the older gentleman ducked down behind his desk to rummage through pillars of files. Amelia had just exhausted all her anecdotes about heavy rain when he held up some papers in triumph.

She duly signed at the bit he'd marked and then he handed her another bulky envelope.

'Here is the property information along with the keys.'

She sat holding it for a moment, her stomach flip-flopping with a mixture or nerves and excitement. This house was a part of Dotty she'd never known. It was wonderful but it also made her incredibly sad realising she wouldn't be able to talk to her about it. They'd talked about everything together, evenings spent in Dotty's flat, sitting either side of the fire in the high-backed overstuffed armchairs, nursing a single malt and discussing everything from politics to the latest storyline on *Emmerdale*. Even months after Dotty's death, whenever anything important or funny or noteworthy happened in her life, Amelia automatically went to the phone to call her godmother, only for reality to kick in like a blow to her stomach.

'Do you not want to take a look?' Mr Armstrong asked gently, interrupting her thoughts.

Amelia brushed her hand over the envelope, feeling the hard bumps of the keys.

'I... um, I don't know if I do,' she said, realising she probably sounded ridiculous, as most people would be eagerly ripping open the envelope. 'I've thought about this a lot and I think I'd quite like to just, well, to turn up and see the property in person for the first time. I never think photographs and room plans show the real character of the place.'

He gave her a bemused smile but nodded. 'I can write the address on the outside of the envelope if you'd prefer. You can use one of those sat nags to find it.'

'Please, that would be very kind of you. And it's sat *nav*, short for navigator.'

'Well, they sound like nags to me.' He gave her an imperceptible wink as he copied out the address in neat copperplate.

But just because she wanted a surprise didn't mean she wasn't curious.

'One thing, if you don't mind telling me. I've had this glorious vision of the little cottage having a real fire, one I can cosy down in front of during cold wintry nights. Do you know if there's a real fire?'

He smiled, giving a little chuckle as he passed her back the envelope. 'If it's a real fire you're after, you won't be disappointed. Now,' he said, more seriously, 'have you had any word from your brother?'

'No, I've emailed him again, but I have no idea where he is or what he's doing.' As far as Amelia knew, her infuriatingly free-spirited brother had fallen off the face of the earth!

It had taken her so long to compose that first email, the one to let him know about Dotty's passing. She remembered how the cursor on her computer had seemed to flash impatiently at her as she'd stared at the blank screen, unable to find the words. She'd started it so many times only to immediately delete what she'd typed. 'Dear Toby' had looked so formal and wrong as she'd never addressed Toby as 'dear' and probably never would, but the normal names she usually greeted him with were wholly inappropriate for the sort of news she had to impart.

She'd looked at the blank bright white screen so long she was worried she'd develop snow-blindness, before eventually plumping for 'Dotty died. Come home,' then adding, 'please.'

Amelia knew an email was a horrible way to break the news but he'd left her no choice as she had no telephone number for him and it was blatantly obvious he'd forgotten hers.

Toby would no doubt think it hilarious that she'd spent sleepless nights worrying about him, but the last novel she'd read had a character who'd gone travelling only to be kidnapped by an underground espionage unit, tortured and brainwashed before being turned into an assassin. Since then, Amelia had visions of Toby wandering unsuspecting into a bar, being chatted up by a Russian agent who, unbeknownst to him, would slip Rohypnol into his drink and then bundle him into the back of a transit heading for a top-secret Siberian training ground. Always so trusting and quick to make friends, it was just the perilous situation he'd be likely to get caught up in. She'd emailed him a personal safety checklist to follow not long after he'd gone but, of course, she'd never heard from him to know if he'd received it. For all she knew he could already have a new name, fake passport and be trying to infiltrate the Oval Office at that very moment.

She'd feared the worst since he'd announced he was off to 'find himself' a few months earlier. Amelia had no idea how bumming around Thailand could help him decide what he wanted to do with his life, but he heartily believed foreign travel held the key to unlocking his inner happiness. In Amelia's opinion a kick up the backside, a copy of the recruitment pages and a highlighter pen would have served him better but she'd long ago learnt to leave well alone when it came to meddling in her younger sibling's life.

He'd sent her another postcard dated a month ago, from Vietnam. He didn't mention Dotty so Amelia guessed he'd not logged on to his email account. If he knew he had a pot of money and a couple of vintage cars waiting for him, Amelia was certain he'd cut short his travels and come home.

'One other thing,' Mr Armstrong said as Amelia got up to leave. 'There's a chap Dorothea told me about, a Mr Jack Temple. It seems she employed him as a sort of handyman. He'd been staying at the property in Glencarlach and she wanted him kept on until the end of the period of employment he'd been contracted for.'

'Oh!' Amelia hadn't factored in a handyman in her 'cosying up to the fire' daydream. 'What is he doing?'

'General maintenance, I believe. I don't have specifics.'

'How long will he be there?'

'He's due to finish up at the end of January. His remuneration had been settled before her death so there's nothing you need to concern yourself with. Mr Temple spent time with Dorothea at her Chelsea property, maybe you met him?'

'No.' Amelia was surprised. She'd visited Dotty every week, and towards the end when the chemotherapy had been stopped, it was every day until she went into hospital. She'd never met anyone else and her godmother had never mentioned anyone. 'Will there be room for us both to stay there as I'd hoped to go up soon to visit?'

'Oh, I wouldn't worry about that,' the lawyer dismissed airily, 'he's not actually living there, he's staying on the land, but in an outbuilding.'

Amelia's heart sank slightly at this news. Maybe Jonathan was right, maybe the property was in such a state of disrepair the handyman didn't even want to live there.

'He does have access to your property though. And remember, Dorothea set aside money specifically for any repairs to the building. Just let me know what you need, when. There's plenty to cover any eventuality.' He cleared his throat. 'I took the liberty of raising a small cheque for you, to get you started when you go up there, in case you need any furnishings or supplies. Or even just to get transport there in the first place.' He handed her a separate envelope.

'Thank you. And thank you for all your help with everything.' Amelia could feel a lump in her throat as she shook hands with the older man.

'My dear, it's been a pleasure.' He grasped her hand warmly in his. 'I knew Dorothea for many years and it was a privilege. She thought so highly of you, considered you and your brother as the family she never had.'

Amelia smiled and hurried away in case she started to cry again.

'And try not to worry about that brother of yours,' James Armstrong called out. 'Dorothea told me she was sure he'd come good in the end.'

With a parting wave and eyes swimming with unshed tears, Amelia made her way back down to the entrance and it was just as she got to the main doors and saw the rain bouncing off the pavement she realised she'd left her umbrella in the lawyer's offices. She ran back to the elevator and jumped in just as the doors closed. She cast a glance at the only other passenger, a man who'd hurried past her in the foyer. He was leaning against the back wall, huddled inside a big black duffle coat and was scratching the rough stubble on his chin, which she could just make out beneath the heavy hood he'd pulled down low over his face, almost completely covering longish lank, blond hair.

And then she couldn't see anything at all; the lift suddenly stopped and they were plummeted into darkness.

3

Amelia stayed silent as her fellow prisoner issued a tirade of expletives aimed, she hoped, at the lift and not her.

There was a sound of boot against lift door and Amelia sucked in her breath, not relishing the prospect of being confined to a four-by-four space with a violent lunatic.

'Don't *do* this to me!'

The cut-glass accent took her by surprise, but she supposed posh folk could be crazy too.

'Did you happen to see a service phone anywhere?'

As he could only be talking to her, Amelia swallowed. 'No, but there might be an alarm somewhere on the panel.'

She heard him feel his way along the wall.

'Christ! I *really* don't need this,' he muttered.

'Are you claustrophobic?'

'No, I just can't stand enclosed spaces,' he drawled and laughed, before it turned into a hacking cough.

'I don't suppose you read braille, do you?' he asked when he'd recovered.

'No. Sorry.' There was something oddly familiar about his voice.

'Where's a fucking blind man when you need one?' he muttered. 'My phone's out of charge and I lost my last packet of matches.'

She really didn't think it was the time or place for a cigarette. 'I don't think you should be smoking, we don't know how long our air will last.'

'Jesus! You're a comfort! I was thinking of lighting up the panel in case there are any instructions for calling help. Have you a phone?'

Again, that voice, she was sure she recognised it.

'Well, *do* you?' he asked again.

'Er, yes.' She got her mobile out of her bag and shone the fascia towards the lift panel. There was a square button with an alarm bell on it. She pressed it. Nothing happened. She tried it again. 'I don't think it's connected.'

'Fucking great.'

She heard a sliding noise and a thud. She hoped he'd just slumped to the floor from annoyance and not fainted from fear or malnutrition, or even worse, a drug overdose! It had been many years since she'd received her Brownie first-aid badge and she wasn't quite sure she remembered the recovery position.

Then a horrible thought struck her. What if cyanide was being pumped into the lift shaft? She'd once read a book that had a scene like that in it. Even worse – what if the entire building had been attacked? What if a terrorist group was trying to kill off Britain's elite lawyers?

She couldn't even hear his wheezy breathing anymore.

'Hello? Are you still there?'

'Where the fuck did you think I'd gone?'

'Oh sorry, I thought you might have die... fainted.'

'I'm not that much of a sissy. FUCK! Of all the *fucking* days to get stuck in a *fucking* lift. I really needed this job.' He let out a sigh.

Amelia nearly had it, she was certain she knew him from somewhere. On the bright side, if she recognised him he probably wasn't an axe murderer. Unless his was one of the voice recordings played on *Crimewatch*.

'Did you have an interview?' she asked. From the brief glimpse she caught of him, it looked as if he hadn't been in work for months.

'Of sorts.'

He startled her by suddenly banging on the side of the lift.

'HELP! We're stuck. HELLO! HELP!'

Nothing.

'What's your name?' he asked after a brief pause.

'Amelia.'

'Well, Amelia, it looks like you and I are stuck here for a while. I don't suppose you've got any booze on you?'

'No.'

'Didn't think so.' He sighed in resignation. 'On a day when I wake up feeling as if I have a pneumatic drill going off in my head, have my career go belly-up and get stuck in a lift on my way to see my lawyer who may be my only salvation, on the proviso I turn up on time, the odds on having a bottle of Scotch stuck in here, too, were stacked against me,' he drawled wearily. 'So then, non-braille-reading Amelia, do you work here? Are you a lawyer? I may need to hire you.'

'No, I'm a receptionist in an advertising agency.'

'You don't sound terribly enthused about it.'

'It's not the sort of job to get enthused about. My office manager could masquerade as an orc from middle earth, most of the directors are a bunch of sexist trolls and the pay is shockingly poor.'

He laughed. 'What on *earth* compels you to stay there then?'

Good question. What the hell, it was dark. It didn't seem so scary telling secrets in the dark.

wondering if anyone would believe that she was stuck in a lift with Gideon Fey!

'No-oo, but I can help being hungover to the eyeballs and wearing the same clothes for the last three days.'

'But everyone knows you're a party animal.'

'Oh yeah, Wey Hey Fey!' he said derisively, referring to his tabloid moniker. 'But there are some people who would like *this* species of party animal big game-hunted and ruled extinct.'

He stood up and began pacing the lift like a caged tiger. 'I was on my last warning. I'd been given a month to get my act together else I'd be fired from this latest film, which is going to be huge. It's my break into Hollywood *evidently*. So for three weeks I lived like a monk and all was well until my friend organised his stag night and it all went rather Pete Tong, as they say. I'm just off the plane from Dublin. My agent is with my lawyer upstairs at this very moment as they plan my next career move. I dread to think what they'll say when they see me. Even my own mother would disown me at the moment. I look and smell as rough as a badger's arse,' he said glibly.

The lift lighting wasn't the most flattering shade of yellow, but he had a point, he wasn't glowing with health.

'You can borrow my concealer if you like,' Amelia suggested.

He laughed without humour.

Then inspiration struck her. 'Oh my God, but look.' Amelia gestured to her bag.

'What, there's an inflatable lookalike me inside?'

'Better than that!'

Always wanting to be prepared in case Jonathan ever invited her back to his for an impromptu night together, Amelia carried around a mini Boots counter in her bag, complete with Ladyshave, in case she had a smooth leg emergency. It had never been used.

'We'll start with your stubble.'

'Whoa, what?' He backed away from her.

'Oh, don't worry, I know what I'm doing.' Amelia opened up her bag wider and Gideon took a cautious look inside.

'Is that all make-up?'

She nodded encouragingly.

Still pressed hard against the lift his eyes flashed wildly. 'I thought you said you were a receptionist.'

'I am, but this is what I call my Optimistic Overnighter. And all this is from my friend Sally who's a make-up artist. She's always giving me odds and ends she's done with, along with tons of tips.'

He relaxed slightly.

Holding his chin firmly in one hand and warning him to be quiet, she shaved him. It wasn't a terribly close shave but it would do and she began searching through her bag, selecting products.

'Not to appear ungrateful, but do you know what you're doing?'

'I do put on make-up every day,' she said as she took out her brush holder. She unrolled the fabric as carefully as a surgeon prepping his instruments for a major operation.

'Hmm, you look nice, if a little pale, but I'll pass on the sparkly-green eyeshadow, thanks. Though it does work sensationally well with your beautiful brown eyes. They really are beautiful eyes, do you know that?'

She could feel her face turn beetroot, which she guessed *wouldn't* look beautiful.

'I expect the married Jonathan tells you all the time.'

She ignored his protestations of pain as she stabbed him slightly harder than necessary as she applied the light-reflecting concealer under his eyes.

~

'You're quite a bit taller than Jonathan, but it'll do.' She thrust the suit at Gideon and he warily removed the cellophane.

'Oh, and put on some of my deodorant first. Don't worry, it's not too feminine.'

He raised an eyebrow as he held up the suit. 'Jonathan likes his boardroom power suits, doesn't he?'

'Jonathan's always very smart,' she said tartly.

'And very dull,' he muttered under his breath, taking in the white shirt and sombre dark-blue tie. He checked the label. 'Hmm, good make. It's very *pinstripey*, isn't it?'

'Look, you can't go in wearing that.' She pointed at his mud-caked jeans and *'I've tried Guinness in Dublin and survived'* T-shirt.

'Fair enough,' he grumbled. 'But they're going to think I've had a style lobotomy whilst sobering up,' he said, holding the suit up against his Puma trainers.

'I think I've got some breath freshener in my bag too,' she said, turning her back as he changed.

Amelia had just tidied away all the make-up when the lift chugged back to life, clunking and groaning back to the ground floor.

Ignoring the crowd gathered by the lift door waiting to see if they were okay, Gideon pushed his way through.

'Will you be long?'

'I hope not, darling! If it goes well I'll want to escape early in case they see through your terrific disguise, and if it all goes belly-up, I'll definitely need a shoulder to cry on.'

Amelia watched him bound up the stairs to his lawyer's office and hoped that the pure alcohol seeping out his pores wouldn't permeate into the fabric of Jonathan's suit. She'd made Gideon rub himself down with her make-up remover wipes but even still, he had three days' worth of alcohol bingeing to sweat out.

After reassuring a lawyer that she wouldn't be suing for emotional distress at being stuck in the lift, she went and collected her umbrella, then paced the floor of the foyer until Gideon reappeared a few minutes later, his tiger-eyes flashing in anger.

'How did it go?' she asked, although she guessed the answer.

'It seems I'm about as welcome in the film industry as a pig in a synagogue.'

'Gideon!' Amelia looked around in case anyone had overheard him, then hurried after him as he was halfway out the door and waving down a taxi.

'I need a drink.'

'I need Jonathan's suit back.'

'My need is greater,' he said tightly as a taxi pulled up beside them.

Amelia started to panic, she couldn't very well strip Gideon Fey naked in the street, but she had to get back to work. 'I can't go back without it.'

'I know. You're coming with me.'

She found herself being bundled into the black cab.

'To Shakedown,' he told the taxi driver – the name of the celebrity hangout Amelia had read about in *Grazia* magazine.

'I can't go for a drink,' she protested. 'I need to get back to work and Jonathan needs his suit and...'

'Belt up.'

'Don't be so rude! I ha–'

'Belt up,' Gideon said, handing her the end of her seat belt. 'Although stopping your protestations would also be lovely as my head is throbbing.'

He sat back against the cab and pinched the bridge of his nose.

'What happened?' she asked.

'I've definitely been chucked off the film, lawyer said there's nothing he can do as I flouted the contract. They've already replaced me with some bloody upstart fresh from RADA. My agent says I'm *persona non grata* as no one's even sending me scripts. Turns out I insulted some minor actress on set and her father's only one of the biggest producers about and he's put the word out I've not to be worked with.'

'Oh, I'm sorry. Looks like my plan didn't work.'

He opened his eyes and turned to look at Amelia. 'Oh, but it did. My agent told me that if I'd turned up looking a wreck, she'd have dumped me as well. Darling, you're the reason I've still got representation. Now I just need work.'

'Isn't there anything?'

He gave a snort of derision and tossed back his blond hair, which now looked lustrous and bouncy thanks to a liberal spray of her dry shampoo. 'Do you know the best they can do?'

She shook her head mutely.

'Suggest a fucking documentary which shows my human, softer side, to try and get the public behind me again. Until then no one will hire me.'

'What's the documentary about?'

'That's the rub! *There isn't one*! They can't think of something suitable at the moment but they'll "get onto it" which means bugger off out my office and keep a low profile until we feel you've been punished enough.'

'Well, why don't you come up with an idea?'

'I find my creative juices flow better after a drink.'

Amelia checked her watch. 'But it's just gone eleven.'

'God, I know. I've usually had at least one Bloody Mary by now.'

Amelia squirmed uncomfortably in her seat as the taxi came to a stop at another red light in London's city centre. 'Gideon, I can't come with you. I need you to give me back Jonathan's suit,' she said as forcefully as possible, using her best schoolmarm voice, the one she used to get her neighbour's cat to stop scratching her front door. It had as much effect on Gideon as it did on the cat.

'Can I borrow your mobile, my battery has died.'

'Uh sure.' She handed it over to him.

For the next few minutes he sent some texts, receiving a couple in reply. Eventually, he handed it back to her. 'There you go. And don't worry, it's all sorted with Jonathan.'

'What have you done?' she said in panic as she searched her sent box to see what he'd written, but he'd deleted the message. 'What did you send?' she wailed just as her phone beeped at her. She opened the text, which was from Jonathan.

Where has this come from? Are you still mad at me?

'What did you send?' Amelia repeated, but Gideon plucked the phone from her hands and held it away from her as he typed a reply.

'Gideon!' She tried to grab it back but the seat belt held her in check.

'Hush now. I'm trying to do you a favour!'

'I don't need a favour, really I don't.'

He looked at her aghast. 'But of course you do!'

When they pulled up to the bar there were already paparazzi lining the pavement.

Amelia looked at him in alarm. 'Oh no! Look at all the photographers! Don't you want to go somewhere else?'

'Whyever would I do that?' He looked at her in bemusement. 'Come on, stomach in, tits out and don't forget to smile.'

'They're hardly going to photograph me,' she scoffed.

'Of course they are, honey; you're with me,' he whispered

into her ear as he opened the door. He got out of the taxi and held out his hand to help Amelia out. As soon as her feet touched the ground, Gideon pulled her towards him and clamped his lips on hers, giving her a smacker of a kiss as a dozen flash bulbs went off in her face.

4

'For the fifth time, I'm *sorry,* darling. I shouldn't have snogged you so publicly. It was very bad of me. Naughty Gideon.'

Amelia covered her burning face with her hands. 'But I've got a boyfriend.'

'Darling, I hate to burst your angsty little bubble, but it *was* purely for publicity.'

She opened her fingers and peeked out at him. 'I know, I mean I didn't think that you...'

'Although it was fun. You have *very* kissable lips, so soft and plump, firm yet supple. Beautiful eyes, kissable lips. Watch out or I may just fall in love with you.' He flashed her a quick grin before licking off the salt around the rim of his margarita glass.

'All those photographers out there, do they just hang around all day waiting to snap celebrities?' she asked, craning her neck to see out the tinted windows. They'd been sitting in their secluded booth for half an hour but none of the hacks seemed to have left.

Gideon grinned. 'There's usually only a couple of paparazzi

waiting for a lucky scoop, but I tipped the wink to a few papers that I was turning up here with a new woman.'

Amelia opened her mouth to object but he popped the slice of lime from his cocktail into it to shut her up.

'Okay, before you start hyperventilating, I didn't mention your name, but apology number six, anyway. Now, let's drink up and not mention the kiss again. And I especially won't mention the fact you slipped me the tongue,' he said lightly.

Amelia floundered for a response. He'd taken her by surprise! It was a knee-jerk reaction to a knee-trembler of a snog!

'Oh God, no! Breathe!' He walloped her on the back, mistaking her apoplexy for choking and the lime slice flew out her mouth and to her dismay, bounced off Jonathan's tie leaving a damp smudge.

Before she could even begin to dream up a comeback for Gideon (and where to start; the kidnapping, the holding Jonathan's clothes to ransom, the fact he'd used her as an accomplice to create a false impression of their relationship...) the beep of her phone indicated another text message had arrived.

Gideon also clocked it and he held up his hands in innocence. 'And for the millionth time, I didn't text anything untoward to Jonathan!'

'Well, why is he bombarding me with texts?' He'd sent so many that Gideon had confiscated her phone again and was reading them as they came in, but wouldn't let her reply. But whatever Gideon had sent had obviously rattled Jonathan; Amelia had never known him to be this attentive.

'Okay, I'll tell you, if it means you'll start enjoying yourself! I merely sent a text saying that you needed some space and you wanted the rest of the day off to think. Now, to me, his reaction is obviously one of a guilty conscience,' Gideon said, playing with the stem of his empty glass.

'He's feeling guilty because he pulled out of our weekend away.'

'Why?'

'He said he has to work.'

He narrowed his eyes. 'But you don't entirely believe him, do you? You're worried the old letch is hiding something.'

She shook her head. 'No I'm not. Not really. And Jonathan's *not a letch*!' She grabbed a napkin and mopped at the splodge of lime juice on the table before Gideon dipped the cuff of Jonathan's shirt in it.

Another text came in.

'Don't be mad at me. I'll make it up to you tonight,' Gideon read.

The phone chirped again.

'The papers should be with you tomorrow, just sent them via courier. Jonathan.' Gideon looked up at her. 'Is this some sort of sex code?'

'No, he must have meant that for someone else. See, you've got him flustered and he's sending things to the wrong people. Let me at least text him to say what he's just done.'

'No! Now come on and finish your drink so I can go and buy another overpriced round from this glorified celebrity-watch bar.' He glanced up and made a rude gesture to a glamour model chatting to a married premier division footballer. 'Look at all the fucking vultures circling, pretending not to watch. God it makes me sick,' he said under his breath.

'We could go somewhere else.' Amelia wouldn't have minded a change of scene. For all its celebrity hangout status the interior of Shakedown wasn't terribly impressive. The velvet seats were a bit worn and tired and the lighting, while clearly aiming for moody, could have used a few extra watts. Quite cavernous in size, on a slow Monday lunchtime it was empty and echoey and Amelia thought there was more of an atmosphere in her local Wetherspoon's.

But Gideon gave her knee a patronising pat and everyone turned to watch.

'If I don't come here, how will people know I'm still in the game. I'm the phoenix rising from the flames!' Gideon loosened Jonathan's tie and undid the top two buttons of the shirt, revealing smooth golden skin beneath. Amelia hated to admit it but Gideon wore the suit better.

'Why don't you see him at weekends?' Gideon asked her and Amelia wished she'd never mentioned the 'no weekend' rule.

'Do you at least call him to have phone sex?' His golden tiger-eyes glittered.

'I don't really call him,' she admitted.

'Why not?' he asked lightly, his long fingers tapping her phone, which he still held out of reach.

'Well, I can't at work as everything goes through his secretary and at home... well, he's never there. He's either working late or at the gym or playing squash...' she trailed off.

'Or shagging his wife,' Gideon added, ignoring Amelia's denials. He reached out and took a swig from Amelia's half full glass. 'When do you ever see him?'

'He calls me. We go out on dates.'

'Where do you go on these *dates*?'

'Somewhere romantic.'

'And out the way, where no one will see you. Or you go to your flat, am I right?'

Amelia nodded reluctantly.

'Honey, you're being taken for a prize ride. Let me guess, the sex is passionate and kinky and he likes you dressing up.' He clicked his tongue. 'That man is married as sure as every Corrs song has a fiddle solo.'

'Can I get the suit back now, please?' Amelia asked.

'But we've only just started our fun.'

'You said a drink. We've had a drink, and now I really need to go.'

'But you've got a free pass for the rest of the day!'

Amelia knew that most people would kill to spend time with the notorious Gideon Fey in a celebrity hangout being plied with drinks, but she felt more like she was being held against her will.

'And actually,' Gideon carried on, 'I do believe I said I needed a drink. This was the drink I needed.' He tapped the rim of the empty glass. 'So now I can move on to the unnecessary ones!'

Amelia couldn't help but laugh, he was very personable. She just didn't understand why he'd chosen her to be his drinking partner when there was a bar full of celebrities he could go and chat to.

'Now,' Gideon said, leaning forward, 'what I'd *really* like to know is what's inside the envelope you've been clutching as if your life depended on it.' He snatched it out of her grasp.

'Don't let me see it!' Amelia put her hand over her eyes as he started to pull out the schedule of her house. 'It's why I was at the lawyers, it's a little cottage I inherited from my godmother. I don't want to have as much of a glimpse of it until I'm standing in front of it.'

'Why?'

'I like surprises,' she said, although the truth was she didn't want to get her hopes raised. She'd rented her shoebox in London on the basis of the photos in the letting agency. The property had looked lovely if a little compact. In an 'up-and-coming area of character' was how the flat had been described. She'd signed in case it was snapped up by anyone else and only after securing a year's lease did she realise everything had been taken through a fish-eye lens and photoshopping had hidden the damp patches and mouldy skirting board. Only on moving in Amelia realised that the 'up-and-coming' referred to the foul stench which emanated from her sink and the 'area of character' tag was due to the hirsute man who stood on the corner of her street in nothing but his underpants and yodelled every morning at 6am.

'So you've no idea what it's like?'

She shook her head.

'Mind if I take a look?'

Amelia wondered how on earth she could possibly stop him, he was a force of nature.

'Fine, just as long as you don't let me know anything about it. Promise?'

'Scout's honour!'

Amelia didn't think that was worth much as she couldn't picture him bivouacking or wearing a toggle. 'I'm off to the loo and when I get back I need the papers to be in there,' she pointed at the envelope, 'and Jonathan's suit back under polythene.'

'Okey-dokey, darling, I'll get us another drink in.'

On her return she found another drink waiting for her, the cottage papers back in the envelope and Gideon still very much wearing Jonathan's suit. There was also a huge circle around their table with Gideon holding court in the centre. Amelia had to squeeze past everyone so she could sit down.

'Now come on, ladies, let Amelia sit down so we can carry on with our date.'

'She's not as glamorous as Veronica,' she heard one woman say as she walked off and Amelia remembered reading an article linking Gideon with Veronica Bliss, the actress in a soap opera.

'Did you and Veronica split up?' Amelia asked.

'We were never really together, darling. All show for the

media. She needed her profile heightened and it never does me any harm to have a pretty girl in tow. We went to Monte Carlo together and blew a million in the casino. We had a blast. My ego needs some fluffing, tell me what you liked best about *Twelve Roses*?'

'I'm going to have to go. Jonathan said he'd be popping round.'

'Stay and get a taxi later. I need you to flatter me. And I hate getting pissed on my own.'

He seemed to be doing a pretty good job of it already she noted as he'd almost finished his latest drink and was already eyeing up her untouched one.

'I'm going now. With the suit.'

Gideon's eyes glittered mischievously. 'Okay, I'll take it off, right here, right now, and walk you to the taxi. Wow! The press will have a field day with that, don't you think? They'll want to know all about the woman who made me strip in public and I am *such* an obliging guy I'd have to tell them all about you. Of course, then I'd have to phone lover boy as I know you would want me to explain about the kiss too. I'm *sure* your terribly loving, unmarried boyfriend will understand,' he said, his hand hovering over the next button on the shirt. 'Oh, hold on, I've got a better idea. Why don't you stay with me for another little drink, we'll get a taxi, I'll drop you off and I'll return the suit to you tomorrow, freshly dry cleaned. In fact, I'll even pretend to be the dry cleaners and say we've mislaid it. What's his work line?'

Knowing when she was fighting a losing battle, Amelia told him the number.

He put the phone on speaker mode and within a couple of rings Doreen answered.

'Mr Harris's office, Doreen speaking.'

'Mr Harris, please.' Gideon spoke in a completely convincing South London accent.

'He's unavailable, can I pass on a message?'

'I really need to speak to him in person, I've a bit of bad news to tell him. Personal, you know.'

Amelia shook her head and mouthed 'just leave a message!'

As Doreen put him through, Gideon covered the bottom of the phone and whispered, 'I'm curious to hear what he sounds like.'

A moment later Jonathan came on the line.

'Jonathan Harris,' he said, using his best professional phone voice that Amelia always teased him about.

'Hello there, Mr Harris, this is Rob from the dry cleaners. I'm afraid there's been a bit of a problem with your suit.'

'What kind of problem?' Jonathan asked stonily.

'The lost kind of problem, I'm afraid. We've had a part-timer in who has managed to mix up all the clothes and we won't get ourselves straight for a few hours.'

'That's unacceptable.'

Gideon raised an eyebrow at Amelia. 'Well, we're working as fast as we can, but it definitely won't be available for today. We'll refund you the money.'

'You certainly will.'

'It'll be available from midday tomorrow. We can even courier it over to you.'

There was a momentary pause. 'No, that's not suitable, I'm away all day tomorrow.'

Amelia nodded to Gideon. He was, she'd been organising his travel arrangements for a meeting in Birmingham.

'But,' Jonathan continued, 'I suppose my wife can pick it up when she collects her own coat tomorrow.'

5

Amelia's blood went cold as Gideon's eyes widened.
'Unless that's lost also?' Jonathan continued, unaware
of the bombshell he'd just dropped.

'No, no,' Gideon said, looking helplessly at Amelia who was
still staring at the phone in shock.

'Um, and what's your wife's name?'

'Alison Taylor.'

Amelia looked at the phone, trying to muddle together what
Jonathan was saying. Alison was the name of his sister. Maybe
he wasn't actually married, she thought despite the horrible sick
feeling in the pit of her stomach which told her that all the
secrecy had to mean something.

'Um, and do you have any children who have clothes to be
picked up too?' Gideon gave Amelia a helpless shrug. Looking
pained, he took a large swig of his drink.

'No, of course we don't buy clothes that need to be dry
cleaned for our children, they make too much mess,' Jonathan
replied tersely.

Children, plural. Amelia felt sick. And a little faint. She bent over, putting her head between her knees and took a couple of deep breaths.

'We'll guarantee we'll have them by tomorrow morning,' Gideon continued, leaning over and rubbing Amelia's back.

'You'd better, we need our clothes as we're going away this weekend.'

Amelia looked up sharply. 'Where,' she mouthed.

'Anywhere nice?' Gideon asked.

'I don't see what business it is of yours.'

'Ah well, you see, some of the chemicals we use alert sniffer dogs in some countries.' He shrugged helplessly at Amelia.

'It's Sweden.'

'Oh, that's fine. Got to go, machine's making funny noises.' Gideon hung up. 'Oh God, darling, are you all right? Here, drink up.' He pushed her margarita over to her.

Amelia numbly accepted the drink and took a swig.

'He told me his sister was called Alison and that *she* had a daughter and a son. He always spent so much time with his niece and nephew. I just thought he was a doting uncle. But it wasn't, it was a cover which could be explained away if I ever saw him with them. He even showed me a photograph. I'm such an idiot,' she added.

'No, you're not, darling. Maybe a little naive and a tad gullible, but you won't have been the first woman in the world to be duped by a lying scumbag.'

'But it was so obvious.' And it was, with hindsight. Gideon, a stranger, saw through it in seconds.

'The only way you'll know for sure is if you phone and ask him yourself.'

'I can't...' But Gideon was already pressing the buttons and was calling Jonathan's mobile.

'No, it's not Amelia, she's here with me, hang on.'

Mutely, she took the phone, her hand shaking as she held it to her ear.

'Amelia!' Jonathan's voice down the phone sounded alien to her. 'What's going on? And who was that?'

'Gideon Fey.'

''Scuse me?'

'Gideon Fey, the actor,' she said. 'I helped him earlier when I was visiting my lawyer and he wanted to repay me by buying me a drink.'

She heard him laugh.

'I thought you were mad at me because of our trip.'

'Why is it you're cancelling again?' she asked in as neutral a tone as she could manage.

'Work. I've got a mountain of paperwork to catch up on and...'

Lies.

'Are you married?' she interrupted.

All the time Gideon watched her from across the table, eyes wide, sipping his drink.

'Where on earth has this come from?' Jonathan asked with a small nervous laugh.

There was no denial, no guffaw at the sheer ridiculousness of such a suggestion, just a panicked cheater wondering how she'd found out.

'Just tell me. Are you married?'

Gideon reached out and squeezed her hand.

Jonathan sighed and she could imagine him weighing up his options. 'Well, technically, yes.' He'd obviously realised she must have found out and there would be no point in pretending he wasn't. 'But we've not really been living as man and wife for...'

'And you have children?'

There was a pause before he confirmed it very quietly.

'And you're going with them to Sweden. This weekend.'

'How did you find out?' he blustered.

'Your dry cleaner told me.'

'What? Are you there? What's...'

'Stop! It doesn't matter how I know. You're obviously still married enough to go on holiday together.'

'It's practically over, we're just going through the motions, for the sake of the kids. She found the tickets and jumped to the conclusion she was the one coming with me.'

'You lied to me.'

'Well, I don't think you're in any position to play the honesty card, I hardly think you're there with Gideon Fey. And let's face it, you believed what you wanted to believe. I presumed you'd realised,' he blustered.

'Don't you dare try and turn this around.' Amelia, bolstered by the half margarita she'd had, smacked the table in front of her as Gideon gave her a thumbs up of encouragement.

'Well, come on, most girls in your position would have realised. Look, nothing has to change, we can go on as before.'

'With the skulking about? You said it was to protect me from office gossip, but it was to protect your lily-livered ass from being rumbled. Well, mister, everything *does* have to change. Take this as my verbal resignation, from the job and from *you*!' She hung up and dropped the phone onto the table.

'Well done, darling. You're not to be messed with, and you've gone adorably pink-cheeked!' Gideon said, taking a swig of her drink. He waved over at the bartender to signal another round.

Amelia sat with her head in her hands for a moment, trying to take in everything that had just happened.

'You were so right. How could he do that? He lied to me and no doubt his wife and children too.'

'A complete and utter scumbag,' Gideon sympathised. 'But you well and truly dumped that bastard's ass.'

'And I resigned,' she said slowly, the reality of what she'd done hitting her. It was all well and good being dramatic but she now had no job.

'You couldn't very well go in and face him every day. And you said it yourself, he was the only reason you stayed.'

All that was true, but it didn't help her out of her current unemployed status. She started to feel light-headed again.

'What am I going to do?' she wailed.

'Well, you're not homeless, are you! If you can't find anything here you can always move into that massive...ly beautiful cottage.' He hiccupped.

Yes, there was always that option. And it seemed a very tempting one. Escaping to a little hideaway in a remote village in Scotland seemed a great way to spend a couple of weeks licking her wounds. She had a little money put aside, coupled with the cheque Mr Armstrong had raised for her. 'Is it really lovely?'

'I could certainly stomach living there,' Gideon said, giving her hand another squeeze.

Amelia guessed that was a seal of approval as she couldn't imagine Gideon living in a hovel that was falling down around his ears.

'I know it will probably need some work done but at least the lawyer has funds put aside for any renovations I want to do.'

'Really!' Gideon leant forward. 'That's great news. In fact, that's amazing news.' His eyes sparkled. 'Could I borrow your phone a moment, poppet?'

She slid it over to him.

'I'll just be a jiffy. And you know,' he said, jumping up and heading outside to make a call, 'I've a good feeling about all of this, I think you're going to be absolutely fine!'

6

Later that evening, Amelia let herself into her flat. Switching on her bedside table lamp, she began getting ready for bed, giggling tipsily at the absurdity of her spending the day drinking cocktails with Gideon Fey. She could just imagine the faces of everyone at work when she told them. Then with sobering clarity she remembered that she wouldn't be going back to work. Ever again. And that meant she wouldn't see Jonathan either. She sat down at her dressing table as a rush of nausea Mexican-waved around her body; partly from the fourth cocktail Gideon had made her drink and partly from the realisation she had become both single and jobless, although Gideon had seemed certain everything would be fine, he'd kept saying it to her in a sing-songy voice.

Taking off her make-up, Amelia suddenly became aware of a soft purring noise coming from her bed. She swivelled around in shock, for the first time noticing a sleeping lump under the duvet.

Jonathan!

He'd never let himself into her flat before. He'd let himself out of it at all times of the night and small hours of the morning, but he'd never waited for her before.

He must have come round to apologise.

Her traitor heart gave an involuntary leap, but she quickly brought herself up to task and quelled any thoughts of snuggling up against his warm, freshly scented body by reminding herself that he was a lying, cheating, *married* bastard.

Heart hardened, she pulled the covers back ready to give him a quick shove out the bed when she realised she was staring at the back of a completely shaved head, save for a peroxide-blond mohawk.

Horrified, her eyes travelled to a Japanese symbol tattooed on what was very obviously *not* Jonathan's shoulder.

Taking slow, measured breaths to keep herself calm, Amelia tried to apply logic to what was before her.

If he was a burglar, why fall asleep in her bed? Unless he was a narcoleptic burglar. A nudist narcoleptic burglar? A quick glance around her room proved that nothing had been stolen, although there wasn't a terribly huge amount worth stealing, apart from her large glass sweetie jar that was now almost full to the brim with twenty-pence pieces. Although maybe he'd tried to nab it, given himself a hernia, then had to lie down to recover. Or maybe he thought he was Goldilocks.

Amelia sobered up at this thought.

What if he *did* think he was Goldilocks. What if he was a serial killer modelling himself on the Goldilocks fairy story! There had been no news articles of any killers waiting for their victim in their own bed, but what if the police were sitting on that kind of detail as they didn't want to cause panic. Or what if she was going to be the first victim?

Amelia steadied herself against her dressing table. Horror of horrors, her post-mortem would show up a lot of alcohol in her system (and she'd read enough crime fiction to know young women with a lot of alcohol in their bloodstream never elicited as much sympathy from the investigating officers) and the two Curly Wurlys she'd scoffed in the back of the taxi would simply compound her stereotype as woman-dumped-by-married-lover-who-seeks-solace-in-alcohol-and-chocolate. She stood looking at the sleeping back as panic continued to build. She did not want to be dispatched by a weird fairy-tale fetishist.

She had to do something.

She picked up her badminton racket from the side of the bed and tentatively prodded the snoring lump with it.

'Right, mister, I want you to sit up nice and slow, no sudden moves and tell me who you are and what you're doing in my bed because I'm kinda guessing you're not Goldilocks.'

The intruder began to chuckle.

She prodded him with the racket again. 'I've called the police and they've got the place surrounded.'

The body continued to shake with mirth.

'I'm warning you. Do it my way and I won't hurt you.'

The body began to turn around and Amelia took a step back, raising her racket.

'What are you going to do, make a grid pattern on my bum?' He laughed.

'Toby!' She stared at her brother as he grinned up at her sleepily. 'What are you doing here?' she said, lowering her racket from above her head.

'Well, I *was* sleeping off my jet lag until you decided to go all vigilante on me.'

She'd played out her meeting with Toby a hundred times in her imagination. It normally consisted of her rendezvousing with him at the airport and them hugging in silence for a moment before meandering slowly through the arrival's area and into a taxi, talking about Dotty in hushed, reverential tones.

46

Instead, Amelia immediately fell back into her usual role of annoyed elder sister.

'It's about bloody time you showed up! Did you get any of my messages?'

He sat up, rubbing his eyes. 'I only picked them up a couple of days ago. I'd not had email where I'd been for months.'

'Or telephones, I take it.'

'Okay, okay, I'm crap. I know. I'm sorry. I got the first flight I could, then went straight round to your work but they said you were away and they weren't sure if you'd be back. I texted you but you didn't get back to me. I still had your spare key so I thought I'd just wait here.'

Amelia inwardly cursed Gideon for not letting her access any of her texts. She sat down on the edge of the bed.

'I'm sorry about Dotty. What happened?'

'The cancer came back.'

They lapsed into silence for a few moments.

'I'm sorry you had to deal with everything on your own.'

'That's okay.' It hadn't been really, not at the time, but she'd gotten through it all. Amelia mustered a smile. 'Did you have a good trip?' She had to bite her tongue from asking if he'd 'found himself'.

'Yeah, it was really enlightening.'

'You know, you didn't have to come all the way home, a phone call would have done.'

He smiled at her, his cheeky chappie face showing no signs of any travel traumas, just an off-the-wall haircut, tattoo and tan. 'I wanted to come back, I think it's time I dealt with things head-on rather than in a fug of incense. And I couldn't actually handle any more green tea. You do have coffee, don't you, I mean proper coffee?'

'You mean the stuff with caffeine in it?' She shook her head.

'Sorry, I gave it up.' His face fell and she laughed. 'For God's sake, as if! Do you want some now?'

He shook his head. 'I really need sleep at the moment. Can we have a proper catch-up in the morning? Over lots of lovely caffeinated coffee. The room is starting to spin.'

Amelia realised it wasn't all that stationary for her either.

'Sure.'

'You don't mind me kipping in your bed, do you?' Before waiting for her answer, he rolled over, cocooning himself in the duvet once more.

Amelia turned off the light and crawled into the other side of the bed, and fell asleep, dreaming of her whitewashed little cottage, which now had roses and sweet peas in the garden, an ornamental birdbath on the lawn and by the front door, a shoe brush in the shape of a hedgehog.

7

*G*lencarloch; *frequently voted one of Scotland's prettiest villages,* Amelia read from her Rough Guide to Scotland Book, *is nestled around the harbour on the banks of Loch Carloch, which leads out into the Minch area of water in the North Atlantic sea in the Wester Ross area of Scotland. Glencarloch village has a population of about 700, almost 900 when taking in the surrounding farms and houses within the parish. The harbour area is a bustling hive for locals and tourists and is home to a variety of shops and cafés as well as the hospitable Whistling Haggis Hotel and bar (est. 1795). Stop off for a lunch or dinner and try their delicious locally caught fish dishes along with their impressive collection of malts. Attractive cobbled streets lined with whitewashed cottages meander in a zigzag fashion leading away from the harbour up through the gradual incline into the hills allowing great views of the loch. Framed by the spectacular Torridon Hills, arriving at Glencarloch by boat shows the village off to its best and on a sunny day one could easily be mistaken for thinking they were arriving at a Mediterranean village.*

There was a fuzzy black-and-white photograph and Amelia had spent hours studying the attractive cottages, wondering if hers was one of them.

What the guide book omitted to mention was just how much of a bugger it was to get to when relying on land-based public transport and not one's private boat. After flying from London to Glasgow, where she caught another flight to Inverness, Amelia had to get a coach to Ullapool and then wait for a tiny local bus, which she'd now been on for well over an hour. There was a banner on the side of the bus which read 'Your Wee Local Happy Bus' but Amelia would have been a hell of a lot happier if the suspension had been better. She was suddenly launched out of her seat as the wheels ran over yet another pothole. Landing back down with a thud, she cupped her hands on the glass window and looked out, but couldn't see a thing as it was almost eight o'clock and pitch dark. She'd left her London flat at just before seven that morning.

She still couldn't quite believe she was on her way towards her new home.

One night she'd fallen asleep with no boyfriend, no job and no idea of what she was going to do with her life only to wake up the next lunchtime to a fuzzy head and DHS delivery containing the plane tickets to Inverness in just over a week's time with a brief note from Gideon.

Luckily, he'd left his number so she'd called him up immediately to tell him she couldn't possibly accept.

'Whyever not?' he said, sounding remarkably chipper considering the amount of alcohol he'd put away in the bar the night before.

'It's too much to accept and I hadn't planned on going up there quite so soon.'

'Why leave it longer? You're desperate to see the place.'

'But I can't just leave now.'

'It's not now, it's a week from now. And let's face it, with no job and no boyfriend you don't really have much going for you at the moment. You need a clean break, darling.'

'Gide...'

'Think of it as a thank you,' he continued.

'Well...'

'Great!' he exclaimed, sensing her weakening. 'And even better, I came up with a fantastic idea for a project and I've been given the go-ahead for a small production team.'

'Wow, that's amazing.' Almost as amazing as his ability to turn everything back to himself again, she mused with a smile as she wandered into her tiny kitchenette where Toby was busy making breakfast.

'You're a fast mover, Gideon, I'll give you that,' she said with a yawn, realising he must have been up at the crack of dawn to get everything organised.

'And I'm not going to let you duck out of this.'

'But Gideon, what am I going to do when I get there?'

'Relax, have a holiday, enjoy your house. You never know what will turn up.'

'But...'

'If I hear that word again, I'm going to come round and kick you on yours! You've also got that cheque from your lawyers to see you through.'

Amelia had forgotten about that. She still hadn't looked at it to see how much it was.

'Now, you'd better not back out of this as I'm going to meet you in Glencarlach the night you arrive so we can have a little jolly before I start work.'

All her protestations were shot down by Gideon. And Toby, who'd decided to get in on the act as he handed her a mug of coffee.

Eventually, to stop Gideon haranguing her and to get off the phone, she agreed.

'Come with me,' she said to Toby as he dished up fluffy

scrambled eggs alongside some crispy rashers of bacon and hot buttered toast, but he shook his head.

'No, I need to get a job and get back to the real world.'

'Oh, are you going back to your course?'

Toby's architecture course had had more false starts than the Grand National on a wet day. He'd been halfway through his third year when he'd deferred it yet again to go travelling.

'Hmmm, I'm going to arrange a meeting with my advisor of studies and talk it through.' He paused to shovel some forkfuls of egg into his mouth. 'I met a guy in Singapore...'

Amelia's eyebrow shot up involuntarily.

Toby smiled. 'No, before you ask, it wasn't serious, just a bit of a fling. But he knows a guy who owns a bar here and told me to drop in whenever I got back and he'd fix me up with bar work. I can get something part-time and weekends to tide me over.'

'They have bars in Scotland.'

'And big welly-boot-wearing hunky farmers too, I'm sure. It's tempting, but no, I'll stay here. If you go up to Scotland, I can stay here and pay your rent.'

And with that, any other argument Amelia could have thought of was blown out of the water. It was as easy as that. Then she nearly fell off her chair when she opened up the envelope containing the cheque from James Armstrong. Not just the couple of hundred pounds Amelia had expected, she found herself staring at a cheque for twenty thousand pounds.

And that's why a few days later Amelia found herself Glencarlach-bound.

'Hey, love,' the bus driver shouted back to her. 'That's us coming into Glencarlach. I'll give you a hand with your bags.'

'Thank you!' She looked out the window again and now could see a whole load of lights dotted up a fairly steep hill. Her stomach turned over a few times in excitement.

They pulled up at the front of the harbour and the guide book had been right, it was one of the prettiest places Amelia thought she'd ever seen, and she understood how it looked as if she could be arriving at a Greek island, with all the white cottages in higgledy-piggledy rows leading up from the main street. The driver took down her heavy case and she slung her large tote bag over her shoulder and walked down the two steps onto the pavement.

And all similarities with the Mediterranean ended right there as a large gust of icy wind almost buffeted her straight back onto the bus.

Amelia gasped for breath as another gust, straight off the North Atlantic, whipped at her face. She tried to gather the edges of her swing coat together but she couldn't hold on to them as they flapped behind her like a flag on a pole at the same time her chiffon scarf flew up over her face and she couldn't see where she was going.

Never in her life had she felt cold like it. All day she'd noticed that the further north she travelled the chillier it got and judging by this temperature dip she'd inadvertently turned up in the Arctic. Finally managing to pull her scarf away from her face, Amelia crossed over to the welcoming lights of The Whistling Haggis, wobbling over the rough cobbles in her black patent stilettos. Thankfully, there was a sheltered porch to the hotel and bar and she took a moment to catch her breath and look a little less wind-ravaged. According to James Armstrong, the lawyer, her house was just under a mile away from the centre of the village, but she had no idea how to get to it, however, she was sure someone in the bar would be able to help. The Whistling Haggis was also where Gideon had told her he'd meet her.

If he bothered to turn up. Amelia still doubted that a famous actor would deign to travel all the way to the north-west of

Scotland to 'take a little holiday' with someone like her, whom he'd met just the once. It would be far more his style to be holidaying on a fellow actor's yacht in the Bahamas or sunning himself in the Côte d'Azur.

Or drying out at an exclusive rehab resort.

Well, even if she never saw Gideon again she was very grateful to him for the plane ticket, for if she was being totally honest with herself she would have hummed and hawed for half an eternity before summoning the courage to visit her new home. She would have waited to get a new job, settle down into it, then held off until she had enough holidays saved up to go; in other words, the *sensible* thing. But this way, just uprooting herself and leaving with no set plans, she felt terribly spontaneous and irresponsible; just the thing she'd get annoyed at her brother for doing. But it also felt incredibly liberating.

Opening the door to the Whistling Haggis, she was almost knocked back by the wall of heat and noise that met her. The place was packed, with everyone trying to compete with being heard over the music which was courtesy of a big, bearded man beating a strange little drum and a diminutive woman beside him furiously bowing a violin. Being on the short side, even with her stilettos, Amelia couldn't see a thing beyond burly chests adorned with chunky knitwear. Pushing forward, she made for the bar, her 'sorry's and 'excuse me's getting lost in the noise.

Finally making her way to the side of the bar, Amelia could see three folk serving. Standing slightly to the side was a sturdy middle-aged man overseeing them all as he thoroughly, and needlessly, dried a glass, ears open for passing gossip.

Amelia managed to get his attention and he wandered over and leant sideways against the bar, his substantial beer belly pressing into the drip trays.

'How can I help, love?'

'I'm looking for someone.'

'Aye, well we've a few folk here, the night.' He smiled.

'He's tall and...' Just then Amelia looked along the bar and saw someone very tall and blond. Could it be Gideon? She hesitated for a second, figuring there would be more than one tall blond man in the village, but then he turned slightly to the side and there was no mistaking Gideon Fey's haughty profile. Or his well-modulated, RADA-trained voice rising above the others to complain, 'If I knew I'd have so much bloody trouble ordering a drink, I would have filled up my hip flask an hour ago. SERVICE!' He clicked his fingers above his head before leaning over the bar, trying to catch the attention of one of the bar staff. He looked far better than the last time she'd seen him as she clocked his non-mud-splattered chinos and a broad, vertically-striped, navy-and-cream blazer. His hair was washed and he was cleanly shaven and despite his casual appearance he still exuded the aura of a film star.

'Found him!' Amelia said to the big man behind the bar as she set off through the throng. When she got next to Gideon she reached up and tapped him on the shoulder. He stared down at her, eyes widening in recognition.

'Oh my GOD! Amelia! So you did decide to turn up after all. I was starting to lose faith.' He leant down to kiss her cheek. 'What's your poison, gorgeous? Gin and tonic? I would say margarita, but I think that's a little beyond them here.'

'A coffee would be fantastic.'

He gave her an exasperated look, then leant forward across the bar. 'I think an ancient jar of Mellow Birds is about the best we can hope for in this godforsaken hole.'

'Oh well, gin and tonic it is then, thanks.'

Gideon snapped his fingers at the middle-aged man Amelia had talked to, but he studiously ignored him as he pulled a pint for someone else.

'Don't they know who I am?' Gideon said tersely and Amelia

was about to laugh when she realised he wasn't being facetious. It was only when Gideon made to vault over the bar to pour his own that the barman quickened his pace and poured the drinks he'd ordered.

Amelia picked hers up, smiling at the barman and took a tentative sip as all around them the bar heaved and groaned as more squeezed into the Whistling Haggis to cheers and bellowing 'hullo's of welcome.

'It seems really busy for a Wednesday night.' She thought of her own local, a wine bar, where the greeting was as chilly as the overpriced Sauvignon Blanc they served.

'Well, apart from incest and sheep-shagging what else is there to do up here?'

Just then a man jostled Amelia's arm.

'Sorry, hen, I'd better keep an eye on what I'm doing,' he said in a lovely sing-song Scottish lilt, raising his voice to be heard above the music.

'Is it usually this busy?' Amelia asked him.

'Nah, we're all here for a nosey.'

'A nosey?' Amelia shouted, wondering if she'd misheard.

'Aye,' he bent his head lower, 'to get us a look at the latest newcomer. There's quite a buzz about...'

'Anyway,' Gideon stepped between them, steering Amelia away from the bar, 'I want to hear all about that dastardly Jonathan. Has he tried to get in touch?'

Amelia felt a pang. He'd been sending text messages all week but so far she'd deleted them all without replying. But not before reading them. They all said how much he missed her and how he couldn't live without her. She took out her phone to check and saw there was no signal. She'd not had one since leaving Ullapool. Maybe it would be a good thing to be unable to use her phone for a couple of weeks, she mused, slipping it back into her bag.

She and Gideon squeezed themselves into a secluded alcove round the corner from the musicians and Gideon tucked Amelia's case against the wall, out the way.

'When did you arrive?' she asked, taking a sip of her gin.

'A car dropped me off a couple of hours ago.'

He must be doing okay for his next project if cars were ferrying him about, Amelia thought.

'Are you staying here at the hotel?'

'No, no, somewhere nearby,' he said evasively but before she could ask where, she became aware of a man waving at them over the sea of people. He was in his early thirties with slightly overlong, jet-black curly hair. He stood out from the other pubgoers as he'd eschewed wool for a deep-plum shirt secured at the wrist with silver cufflinks.

'I think someone's trying to get our attention,' Amelia said.

'Oh? Probably just a fan,' Gideon said with a world-weary sigh, turning to have a look. He quickly turned back, downing his drink in one. 'Come on, poppet, drink up and I'll show you the bright lights of Glencarlach.' Grabbing hold of her arm he started to drag her away and Amelia just had enough time to pick up the handle of her case. Pulling it along behind her and apologising to everyone whose ankles she bashed with it, Amelia teetered along on her high heels in a bid to keep up. They got to the front door.

'Hang on, Gideon, I don't know where my house is, I'll need to go back and ask someone local.'

'No need, I've scouted it out for you already. I'll lead the way. Brace yourself.' Gideon had to push his entire body against the door before it budged slightly with the gusting wind.

This time, forewarned, Amelia buttoned up her jacket, securing her scarf beneath her collar, before venturing out, although the light fabric did nothing to keep out the cold.

Lifting up Amelia's case Gideon marched ahead, his long legs taking easy strides as Amelia half jogged to keep up with him.

'Can you slow down a bit,' she puffed.

'Don't want to risk bumping into anyone else, it's such a pain being asked for my autograph all the time.'

Amelia smiled, he seemed to be fairly incognito in the bar.

They reached the corner of the pub and turned up a lane which was riddled with potholes and puddles and seemed to be turning away from the village, almost going in the direction Amelia had come from. But at least they were slightly more sheltered from the wind. About 200 yards along the lane the street lighting ran out.

'Hang on,' Amelia said as Gideon swore after stubbing his toe on a large boulder. She dug inside her big shoulder bag and brought out a slimline scarlet Maglite. 'This will help.'

Gideon gave her a look of incredulity. 'You carry a torch in your bag?'

'Of course! It's ideal for those times when I'm being led up a dark path with no street lights.'

'Fair dos,' he said with a shrug.

With Amelia's torch beam lighting the way, they walked along the lane for another few minutes until they came across two rather imposing stone pillars and an eight-foot-high gate. With the village lighting now far behind them and the moon and stars playing coy behind the clouds, Amelia swept her torch either side of the pillars and could see a six-foot-high wall ran round the perimeter of whatever it was it concealed.

'Friendly!' Amelia said, trying not to show her disappointment. Her cottage lay beyond the wall and judging by the smooth, if slightly weathered and cracked appearance, she wasn't going to be able to scale it without a set of ladders.

'Don't worry, they're not locked, just heavy,' Gideon said, putting his shoulder against one of the gates and leaning all his weight against it. Very slowly it opened, rusted metal grating against the stone path.

Heart beating a little faster at the thought of what lay beyond, Amelia followed Gideon through. The lane now narrowed to a driveway, probably not much more than one car width, and either side was a deep verge, with tall, mature trees a few feet back, and beyond that more trees, as far as her torch would let her see.

'Is my house in the middle of a forest?'

'Yes, it does look a little Brothers Grimm in the dark, much friendlier by daylight, I assure you.'

A fox barked and Gideon and Amelia both jumped.

'Give me your hand,' Gideon said.

'I'll be fine, I'm not scared of some nocturnal animals.'

'You might not be, but I'm bloody terrified,' Gideon whimpered.

An owl hooting made Amelia re-evaluate her 'brave' status as she tried not to think of all the thrillers she'd read where a night walk in the woods ended very badly. Especially when the heroine was wearing a pair of vertiginous heels.

Progress was slow, between them stumbling into potholes and Gideon pausing to rest every few steps complaining she'd packed everything into her case *including* the kitchen sink.

Eventually, they rounded a corner and there, in a little clearing of trees, sat a beautiful cottage exactly as Amelia had imagined. Set back from the lane, it was small and squat with whitewashed stone walls and a slate roof. The front door was in the centre and either side sat two sturdy and slightly bowed windows. Shining the torchlight up to the roof she could see a proper chimney stack. It was fairy-tale book perfect.

'It's lovely,' she said, a lump forming in her throat.

'But...'

'It's exactly as I hoped it would be. I can't wait to see inside!'

'Amelia–'

'No, wait, Gideon, don't tell me anything about it, let me find out for myself.'

'Okay.' He held his hands up as she dug into her bag and pulled out the envelope with the house details and bunch of keys. Picking the one that looked most likely to fit she tried it in the door. It didn't turn.

She tried the next. It didn't even go in properly. She systematically went through all the others but not one of them opened the door to her charming cottage.

She gave a wail in frustration.

Gideon, who'd been leaning against the door jamb, gave her shoulder a squeeze. 'Um, darling, I'm not sure how to break this to you, but this isn't your house.'

'What? But...' She looked up at the door, it even had a brass knocker in the shape of a horseshoe.

'You asked me to let you find out for yourself.'

Amelia swallowed her disappointment. 'Where is my house then?'

'Slightly further along.'

'Is it as nice as this?'

'I do believe that when you see it all thoughts of this quaint little dwelling will go out your mind, darling.'

Just then Amelia's torch flickered, then went out.

An owl hooted and both she and Gideon clutched each other in fright.

'Shall we just pretend this is your cottage and break the door down,' Gideon whispered.

Tempted to go back to the cosy warmth of the Whistling Haggis, Amelia took a deep breath, the cold air biting at her lungs. Within a few moments her eyes started to get used to the dark and she could make out the lane and the shapes of the trees either side. A spooky forest was not going to put her off.

Linking arms, they set off again, this time a little more gingerly. They remained silent, as if their voices were too loud for the darkness. After a couple more minutes, Amelia became aware of another dark shadow looming up before them, breaking through the top line of the trees.

'I think there's something up ahead,' she whispered.

As they continued, the shadow grew higher and larger and engulfed the sky above them. Turning the last bend, Amelia realised it wasn't a house but a hotel. It was a large, rectangular, flat-fronted building, two storeys high. Very symmetrical, there was a large stone portico slap bang in the middle with many tall windows spaced evenly either side, looking very much like a house in a Jane Austen television adaptation. 'Have we come too far?' Amelia asked, but if it was a hotel in front of them, why was it in complete darkness, with no welcoming light to guide the way?

'No, this is it,' Gideon whispered back.

The feeling of expectant exhilaration in the pit of Amelia's tummy was now replaced by confusion and the sense that they were trespassing. There was no way this, this *mansion*, would be hers. It was surely a stately home or other national trust property and any second now the angry owner would appear on the threshold with a twelve-bore.

'Come on.' Gideon tugged at her arm.

'I really don't think so, there must be a mistake. Why don't we go back to the pub and I'll ask someone else, and I'll open up this envelope and have a proper look at the house details,' Amelia said.

'Only if you try the keys first. Remember, I've seen the house particulars.'

Now she knew how Elizabeth Bennet must have felt on seeing Pemberley for the first time. Slowly, Amelia walked up the wide stone steps towards the heavy wood-panelled double doors which were flanked by large stone columns. Digging out the bunch of keys, Amelia noticed her hand trembling and it wasn't just from the cold; it was one thing to imagine inheriting a lovely little two-room cottage but another entirely to be the benefactor of a fuck-off huge, imposing stone mausoleum.

She took her phone from her pocket and switched it on. There was enough light from the facia to see the keyhole. She picked out the biggest key and it slipped in easily and with a bit of pressure turned in the lock with a satisfying clunk.

Butterflies going into overdrive in her stomach, Amelia wondered what on earth she was going to find on the other side; some draughty relic fit for Miss Havisham, with all the furniture covered in dust cloths? Ancient grandfather clocks ticking solemnly in a dark and dank hallway? Ghosts silently traversing the stairs? More practically, was there damp rot, dry rot, mice?

Gideon cleared his throat beside her. 'I know this is a really momentous point in your life, darling, but do you think you could get on with it, I'm bursting for a pee.'

Amelia pushed the door open and stood momentarily in the doorway, breathing in dust and mothballs, the smell of history and secrets. Then a few seconds later the night air was ripped into by a very modern alarm sounding off as floodlights lit up the front of the house.

8

'Jesus! Turn it off!' Gideon shouted, holding his hands over his ears and squinting through the sudden brightness.

'I don't know how!' Amelia shouted back. She pulled out the particulars of the house, taking a moment to stare at the photo on the front page. Yup, the house was huge and quite beautiful. And all hers it would seem. Gideon grabbed the papers from her.

'Alarm code, alarm code, where's the bloody alarm code,' he said as he scanned the front page.

Amelia saw movement from the corner of her eye and turned to see a hooded figure running towards them brandishing a baseball bat.

Too paralysed with fear to scream, she clutched Gideon's arm as the figure bounded up the front-door steps, but instead of bashing them over the head with the weapon, the man went over to a panel and punched in a series of numbers. The piercing ringing stopped and the man turned to them.

'What the hell do you think you're doing?' he said in an American accent.

Gideon stepped forward, his nostrils flaring angrily. 'This is the owner of the house, claiming her rightful inheritance. And just who the hell are *you*?'

Standing a good couple of inches taller than Gideon, the man pulled his hood down, revealing shortish sandy-coloured hair and green eyes which appraised them coolly.

'The owner's dead.'

'I assure you I'm very much alive, despite your best efforts to scare us to death!' Amelia said. 'My godmother used to own this house but she died and left it to me.'

If she thought the American would back down and apologise for the mistake, Amelia was sorely deluded as he folded his arms across his chest and glowered at them.

'What's your name?'

'Amelia Adams.'

'I don't think so.'

'Yes it is!' both she and Gideon said in unison.

Then Gideon turned to Amelia. 'Well, I'm assuming it is unless you've fooled me with a very elaborate lie and lured me here under false pretences. Ooh, am I an accessory to your fiendish plot? This is getting very excit–'

'I've seen Amelia Adams and you are not her,' the American continued stonily.

'But of course I am!' Amelia said. 'And if you've met *her* before, it would have been *me*, and you would recognise me because I'm here, but that's all redundant because I've never seen *you* before!' She turned to Gideon. 'Of course there is no fiendish plot!'

The American shook his head. 'No way. I knew Dorothea and you are not the same Amelia that was in her photograph.'

Gideon looked back to Amelia.

'What...?' Amelia was so confused. 'Hang on, if you knew Dorothea how come I don't know you?' Then she remembered the lawyer telling her about the handyman and how he'd spent time with her. And it would explain why he knew the alarm code for the house.

'Are you Jack?'

His eyes narrowed slightly.

'We've never met,' Amelia said.

'Oh shit, the rozzers are here.' Gideon nodded at a police car roaring along the drive, blue lights flashing. It braked to a stop, sending chip stones flying. A policeman got out the driver's side and walked over.

'Trouble, Jack?' he said, hoisting up his belt.

'Yup, these two were trying to break in here but not before trying the gatehouse first.'

'Did they get in?'

'Nope, I was waiting for them if they had.' Jack smacked the baseball bat into his open hand. 'That's when I called you and followed them up here.'

'But this is my home!' Amelia said.

'Aye, and did you think the cottage was your home too?' the policeman asked, his thumbs hooked into his belt.

'Well, I did actually. Look, I've got keys!' She pointed to the large bunch, still hanging from the keyhole.

'So, you came into possession of a bunch of keys and thought you'd try all the local houses until you found one that they fit?'

'No! I really am the owner...'

'She's claiming to be Amelia Adams,' Jack said to the policeman, then he turned to Amelia, stony-faced, 'but I've seen a photograph of Amelia and you are clearly not the woman in it.'

Amelia thought back to her godmother's living room. Dorothea didn't have many photographs around the place, and the only one of Amelia was the one where...

Amelia started to laugh. 'Oh my God, no wonder you don't recognise me! That's not me as *me*, I'm Miss Marple!'

'Impersonating someone else?' The policeman's eyebrows shot up into his hat. So, now you're claiming not to be Amelia Adams but a Miss Marple, first name?' the policeman asked.

'Well, it's Jane, Jane Marple, but she's not real, she's the creation of Agatha Christie.'

'And this Agatha Christie, she's the mastermind behind your attempted breaking and entering?'

'What? No!'

Amelia looked to Gideon for some backup but he was leaning against one of the stone pillars at the top of the stairs, helpless with laughter. Amelia looked to Jack who was frowning at her.

'I know the photograph you're talking about,' Amelia said, trying to remain calm. 'It's of a little old lady with a tight grey perm and half-moon spectacles wearing a lavender twinset and pearls. And she's holding a carved pumpkin?'

'Uh, yeah.'

'That was me dressed up as Miss Marple for a Hallowe'en party! It was a very convincing costume. Someone even gave up a seat for me on the Tube! My friend Sally is a make-up artist and she was the one who transformed me with some latex and a ton of stage make-up. I even won a prize, which was a really nasty bottle of vodka.' She could see doubt flicker across Jack's face. She wouldn't exactly say he was thawing, but he definitely looked less certain of her guilt at attempting breaking and entering. 'And look, here are the particulars and keys I got from the lawyer. Why would I have them if I didn't own the place?'

'I think you should leave the questioning to me, Miss Adams or Miss Marple or whoever you are. I'm going to have to ask you to accompany me to the station while I find out what's going on.'

Amelia felt her knees go weak. She'd never had so much as a

parking ticket before. 'Are you arresting me?' she asked, feeling close to tears.

'I'll decide that once we establish who you are and if you do own this house.'

Gideon had suddenly stopped laughing. 'Oh, darling, don't worry, I'll get you out when they set bail or I can bake a cake and put a file in it, well it'll probably have to be a nail file because I don't have anything larger. I don't really bake either, but I can get a muffin from the bakers tomorrow.'

'No need, you'll be coming along too.'

'Me? But I've got nothing to do with this!' he said, outraged.

'Is it possible we could sort it out here?' Amelia asked.

'We'd need to verify your identity and have a look through all those documents of yours.' The policeman stood looking at her standing shivering in her flimsy coat with her large fuchsia-pink suitcase by her side, clearly weighing up how much of a criminal mastermind she looked.

'Let's go inside. If you are who you say you are, you have nothing to worry about.'

They walked in and Amelia was momentarily taken aback by the grandness. The vestibule itself could have easily housed most of her tiny flat. She paused, not having a clue where to go.

'I suppose I'd better lead the way then,' Jack said gruffly as he strode by them, leading them through the house.

They walked into a beautiful hall with a large sweeping staircase leading up to the first floor, which had an open gallery running round the corridor which allowed Amelia to see all the way around the floor above, with only the occasional column breaking up the open effect. There seemed to be a lot of bedroom doors, she thought as she turned round full circle. Directly up above her was a domed glass cupola and she could only imagine how bright the house would be during daylight hours. Amelia didn't have time to stop for long as they had to hurry along a wood-panelled passageway lined with serious-looking subjects in portraits and lots of dark, moody landscapes. She snuck a glance into a couple of rooms where the door was open and was thankful not to see one single dust sheet. They were now at the back of the house and Jack opened the door to the kitchen. It was another impressively-sized room, but the most standout feature was the retro cupboards. Actual retro, not a cool interpretation with a modern twist. It was a place of worship to 1960s orange Formica. The floor tiles were a hallucination-inducing intricate pattern of brown, yellow and orange which either clashed or complemented – Amelia couldn't be sure which because her eyes were jumping about and unable to focus – with the wall tiles which were in similar shades but a different frenetic pattern.

It was with blessed relief that Amelia saw a kettle and beside it a jar of Nescafé. She hoped it wasn't going to be a long night.

Thankfully, it all got sorted out reasonably quickly. Amelia produced her passport which she'd had the foresight to pack, and a quick call to dear old Mr Armstrong the lawyer had cleared everything up. Once she was no longer on Scotland's most wanted list, Constable Raymond Williams, or Ray as he asked them to call him, was actually very genial, welcoming them to the village and letting them know about the various forthcoming events planned, particularly the Christmas pantomime in which he'd been cast as one of Cinderella's ugly sisters. Cast every year by the Reverend McDade, Ray went on to say it was always a hotly fought battle for the main roles and Big Davey, the owner of the Whistling Haggis, had been cast as the other ugly sister. Ray had even shared his thermos of Heinz tomato soup after Amelia and Gideon promised to get tickets.

The entire time Jack sat on one of the counters, watching them.

With Ray bidding them a goodnight and Gideon seeing him to the door, Amelia spread the house particulars over the kitchen table. Jack wandered over and sat down in the chair opposite. Now he'd lost the ASBO hoodie and suspicious glower, he didn't look quite as threatening. Putting his age as early thirties, Jack Temple could be described as quite good-looking, Amelia supposed, if you went for a rugged alpha-male type with a strong chin and jaw, who clearly didn't feel the need to shave seeing as he had quite a few days' build-up of stubble. His sandy hair was also still sticking up from his head at odd angles. But it was Jack's eyes that caught Amelia's interest; a light green, they moved over the room, taking everything in and assessing. Clever eyes, Dotty would have described them as. And now those eyes were focused on Amelia with an unblinking frankness.

'You really didn't look at the plans once?' he asked, leaning back in his chair, one ankle resting on his other knee.

'I wanted to be surprised.'

'Are you?'

'Just a bit. I was expecting a little cottage, rather like the one slightly further up the road.'

'The gatehouse, where I'm staying.'

'Oh, is it nice?'

'Great. Real cosy.'

Amelia glanced back at the floor plan of Stone Manor. Impressive. Stunning. Full of architectural merit. Yes, her house was all this and more, but cosy it wasn't. Even the name Stone Manor didn't radiate warm and fuzzy feelings. Then she immediately felt guilty for such an ungracious thought.

'The lawyer mentioned my godmother employed you as a handyman and you'll be staying on for a bit.'

'Until the end of January.'

'Right. Are you enjoying it here?' With not much conversational input from Jack, Amelia was left with inconsequential small talk, although even that was also proving a challenge for Amelia as she could feel tiredness engulfing her.

'I'm having a swell time,' Jack said dryly, rising to his feet. 'I've written the alarm code instructions on the pad by the kettle and there are some candles and torches under the sink. The electrics aren't the best and sometimes fuse. All the rooms are regularly cleaned and aired so should be fine for you to take your pick of the bedrooms.'

Amelia tried to smile but just felt overwhelmed by the events of that day.

'Don't worry, this place is a lot less intimidating in the daylight.'

'Are you?' she fired back.

He gave her a ghost of a smile. 'Sometimes.'

'Well, aren't you Mr Congeniality!' Gideon said, returning to the kitchen. He reached into the inside pocket of his blazer and pulled out a hip flask and took a long swallow from it. 'Well, we don't want to keep you, I'm sure there are some light bulbs to replace somewhere or some equally handy handyman task to perform.'

'Gideon!' Amelia warned, although Jack wasn't doing very much to endear himself to her either.

But Jack just gave him a wry smile, unfazed. 'I'll leave you to finish your hip flask in peace. I'll see you tomorrow.' Amelia walked him to the door, with Gideon trailing laconically behind and they watched as Jack made his way back along the lane.

Closing the door, Gideon turned round, clapped his hands and rubbed them together. 'Righty-ho! Let's unpack and get wellied into my bottle of vodka!'

'It's almost midnight.'

'Exactly! Party time!'

It was only then that Amelia noticed four large cases lying in the hall.

'Where did these come from?'

'The car dropped these off with me when I came to do the recce earlier. I hid them round the side of the house.'

'You said you were staying locally.'

'I am. Here. With you.'

'But, your documentary? Don't you need to be with the rest of the crew?'

'They're not far from here.' Seeing her eyes widen, he gave her a reassuring smile. 'Oh, don't worry, they're not staying here, too, darling. I just thought you'd like a little bit of company.' She looked around her, at the imposing staircase, the wood panelling and impressive chandeliers and the scale of the room sizes. She hated to admit it but another living, breathing person in the house with her was a reassuring presence, even if that person was three sheets to the wind already.

'Let's go pick our rooms. And get the place a little more welcoming,' he said, flicking on an art deco table lamp. There was a loud bang and a flash from the wall socket and all the lights on the ground floor went out.

'Or we could go and light some candles,' Amelia suggested with a sigh.

'And say a prayer while we're at it. Look, the first-floor lights still seem to be on. Come on.'

Amelia followed Gideon up the stairs. Although the lights were on, they weren't the brightest wattage, and with the walls painted a dark brown, which matched the heavy oak panelling, the overall impression Amelia had was of gloom. At that moment Amelia would have gladly swapped the sheer scale of her new home for a modern en-suite room at the local pub.

At the top of the stairs, Amelia stopped at the first room. 'I may as well take this one.'

'Okay, I'll go in the next one along.'

Amelia pushed open her door. It creaked ominously. It was another huge room which was by no means dwarfed by the large oak four-poster bed nestled against the left wall. Reassuringly, when she pulled back the bedspread she was met with the fragrance of Lenor and not musty old dustballs. Despite the wood panelling and dark burgundy-and-gold regency stripe wallpaper she realised the room did have a quaint, antiquated charm to it. The walls were adorned with paintings of flora and fauna apart from the wall at the side of the bed which had a six-by-four-foot painting of a woman. The little brass plaque on the frame named her as 'Flora'. Flora in amongst the flora, Amelia thought and gave a little chuckle. Amelia stared at it for a few moments, trying to figure out the woman's facial expression but couldn't quite fathom what was going on behind the woman's eyes. She could certainly give the Mona Lisa a run for her money on enigmatic!

She liked it, though, even if she did feel as though she was being watched. Pushing away thoughts of Gothic horror novels where paintings came to life and the eyes followed the heroine around the room, Amelia opened up her case and pulled out a few things, including the new Denholm Armitage crime thriller which she'd still not managed to start, unable to give it her undivided attention with Toby living with her at the flat. Amelia walked over to the window to draw the curtains and as she looked out into the night the clouds parted to reveal the moon. With just that extra little shaft of light she could make out the silhouette of the treeline and nestled amongst it, reaching high up into the sky, there looked to be a tall tower. She was about to turn away when she saw a flicker of light coming from what must be a window. She stared. It wasn't an electric light being switched on, it was fainter than that.

There it was again! A faint light sweeping back and forth – like torchlight. A second later it went out.

Maybe someone was living there. It may not even be part of her garden, but a neighbour's. She would check it out tomorrow. Walking over to the bed, Amelia flicked on the bedside light only for there to be a large bang, darkness, then a shout from Gideon's room next door.

'Sorry!' she hollered back. Not bothering to change into pyjamas, or brush her teeth, shivering with cold and tiredness, Amelia crawled under the covers fully clothed. She glanced at her phone. No signal.

She wondered if she had any waiting text messages or phone calls. Toby would probably want to know how she was, and she'd promised to tell Sally about her new house too... and, of course, there was Jonathan...

She stared up into the darkness, willing herself not to cry. How was it possible to miss someone who wasn't ever really there for her? Things would look better in the morning, she told herself. Mr Armstrong held money in trust for the house to be done up and she was sure some new paint, IKEA furniture and a complete overhaul of the electrics would make a difference. Along with some heating, she thought as she pulled the bedclothes tighter around her. She would start a new to-do list tomorrow. She rolled over, hoping sleep would come quickly as she tried not to think of ghosts, ghouls and other things that went bump in the night.

9

Jack was already in the kitchen, cleaning grass off a lawnmower blade at the sink, when Amelia wandered in from a walk around the garden the next morning. She paused for a moment, distracted by Jack's physique, which last night had been hidden under a shapeless hoodie. The sleeves of the grey T-shirt he was wearing cut across at the widest part of his biceps, which were really rather bulgy, and she could see the muscles flexing under his tanned skin as he worked. His shoulders were broad and solid and down the middle of his T-shirt, in between his shoulder blades, ran a thin, slightly darker line of sweat.

'Are you going to say anything or just stand there checking me out in silence for another few minutes?' he said conversationally, without even turning round.

Amelia could feel her cheeks get warm. It wasn't as if she'd been ogling him!

'I just wondered how long you were going to be, so I could start making breakfast.'

He turned and flashed her a smile. 'Asking me would get you the answer a lot quicker.'

God, he was insufferably rude!

'What are you doing?'

'I was starting on the last cut of the season when it jammed, think it's okay now, so I'll be out your hair soon.'

'How big is the garden?' In fact, Amelia didn't even know if it constituted as a 'garden', with no visible boundary she was possibly venturing into owning 'grounds'.

'About thirty acres or so.'

Amelia had no real idea of how big an acre was but thirty of them sounded a lot. She also had no idea about gardening. On her walk she saw lots of lovely vast grassy areas with old trees and bushes. It looked very pretty in the pale morning sunshine, but as someone who couldn't even keep a supermarket basil plant alive for more than a couple of days on a window ledge, owning so much green space was a little daunting.

Jack turned to face her, drying his hands on a dishtowel. 'I'm sorry about your godmother. She was a nice lady.'

'Thanks. Yes, she was,' Amelia said, looking through the cupboards and finding the coffee and a mug. She leant over the sink to fill the kettle. Last night Amelia hadn't realised just how tall Jack was, but now standing eye level to his pectorals she figured he must be over the six foot mark by a couple of inches. 'How did you meet her?'

'She'd placed an advert for a handyman, I saw it and answered.' Jack picked up the piece of machinery and began to inspect it.

'Right. Only, the lawyer said you'd been visiting her at home while she was sick.'

'Yeah, she had a lot of things to tell me about this place before I started here. Because she got tired easily, I couldn't visit her for long periods of time.'

Amelia mulled this over for a moment before blurting out, 'It's just... she didn't mention you to me once.'

'Why would she?' He shrugged. 'I was just the handyman she'd hired.'

Despite telling herself not to be silly, Amelia was upset. Towards the end, her godmother's life was so insular she would have thought that any change to her normal routine would have merited a mention. It was almost as if she'd kept Jack a secret. Amelia never thought she and Dotty had any secrets from each other but between Jack's daily visits and a huge house in the north of Scotland, Amelia now wondered if anything else was about to rear its head.

'Did you enjoy your exploring?' Jack asked, breaking into her thoughts. 'I saw you wandering about.'

As soon as she woke she'd gone to look for the tower. Having no idea of its size from last night she was a little taken aback to see just how imposing it was, perched on top of a steep hill. A path led up to it from the main part of the garden, winding its way past some eight-foot-tall hedges and interesting-looking bushy plants. About halfway up the route became steeper, with a few large tree roots to manoeuvre around. Finally, when Amelia came out at the top, the tower loomed above her. About fifty feet high, the base was about thirty feet in diameter but then it tapered inwards towards the top. The building was encircled by a gravelly path and there was a large solid stone bench placed a few feet away, positioned to face out towards the stunning views of the Torridon Hills. The tower had clearly seen better days as the top section had crumbled away and it looked as if it was sitting at a bit of an angle. She'd walked all the way around it but couldn't find a door. She'd taken a few steps back and walked around it again in case the entrance was slightly higher up but there was still nothing, apart from a few narrow arched windows she'd have no hope of ever fitting through. There seemed to be a larger window at the top but unless Rapunzel was the princess in residence, Amelia couldn't see any way to get in. Jack would surely know about it.

'I just went for a quick walk, I didn't go very far. You know the tower?'

'Yup.'

'How do you get into it?'

He shook his head. 'You don't. It's a folly.'

'A what-y?'

'A folly. They were popular in the eighteenth and nineteenth centuries. They were built as ornamental buildings, often in the style of a Roman temple or a mock Gothic ruin, like the tower out there. Just something pretty with no real use.'

Gideon chose that moment to flounce in, narrowing his eyes at Jack.

'I need a coffee,' he said, knotting his dark-grey silk dressing gown at the waist.

'Sleep well?' Amelia asked.

'No, I did not. All that noise out there! Screeches and hooting and yelps and God knows what else! It was horrific.'

'It's called nature,' Jack said.

'Bloody intrusive is what it is.' Gideon sat down heavily on a chair laying his head on his arms just as there was a shrill ringing noise.

'That's the doorbell,' Jack said.

Gideon's head shot up. 'I'll get it,' he said, bolting for the front door.

A couple of minutes later he was back with someone else in tow, and Amelia recognised him as the man with the black curly hair who'd tried to speak to them in the pub the previous night. There were another three men with him.

'You must be Amelia!' the first man said in a husky, accented voice.

'Um, yes.'

He stuck out his hand and shook hers. I'm Beniamino Vincenzi, the director.'

She looked at Gideon who in turn sloped off towards the kettle.

'Oh! Are you the director of Gideon's new project?'

'Yes! But don't be so modest, we wouldn't have a project if it wasn't for you.'

'What?'

'You came to Gideon's rescue!'

Amelia laughed. 'Oh, that day in the lift? Please, all I did was pop on a bit of concealer and let him borrow a suit for a few hours.'

Beniamino's smile faltered and Amelia wondered if his English wasn't all that good.

'Are you filming close to here?' she asked him, a little more slowly.

Beniamino frowned and nodded, his black curly hair bouncing around his head.

'When Gideon arranged to meet me here I didn't realise it was because he'd be working locally,' Amelia said, glancing over at Gideon who was studiously ignoring them all.

Beniamino looked very confused. Okay, maybe his English was worse than Amelia thought. No wonder Gideon hadn't looked that happy to see him.

'I'd love you to tell me more about your documentary,' Amelia added.

'Fantastic! That is why I am here. We need to sit down together and have a good old chinwag about it,' Beniamino said in fluent English, the smile returning to his face.

It was now Amelia's turn to look confused. Why on earth would the director of Gideon's documentary want to sit down with her?

'We have so much to discuss and plan,' Beniamino added as

the other three men nodded in agreement, 'but first I'd like to set up in here and do a quick interview to get a feel for your emotions at finding all of this.'

'Um... me?' Amelia said, thinking she'd misheard.

'Si. It's a shame we couldn't be here last night to get your very first reaction shot but this morning is good enough. Mike has taken a few exterior shots already, where you are walking thoughtfully, with a touch of melancholy, through the garden.'

The muscular black man to Beniamino's right gave her a small wave and Amelia realised he was holding a camera in his hand.

'Oh, and this is Lawrence, lighting, and Ross, sound and editing.' He patted both the other men on the shoulder, one a tall, skinny guy with floppy blond hair and glasses and the other a sturdy man with short reddish hair who gave her a friendly wink.

'I'm sorry, I don't understand,' Amelia said, feeling very confused.

Beniamino looked to Gideon who put down his mug and turned around.

'Amelia, my darling, I've got an itsy-bitsy little confession to make...'

Amelia looked from Gideon to the film guys. She glanced at Jack who was now leaning back against the sink, arms folded, watching the unfolding drama with amusement.

'A word, Gideon. Outside.'

Gideon followed her into the hallway.

'You didn't tell me I'm going to be in your documentary,' she hissed so the others wouldn't hear.

'It's a bit more than that, poppet, you *are* the documentary.'

10

Amelia tried to remain calm as Gideon's words sank in.

'What exactly do you mean, *I'm the documentary*?'

'Well, when I saw the particulars of the house and you told me your lawyer had money put aside for refurbishing, I thought this would be a sensational story for a documentary. A rags to riches fairy tale. With me helping you along the way.'

'You are a far cry from my idea of a fairy godmother, Gideon,' Amelia said, struggling to keep her voice calm.

'You see, this is what they want!' He clapped his hands in delight. 'Witty retorts like that! With your spirit and my looks, we are perfect documentary fodder.'

Amelia pinched the bridge of her nose, and tried to breathe deeply.

'I really didn't think you'd mind,' Gideon said.

'But you didn't even ask! I thought you'd arranged my flight to help me out.'

'I did!' he said, clutching his chest, sounding wounded. 'When would you have done this yourself? I gave you the push you needed. You had no job, no boyfriend...'

'Which all came about because of your interference!'

'Are you seriously trying to tell me you'd rather be in a job you hate, having secretive dates with your married boyfriend than claiming your inheritance and becoming lady of the manor?'

Obviously not, but she didn't want Gideon to think he was in the right.

'Why didn't you ask me first?'

'You might not have said yes.'

Amelia sighed. It was impossible to argue with someone who applied a toddler's logic to the situation.

'I just wished you'd at least warned me!'

'I intended to but the situation never really arose, darling.'

'We saw Beniamino, the director of this thing, last night! It was the *ideal* situation.' Despite her best intentions to stay calm, Amelia could feel her voice rising.

'You'd had a long journey, I didn't want to bother you.'

'So you thought them rocking up with the cameras and fuzzy microphones was a better way to break it to me?'

'Darling, please don't make a fuss,' Gideon appeased. 'I am truly sorry for upsetting you. I know I've gone entirely the wrong way about it, but I really need this to work for me. And I like you, I wanted to save you from your drudgery. I want us to do this together.'

Drudgery! She didn't think her circumstances were *that* dire. 'Gideon,' she said in a much calmer voice, 'what if I say no?'

Gideon visibly slumped. 'Obviously it's your house and your call. I'm sorry. Yes, I do need something to save my skin, I'll be honest about that. I'm fucking terrified I've blown it and I won't have a career anymore. And that means everything is over for me. If I don't come up with something for a documentary I'm dead in the water. I could, of course, pitch a trip to Africa to save some poor, almost extinct animal or say I'll sell my soul to take part in a cookery programme or a dancing competition but it will be ten a penny and dull and what's the point in that? But this here, you and me, is far more real.' He looked at her imploringly. 'But this isn't just about me. I honestly believe we'll have fun. I saw the opportunity and I took advantage of it. And I know I took advantage of you and I'm sorry for that, but think it through; this house is huge, yes? You want to do it up, make the most of it? Unless you're superwoman you'll need some help, right? Okay, I'll 'fess up to being pretty crap at stripping wallpaper and I have no discernible DIY skills. I'm also pretty useless in an emergency. But I *can* make people laugh, I'm a boon at any gathering and my cocktail making skills are second to none. This place is going to take a lot of work so why not have a little fun while you're doing it? The only catch is it will be documented along the way, helmed by a jobsworth Italian, but the film crew will be in the background. You won't even realise they're there half the time.'

'Could you do that bit again?'

'What?' Amelia whirled around to see Mike filming them from behind the half-open doorway.

'Could you repeat it from "It's your house and your call". The sound got a bit muffled.'

'No, I had no idea Dotty left me this house.'

'This is Dorothea, your aunt?' Beniamino stood a little way behind Mike, the cameraman, and was asking her the questions. They'd gone for an informal setting, with Amelia standing in the kitchen, coffee in hand. Wanting to get Amelia's reaction as soon as possible so it was fresh, they'd given her just five minutes to get ready before following her around the house as she talked them through each room before returning to the kitchen for her interview on camera. She'd hurried to put on some make-up, as Amelia wanted to look as kick-ass as possible in case Jonathan ever saw the documentary. She didn't want him to think she was pining for him and decided nobody 'pines' wearing a daring shade of scarlet lipstick. She'd also added another layer of black kohl eyeliner for good measure. Whoever said you should make a feature of either eyes or lips but not both had clearly never wanted to show their pathetic cheating ex they'd been well and truly kicked to the kerb. With a quick ruffle up of her short hair to give it a cute, choppy look, Amelia was camera ready.

'She wasn't my real aunt, although I called her that,' Amelia continued, trying not to be too self-conscious of the camera pointing right at her. 'She was actually my godmother and looked after me and my brother when our parents died.'

'Did she bring you up as her own?'

'To an extent. I mean, we didn't live with her all the time, we went to boarding school, but she came and fetched us and we stayed with her in the holidays and most weekends. She'd often pop down to take us for lunch or to the cinema or just to see how we were doing. She was forever bringing us emergency chocolates and magazines and books and things like that.'

'But it must have been very tough being on your own.'

'I wasn't on my own, I had my brother Toby and we're very close in age.'

'Boarding school must have been a lonely time for you.'

'Not at all! I had an absolute blast.'

Jack, who'd been sitting on a kitchen countertop out of shot, burst out laughing.

Amelia cleared her throat. 'I made some great friends there. One girl, Sally Bishop, is still my best friend to this day. We've had a lot of fun together over the years. In fact, she's a make-up artist, one of you may have worked with her at some point.'

'And cut,' Beniamino said. 'We'll leave it there for now. Don't know if we'll use this or not,' he added to Mike in a quiet voice. They all trooped out with their filming paraphernalia.

'Did I do something wrong?' Amelia said to Jack. 'Beniamino didn't look very happy.'

'I think he was after more of an emotional impact,' he said, jumping down from the countertop. 'Probably something along the lines of how your upbringing was miserable because you were an orphan and you ended up in a Dickensian-style school where they offered gruel at mealtimes and your only source of comfort was the distant woman who looked after you for two weeks out of every year.'

'But it wasn't like that at all! My school was fantastic, and the food was great, still the best sticky toffee pudding I've ever tasted. Oh bugger, I knew this documentary was a bad idea.' Amelia took a sip of her now lukewarm coffee and silently cursed Gideon.

'Shouldn't have said yes then,' Jack retorted as he walked out the back door, his big heavy boots scuffing over the tiles.

'Yes, well, thank you for stating the obvious,' Amelia replied hotly to his retreating back. All he did was give her a backhanded wave in return.

'SIGNAL! I've got a signal!' The cry went out and reverberated around the entire house. Amelia dumped her mug on the draining board and ran to where Gideon had called from. She could hear a thundering stampede of feet from other rooms.

'Gideon?' Amelia, called out, phone at the ready.

'In here!' Following his voice she found him in the library, a beautiful room she'd already discovered and looked forward to spending more time in. A large bay window, with a French door insert, overlooked one of the prettiest parts of the garden and was crying out for a chaise longue to be nestled there where Amelia could sit and read and while away a few hours. There was also a set of stairs which led to a mezzanine balcony which housed the books in their solid, floor-to-ceiling bookshelves. When she'd been in the library earlier Amelia hadn't had time to explore fully, she'd been too busy honing her 'reaction' for Beniamino which consisted of her opening the door, making a shocked expression and going 'Oh my God, *another* huge room.' Although she didn't have time to linger in any of the rooms, she'd marvelled at what on earth she was going to do with all the space. Was there any call for a twenty-first-century woman to make use of two drawing rooms, a billiard room, music room, dining room, library and kitchen with various pantries off of it? Then there were the bedrooms. She was pretty sure she'd counted seventeen of them.

This time, though, she didn't even glance at the room, but made a beeline for Gideon who stood at the window. Amelia joined him and turned on her phone to see two bars of signal light up the facia. Within a few seconds it was beeping and chirping at her as text messages and voicemails registered on her phone.

Beniamino, Mike and the tall, blond one – she still hadn't worked out which was Lawrence and which was Ross – were close behind and started making phone calls as soon as they joined her.

Amelia quickly fired off a text to Toby, briefly explaining about the house and the documentary. Then, fearing the signal would disappear again, she just cut and pasted it and sent it to Sally. Then she tackled her newly received texts. Sifting through the usual nonsense of spa offers and shoe sale notifications, there were a few from Toby, asking how she was, wanting photos of her house, wondering if she'd had problems with her washing machine and then, rather worryingly, one asking if she had the number of a plumber. Two from Sally, the first asking how she was, then another telling all about a cute guy who was sitting beside her on the flight from LA to London. And five from Jonathan. Her stomach tightened in anticipation as she opened them. They were short and to the point.

I miss you. I need you.

They all said the same. She looked at them fairly dispassionately. Okay, so she wasn't expecting a Byronesque love poem or even a thousand-word essay on why he wanted them to get back together, but something a little more personal would have been nice. Looking at those six words again, Amelia started to get annoyed; they were all about him. *His* wants and *his* needs. On repeat. She wondered if he'd cut and pasted them all too.

She stuffed her phone back into her pocket. With the others still texting and reading their messages, Amelia took a moment to walk up the steps to have a proper look at the books. The first few bays she bypassed when she saw they contained lists of crew and shipping routes of the merchant navy from 1860 along with some other very dry-sounding titles. There were rows of books on Egypt covering the country's geography and history but mostly archaeology. There was the same again for Asia. A few books on the archaeology of Pompeii and Herculaneum too. Then she came across some beautiful leather-bound editions of Dickens, Austen and everything Shakespeare had ever written. The farther round she got the more interesting the books became for her. Classics morphed into modern classics and then ended with row upon row of crime, including the Agatha Christies. All of them. Now would be a perfect time for Amelia to revisit the comforting pages of the crime books Dotty had introduced her to. She found *Murder on the Orient Express*, the first one she'd read. Slipping it from the shelf, Amelia could smell the musty, papery smell she loved from old books. She carefully opened it and a piece of cream card fell out and landed at her feet. Expecting it to be a bookmark, Amelia bent to pick it up but discovered it was an envelope.

Turning it over she saw there was a name written on the front...

Amelia.

11

Amelia's heart pounded as she stood looking at the envelope. She wasn't imagining it, the letter was addressed to 'Amelia' and she was pretty certain it was her godmother's handwriting. But could it really be meant for her? She didn't know of any other Amelias in Dorothea's life. The fact it was in her favourite Agatha Christie book, the one Dotty had given her to introduce her to the genre was too much of a coincidence. Taking both the book and her letter, Amelia slipped out the library and ran back upstairs to her room and closed the door behind her.

Her hands were shaking so much Amelia ripped the envelope slightly as she removed the letter. Sitting on the edge of the bed, she unfolded the letter and started to read.

My darling Amelia

You've found it! Well done. I thought this was the most likely book you'd look in first, despite there being so many to choose from. Christie's work really does still stand the test of time.

Amelia had to look up for a second and blink furiously as the words were swimming in front of her. Through her tears she also managed to laugh; she should have known that even death was never going to stop Dotty from getting in touch with her. With a shaky breath she carried on reading.

I know I could have given this to Mr Armstrong but I thought you'd find this way of communicating far more satisfying! (James is a dear, isn't he? Did I ever tell you he once tried to court me? What a disastrous fit we would have been.)

So, let's cut to the nasty bit. The cancer's back. I won't be surviving it this time. I've made my peace with it but it's still so infuriating as I still have so much to say to you. Yes, I know we could have talked but this way is so much more fun!

Clearly, the fact you're reading this means I'm dead, turned to dust, etc., etc. Please don't be too sad, I've had a good innings as they say. I do regret not being able to know what kind of turnout I had at my funeral. I hope it was enough to be an event but not too much to be vulgar. I also hope that peculiar neighbour with the bow tie collection and love of playing Wagner at one in the morning didn't make an appearance, he was such an oddity.

So, Stone Manor is all yours. I hope you like it... or is it even a house that can be liked, I wonder? It holds many, many secrets, some good and some bad. It likes its secrets so much it is still holding on to some of them. You see, my dear Amelia, the house has hidden treasure.

'Treasure?' Amelia said aloud in disbelief.

Yes, darling, you did read that correctly; treasure. Of course, it could just be equal measures of romanticism, folklore and optimism but I've always believed there's enough evidence to support it being here.

Why didn't I tell you about this sooner? Well, I certainly thought about it many times but something always held me back. There is a belief that there's a curse attached to the treasure and I have to say it has sent some of the family a little mad in their desire to find it. I, too, was briefly touched by the obsession. On inheriting the house from his brother, my father kept Stone Manor on with a skeleton staff and we only ever holidayed in it during the summer as we lived permanently in London. In 1958 I contracted glandular fever and had to defer my university placement and it was decided I would recuperate away from the city with some clean fresh air and so I came to Glencarlach. I stumbled upon the legend of the hidden treasure which I'd never heard of before. (My father refused to speak of it and when I pressed him on it said nothing good could come of finding it.) In 1958 I gave myself a full year in which to find it and when I didn't, I walked away. In the passing years I have thought of it many times, but I didn't want to risk getting caught up in it again. I thought by telling you about it I would become absorbed once again and feared I'd take you with me.

I do believe you have far more sense than to let a treasure hunt take over your life. If you find this letter, please start to look for it but always remember it is for fun, don't let it obsess you.

The other reason I didn't tell you about the treasure before is because this way is so much fun, wouldn't you agree? Of course, there could be no actual treasure at all, but just in case there is, I didn't want the house to be sold on to a stranger. That's why I put the clause in the will that it must stay in your possession.

Although you and your brother are not my blood relations, I love you both as if you are.

I'd love to tell you more about the treasure and the secrets of the house but I have a feeling you'll enjoy finding it out for yourself.

I will tell you that it is Montgomery Campbell who would be the one responsible for the treasure. I shall leave other letters and information hidden for you. I know how much you love a mystery so

*I'm not going to tell you where they are, but you're a bright girl and I
have every faith you'll find them.*

All my love,

Dotty

*P.S. Apologies about the kitchen, my mother decided to have it
replaced in the late sixties, I always meant to modernise it but never
quite got round to it. It really is rather hideous!*

*P.P.S. Remember that the house has its secrets — I always
thought my grandmother Flora looked as if she knew a few too.*

XXX

Amelia read it again and let it all sink in.

What if she didn't manage to find any of the other letters?
She desperately wanted to know what else Dotty was going to
tell her. And what on earth was all this about treasure?

A loud knock on her door made Amelia jump.

Gideon poked his head round the door.

'Come on, we're all going to the pub.'

'Now?'

'Yes, it's bloody freezing, there's no food and Beniamino
wants to get some "local colour" recorded.' He made air quotes
with his index fingers.

Amelia folded the letter and slipped it into the pocket of her
pencil skirt.

'And more to the point,' Gideon added, 'I'm desperate for a
drink.'

Despite wanting to stay in the house and start looking for
Dotty's next letter, Amelia found herself cajoled into joining the

others in the Whistling Haggis. By the time she sat down at a table near the fire, so welcoming after the cold house, and the even colder walk to get there, she was very glad Gideon had persuaded her as her stomach was growling in annoyance at having had nothing more than a Twix and a Pot Noodle all day. Her decision to eat out was further vindicated when she saw a waitress walking past with a plate of delicious-looking, and smelling, fish and chips.

Two gin and tonics later and she was positive she'd never been in a nicer pub in her life.

'You're really not much of a drinker, are you, poppet?' Gideon said, patting her hand.

'Not really, but you know the thing I love most about this place? It's our local!'

'Well, it's *your* local. I am merely a ship passing through in the night.'

'Well, I suppose I am too then,' she said, suddenly feeling sad.

'You don't have to be. What's back in London for you? You can carve a beautiful new life up here.'

'But doing what?'

'That's the beauty of it, darling, you can make it whatever you like and luxuriate in that lovely big house while you decide.'

At that point Amelia glanced over to the nearby table where Beniamino, Mike, Lawrence and Ross were sitting. Mike was surreptitiously filming Amelia and Gideon as they talked.

Amelia waved them over. 'Come over here. Stick the tables together. You don't have to eat separately.'

Beniamino quickly obliged as Mike carried on filming.

'Okay, I have a question,' Amelia said, emboldened by the gin. 'Which one of you is Lawrence and which one of you is Ross, as I've been getting you confused all morning?'

'I'm Lawrence,' said the taller of the two with the blond hair.

'And I'm Ross,' said Ross.

'Okay. Ooh, I've got a good way to remember! *Ross* is the *rrr*redhead, with the *rrr*rougish good looks and the *rrrr*rugby player physique. Who's from *rrr*round here,' she said, rolling her 'r's to imitate his Scottish accent.

'Well, Glasgow actually, but yes, I can live with those descriptions.' He gave her a cheeky wink.

'And *Lllawrence* is from Lllllondon and is *lllllanky* and *lllllosing* his hair...'

Gideon guffawed. 'And I'm accused of lacking diplomacy at times!'

'... and *lllllovely*,' Amelia finished. 'Oh, I don't mean it in a bad way, just an observant way.'

'Charming,' Lawrence said, none too pleased with the description.

Amelia tried to think of a word beginning with 'L' that also meant grumpy sod. She'd not seen him smile once.

'And, of course, there's Mike, *Mmmmike* from *Mmmmmanchester*. You take your job very seriously. I don't think I've ever seen you without your camera in your hands.' She picked up her napkin and waved it at him. 'If you stick around you can see me make a swan out of this!'

As the meal went on, Amelia relaxed into the documentary crew's company. They were actually a really nice group and even Lawrence was starting to thaw.

'A toast!' she said, lifting her glass. Everyone lifted theirs too.

'At first, I thought this documentary thing was going to be a nightmare but I'm really glad we've all gotten to know one another a bit better and I definitely feel more comfortable with you all. Here's to a very successful documentary!'

'To a very successful documentary,' they all chorused and chinked their glasses together.

'I agree,' said Ross, the red-headed one. 'This has really

helped us bond. The better a crew and the subjects get on, the better the documentary will be.'

Beniamino nodded. 'Exactly. You break down the barriers and the interviews become much more open and honest, which in turn makes the viewer believe in the process far more.' He took a breath. 'You know, if we moved in with you, we would have a much more seamless filming process. There wouldn't be an obvious beginning and end to filming time, you would see us as an extension of your home. Obviously, you would still have your privacy and we would respect that completely. But by having a closer rapport with you we would have a far better idea of when to approach you and when to leave you alone with the filming. And it would be really helpful if we had a room to use for our editing.'

Amelia didn't know what to say. In some ways she still hated the idea of the documentary but she had agreed to it for Gideon's sake and she didn't want to make the process any more difficult than it was already. And the house was so large... it might be nice to have more people staying in it. She certainly had enough room.

'Sure! Why not. The more the merrier.'

'Fantastico!' Beniamino said effusively, leaning over and kissing her on both cheeks, not caring that the sleeves of his cashmere jumper had landed in the remains of Amelia's tartare sauce.

'Right!' Amelia said, standing up, 'I'm off to get us some more drinks in.' She walked over to the bar, turning to check what everyone was drinking. Not paying attention to where she was going, she managed to trip over someone's bag lying on the ground. Stumbling forward she careered head-first towards the bar, buffeting against someone's hard stomach muscles, seconds before a glass of something cold, wet and alcoholic landed on her head.

'Argh!'

'Whoa there!' Two strong arms helped her to her feet.

Wiping beer from her eyes, Amelia looked up at Jack. Bugger it! Of all the people she had to land on.

'It's not every day I have women literally falling at my feet!' He immediately started mopping at her hair with the sleeve of his woolly jumper. She felt as if she was a damp dog being dried off after a walk.

'I tripped.'

'Yeah, so you say.' He laughed.

Uh, he really had tickets on himself, Amelia thought as she wafted her blouse away from her skirt, feeling the beer seeping through the layers of her clothes and settling in her underwear.

'Aren't beer shampoos good for the hair? Davey, can I get a towel or something?'

Davey, the big man from behind the bar that Amelia had spoken to the night she arrived, obliged and handed over a clean dish towel.

'Amelia, this is Big Davey, Big Davey, Amelia. And that guy over there is Wee Davey.'

'My son,' Big Davey elaborated, although he didn't have to as the younger man changing one of the optics was a mini-me of his father, just a little less jowly and a couple of stone lighter.

'Hi, nice to meet you,' Amelia said, trying to soak up the worst of the spill from her clothes.

'Hang on,' Jack said, bending over to pick something off the floor. He looked at it, then held it out for Amelia. 'It's yours.'

It was Dotty's letter. It must have fallen out of her pocket when she tripped. Amelia quickly returned it to her pocket.

'Oh, darling, are you okay? That was quite a spectacular nosedive,' Gideon said, coming over and draping his woollen scarf over her shoulders. 'Let's get you home.'

'But we're celebrating,' Amelia said, not wanting to force the others to leave.

'Don't worry, I'll grab some bottles to go. We can't have you wandering about soaked in beer, you'll be sending the local men crazy with your impromptu wet T-shirt look.'

Amelia lifted off Gideon's thoughtfully placed scarf. Right enough, her white silk blouse was almost transparent and her lace bra was showing. At least it had been her good underwear, was the only salvageable thought she could take away from her embarrassment.

'You're celebrating?' Jack asked.

'Yes, I've said for the others to move into the house. It'll make filming easier if they have twenty-four-hour access.'

Jack gave her a wry smile and took a large swallow of the remains of his pint.

'I'll go and get my jacket,' Amelia said as she and Gideon headed back to their table. Amelia tried to ignore the feeling of beer running down her legs and puddling in her stilettos.

'Listen to this!' Beniamino said, ushering for Amelia and Gideon to sit down again. 'This is Archie.'

They'd been joined by a man Amelia judged to be well in his seventies, with a weather-beaten face and a twinkle in his eye. Mike was already filming him.

'Archie is here to tell us about the legend of Stone Manor!' Beniamino said in delight.

Archie gave a little wink at the camera. 'Aye, I certainly am.' He reached out to shake Amelia's hand; it was rough and calloused and he clearly worked outdoors. 'A pleasure to meet the new owner.'

'So, what can you tell me about this legend?' Amelia asked, her heartbeat quickening, instantly forgetting about her beer-dampened clothes.

'Well, it's just what people say. My family have lived around here for generations, long before the house was built,' he said in his lovely Scottish lilt.

'Oh, and what was here before the house, Archie?' Beniamino interjected.

'Fields, Ben, fields.'

'Just fields, no burial sites or anything like that?' Beniamino pressed.

'Och, we're no in a Stephen King novel here, Ben!' Archie scoffed. 'But once the house was built there were a fair few rumours flying round. It was built in the 1700s and word is there were a couple of extra nooks and crannies built in.'

'Nooks and...?'

'Hidden bits, Ben, secret rooms and the like,' Archie explained. 'Aye, and they managed to successfully hide more than a couple of Jacobites on the run from the king's soldiers. One of the previous owners, Montgomery, did a fair bit of travelling but contracted something that made him go a bit doolally every so often. The story is he found quite a bit of treasure on his travels and buried it here, in the house.'

'Where?' Beniamino asked as Amelia leant in to listen carefully. So far, everything Archie said had matched what Dotty had put in her letter.

Archie laughed. 'Do you think if I knew that I'd have no tried to dig it up by now? He either forgot where it was or died before he could tell anyone.' He leaned a bit closer to Amelia and the camera, and everyone round the table did the same.

'His son, Archibald, he was a rum 'un. A ne'er-do-well if ever there was one. A gambler and a drinker. His father tried to palm him off on a few different lassies and eventually some unsuspecting poor girl agreed. Archibald spent his whole life hunting down the treasure but couldnae find it anywhere. He went insane trying to find it and then he threw himsel down the stairs an' broke his neck.' Archie gave a very convincing impression of someone breaking their neck, complete with tongue sticking out the side of his mouth in a grotesque fashion. 'Although there were rumours that his wife had a hand in it, if you ken,' he tapped the side of his nose, 'and no one would ah blamed her if she'd thrown him doon the stairs hersel. Anyway, Archibald's firstborn son, Charles, also became obsessed with the legend and spent his life looking for it, too, until one day he disappeared. No one ever found the body. Some say he found the treasure but ended up getting buried with it. Some say he went mad and hanged himself in the woods and crows pecked away at his head until only his body was left, and his headless ghostly corpse rides through the woods on his horse. There's a spot in the woods we locals call Hangman's Gorge, you know.' Archie's eyes widened and he arched his brows as he let that little titbit of information sink in. 'Some say he was attacked by the father of a young village girl he'd raped and he was the one who cut off his head with a sword. Some say there was already a crazed axeman roaming around the woods and Charles was in the wrong place at the wrong time an' became the next victim.'

Amelia felt herself shiver.

'But however he died, because that is in no doubt, people still hear him at night, through these woods, wailing and screaming. When ah was only a nipper ma folks wouldnae let me near the house in case the ghosts of Stone Manor would get me, which was a right shame cos you could find yoursel some great rabbits there. Ahh...' he looked at Amelia with a slightly worried expression, '... but obviously no one poaches up there now.'

'Wow! Treasure and ghosts! Fantastico!' Beniamino said with a grin as Mike gave him the thumbs up to show he'd caught it all and it was a cut. 'Let me buy you a drink, Archie.'

'Why that's very kind of you,' Archie said as they went up to the bar together.

So the hidden treasure wasn't all that much of a secret then if any random farmer knew about it, Amelia thought. But at least she'd gleaned a little more information. She glanced up at the bar to see Jack watching them. He gave her an assured grin before turning back to the bar and his pint.

'Come on, Gideon,' she said, 'let's go home.'

They were a far more subdued little group on the walk back to the house. The filming crew had decided to walk back with Amelia and Gideon and they all trooped along the dark path from the Whistling Haggis. All of them had a torch to help light the way except Gideon whose hands were taken up with carrying bags full of bottles he'd bought at the bar. The wind had picked up again and Amelia pulled her ineffectual coat around her beer-damp clothes.

Ross, who was at the front, turned around and put the torch under his chin.

'We'd best not dilly-dally, we don't want the ghost of the headless horseman to get us!'

There were a few spooky wails from the others.

Ross shushed them, then carried on. 'The night we arrived here I got talking to some locals at the bar and I heard a couple of variations on the ghost story. A few people have gone missing along this stretch of woods over the centuries. Many more have witnessed strange occurrences.'

'Ooh, like what?' Amelia asked, intrigued as she teetered along, trying to keep up in her high heels.

'Like at certain points of the path, have you noticed that the wind picks up, and it whistles slightly? If you listen carefully it's almost like a voice, beseeching you to step off the path and go deeper into the trees.'

Amelia briefly shone her torch out to the side and into the dense woods.

'No, I've not heard ghostly voices!' Gideon said. 'Anyway, it's the ghost of the axe-wielding man who cut the head off the headless horseman in the first place we should be keeping an eye out for!'

'Someone else told me there was a man of the cloth who had a gambling problem and when he had nothing left, he sold his soul to the devil and it was the devil who chopped off his head,' Ross continued. 'Another said it was a highwayman who'd fallen into a trap set by the locals. He thought he was escaping but he rode straight into a broadsword which had been balanced across the branches at the trees at the entrance of the woods.'

'Well, clearly all the stories can't be true,' Gideon said, 'otherwise this wood would be as busy as Piccadilly Circus with all these headless horsemen galloping about and bumping into each other because without any heads how would they know which way to go!'

'How often does he appear?' Amelia wondered aloud, her body tingling with intrigue. 'Is he a harbinger of doom or does he warn people of impending danger?'

'Oh darling! Only you could think that a headless apparition would appear so it could help someone, just like Casper the friendly ghost!' Gideon laughed.

'Well, there may well be a ghost, but I doubt it's got anything to do with buried treasure,' Ross said firmly. 'I'd put my money on it being a mad local. There'll be a fair amount of inbreeding up here. Anyone seen *The Wicker Man*?'

There was a ripple of uneasy laughter. 'Christ, Ross, you're a comfort!' Mike piped up.

Any previous jollity had now left the group and they walked the last stretch in silence. Amelia was glad to see the house lit up and welcoming when they rounded the last bend in the path. It wasn't a very long walk from the village but it was a little eerie and she wondered how difficult it would be to get some subtle lighting organised for the drive, the kind that posh hotels had. She'd add it to her to-do list.

As everyone piled into the drawing room, Amelia went upstairs, desperate to get out of her beer-soaked clothes, very aware that now it had started to dry in, she was smelling like a brewery and felt very sticky.

Freshly showered and changed into her pyjamas and dressing gown – an inappropriately weighted silk kimono for the temperature, which she guessed was now dropping to single figures – Amelia padded back downstairs and made for the kitchen, bypassing the drawing room with the gales of drunken laughter emanating from it. The walk home and shower – far cooler than she'd have liked thanks to the antiquated plumbing – had sobered her up and now the only drink she fancied was a hot one to warm her up while she read another couple of chapters of her Denholm Armitage. She'd finally started into it and was thoroughly enjoying losing herself in the English detective crime thriller and its familiar world of picturesque thatched cottages and the quaintly proper police chief and all the other usual characters she'd grown to love throughout the series of books.

She boiled the kettle and checked out the cupboards, finding tea, coffee, sugar and a jar of Ovaltine so old it was no longer a powder but had become one solid lump. She attempted to chisel off some but realised she'd need a pneumatic drill rather than a spoon. She grabbed the teabags and went to put the Ovaltine jar in the bin, and that's when she heard a noise from outside; a thump and something scraping across gravel. The beauty of single glazing meant she could hear everything. She opened the back door. It was dark. And bloody freezing!

She was about to go back inside when she heard the noise

again. Was there someone out there? She took a couple of steps out onto the patio... Nothing... She continued over to the farthest edge, past a nice set of wrought-iron table and chairs, to where a chest-height box hedge ran round the perimeter. She stood, barely breathing, waiting to hear if there was another noise. Behind her the back door slowly creaked closed, cutting off a big chunk of light. Amelia's teeth started an involuntary castanet chatter as her eyes tried to get used to the dark. Fingers crossed it would just be a fox, or a hedgehog, or anything rather than the headless horseman.

Oh bugger, why did she have to go and think of the headless horseman?

She willed herself to think of something else, but now she'd thought of him that's all she could think of, the vision growing in intensity as she imagined him galloping towards her...

And what if there was a ghostly axeman too! The pair forever doomed to re-enact their ghostly last encounter.

He could be standing right behind her now, axe hanging by his side, blood running down the rusted blade, the rusted, *blunt* blade...

There was another rustle in the foliage.

Oh God! There *was* someone or some*thing* out there! The ghost was going to hack her to pieces and ride off with her body parts, and everyone would think she'd just run away because she was daunted by the amount of work she'd have to do to get the house in order with all the new plumbing and central heating and a nicely lit driveway...

Another rustle! Closer this time.

Senses tingling, Amelia's fight or flight instincts kicked in and ramped up all the way to flight.

She turned to run back to the house, but something had grabbed hold of her kimono and was pulling her back. She screamed and flailed, smashing against a decorative Grecian urn-style planter and falling over the top of it.

Still struggling against the unseen force pulling her back, she got up and looked over her shoulder in time to see a figure bear down on her. Closing her eyes, Amelia screamed.

12

She managed to get a couple of punches in before she realised it wasn't a ghost but a warm body, a warm, muscular body belonging to someone who was holding the tops of her arms in a bid to stop the onslaught of her fists against their chest.

'Whoa, whoa! Calm down,' a familiar American voice said. 'What's happened?'

Amelia stopped struggling, relieved that it wasn't the headless horseman but dismayed it had to be Jack that she'd launched herself at. Again.

'You know, we really have to stop meeting like this, with you continually throwing yourself at me,' he said. In the darkness Amelia could just imagine the self-satisfied smirk on his face.

'I heard a noise.'

'What kind of noise?'

'A rustling.'

'A fox? Or maybe it was me, I've been doing a walk round the perimeter. Come on, let's get you inside.' He grabbed the end of her kimono and gave it a tug. Rather than it being in the clutches of a malevolent ghost, Amelia saw that the hem had got snagged on the rough branches of the hedge.

Jack bustled her into the relative warmth of the house – it wasn't really *warm*, just slightly less cold than outside.

'You heard a noise and you thought you'd go play Nancy Drew and investigate? Alone. In the dark. In an almost freezing temperature in completely inappropriate clothing?' he said in disbelief.

Saying it like that did make it sound a bit of a stupid plan.

He pulled off his thick, chunky knitted jumper, revealing another muscle-hugging T-shirt underneath. 'Here.' He held it out to her.

'I'm fine,' she said, trying not to shiver too noticeably. There was something about Jack's attitude that rubbed Amelia up the wrong way and she'd prefer if he didn't do her any favours.

He sighed. 'Take it or I'll ram it over your head.' His expression made it clear he wouldn't hesitate to do so.

She took it and pulled it on, immediately enveloped in lovely pre-warmed wool. Being a fair bit bigger than she was, Jack's jumper reached down to almost her knees.

'Thank you,' she said through gritted teeth. 'Won't you be cold?'

'Don't worry about me, I've got plenty more of these at mine.' He walked over to the kettle and finished off making the cup of tea she'd started.

Amelia bristled as she realised he was making himself one too; she hadn't asked him to stay.

She got the milk out of the fridge – the only item inside that wasn't alcohol – and poured some into her mug.

'Goodnight,' she said, taking her mug and picking up her book on the way out of the kitchen. She couldn't hear the others anymore so she went into the drawing room so she could sit and read in peace.

She'd barely spent a moment in the drawing room, which was a shame as it was stunning, with huge ceilings and ornate cornicing and large leaded windows which let the light stream in during the day. A real fire, although currently unlit, held centre court with a mantlepiece so grand, Amelia could imagine the previous owners of the house, standing leaning against it in their black-tie attire, nursing a single malt. Around the room was littered a few comfortable and slightly shabby leather sofas and wing-backed chairs with a bridge table off to one corner. Amelia remembered fondly when Dotty had taught her and Toby to play. So many years ago now, she wondered if she could dredge up the rules. With a bit of decor know-how, Amelia could only imagine the room's potential. Sitting in the softest, squashiest-looking chair and putting her feet up on a pouffe, Amelia opened her Denholm Armitage and began to read.

Suddenly the door barged open and Amelia jumped, almost knocking over the pouffe, as Jack strode in.

'You should get into the habit of always locking the back door,' he said.

'But then how would you manage to sneak in and half scare me to death!' Amelia said hotly, dabbing at some tea that had slopped over the sides of the mug and splattered onto her pyjama bottoms when she'd jumped. 'Do you do nightly rounds inside the house too?'

Ignoring her jibe, he pulled another chair over. 'You need to sort out your clothes,' he said, sitting down opposite her and taking a slurp of tea.

'There's nothing wrong with my clothes!' Amelia said indignantly. She prided herself on always looking nice.

'No, no, there isn't. If you live a few hundred miles south of here and you're going to work and going on dates and meeting friends for lunches in stylish gastropubs. For wandering around the Scottish countryside in the cold, wet and dark, they are a whole world of wrong.'

'But I don't have anything else with me.'

He looked at her levelly, with his frank green-eyed stare. 'Do you not possess a pair of shoes that aren't high heels?'

'I have my Uggs.' She showed him her feet. She'd been wearing them as slippers.

'That's a start. Now you need waterproof boots, like wellingtons and a pair of hiking boots, probably some sneakers too.'

'But where...'

'Luckily, the village has a great shop you can find all these things in. As well as fleeces and waterproof coats and these amazing inventions called gloves and hats.'

'I'll take a look.' She didn't want to show how relieved she was at hearing someone local stocked warmer clothes.

'Great, just try not to die of exposure or hypothermia in the meantime. I'm guessing your godmother would not like to think of you wandering around the moors like a windswept Cathy in nothing but a flimsy bit of cheap fabric.'

'It's a very expensive pure silk kimono!' Amelia retorted.

'Great, I'll make sure to put that in your obituary.'

He gave her a cocksure smile, and Amelia threw down her book and marched over to the fire. She'd spotted a wooden crate of logs beside it. She'd show him that she was perfectly capable of keeping herself warm. Although she'd never actually lit one before, she'd seen Dotty do it a couple of times.

She knelt down and began to pile the logs up on the grate, acutely aware of Jack watching what she was doing. There was a paper lying nearby so she grabbed a couple of pages and scrunched them up and placed them on top. Without saying a word, he got up and walked over to her, handing her a box of matches. She lit one and set it against the paper and it immediately ignited, burned up and went out. She was about to light another match when Jack gently prised the box from her fingers.

'Much as this is amusing the hell out of me, can I give you some pointers on lighting a fire, otherwise we'll both be dead from hypothermia and smoke inhalation before that gets lit.'

Amelia sat back on her heels in annoyance as Jack leant across her body to reach down into the fire.

'First, we have to check the damper valve is open because that controls the amount of air which flows through the flue.' He took off the logs then started to scrunch up the paper, putting a layer of them over the grate. 'We don't want too much of this otherwise it will generate a lot of smoke. Now we stack the kindling,' he added a layer of smaller twigs, 'and a couple of logs. Now we light the paper.' He struck a match and the paper ignited and before the flame was extinguished it set off the kindling.

'Great, I'll know that for next time.'

Jack stood up and went over to the chair Amelia had been sitting in and lifted up her book, studying the cover. 'We should throw this piece of shit onto the top.'

Amelia jumped up and snatched it back off him.

'No you will not! First, you find fault with my clothes, then my fire-making ability and now it's my reading choice you have issue with. Is there anything else you'd like to criticise while you're at it?'

He slowly looked her up and down. 'Nope, I think we're good.' He grinned. 'But give me time and I'm sure I'll find something else.'

'Uh! God, you're so rude!'

He continued to smile. 'You're not the first to come to this conclusion.'

'Why am I not surprised?' She brandished the book at him. 'Have you even read Denholm Armitage's books before?'

'Unfortunately, yes.'

'He's a fine author!' she said hotly, jumping to the English gentleman author's defence. 'I love his Inspector Grayson books.' She hugged the book to her chest in case Jack tried to grab it from her.

'They're twee!' he said in exasperation.

'They're comforting to read.'

'He writes bland, one-dimensional stereotypes!'

'He doesn't. He writes interesting, quaint characters! Maybe you haven't been able to pick up on the subtleties of his writing.'

'Wow, you're so defensive, you must really love these books. Denholm must be sitting in his rocking chair, sipping a cup of tea, in his slightly threadbare smoking jacket, chuffed to bits,' he mocked, putting on an upper-class English accent.

'Now who's being stereotypical?'

'But even the name. Denholm Armitage? Come on!'

'And Jack Temple's any better? You sound like you're a gumshoe from an American crime-noir book!'

Jack threw his head back and laughed. 'I'll take that as a compliment.'

'I didn't mean it as one,' she fired back.

'Oh, I know.'

Amelia took a deep breath in an attempt to calm down. She never usually argued with people. 'Sorry, I shouldn't have snapped.'

Jack grinned, running his fingers through his sandy hair. 'Don't worry, I seem to bring it out in people. Shall we start off this evening again?'

'If you learn a little diplomacy.'

'And if you learn to loosen up a little.'

'I'm perfectly loose!' Amelia said, feeling her annoyance at him build up again.

'Yeah, right!' He laughed, then stopped. 'Okay, yeah, I see your point. That could be construed as rude. Hang on.' He walked over to the glass cabinet and returned with two lovely crystal tumblers and a bottle of whisky. 'I hid this in here a while ago, I'm just glad your lush friend didn't find it first.'

He handed Amelia the bottle and she glanced at the label. 'Eighteen-year-old Dalmore. Nice.' Dotty had also given her an appreciation of malts.

'Glad you approve. There you go! There's something we agree on. We can drink to that. Get stuck in,' he said as he bent down to prod the fire.

Amelia poured two hearty measures, then sat down cross-legged on the floor beside him, determined to get through the next few minutes without bickering with him. He was definitely one of the most annoying people she'd met. Clearly her godmother had liked him enough to hire him and she'd always thought of Dotty as a good judge of character. She would give him another chance.

'Here's your dram,' she said, handing him a glass.

He held it up, swirling the rich amber spirit around. 'I've often wondered what constitutes a dram.'

'It's a measure which is as pleasing to the host as it is to the guest.'

He smiled, his eyes crinkling attractively. 'Well, this is pleasing to me.'

'And this fire is very pleasing to me.' There, she was being nice.

Jack took a swig of his whisky, tapping his index fingernail against the cut crystal markings of the glass and Amelia noticed how long his fingers were.

He sat, looking into the fire, his arm that was holding the

whisky resting on his knee, as he absent-mindedly swirled the spirit round in its glass.

What was it about him, he seemed to take up so much space, just sprawling himself over the carpet beside her. He wasn't overly muscly like a bodybuilder although he clearly did work out. He certainly wasn't fat, as she could see by the way his T-shirt lay against his abdomen he had a washboard stomach – she'd also felt his hard stomach muscles when she'd hit him, mistakenly thinking he was the ghostly headless horseman – but he seemed to fill up every room he was in, in a big, overbearing way.

'I think we got off on the wrong foot when we first met,' Jack said suddenly, still looking into the fire.

'I didn't mind you thinking I was a housebreaker nearly as much as you thinking of me as some little old lady with a blue rinse and twinset and pearl fetish. That insult will take a hell of a lot more whisky and fire-starting to get over.'

He turned and smiled at her. Not his usual cocky grin, but a genuine smile which made his eyes crinkle attractively.

'What do you really think about the documentary?' Jack asked lightly, after a moment.

'Um, well, it's not my ideal scenario,' Amelia said, now slightly regretting her spur-of-the-moment decision to invite the documentary crew to stay at the house.

'Why agree to it?'

Amelia looked at the amber whisky in her glass for a moment.

'Gideon's relying on it. He needs it.'

'And what about you, Amelia Adams,' he asked softly, 'what do you need?'

They locked eyes and Amelia started to feel a little hot. From the effect of the whisky, the heat of the fire or the weight of the woollen jumper she had no idea. But the way Jack asked what she needed, with that warm American drawl, seemed so intimate, like he was looking into her soul.

The fire gave a pop. Jack cleared his throat.

And something smashed through one of the panes of glass of the drawing room window.

13

'Jesus!' Jack leapt to his feet. 'You okay?' he asked Amelia.

She nodded, looking at the gigantic stone sitting in the middle of the tartan Axminster.

'Wait there!' He bolted for the door.

Amelia stayed in the middle of the room clutching her glass of whisky for a moment or two, then put her glass down on the side table, damned if she was going act like a helpless damsel in distress while she let someone else find out what had happened.

Jack had switched on the outside lights which illuminated the driveway and gravel but not any further. Grabbing a torch from the hall table, she ran down the steps and round the side of the house, but the torch beam revealed nothing. She stopped, holding her breath in case she heard something, but the wind had picked up and was whipping through the trees and drowned out anything else. She ran to the back of the house, to the patio and looked beyond the hedge to the rest of the garden, but she couldn't see anything beyond the reach of the torch beam. She searched for a few more minutes, then, disappointed, walked back round to the entrance of the house where Jack was already at the front steps, bent over, hands on knees, trying to catch his breath.

'I couldn't see anyone,' he said, straightening up. 'I ran along the drive towards the village. Someone could have easily jumped off into the woods.'

'I checked round the back, but nothing.'

'I thought you were going to stay in the house.'

Amelia gave him a look. 'I'm not about to wait inside and play the role of helpless female.'

He grinned. 'Are you sure you're not a blood relation to Dorothea? You sound awfully like her.'

They walked back up the steps to the house to find Gideon standing at the bottom of the stairs.

'What was that smash?'

'The window.' Amelia pointed to the drawing room and they all trooped in and stood staring at the large rock in the middle of the floor.

'Shit!' Gideon said. 'Who did it?'

'Don't know. I didn't get a look,' Jack said, running his hand through his hair.

Amelia picked it up. It was the size of a small melon and very heavy.

'It must have been kids larking about,' Jack added.

'That's some serious fucking larking!' Gideon exclaimed. 'It's a boulder. They could have killed you with it.'

Amelia shook her head. 'No, they didn't want to kill us.'

'Hey, come on! No one's talking about killing, okay, it was an accident,' Jack interjected.

Amelia pointed to the window. 'The lights were all on inside so whoever was standing looking in would have seen Jack and I, but it was thrown over to the other side of the room, so it wasn't meant to hit us.'

'That's hardly a comfort,' Gideon said in alarm. 'What if they just had a dreadful aim?'

'Maybe it was a warning?' Amelia said.

'What could they be warning us about?' Jack asked.

'Clearly to take cover, because there was a ruddy great big boulder coming through the window!' Gideon said, eyes wild. He clutched his chest. 'The warning! Is it for me? I can't help it if I make enemies wherever I go! It is me! Oh God! Someone's followed me up from London.'

'Gideon, calm down! This may not be about you! It could as easily be a warning to me,' Amelia said.

'How so?'

'Well, what if someone local doesn't like me coming up from London and taking over a historical building and bringing with me a documentary crew?'

'Oh. Oh God, yeah!' Gideon plastered his palms against his cheeks. 'You're the intended target.'

'Can we all stop running away with our imaginations?' Jack said. 'I really don't think this is a warning to anyone. It will have been kids mucking about and daring each other. It got slightly out of hand and they scarpered.'

Amelia made a non-committal noise.

Just then Ross and Mike came down the stairs.

'What's going on?' Ross asked.

'Kids have thrown a rock through the window and they've made a hell of a mess,' Jack said. 'I'll go grab a piece of plywood and some nails and board it up before calling out a glazier in the morning.'

'Oh, so you are good for something then,' Gideon said, flaring his nostrils and strutting out of the room.

'Ben and Lawrence are coming back with the last load,' Mike said. 'We'll just be upstairs unpacking our gear if you need us.'

'I shall never be able to sleep with all this drama!' Gideon called out at the top of the stairs. Jack turned to Amelia. 'I'll not be long.'

Once Jack had gone, Amelia surveyed the mess, then spotted something. Lying a couple of feet away she could see a folded and slightly crumpled piece of paper with an elastic band round it. Carefully picking her way through the broken glass she retrieved it. It looked like a note had been attached to the rock, with the elastic band holding it place, but had pinged off on impact. She unfolded the paper. It was one word, composed from letters cut out from newspapers and stuck down on a plain white sheet of A4.

It said 'LEAVE'.

With the window boarded up and all doors locked, Amelia went up to bed. She'd decided not to tell Jack or Gideon about the note. She hated to admit it but it had shaken her slightly. Of course, it could be for Gideon or the documentary crew but Amelia had a gut instinct she was the intended recipient. But why would someone want her to leave? Was it possibly the work of a local who didn't like the idea of her taking on Stone Manor and renovating it? As she paced the bedroom floor her gaze happened upon the photograph of Dotty she'd brought with her. It was black and white, taken at her graduation in 1963. She was a handsome woman, tall and elegant, with quite an air of dignity about her even in her twenties.

'Well, Dotty, I presume you knew what you were doing, not telling me about this place, but oh my, I could really have appreciated a bit of a heads-up. And why did you keep Jack a secret?' She studied the picture for a second, as if willing it to answer. She fetched the letter and reread it again, pausing on the passage about the house having secrets, especially Flora.

Then, ever so faintly, Amelia heard a scuffling noise. She looked over at the painting of the enigmatic woman. The noise seemed to be coming from that direction. She slowly walked towards it, heart pounding.

'Dotty?' She felt foolish saying her name out loud. As if the spirit of her godmother was here with her, sitting behind the painting, all ready for a chinwag! Really... It was probably just a mouse.

She gasped as she heard the scuffling noise again.

'Dotty? Is that you?'

She was now standing directly in front of the painting. Taking a step closer, she ran her fingers across the canvas, feeling the slight raised grooves of the brushstrokes of the paint and varnish overlay. There was an agonisingly long moment of silence, then a very faint scraping noise again, just to the left of frame. She touched the wood panelling.

'Give me a sign, Dotty, if that's you.' She pressed her forehead against the section of wood panelling and closed her eyes, breathing in the centuries-old smells of wood and dust and secrets...

Her eyes flew open. An old house... wood panelling... secrets. In any mystery worth its salt where an old house was involved, there was always a hidden panel. Was Archie right, could there really be hidden rooms in Stone Manor and could Dotty be telling her about one of them right now?

Dotty alluded to Flora knowing secrets. Very carefully, Amelia pushed the portrait of the woman to the side, releasing an avalanche of dust in the process. She started to run her fingers under the edge of the panelling, applying a little pressure, looking for a switch or a raised section. She'd gone three panels in when she felt the wood give, ever so slightly. She pushed upwards until she heard a click, and at the same time the panel below sprung open. Terrified of seeing a vision of her dead godmother's face, she bent down and looked inside but instead of Dotty, she saw a leather-bound book and another cream envelope on the top. She carefully took it out of its hiding place, wiping away a layer of dust and cobwebs, then put the painting back.

Her hand was shaking with excitement as she opened the letter.

Good Girl!

I knew you'd do it! Here's a scrapbook I put together of some interesting articles. There's a little museum in Ullapool which has quite a few historical gems. I have most of them here but if you're at a loose end you could always go and check it out and see if there's anything else you can find.

There's also a book I hope you find interesting!

It's terribly frustrating writing these in advance, not knowing for sure if you'll even find them. It makes me want to come and haunt the house to check on you and make sure you're okay. If I can't make an appearance myself, I'll try and arrange for a guardian angel to look out for you. Happy hunting, and possibly happy hauntings!

D

xxx

Carrying over all the papers and the book, Amelia hopped into bed and snuggled under the blankets, keeping the woolly jumper on for extra warmth. Although she'd been terrified at the thought of a headless-horseman ghost standing behind her, she didn't feel at all scared at the notion of Dotty's ghost in her bedroom. She knew the scuffling could more than likely be attributed to a mouse but what if...

'Hello?' she said quietly. 'If that is you, Dotty, thank you for all the papers you left me. I'm going to read them now. Maybe you're not actually a ghost and I'm talking to a mouse... or maybe I'm going a little crazy.' She figured it could very well be the latter. But regardless, she liked speaking out loud to, to... whatever. It made her feel slightly less alone. 'We've got a few more house guests staying with us for a bit,' she continued. 'They're making a film about your beautiful house. *My* beautiful house, I suppose it is now, and how I'm going to help renovate it and bring it back to its full glory.'

She paused, waiting to see if there would be any kind of thud or bang or acknowledgement to her little speech. Nothing. She'd once read that in the presence of a ghost the temperature took a sudden drop, but in her house it was permanently chilly and she wouldn't notice a couple of extra degrees cooler.

Opening up the scrapbook, Amelia began to read.

14

'I think I'll wear them, if that's okay.'

Standing in Mrs McGuthrie's outdoor equipment and clothing shop, which also had the village post office attached, Amelia was now decked out in winter weather attire, and she'd never felt less attractive. Everything she now wore was either waterproof or thermal, and in some cases both. As well as wanting to be equipped for the weather, another reason Amelia wanted to keep all her new clothes on was because there were so many bloody layers of them she'd take forever to remove them all and she was getting hungry for lunch. At the counter she added a pair of waterproof gloves to her haul along with yet another torch, a penknife and a pocket-sized bird-watching monocular.

Mrs McGuthrie nodded in approval as she rang everything through. 'You bought these just in time, it's due to turn a bit chilly tonight.'

Turn? Surely it had turned already!

Laden with bags full of more fleeces, an array of warm and waterproof trousers and sturdy boots, Amelia left the shop and made her way down the cobblestone path onto the main street and walked the short distance to the pub. She may not have felt attractive but she certainly felt comfortable, as everything was warm and stretchy, so stretchy she decided she'd have a bowl of the pub's sticky toffee pudding for dessert as there would be no tight waistband digging in to deter her.

With it just being before midday it was still quiet enough to find a booth in the Whistling Haggis. Squashing all her bags into the corner, she sat down with a Diet Coke and got out a pad and pen.

It was time for her 'Stone Manor To-Do List'. Then she turned the page and put another heading of 'Other Stuff To-Do list'.

First up, under the Stone Manor heading she wrote 'Contact Electrician', then 'Contact Heating Company', then 'Contact Lawyer about releasing funds'. She'd need to find someone local for the work. Without her phone to use for its internet app she was a bit stuck, then she looked over at the bar where Big Davey stood surveying his lunchtime clientele. If anyone was likely to know the village goings-on of the local tradesman, it would be him.

As it transpired, Tom Hastie, the plumber and heating expert Davey recommended, came into the Whistling Haggis for lunch and seemed delighted at the prospect of going out to the house to give a quote. He also seemed quite excited about the possibility of being in the documentary.

'I know Jack from drinking in here, good sort, he can show me around later if you're not available.' Surprised that anyone thought Jack as anything other than deeply annoying astounded her, but Amelia simply smiled as he handed her his business card and left.

Amelia had also managed to get hold of Mr Armstrong on the public payphone on the bar and nearly fainted when the lawyer told her the amount which was aside for her disposal, paling her cheque for twenty thousand into insignificance. She'd clearly looked in shock as Davey came over to ask if she was feeling all right.

'Could I have a double gin and tonic, please,' she whispered as Mr Armstrong went into more detail about the refurbishment money. Her aunt had been purposefully vague on the terms and conditions. If Amelia wanted to fly off to Italy, first class, to pick a Carrara marble worktop for the kitchen, that would be absolutely fine, he'd explained. In fact, there was nothing in place for receipts to be checked so even if she just flew off to Italy, first class, to look at Carrara marble worktops and not actually buy one, that would also be fine.

Just then Gideon walked in and waved over to her. She pointed to the booth she was sitting at and he sidled into the seat.

'Amelia! Are you still there?' Mr Armstrong asked.

'Yes,' she took a long gulp of her gin.

'Have you decided what to do with the house?'

'Not really. I mean, I want to get it looking the best it can. I'll get in touch with an architect or a planner or someone like that to see what can be done in case it's a listed building, but I haven't really thought beyond that.'

'You know you can't sell it on.'

'Yes, and I don't want to.' And she didn't. Of course, the allure of the hidden treasure was a bonus but Amelia could see beyond that. At first, the house had seemed cold and austere, but in just the short time she'd been there, Amelia had fallen for its old-fashioned charm and rather shabby grandness.

'I'd maybe look at it being a B and B, or a posh guest house,' she said, realising she liked that idea very much.

'I think it would lend itself very well to that judging by the floorplans.'

'Have you ever visited the house?' she asked him.

'No, sadly not, but maybe when you're up and running as a business I'll be able to pay you a visit and see the house for myself,' Mr Armstrong said, adding, 'and remember, I can organise any licences you would need for that.'

After thanking him and promising to be in touch if she needed anything, she hung up, taking her gin back to her table.

She sat down, trying to process the fact she was now a very wealthy woman.

'Darling!' Gideon said in alarm, looking up from taking a peek in her bags. 'Have you been through one of those makeovers, but in reverse?'

'Mmm?'

He rubbed her arm. 'You're fuzzy! And purple! What happened to the Dita Von Teese look, your pencil skirts and sexy killer heels?'

'I realised I was going to freeze if I didn't dress for the climate.'

'But who cares if you're a beautiful corpse?' He gave her an appraising look. 'You do manage to get away with it. Beneath all that Gore-Tex and Thinsulate I just hope to hell you're wearing a pair of French knickers and a racy bra!' He sighed. 'Maybe I'll need to embrace the look too.'

Amelia raised an eyebrow suggestively.

'I mean the thermal fleece look. Although I bet I'd look fabulous in a spangly basque à la *Rocky Horror Picture Show*.' He winked.

The pub door opened and Gideon gave an exaggerated shiver. 'I've never been so cold in my life! I honestly thought this scarf would be all I'd need,' he said, unwinding the length of wool from around his neck and draping it over the back of his chair.

'What have you got there?' he asked, looking at her notepad.

She turned towards him. 'My to-do list.'

He had a quick scan. 'That's a lot of dos.'

'I know, but I've already spoken to a couple of people so I'm making progress.'

'You do know Beniamino will probably demand you go through the entire conversations with these people again so he can film it all.'

'That's fine.'

'Really?' His eyebrow shot up and disappeared into his blond hair.

'Really.'

'And you're not mad at me.'

'Not anymore, Gideon.' And she wasn't.

'Thank God for that! I know the documentary seems such a trite little thing but I'm so grateful for this chance. I really thought that was me out of this business they call show.' He gave a small laugh. 'After managing to pitch it, it very nearly didn't go ahead at all when one of the original crew was... well... I honestly thought I was cursed. But there's something about this place... I think it was always meant to be. The way we met, all of it. God, darling, I'd best go and get another round in before I get emotional!'

Amelia watched as Gideon went up to the bar, then she pulled out the second letter and bundle of papers Dotty had hidden for her.

There was an old newspaper clipping from the *Herald* in 1897, which covered the return of the landowner and gentleman Montgomery Campbell. It reported that he'd travelled to Asia in

1850 when twenty-five years old, then Egypt in 1853. He married Iris Cuthbertson in 1855 and had a son, Archibald in 1857 but tragically his wife died in childbirth. Montgomery left for Egypt shortly after this loss and, apart from a few brief returns to Scotland, had stayed in Egypt for the best part of three decades overseeing excavations at various archaeological sites throughout the country before latterly focusing on the Valley of the Kings. The cuttings had been tucked into a leather-bound book with an inscription of the family tree written on the inside cover:

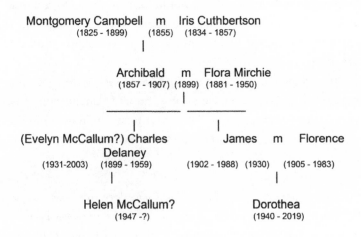

Montgomery Campbell   m   Iris Cuthbertson
(1825 - 1899)   (1855)   (1834 - 1857)

Archibald   m   Flora Mirchie
(1857 - 1907) (1899)   (1881 - 1950)

(Evelyn McCallum?) Charles Delaney
(1931-2003)   (1899 - 1959)

James   m   Florence
(1902 - 1988) (1930)   (1905 - 1983)

Helen McCallum?
(1947 -?)

Dorothea
(1940 - 2019)

The handwriting was all the same and looked pretty fresh. Because Dotty's dates had been filled in, someone had clearly done it after her death and then hidden the book. This made Amelia feel a little strange. She'd wondered if it had been Mr Armstrong, as a last request to the woman he was clearly very fond of, but he'd told Amelia he'd never been to the house and she had no reason to think he'd lie. Possibly, because Dotty knew the cancer was terminal, her godmother filled it in herself and then enclosed it in the secret space. But *had* she been the one to hide the letters or was there someone else helping her? And why was Evelyn McCallum's name in brackets with a question mark? Had Charles not married her and was Helen illegitimate? Or was there a question mark over the parentage? The book itself, Amelia had high hopes for; it was the diary of Flora Mirchie, who then became Flora Campbell, the woman whose painting hung in her room.

Amelia's excitement soon evaporated when it became clear that life for a young, middle-class woman in the late 1890s was draggingly uneventful. Amelia would have preferred to continue with her Denholm Armitage but persevered, although she'd started to skim-read whole chunks of it. A saucy potboiler it was not.

Amelia looked up at the bar and could see Gideon was now engaged in conversation with someone and Amelia hoped he wasn't antagonising anyone. With him busy, she pulled out the diary from her tote bag and opened it at the next entry.

10th November 1898

It finally happened! The meeting I have been tremulous over from nerves and excitement came about last night! I was too much in a fever to write about conjectures in case they did not come to pass but now I can tell all. Mr Campbell made a call upon my father on the last day of October, which was but a week ago, but seems as if it were forever and a day. This time the call was not of a business nature, as father had already completed Mr Campbell's accounts for the month, but Mr Campbell wished me to meet with his son, Archibald. We had but a brief exchange at the summer party at Stone Manor all those months ago, but I had made a favourable impression on both the father and son. I can barely remember what I talked of; mother and father and visiting poor sick Mrs Galbraith and playing with the gardener's puppy, that is all, I am sure. A further engagement was made and yesterday Archibald Campbell called on me. We took a turn in the garden – I am so thankful for a cool autumn for he is so handsome and how I blushed whenever he addressed me – had it been any warmer I fear I would have fainted.

And what of Archibald Campbell? Well, he is handsome and of strong character and he sits well on a horse. His eyes constantly look to the horizon as if he senses excitement in the air. I swear I did not know what to speak of and fear I came across as foolish, but he must like my foolishness because he sent me his card this morning and has asked me to dine at their house. Without father and mother. I do not know how I will manage a morsel of food, as I cannot contain my excitement!

Now it was getting interesting! Amelia looked up to the bar but it seemed Gideon was now talking to Big Davey. She quickly flipped over to the next entry.

28th December 1898

He asked! He called on father before luncheon and asked for a private meeting. I knew why he had come as soon as I set eyes on him. He looked pale and he was shaking slightly. To be true, I had worried there had been a breaking in his feelings towards me. He had not called me for ten days and I had almost taken to my bed, I felt so sick with unhappiness. But he came, and he asked, and father said yes. Even if he had not said yes, my answer was a thousand yeses and that would have won out. Archibald was very quiet and I could not begin to fathom the emotions of his heart but he kissed my hand and I felt a passion I knew not existed. Archibald Campbell makes me tremble with his intensity and I am to become his wife.

Crikey! That was all a bit sudden, Amelia thought. A couple of walks in the garden, a dinner in the family home and Bob's your uncle, that was you in love and engaged to be married. Mind you, if some mutton stew and two trips to church on a Sunday were all she had to look forward to, like Flora, Amelia wondered if her head would also be turned by a man who looked good on a horse and had a wistful look in his eye.

15

Gideon had been right, Beniamino did indeed want to film the exchanges. As soon as Amelia and Gideon returned to Glencarlach House they were met by Beniamino and Tom, the plumber, who'd changed out of his mucky overalls from earlier and was now wearing a pair of box-fresh chinos and well-pressed red shirt. Standing beside him was a rotund, ruddy-faced man in a suit who was introduced as Angus, a planner from the local council. Tom was quite delighted at being filmed and had many anecdotes about botched-up plumbing jobs which resulted in flooding and fires. He repeated many times that he was an honest workman and took great pains to keep dropping his business name into conversation as much as possible along with the dreadfully clunky tag line, 'The name may be Hastie, but my work is careful'.

Far more uncomfortable with a cameraman following him around was Angus, the planner. Each time he had to talk about the house and what would be permitted without any extra permission being required, Angus got even ruddier and would run his finger around the collar of his shirt.

'With your windows, they're classic eight panes over eight

panes sash. Um, you wouldn't be able to replace them with uPVC but you could get a restoration company to take any damaged windows away and repair them, then put them back in. The same goes for the surrounds. Some are a bit draughty and you could get them restored and, um, make sure that the original workmanship is kept,' Angus said, trying to turn away from the camera at every opportunity.

'I've been thinking about opening the house as a B and B or a guest house. Would I be able to make the bathrooms into en suites?'

'Yes,' Angus said stiffly.

'Cut,' Beniamino called out. 'I don't think we need any more of this. Amelia, would you be able to do a piece to camera later, just a quick recap over the information?'

'Sure.'

Now the camera was switched off and Lawrence and Ross were removing their equipment, Angus was visibly more at ease as he studied the plans of the house. 'Most of the bathrooms are beside the bedrooms so it would be perfectly acceptable to make a doorway to connect them. And with these two rooms here,' he pointed to two of the larger bedrooms, 'the footage of the room could easily incorporate an internal shower room. You'd need to apply for permission for that, but I can't see any problem with it being passed.'

They headed down the stairs to the hall as Angus continued, 'Luckily, there's nothing I've found in the archives which would prevent any design work on the interior being carried out. You'd be able to change the interior as you see fit. Well, all apart from this staircase.' He patted the solid mahogany bannister as they walked down the stairs. 'This is protected under the Listed Buildings Act due to the carpentry skills of the artist. It was a local tradesman who went on to produce some noteworthy staircases in his career, he actually went over to France. Stone Manor is one of the very first examples of his work.'

'I wouldn't dream of changing this,' Amelia said. She loved the way it swept majestically up to the first floor. The spindles on the bannister were intricately carved and there were four elaborate carvings which topped the bannisters. There was a pineapple on the bottom right, a parrot on the bottom left and upstairs there was a monkey and a palm tree.

'And, of course, you'll no doubt find some of the old priest holes and hidden passageways.'

Amelia stopped. 'The what?'

'Priest holes. They're quite common. They were built to hide priests when they were being persecuted in the 16th century but they carried on being built through the centuries. Handy to have a hiding place. Oh yes, this house is allegedly riddled with secret rooms and passageways.'

'Could some have hidden those from the Jacobite rebellion?' she asked, remembering what Archie had told them in the pub. As she'd already found a small hidden cupboard it was reasonable to assume there were other secret hiding places, even if on a larger scale.

Angus nodded. 'Very probably. The original house was built in the 1730s and it's a classic example of Georgian architecture, but there were a few changes made over the next hundred years or so. Around 1880 the owner, Montgomery Campbell, had the final work commissioned, this staircase being one of the additions. He also had the back extension to the house added. He was seen as being a local eccentric and wanted hideaways laid into the foundations, connecting to the older part of the house. Behind these walls there could be a myriad of secret passageways. Or so legend has it.'

'Are there any plans of this?'

Angus shook his head. 'Not that I know of. It's quite possible plans were made and they're still somewhere in this house, but who knows. Let me know if I can be of any help, but maybe just if you could come for a meeting at my office, without... you know.' He gestured to the documentary crew behind him.

'Of course,' Amelia said, showing him out. Closing the door, she turned and almost walked into a beaming Beniamino.

'Fantastico! We've got some great footage.'

'But I thought you'd turned the cameras off.'

Mike piped up from behind the director. 'That's what we wanted him to think. He was much more at ease when he thought we'd stopped filming. What a great story for the documentary too! The sound may be a little patchy but Ross can work on that in the editing suite.'

'Come on, Mike,' Beniamino said, ushering his cameraman to follow him. 'Let's get Gideon to do a piece.'

Amelia watched them go, feeling a little uneasy about their underhand tactics for filming. If this was how she felt, only having owned Stone Manor for a short period of time, she wondered how all the ghosts were going to cope with having their secrets and privacy ripped away by an unscrupulous documentary crew.

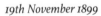

19th November 1899

I had hoped producing a male heir would keep Archibald from his disappearances. Charles is now two weeks old but apart from a cursory glance at the boy, his father has neither been near him nor myself. With Mama too ill to call on me I am without counsel at this time. McPherson, the nanny, is a very capable woman and I know Charles will be well cared for by her but there is no warmth extended to me. The walls are becoming oppressive and I have taken to seeking solace by walking in the grounds. My recuperation is coming along well and I hope to be at my full fitness soon. I often wish my father-in-law had lived to see his grandson but I think any joy would be destroyed by his son's behaviour. In many ways it was a blessing when Montgomery died. He had become so weak and unwell in the weeks before he took his final breath. I do not even know if he recognised his own son, his fever was so great. In the short time I knew him, I saw how he was plagued when the madness gripped his mind. I sometimes see that same delirious look in Archibald and it shakes me to my core.

...Earlier I wrote of Archibald having stayed away from his son and his home. I wish it had stayed that way. Earlier this evening he returned to us. Having not seen us in nearly two weeks he arrived inebriated and immediately asked to see Charles. Luckily, McPherson was able to encourage but the briefest of visits but then I heard him come for me. I have known him in this mood and I hid from him in one of the bedchambers. I stumbled over my skirts and fell against the fireplace, pulling down the edge of the woodwork and was taken aback to see a door spring open. I had just enough time to slip through and close it behind me when I heard Archibald enter the room I had been in but a moment before. He called my name and when he heard no answer, left, but not before smashing a glass trinket bowl my mama gave me as a gift. I cowered in the dark for a few minutes before I had a chance to observe my surroundings. It was a space a little taller than my height as I could just reach up and touch the ceiling with my hand. There did not seem to be any light available and for a moment I panicked that I would not manage to escape. After a few moments my eyes became accustomed to the gloom and I could make out a handle jutting from the wall. I pulled at it and the small doorway opened once again and I slipped back out. With the door now open I could see from the lamplight that there was a smaller tunnel leading away from my hiding space, into the depths of the house. In the past I have taken a fancy that this house is against me with its

dark, foreboding passages, but tonight the house became my salvation.

Amelia put the diary down. A secret passage? She jumped up and went over to the fireplace in her room. *Edge of the woodwork, edge of the woodwork...* Her fireplace was more tiles than wood, but she had a good feel and a prod around the surround and mantlepiece anyway. Nothing. She pressed along a few of the wood panels just for good measure but nothing yielded to her touch. Although disappointed she hadn't found the secret room and passage first off, she knew there were plenty of other bedrooms to try, but that would be a job for the morning. She looked back at the diary, feeling a pang of unease. She was caught up in the mystery of the house and the exciting notion of unearthing secret passageways and possibly treasure, but for Flora, the isolation must have been crushing. Dotty's ancestor wouldn't have been able to pop down to the Whistling Haggis if she needed some company and a gin and tonic.

Ready to turn in for an early night, Amelia went to the window and started to draw her curtains when something caught her eye. Cupping her hands around her eyes, she pressed up against the window so the light from the room behind didn't interfere. It was a light in the tower! Or folly, or whatever the hell it was. The building she couldn't seem to find a way into. Well, someone was definitely getting up into it and Amelia damn well wanted to know who it was and how they did it.

She threw on her fleece on top of her pyjamas and jammed her feet into her Ugg boots before grabbing her hat, gloves and torch. She flew down the stairs, almost tripping on her overly long pyjama bottoms. Pausing briefly to tuck the ends of them into her boots, she then ran through the house and out the back door.

The temperature seemed to have dropped by another couple

of degrees, if that was even possible, and Amelia wished she'd grabbed her new padded coat instead of making do with just her fleece. Thank God she had her hat and gloves, although something better than her Uggs on her feet would have been good, as the grass beyond the patio was marshy from the earlier rain and she kept sinking into it, which slowed down her progress. She got to the path at the foot of the incline to the tower and started up it, wet foliage from the large bushes slapping at her face as the branches danced in the wind. The incline seemed far steeper than it had the first day when she'd been out for a leisurely exploration. So as not to announce her arrival Amelia turned off her torch and put it in the pocket of her fleece. Now, without the light as a guide, her progress was slow as she kept tripping over tree roots. It didn't help that the rain had also caused mini mudslides, and for every few feet she ascended, she managed to slither back one, her boots giving her little tread. Pausing halfway up, she removed her gloves so as she didn't ruin them, and then, using her hands for traction, ploughed on up to the top.

Breaking free of the undergrowth she suddenly found herself at the top, the tower looming up in front of her in dark relief against the sky. She tried to catch her breath, knowing she'd hardly be able to sneak up on someone inconspicuously if she was breathing like an asthmatic making a dirty phone call. Bloody hell, it was cold, she thought as the wind whipped around her, causing her pyjamas to flap against her legs. She took a few paces back and looked up to see if the light was still on, but she couldn't see anything.

But then she heard something. Despite the wind she could hear footsteps crunching on gravel. Then they stopped. Then she could hear choral music, beautiful voices harmonising. Was she about to have a moment of divine intervention?

Amelia was paralysed with fear, every nerve ending standing

to attention. She'd never been so scared and couldn't help wonder if she was about to be visited by an angel. Or what if it was the headless horseman axeman-murderer out on an evening prowl and he liked to announce himself with a soundtrack? What if it was the ghost of Archibald wreaking his revenge and about to unleash unholy terror? Amelia wrapped her hand round the torch in her pocket and drew it out, ready. Then the music stopped and she heard the footsteps again. She would have to make a run for it. But which way? Left or right? She couldn't make out which direction the footsteps were coming in as they were being distorted by the wind. She plumped for left, the way she'd come, hoping to make a beeline towards the undergrowth and the path leading back to the house. She ran, full pelt, just as someone loped round the side, coming towards her. Adrenaline pumping, she gave a banshee-like yell and threw the torch as hard as she could…

… and smacked Jack square in the face.

She watched helplessly as he staggered back a few paces before collapsing to the ground.

16

Amelia's first thought was that she'd killed him as she stared in horror at his motionless body.

She bent down at his head just as his eyes flickered open and focused on her. 'I'm so sorry!' she gasped. 'Is anything broken?'

'I seem to have landed rather awkwardly on my keys.' He winced. 'And my pride is seriously dented from getting mowed down by a petite, five-foot-nothing female, but I think everything else is intact.' He touched the back of his hand to under his nose and when he pulled it away there was a dark smear of blood. 'That's some throw you've got there, I've seen worse at pro baseball.' He pinched the bridge of his nose.

'Is it painful?'

'When I get the feeling back, I'll let you know.' He gave her a wry smile and struggled to his feet.

'Did you hear it?' Amelia said, looking around them.

'Hear what? The crack of bone?'

'No, the music, like a choir. It was terrifying.'

Jack started to laugh; not the reaction Amelia expected.

He took out his phone and pressed a button and the same music started up.

'It's the start of 'This Corrosion' by Sisters of Mercy, an eighties goth band. I have it as my ringtone.'

'Oh.' Amelia felt both relief and deflation. 'I thought it was a ghost.'

'A ghost with an accompanying choir for walk-on music to announce his arrival? But good thinking to throw the torch, clearly it's a spectre's greatest nemesis.'

Amelia bristled, hating that he always seemed to be mocking her. 'And what would you battle one with, your sharp wit and clever put-downs?'

He just laughed.

'You know, I'm sorely tempted to hit you again,' Amelia warned. 'It was very freaky.'

'Okay, okay, I'm sorry!' He held his hands up.

She did feel quite guilty about hitting him. 'You need ice on that straight away. We've got some at the house.'

'You sure Gideon won't have used it all for his gin and tonics?'

'Don't worry, he's moved to drinking straight from the bottle by this point in the evening.'

They slowly began to make their way down the treacherously slippy path. After nearly losing her footing a couple of times, Jack reached out his hand to her.

'I can manage,' she said just as she slipped on a wet tree root.

He grabbed hold of her seconds before she hit the ground and she was annoyed to realise she did have better balance now he had a firm grip of her mud-caked frozen hand enveloped in his leather-gloved one. She thought back idly to the last Denholm Armitage book she'd read, where the murderer had worn an almost identical glove; black cracked leather with visible seams running from the finger along the back of the hand to the wrist where there was a little worn-away section from where it had rubbed against his watch...

They reached the bottom of the slope and squelched their way over the grass to the patio.

'Come on in, I'll get that ice,' Amelia said.

'Will you continue to hold my hand if I whimper in pain?'

She quickly dropped it. Jack grinned, then winced.

'And I think you also owe me a nightcap,' Jack said. 'I'm starting to get some feeling back and I definitely preferred it when it was numb.'

In the kitchen Amelia peeled off her boots, now more Ugh than Ugg, the two-tone sheepskin caked with mud and what looked suspiciously like animal droppings.

'Sit,' she said, pointing to a chair on her way to the freezer. Gideon was a thoroughly annoying housemate due to his habits of forgetting to put the milk back in the fridge, never washing his coffee cups and leaving empty bottles of booze littered around the drawing-room floor for her to dig out from under the sofa and chairs, but the one thing he was always on top of was making sure there was plenty of fresh ice. She found a relatively clean dish towel and loaded a few cubes into it before twisting the ends and pressing it gently on Jack's nose.

'Yoahw.' He lifted off the chair slightly.

'Don't be such a big girl's blouse.'

'You're not very remorseful anymore!'

'I was, until you started mocking me, at which point I realised you must be fine.' She lifted the ice away to have a look at his nose. 'Don't worry, I haven't done any permanent damage to your looks.'

'So you think I have looks?'

'I didn't say they were good ones,' she fired back.

'You didn't say they weren't.'

He really was the most infuriating man, she thought as she got up to fetch some damp kitchen roll. Returning, she found Jack tentatively touching his nose. Sitting down opposite him, she dabbed at the dried blood.

'I am sorry. I was just a bit jumpy, and you got in the way.'

Then they both said in unison:

'Why were you up at the folly?'

They stared at each other for a moment, neither answering.

Amelia sat back in her chair. 'You first,' she said, wondering what he was going to say. It seemed obvious to assume he'd been the one in the tower; therefore, he'd lied to her before when he said he had no idea how to get in.

Jack didn't break eye contact. 'I was just doing my nightly rounds.'

'How long do these nightly rounds last for, you must cover a lot of ground?'

'I don't go up to the folly every night. I mix the route up. Now you.'

Amelia hesitated. Jack was a cool customer, but she could play this game too. She shrugged. 'I fancied a walk.'

'At this time? In those clothes?' Jack's eyebrows shot up.

'I couldn't sleep.'

'You must have some serious insomnia if you think a hike up *that* hill in the freezing temperatures will help you nod off.'

'Well, we're out of Horlicks.' She gestured to the open cupboard where there sat a jar of coffee, a caddy of tea and a Tate and Lyle bag of caster sugar, now all very much depleted since they'd arrived.

'Have you guys seriously not bought any more food yet?' Jack said, looking over at the cupboard.

'We manage.'

'On caffeine and pub meals?'

'Not just those,' she said indignantly. She'd had a Pot Noodle earlier on in the day too.

'Can we be honest for just a moment?' he said with a sigh. Amelia noticed how his accent became very husky when he became serious.

Amelia held her breath, wondering what he was going to say; was he going to admit he was in the folly?

'Were you out looking to see if you could find the treasure?'

'What treasure?' she bluffed, with what she hoped was a good poker face.

Jack gave her a look. 'I heard Archie telling you all about it in the pub.'

'Oh, well no, I wasn't.' She paused. 'Were you? Because I *know* it was you inside the folly!' Haha! She sat back after her big reveal. To her disappointment Jack didn't look like he'd been rumbled, he just shook his head.

'Wasn't me inside. I have no idea who it was up there and I'm equally clueless on how they got in. But I guess you saw the lights, too, and came to investigate and not just because you fancied a walk.'

Amelia felt slightly deflated. She'd hoped he'd stammer awkwardly and then confess all. She tried to read him to see if he was lying. He could be annoying and condescending, yes, but she didn't think he was lying over this.

'Who do you think was up there? And why?' she said.

He shrugged. 'Beats me. If we knew what was inside the folly it might make more sense.'

They lapsed into silence for a moment.

'Did you already know about the buried treasure?' Amelia said eventually.

'It's hard to avoid hearing about it. Anyone new, especially if connected to this place, hears about it from someone in the

Whistling Haggis. I think it has to be Glencarlach's worst kept secret.'

'Have you heard there are meant to be secret passages?'

'Yup, that's the rumour.'

Amelia couldn't help but smile. Dotty had gone to a lot of trouble to leave hints and clues for her, but really all Amelia had to do was pop into the local pub for a catch-up on the mysterious history of her new house.

'If everyone knows about it, why hasn't anyone found it yet?' Amelia wondered out loud.

'I honestly don't think people are trying to find it. I think they just like to retell the story, a torrid tale of treasure and ghosts to be told on a wintry night by the fire. It's a bit like the Loch Ness monster; people love to tell stories about her but most of them wouldn't dream of going as far as to hire a boat and an extra-large fishing rod.'

'Do you think the treasure exists?'

He smiled. 'I'd like to think so.'

'I'm pretty certain someone else must also believe in the treasure and is hunting for it at this moment.'

'Possibly, but I'm now starting to doubt what I saw,' Jack said. 'What if it was a low-flying plane or–'

'I know the difference between aviation and a torch,' Amelia cut in firmly. 'How long had you been up there before I saw you?'

'Barely a minute.'

'I came up the same way we went back down and you–'

'Came up from the east side, it's a bit steeper but more exposed and I would definitely have noticed if I'd passed anyone.'

'But surely if we both got there from different directions, one of us would have seen whoever was there.'

'Unless–'

'It was a ghost?' Amelia interjected.

'Jeez, you and your ghosts! I was actually going to say, unless whoever it was was still there, but even so, they'll be long gone now.'

'Not necessarily. They may have heard us leave, thought the coast was clear and decided to stay and carry on doing whatever it was they were doing.'

'The first thing we do is find out how to get in. There must be something like a loose brick or, or a secret entrance located nearby. What else is up there?' Jack said, tapping his forehead, trying to remember. He'd now leant forward, staring at her, his face only a few inches from hers, his eyes narrowing thoughtfully, accentuating the fine crow's feet, as he rasped the palm of his hand against the stubble on his chin. Even with his bloodied nose, he was quite sexy, in a brooding, curmudgeonly way, Amelia thought, then immediately pushed the thought from her head, as she did not want to be thinking those thoughts about Jack Temple! She reminded herself just how much he irritated her.

'Come on! Let's go!' Amelia jumped up, knocking her chair over. 'We need to get back up there now,' she said, excitement bubbling in her stomach at the thought of an adventure.

Jack, too, was on his feet, heading to the door but then he stopped abruptly and turned. 'Whoa, hang on just a minute.'

'But we might lose them.'

'We don't know who's up there or what they're doing. It may be harmless kids larking about or it may be something else.'

'I have my torch!' She grinned, holding it up.

Jack smiled. 'Despite being pretty nifty with it, I think we should leave it for tonight. For a start, look...' He gestured to Amelia's clothes. She looked down. There was dried-in, caked mud all over her pyjamas and fleece from where she'd wiped her hands after making the ascent. She also had splatters of mud all over her pyjama bottoms, the ends of which were sodden from becoming untucked from her boots when she'd trampled over the grass.

'You need a bath and a good night's sleep,' Jack said firmly.

She hated to admit it but she *was* bone tired and her calf muscles ached from trying to sprint up such a steep hill.

'We're gonna be able to look better in the daylight.'

Annoyingly, he had a point.

'Just promise me you're not going to go all super sleuth on me and head off out there on your own?'

Amelia bristled slightly. 'I don't need protection.'

'I just don't want you to do anything stupid.'

'I'm not stupid.' Amelia gave a frustrated laugh. 'That's what's so funny. I'm always the sensible one, I never take risks. My brother Toby's the one who wanders off halfway round the world without a second thought, but I've always made sensible choices and thought things through carefully before acting. Maybe I do want to do something spontaneous like go off up to the folly in the middle of the night. Maybe I want to take a break from making massive to-do lists and planning for every eventuality. My cautious life has suddenly changed into one where I find myself in the middle of a documentary, working out how to make this place work as a potential business in a new part of the world where I know absolutely no one, while carefree Toby is now living in my old flat, paying my old rent and getting a job sorted so he has some sort of stability. Pardon me if I don't know how to act, because I'm new to it all.' Amelia stopped, not knowing where the outburst had come from. Even worse, she could feel her eyes get hot and prickly as tears threatened. 'It should be the other way around. Toby would make a better go of all this,' she added.

'Look at me.'

Jack marched over to her and stood directly in front of her.

He lifted up her chin so she was looking straight into his eyes. 'Dotty knew exactly what she was doing. She made the right decision. You'll see. Wanting to unravel a mystery is one thing but throwing yourself into an unknown situation which could end up dangerous is something else. Clearly, there is someone sneaking around out there. We don't know who or why. I'm suggesting biding time and unravelling it at a safe distance. Watching and waiting, rather than running in, all guns blazing. Obviously, I can't tell you what to do, I'm sorry if it has meant I've come across as–'

'A patronising, chauvinistic, overbearing–'

'I was going to say overprotective,' he cut in, with a small smile.

'And that.' She waited for a beat to see what he'd add, something rude or something that would get her hackles up or start an argument, but he didn't say anything else. He took his hand away from her chin.

'I'm going to bed. I'll see you in the morning.' He opened up the back door and turned. 'You still owe me a nightcap.'

'Rain check?'

'I'll hold you to it,' he said with a wave and disappeared into the night.

Amelia closed the door behind him and locked it, then dragged herself upstairs to her room, not even bothering to check the tower to see if there was a light on in it.

She threw off her pyjamas into a soggy, muddy pile to be dealt with in the morning, then after a very quick and not very warm shower, pulled on a fresh pair of pyjamas and crawled into bed. Not even bothering to read another diary extract, Amelia switched off the light, that evening's happenings replaying through her mind as she fell asleep.

17

'Amelia, *pst*, Amelia! Wake up!'

Amelia became aware of someone shaking her shoulder. She opened her eyes to see Gideon sitting on the edge of her bed.

'Thank God you're awake,' he whispered. 'I think someone's trying to break in.'

Amelia sat up. 'What?' she said, trying to unjumble her sleep brain. 'Is it someone from the tower?'

'What?'

'I, uh,' she shook her head to shake off the dream she'd been having about the folly, 'what's happened?'

'There was a tapping noise on my window. At first I thought it was hailstones but it wasn't.'

'Maybe it was a bat?'

Gideon recoiled. 'That's really not the best way to reassure me, darling. I detest bats and their little squashed-up noses and ratty-type pretendy human hands. But no, it wasn't a bat either because I snuck a peek outside in time to see two figures walk off, towards the back of the house.'

'Why are you whispering?'

'I don't want to wake everyone up.'

'But if everyone's awake, it might scare the intruders off?'

Gideon didn't look convinced.

'Come on then!' she said, throwing back the blankets.

'What are you doing?' Gideon said in alarm.

'Going to investigate.'

He looked horrified at the suggestion.

'Gideon,' Amelia tried to appease, 'they're hardly going to be high-end criminals if they were trying to wake you up by throwing gravel at your window. It'll probably just be fans trying to catch sight of you.'

'Great, just what we need in the mix, a stalker!'

Nonetheless, he followed her down the stairs.

'They were heading towards the back of the house?' Amelia checked.

Gideon nodded.

Grabbing a golf umbrella which was propped against the bannister, Amelia tiptoed through to the back of the house. Passing the hall table, Gideon lifted a copy of the local paper, *The Wester Ross Chronicle*, and rolled it up. 'You can thrust and I'll jab if it gets nasty,' he said, brandishing it.

In the kitchen they could hear muffled noises along with some scraping sounds.

'What are they doing? Are they moving those ceramic planters?' Gideon whispered, referring to the ones either side of the back door which housed slightly past-it geraniums. 'Surely there isn't a back-door key under one of them?'

Amelia shook her head. No one would be stupid enough to leave a spare key there.

Seconds later they heard a key turning in the back door. Gideon clutched Amelia's arm as the back door inched open. Amelia raised the golf umbrella over her head.

'ARGHHHHHHHHHH,' she bellowed at the figure coming in.

'ARGHHHHHHHH,' the intruder yelled back.

'ARGHHHHHHHH,' Gideon screamed in Amelia's ear before shoving her in front of him just as the overhead strip light flickered to life.

'Oh my God! Why do you keep insisting on trying to kill me every time you see me!'

'Toby!' Amelia exclaimed, never being so happy to see her brother.

She had barely time to register what was happening when she was engulfed in a bone-crunching hug by a woman with masses of waist-length, glossy brunette hair, subtly highlighted with every shade and tone of bronze, copper and gold.

'Oh my goodness, Amelia Adams, I thought we'd never get here!' said a throatily warm voice with an unmistakable Cornish twang.

'Sally? I don't believe it!' Amelia laughed, hugging her back. 'What are you both doing here? Aren't you meant to be off in Ireland? When does your new job start?' Sally had been working the previous three months in LA as a make-up artist on the set of a new horror film and was only meant to have had one day between it finishing and a new television series starting in Dublin, something Sally had complained about, worrying she'd have no time to recover from the jet lag.

'I was meant to have started yesterday but I'd just touched down at Heathrow when I got a call from the production team,' Sally said. 'The studio bosses are getting a bit anxious about their leading man over some minor drug misdemeanour and they've put the series on hold until after the court hearing, just in case he gets jail time. So there I was wondering what to do with all my free time when I got your text, so I decided to hotfoot it up here. I texted Toby to give me the address and as luck would have it he was coming up, too, so we had ourselves a road trip. I also thought with a documentary crew on the prowl, a highly skilled make-up artist would be a welcome addition.'

'That would be brilliant. We've got plenty of room.'

'You're not joking,' Toby said with a grin.

Amelia was so pleased to see them she hugged them both tightly, feeling tears spring up into her eyes. 'It's so nice to have a friendly face around here.'

'And what am I, chopped liver?' Gideon huffed from behind her.

'Oh, Gideon, this is Sally Bishop. She's my best friend, the make-up artist.'

'Oh, I've heard all about you! You're the one who inadvertently helped me out of a tight spot due to all your magical lotions and potions.' He narrowed his eyes. 'I haven't ever worked with you, have I?'

'No, not as yet.'

'Oh good, turns out I can be quite beastly to folk on set when I'm hungover.'

'And this is my brother, Toby.'

'Pleased to meet you,' Toby said, shaking Gideon's hand.

'Yes, well, I'm going to head to bed and for once I don't have to worry about my grey pallor in the morning appearing on film,' Gideon said, blowing them a kiss and sauntering off.

With great delight Amelia showed them to another two spare rooms. The few days they'd spent together in London when Toby returned from his travels had been lovely, and they'd barely bickered at all, and being able to share her new, crazy life with her best friend was the icing on the cake. From initially being worried about rattling around the house on her own, it was fast becoming full.

18

'I think I'll need to invest in a large bag of crumbs to help me find my way about,' Sally said as she joined Amelia in the kitchen the next morning. She ran her hand over the orange Formica worktops. 'I'd wondered if all this colour had been a bad dream, but no! Wow, it really takes retro to a whole new level.' She went over to the cupboard. 'Oh, great, proper tea! I missed this in the States,' she said, pouncing on a bag of Tetley's.

'How have you been?' Amelia asked as she boiled the kettle. She still couldn't quite believe Sally and Toby had turned up.

'Still single.' Sally grimaced, this being the one definitive yardstick of her life and happiness. As long as Amelia had known her, Sally was either falling in love or out of love and always in as highly a dramatic way as possible. Amelia often wondered if Sally could manage to cope with maintaining the status of being *in* love.

'I thought you and that set designer were pretty serious.'

Sally looked horrified. 'Grant? Oh my God, no! He was no good for me whatsoever.' She pulled a face. 'Well, that's what I had to tell myself when I found out he'd been notching up more conquests than I'd been dotting concealer. Then after him was

Sebastian, a rather minor actor from that awful science fiction thing I worked on – I knew it was on the rocks when I found him more attractive as an alien than when he wasn't in make-up.' She ticked off another on her finger. 'Then were was Adam who was bi, and *I* had to say bye-bye when I found him in bed with my postman. Oh, and there were two beer bonks and a champagne shag.'

Amelia laughed as she remembered Sally's sliding scale of drunken one-nighters.

'What about you? Any word from Jonathan?'

In the immediate aftermath of breaking up with Jonathan, Amelia had told Sally everything that had happened as she'd deconstructed their entire relationship in detail, and clocked up quite a large phone bill in the process. 'He's sent a few texts. He needs me and misses me.'

'And?'

'And that was it.'

'Did you reply?'

'There isn't really a signal here, to be honest.'

'Good. You don't need that arsehole in your life. Have you met anyone interesting since you've been here?'

Sally didn't believe in long periods of abstinence between relationships.

Just then she glanced out the window and saw Jack dragging some stepladders over to the side of the house.

'Ooh, who's that hunk of delight?' Sally asked appreciatively.

'Jack, he's the handyman.'

'I bet he is,' she said with a small growl. 'Now, *that* is someone who could make you forget about whatshisname.'

Amelia watched Jack working for a moment or two, as he rubbed his arm over his forehead, making his sandy hair stick up at odd angles.

'He's actually rather annoying.' Although Amelia had been

surprised to find he'd been as excited as she'd been at trying to find the secret entrance to the folly and they'd left it on far friendlier terms.

'Doesn't matter if he looks like that!'

Amelia made a non-committal noise as she handed the mug of tea to Sally who was standing in her lightweight, multicoloured poncho, noticeably shivering. 'You're going to need something a lot warmer than that to wear. The weather's going to turn.'

'Turn?' Sally said, aghast. 'Turn into what, Siberia?'

Unsurprisingly, Gideon suggested everyone head to the Whistling Haggis to celebrate welcoming the new arrivals. Amelia had fully intended on searching the house for secret passages but any excuse she cited for staying was soon shouted down by the others.

They all trooped along the drive to the village, kicking through the fallen leaves. The sun had also made a welcome appearance and shafts of light fell on the path before them and filtered through the branches of the trees which were becoming more sparse daily from the autumn winds. Amelia was pleased to be able to show Stone Manor's estate off to Toby and Sally on such a beautiful day.

Inside the pub, the fire had been lit and the whole place exuded a warming ambience of bonhomie.

They were becoming such regular fixtures a couple of the locals acknowledged them with a raised hand of welcome as Mike joined a couple of the tables together to accommodate them all.

Amelia sat down and dragged Toby beside her so she could have a quick word.

'Lovely as it is to see you, shouldn't you be starting back on your architecture course now, you'll only have missed the first week or so of term, surely?'

Toby pulled a face and scratched the side of his head where his hair was starting to grow back in, his natural dark-brown a stark contrast to the shocking dyed-blond stripe down the middle. 'I would, if I was going back.'

'But you were going to meet your advisor. If they won't let you back I'm sure you could appeal and–'

'I told them I wasn't coming back. Ever.'

'But–'

He took a breath. 'I don't want to be an architect. I hate it. I knew early on it wasn't for me but I kept trying to like it.'

'But what about your bar work?'

'The guy could only promise me a few hours a week but then I went to see James Armstrong and everything changed when he handed me a cheque for more money than I'd ever imagined having. I've suddenly got choices, Ames.'

'But what are you going to do?'

'Well, not panic for a start.' He grinned, making fun of Amelia's stricken expression. By now Sally, Gideon and Beniamino were also listening in to their conversation. 'When I was travelling I realised what it is I want to do.'

'Sleep late and drink beer?' Gideon hazarded.

'There is that, yes, but while I was travelling about I ended up working in some kitchens to make extra money. I really love cooking, and it seems I've got a bit of a knack for it. Now I've got the chance to do something I love. I've still not worked all the details out, I'll probably need to look at honing my skills before I open my own place or I may even just get a mobile van and offer street food, but I could start with cooking for you guys.'

Now he had everyone's attention.

'And don't tell me you don't need me. What have you guys

been surviving on? I couldn't even make a simple breakfast this morning as you've got nothing apart from booze and a carton of milk a day past its use-by date.'

'I get my five a day,' Gideon said. 'Tomato juice in my Bloody Mary, olives in my martini, lime and lemon in my gin...'

'At least you're not at risk from scurvy.' Toby smiled.

'It's all on my to-do list,' Amelia said. 'I just haven't got round to organising food yet.'

'You're trying to get the house up and running, yeah? Beniamino said you've been thinking about turning it into a hotel?'

Amelia nodded. 'We've booked electricians and plumbers to start renovations.'

'Why don't you spend your time focusing on that while I make sure none of you keel over from malnutrition.'

There was a chorus of whoops and cheers and requests for curry from their little group. Amelia was just about to say yes when a thought struck her.

'What about my flat?'

'Uh-oh!' Sally said, chuckling into her gin and tonic as Toby looked uncomfortable.

'The thing is... your landlord is an arsehole,' he said.

'I know that. What did you do?' Amelia felt her anxiety levels rising.

'Your washing machine started to leak and I asked him to fix it. He refused and we got into an argument, and I told him he could stuff his lease.'

'But–'

'I hired a storage facility and everything you own is in it.'

'But what–'

'You don't need a pokey, damp, smelly little flat in London anymore when you've got a sprawling country estate up here, do you? And if you do want to move back I have more than enough money to rent you something really nice in the interim.'

So many thoughts were vying for first place to panic over, Amelia didn't know what to settle on first. Up until now, she knew she had the safety net of returning to her flat if the sheer magnitude of what she was undertaking overwhelmed her. Now the comfort of an escape route was gone, Amelia had to make Stone Manor work as her future livelihood.

'Sorry, sis,' Toby said. 'But now I'm here, I can help you.'

'And me, my love,' Sally added, giving her hand a squeeze.

This was it. There really was no going back now.

And it didn't seem nearly as scary as she thought it would be.

'Ooh, look, there's your handyman!' Sally said, craning her neck to see out the window.

'He's hot!' Toby said approvingly.

'He's really not all that,' Amelia said as she turned in time to see Jack coming out the hardware store clutching a bag. Although from a distance he did look quite windswept and manly, with his rough stubbled jaw and muscly physique encased in well-fitting jeans and a chunky knitted jumper. Although best kept at a distance so he didn't open his mouth and ruin it by being cocky and rude. But she did need to talk to him about the folly.

'Back in a sec,' Amelia said as she squeezed past her brother and ran out the door. It was only as she was darting along the pavement Amelia realised she wasn't sure what she was going to say to him.

'Hi,' she said, a little breathless from her run.

'Hey.' Jack pretended to duck and cower from her. 'I come in peace.'

'How's your nose?'

'Broken in four places and causing me breathing difficulties.' He gave her his cocksure grin.

He was fine.

'My brother Toby and best friend Sally turned up in the middle of the night. Do you want to join us for a drink and meet them?'

He hesitated. 'I'd love to but I've got some things I need to take care of first.' He lifted up the bag he was holding. 'I've just bought a new lock, I need to replace the one to the cellar. They can get a bit rusty, especially at this time of year.'

'Okay.' Amelia couldn't understand why she felt a little deflated. 'I also wondered if you wanted to head up to the folly to see if we can find the secret entrance.' She cringed inwardly at just how 'Enid Blyton' it all sounded.

Rather than jump at the idea Jack seemed to hesitate, thrusting his hands in his jeans pockets. 'Are you sure you still want to?'

'Yes! Don't you?'

'I know it seemed exciting last night but...'

'Don't worry, if you're scared, I'll go on my own.'

He looked at her for a second, then smiled. 'Aw shit, I never could resist a challenge. Fine. How about we meet up there tomorrow morning, about ten?'

'I'll see you then.' Amelia turned and headed back to the pub, unable to keep the grin from her face, even when a van drove past her through a puddle, sending up a wall of water that soaked her from the knees down.

'Amelia! Over here!' On re-entering The Whistling Haggis, Amelia saw Sally wave over to her from the bar. She'd moved away from the rest of their group and had commandeered two bar stools.

'I wasn't sure how long I could hold on to these. I've had a few angry looks from the locals – it's a little *Wicker Man*, don't you think?' She gasped in excitement. 'The place is heaving with big Scottish men with pitchforks and dark secrets.' She gave a happy shudder.

Amelia glanced around the bar. There were a few farmers in wellies but none of them were in possession of a pitchfork or an iota of desire to pounce on their stools which Sally had so steadfastly clung on to.

'I thought you and I could have a really good catch-up and I wanted to bend your ear on the single men.'

Sally slid a fresh gin and tonic over to Amelia with a grin, her blue eyes sparkling in anticipation.

'Jack?' Amelia asked lightly, not knowing why she was holding her breath, waiting for Sally's reply.

Sally shook her head. 'I'm thinking more of Mike. You know I like my men like I like my kohl eyeliner; black, smooth and can stay on for twelve hours.'

'Sal!' Her friend really was incorrigible.

'What?' she said in mock innocence. 'So, what's the deal with him?'

'I, um, I don't really know. He's never mentioned a girlfriend...'

'That's good. He's been quite flirty with me. Beniamino's quite sexy in that Latin way, Lawrence is a bit stand-offish and possibly scared of me, Ross, I'm not getting any vibes off him, which could mean he's spoken for.'

Amelia always marvelled at how quickly Sally could work out potential date material.

'If only your brother was straight.' She sighed.

'What about Gideon?'

'Oh Lordy, he's too much of a train wreck even for me. Actors are really the worst and I'm doing my best to avoid them from now on. I also think he's on a bit of a bender.' She nodded along the bar.

Amelia turned to see Gideon leaning over the bar, clicking his fingers for service.

'If there's one thing that pisses me off, it's not getting served at the bar!' he said, his well-modulated voice rising above the cacophony of lunchtime chatter. 'Excuse me, you retarded Neanderthal nonce, but can I get some service here!' he shouted to Big Davey who was pouring two exports, a lager and taking a food order.

'Oh bugger!' Amelia slid off her bar stool and hot-footed it over to him. She tapped him on the back. 'You go sit down and I'll get the round in. What are you having?'

'I'll tell you what I'm having! I'm having difficulty being served,' he said in clipped tones. 'This place is full of inbreds and I don't even think they understand English.'

The bar had become eerily quiet. The farmer on the bar stool next to them put his pint down and turned to look at Gideon.

Amelia hoped there wasn't going to be a fight. Just then, Toby slipped in between Gideon and the local, who was still eyeballing Gideon.

'Hello!' Toby said, giving Davey a smile. 'Lovely day outside, isn't it? Cold, though, so your fire's lovely and welcoming.'

Toby's random chat about the weather seemed to deflate the atmosphere a little.

'Have you tried any of the malts here yet?' Toby asked Gideon. Not waiting for an answer, he carried on, addressing Davey. 'You've got a terrific selection. I'm normally a Islay fan but I think I could be converted to some of your local highland malts. I'm Toby, by the way, this is Gideon. I know he came across as being offensively rude there but sometimes, in London, people click fingers for service. Luckily, because I've travelled a bit, I realise social customs change from place to place and know it's not a cool thing to do.' He bent his head chummily towards Big Davey as an aside, but kept his voice loud enough for most of the folk in the bar to hear. 'We're actually *all* from London. It's an all right place, bit trendy, bit impersonal, nothing like your lovely village. Some things my friend has done could be misconstrued as rude, he doesn't really mean them to be because we all know pissing off the bar staff is never a good idea, wherever you are.' He clapped Gideon on the back, ignoring the look he was getting. 'Right, so I'm going to buy myself and my friend here one of those lovely malts, if you could recommend one for us? In fact, why don't I buy everyone in here a drink. A friendly gesture from the new guys. How does that sound?'

There were mumbles of agreement.

'It sounds like you're being a patronising arsehole,' Gideon said to Toby, his tiger-eyes flashing in anger.

'And it sounded like you were being a rude dickhead to these nice people,' Toby replied in a low voice. 'If you want to get barred from the only place around here to spend an evening go right ahead but don't bring us down with you. You've already taken advantage of my sister's good nature, don't be mistaken into thinking you can do that with me. Now, I would love it if we could all get along. Shall we start this again?'

Gideon stood up and looked down imperiously at Toby. 'I am very fond of your sister and I'm willing to stretch that friendship to you, too, but don't push your luck.' He stormed off towards the toilets.

'Wow!' Amelia said.

'I'm sure his bark is worse than his bite,' Toby said, watching him go.

'His bark isn't really that bad either to be honest.'

'He was being an ass.'

'I know...' But as Amelia watched Gideon strut off, she couldn't help but think he was a bit lost at the moment.

19

Standing at her bedroom door, Amelia opened it a crack and listened for a moment before peering out into the corridor. Silence.

Knowing that the documentary crew had wanted to get some early morning shots, Amelia hoped they'd be long gone and that everyone else was downstairs in the kitchen. It was time to check out the fireplaces in all the bedrooms in search of any levers or handles or oddly-shaped carvings which on being depressed would open up an entire new world of mystery and intrigue.

Since reading the diary extract where Flora described her adventure, Amelia had been desperate to look for the hidden passageway herself but with such a busy house it wasn't easy to get alone time. She slipped out her room and ran along the corridor and knocked quietly on Gideon's door, then a little louder on weighing up how much alcohol he'd sunk the previous night. After a couple of minutes of no response she let herself in. The bedcovers were pulled right back and there was no sleeping actor in the middle of them. She was alone. After a thorough feel along his fireplace and surround, Amelia concluded there was no secret lever.

Two down, fifteen to go.

Next along was Mike's room but she could hear him singing inside so gave it a miss for now. Ross was just coming out of his room so she shouted a friendly 'Good morning' and carried on walking along the corridor. Once she was sure he'd gone downstairs she double-backed and turned his door handle...

'What are you doing, poppet?'

She whirled around to see Gideon standing at his door, hand resting on the doorknob about to go in.

'Just looking for Sally.'

'In Ross's room?' He raised an eyebrow questioningly.

Amelia looked at the door. 'This is Ross's room?' she said in faux surprise. 'Oops, silly me!'

Gideon folded his arms. 'I do believe you're up to something, Amelia Adams.'

'Nope! Just being a bit dizzy, that's all.'

At that moment Sally opened her door. 'Morning.'

Amelia looked from Sally to Gideon and back to Sally.

'Morning! Just thought I'd see how you slept.'

'Oh, like a log!' Sally smiled.

'Fabulous. I'll just go and stick the kettle on then,' Amelia said, turning and walking back along the corridor.

'I slept well, too, darling,' Gideon said to Amelia as she walked past him.

'Good to know, Gideon, good to know.'

'Oh, Ben's wanting to hold a house meeting in five,' Gideon called after her.

'What about?'

He shrugged. 'No idea, maybe someone's made fun of his cashmere jumper collection.'

❧

'A party?' Amelia said.

'Si, yes! I think it will really pique people's interest.' Beniamino's dark curls bounced against his forehead as he nodded emphatically. 'The footage we have is already fantastic but we need something to aim for.'

'Surely turning the house into a hotel is an aim?' Amelia said.

'The main aim, yes, but we need little stories along the way to keep it interesting. Think of them as instalments all leading up to the big reveal.'

Beniamino took a sip of his coffee, moving his elbows out the way as Toby set the table in preparation for the full-cooked breakfast he was about to serve.

Gideon, who was slumped in the corner, raised the sunglasses he now donned to exhibit bloodshot eyes. 'I'm always up for a party.'

'When are you thinking? It will take a lot of planning,' Amelia pointed out.

'It's nearly Hallowe'en. We can have it for that.'

'Won't it interfere with the plumbers and electricians?' Amelia queried. The work was due to start that day and Tom had warned her about all the floorboards he'd be ripping up and areas which were designated as 'no go'.

'We'll liaise with the workmen and see what areas will be finished or can be left alone until afterwards,' Beniamino said.

'But who do we invite?' Amelia asked. 'I don't really know anyone here yet.'

'We say it to Davey in the Whistling Haggis. Tom, Archie, all the locals, word of mouth will be fine. Even more if it's a free bar,' Mike said.

'Excellent!' Beniamino drummed the table with his hands in delight.

'But I've never organised a party on this scale before, and with everything else going on...' Amelia started to say.

'Leave it to me, darling,' Gideon piped up from his corner. 'I can throw a party in my sleep. Sally, you look like a good-time girl. Want to be on party duty with me?'

'Do I ever!' Sally bounced in her seat and clapped her hands.

'Sorted.' Gideon reached out for Amelia's to-do list, which was never far from her side, and scrawled 'Delegate party organisation to Gideon and Sally' and put a tick beside it. He slid it back to her. 'Clearly, it will have to be fancy dress. Luckily I have fabulous contacts in the BBC costume department.'

'Bravissimo!' Beniamino exclaimed.

'When?' Amelia asked, still unsure how a major fancy dress party could occur, fairly last minute, without her having to do anything.

'A week on Saturday,' Gideon said.

'But that's just under two weeks,' Amelia said, trying to get Beniamino's attention, but no one listened to her.

'Great, I'll go let Big Davey know to spread the word.' Mike nodded. 'I'll be in at lunchtime to get some thoughts from the locals.'

'Thoughts about what?' Amelia asked.

'To hear what they think of changing Stone Manor into a hotel.'

'Are some people not happy?'

'You thinking of the brick-through-the-window incident?' Ross said.

'What brick-through-the-window incident?' Toby asked, appearing at the table, spatula in one hand, massive plate groaning with sausages, bacon, hash browns and black pudding in the other.

'Someone threw a brick through the main drawing-room window,' Amelia said lightly.

'While she was in it,' Ross added.

'Why didn't you say anything?' Toby frowned.

'I just did!'

'Oh, don't get your striped apron in a twist,' Gideon said as he leant over and skewered a sausage off the plate Toby was holding.

'It must have been kids larking about, that's all,' Amelia said with a shrug, hoping to play it down. She still hadn't told anyone about the 'LEAVE' sign attached to it.

Toby put the plate down on the table, standing back quickly as everyone pounced on it like starving hyenas.

Lawrence flicked his long hair back as he said, 'Probably the same ones that broke into the cellar.'

Everyone stopped to look at him.

'What?' Gideon said through a mouthful of bacon.

'Someone broke into the cellar?' Amelia asked.

Lawrence nodded. 'I was out having a look around and when I opened the door, I realised the lock had been broken. Don't worry, I went to find Jack to report it.'

'So Jack knew?' Amelia asked. Jack had told her he was replacing the lock but said it had rusted, he didn't mention anything about it being broken.

'Yeah, well, he's the handyman, isn't he? He said he'd fix it.'

'So, what's in this cellar?' Gideon asked.

'Dunno, I didn't have a proper look,' Lawrence said, focusing back on his breakfast, all conversation exhausted from that source.

'Ooh, I wonder if the treasure will turn out to be a few hundred bottles of malt,' Gideon said cheerily.

'Treasure?' Toby looked at Amelia.

'Turns out this house and your sports car weren't the only things Dotty kept secret from us. There's meant to be buried treasure somewhere around here.'

'But no one knows where it is or even what it is,' Gideon said. 'Oh, can't you put it away for once!' he added as he gave Mike the finger, and Amelia realised that once again Mike had been recording the entire thing and she'd had no idea. Mike and his camera had a way of blending in, unnoticed.

'Come on, let's talk more about this party!' Sally said, changing the subject. 'What's everyone going as, should there be a theme or just general fancy dress?'

There started a general murmur about costumes around the table.

'Ooh, could you do me up as Miss Marple again?' Amelia said to Sally. She had loved that costume, it had been so convincing.

'Absolutely not!' Sally said firmly.

'Poirot then?' Amelia suggested.

Sally sighed theatrically. 'Not this time. No little old women, no French detectives–'

'He's Belgian.'

Sally gave her a withering look. 'You need to go sexy.'

'I can sex up a waxed moustache.'

'I'm sure you could, but for this party it's time to put the waterproofs and comfies away and bring out those heels again. As your best friend and make-up artist it's my duty to tell you you're going to go knock-out sexy.'

Amelia excused herself as soon as she could to head up to the folly as she hoped to read a few more diary extracts before Jack joined her. It was another cold, bright day. The ground had hardened and dried with the continuous drop in temperature and Amelia managed to scramble up the hill towards the folly without any mudslide-related difficulties. At the top, she walked once around the folly, running her hand along the uneven brick wall as she went, just in case a door suddenly made itself known to her, but after a few good prods and pushes uncovered nothing, she went to sit on the small stone bench a few feet away and looked out onto the glen before her as she waited for Jack. There was a little stone pillar beside her with an engraved plaque at the top. 'Folly View', it read.

She opened up Flora's diary. Annoyingly, there was nothing interesting for pages, just the usual listings of meals, church visits and her walks in the garden. She didn't really even mention her son Charles very much apart to say he was growing and had blond hair. The only person that seemed to get a namecheck was Gemmell, the gardener. He seemed to be Flora's new confidante as she took her daily perambulation, as she called it. Amelia had at first wondered if it was going to get steamy, imagining Gemmell as a sexy Mellors-type figure until Flora mentioned Gemmell was almost seventy and had an arthritic hip. And it seemed all he ever talked about was the weather, the changing seasons and the dead Campbell ancestors.

Then she got to:

14th September 1901

He returned. But not to me, his son or his house. He came to find IT. Gemmell had told me the stories, the facts being muddled with the rumours through the passage of time. Most of the treasure was returned, a little was sold, but most of it accounted for apart from some trinkets and the Amor Rubra, and this is what has incensed Archibald. This is what has caused the black moods, the drinking and the disappearances. He needs to find it. His father did not tell him its location. I realised I was now a commodity. To trade respectability and an heir for the location of the treasure. Montgomery's brain was too addled to know his own name towards the end and it is no wonder that he did not divulge the hiding place to his son. It has now become my husband's obsession to find it. He came calling for me after supper, after he had imbibed. I did not manage to hide this time and he forced me down and took what was legally his. There was no love or tenderness, just anger. He is an animal and I pray to God that he leaves and I don't see him for some time.

Amelia looked up, feeling ill at what she'd just read. Trying to second-guess from the roundabout terminology, she figured that bastard Archibald must have raped Flora. That poor, poor woman. No wonder she took solace in the nice grandfather figure, Gemmell. But it also talked of this Amor Rubra. Amelia's Latin was a bit rusty but she was sure that translated as something like The Red Love? She carried on reading, skipping over some of the rather dull and factual entries. They did seem to eat an awful lot of mutton...

3rd June 1902

I am so weary but I must write. It is another boy. How can so much love and beauty come from such a hateful act. James is heaven sent. My heart is so full of love.

Well, Amelia had never read anything quite so poetic about James. Either completely high from a hormone surge or Flora clearly had a favourite already! Then there was page upon page of entries about James, and Charles, too, to be fair, but not as many. It seemed that a new nanny had been employed and was a bit more understanding about letting the mother get in on the act occasionally in the raising of the children. And so the years rolled on. Very occasionally Archibald got a mention but luckily it didn't seem that he did anything heinous when he turned up, although he was normally drunk and a bit crazed.

19th October 1907

I am trembling so hard I can barely write. I have done such a terrible thing, I never thought it possible. He had been drinking all day, shouting at me, shouting at what invisible demons follow him. He had a rage I have never seen before take hold of him. He talked of searching all through his father's belongings in India and Turkey, how he'd exhausted all potential sources and he was no further forward than when he started. His ramblings were those of a madman. I had excused myself and went to retire to bed but he came after me. He began talking of his father liking me more than he, how his father must have told me where the treasure was. I tried to get away but he held my wrists so hard I feared they would break. I begged for him to stop but he kept at me. I screamed but he would not stop hurting me or shouting words I could not understand. I still screamed, in part to block out the hateful names he called me. Then it stopped. His body fell away and my wrists were released. He had taken a dive over the top bannister and landed on the floor below. And then I saw Gemmell standing just behind where Archibald had been. He was out of breath, having been the one who had pushed him to save me. I looked down at my husband and knew he was dead by the angle he lay at. Gemmell looked in shock. He had saved me. I heard stirrings downstairs as the other staff came to investigate the noise. I vowed to protect Gemmell and took him through to the secret passage out of the house. He was shaking so badly but there was not a moment that could be wasted and I bade him go back home and tell no one what had occurred. I made him swear. I, too, then appeared at the stairs and looked down at my dead husband, feigning shock and horror. No one questioned me as all the staff knew of his erratic behaviour and how much he'd been drinking.

25th October 1907

It was decided he was not in fit mind and had acted in a dangerous fashion. The verdict was accidental death.

I fear we will still be punished for this. But my relief at no longer living under a tyrant is greater than my fear or guilt.

Amelia had to reread the last two entries a couple of times. She looked up and out over the glen, thinking of Flora and the secrets she had kept. No wonder she hid the diary. In fact, Amelia couldn't believe she hadn't burned it to remove all evidence. She looked over the glen, thinking how beautiful and peaceful it was. Had it changed much in the decades since Flora lived here? Had Flora herself come up to sit and look out at the same view...?

'Don't do it!'

Amelia let out a slight yelp of surprise. She whirled round on her bench to see Jack leaning against the tower, watching her.

'You looked so serious, I was worried you were about to hurl yourself off down the side,' he remarked, pushing himself off the tower and ambling over as Amelia marvelled at how he actually suited jeans, wellies and an oversized orange-and-brown Fair Isle jumper.

'Just thinking.'

'Anything good?'

'Just thinking why you wouldn't want to tell me the cellar was broken into?' She studied him for a reaction but he continued looking out at the view, his eyes squinting slightly against the morning sun.

'I didn't want to bother you–'

'It's the sort of thing I should know about.'

'–or worry you.'

'I'm not worried.'

He turned to look at her. 'Well, that's fine then. Shall we go look for this entrance?'

'Hang on. So, was anything taken? Any damage done?'

'It was the cellar and it was used for storage and I'm not sure what was in there to start with, but it didn't look as if anything had been disturbed. Nothing was damaged. You've all generated quite a bit of interest since you arrived and people know you've got filming equipment. Maybe it was thieves taking a chance that there were valuable things stored in there.'

'Did you call the police?'

'Yes, I spoke to Ray, he thinks the same. So, we going to do this thing?' He nodded at the folly.

'Sure.' She stood up and realised her bootlace had come undone. She lifted her foot up and rested it against the stone pillar and started to retie it.

'If you want to take the–' Jack was interrupted by a low grating noise, like two slabs of concrete rubbing together.

Amelia stopped tying her lace and stood up straight. 'What was that?'

'Do that again,' Jack said, pointing to her boot.

Amelia put her leg back on the pillar, this time adding some more pressure. There was the same noise and they could see the concrete slab the little pillar sat on move slightly.

20

Amelia pushed the pillar again, this time with Jack's help and it gave with surprising ease. With the slab moved to the side, it revealed stone steps leading into the ground.

'I think we just found ourselves a way in to the tower,' Amelia said breathlessly, staring down into the dark. 'Come on.'

'Whoa!' Jack held her arm. 'You want go down there, now?'

'I could pencil in a slot a week on Tuesday... of *course* I want to go in there now!'

'We got torches?'

'Always.' She felt around in her pocket and then held up her Maglite.

He puffed out his cheeks.

Amelia stood back slightly, unable to keep the grin from spreading. 'Are you scared?'

'What? No.'

'Really?'

'Well, okay, I'm just not that fond of spiders and down there looks like a place we'd find spiders.'

She looked at him, eyebrows raised.

'Hey, it's my only flaw. Indiana Jones had snakes, I've got

spiders.'

'I'll protect you.'

'Thanks, you're doing wonders for my street cred.'

'Or you can stay up here and keep lookout?'

Jack peered further into the dark entrance.

'Hell no! I'm coming with you. I'll go first,' Jack said.

'What, and have you scream like a girl every time you walk into a cobweb, no chance,' Amelia said, making her way down. The smell of mustiness was almost overpowering and the damp clung to her face like a veil as she descended further. By the time she reached the bottom of the steps the temperature had also dropped another few degrees.

'Hang on, I'll see if I can close this over,' Jack called down.

Amelia shone her torch back up towards the entrance and illuminated a smoothed-out groove cut into the slab which moved back into place easily under Jack's touch.

'Watch, it's slippy,' Amelia said as Jack made his way down the steps to join her. Shining the torch in front of her, Amelia could see the levelled out earthen floor stretched for a few feet. Amelia led the way along the narrow tunnel as she started to sing 'Incy Wincy Spider' under her breath. The further they went, the narrower the tunnel became. It wasn't that tall either and although Amelia could walk along easily Jack had to stoop. After a few feet they came to another set of steps, this time leading up.

'These must lead up into the tower,' Amelia said, her heart hammering with excitement. The steps were narrow and the walls wet and slimy under her touch as she tried to steady herself as she ascended.

'Hey, what do you know, it seems I'm also slightly claustrophobic!' Jack laughed ruefully as he climbed the steps behind her.

'Don't worry, I think I can see a bit of daylight above us, must

be coming from the window at the top of the tower. Keep going!'
Amelia continued to climb until she eventually came out onto a
level stone floor. She'd got to the top of the tower! It was about
twelve feet in diameter and along the wall there were small
arches gouged out where deposits of hardened wax were
evident.

'Wow!'

'Wow indeed,' Jack agreed as he joined her. They were both
slightly out of breath from the climb.

Amelia couldn't see over the top of the opening of the tower.
Jack could. 'It's some view, you can see for miles.' He walked
round. 'And the house.'

'But what's this for?'

'Well, the whole point of a folly is that it *has* no use.'

'But in that case, just keep it as a folly, surely? Someone went
to a whole lot of bother to build a folly which wasn't a folly,'
Amelia pointed out. 'And I'd love to know why.'

They stood looking around them.

'Maybe a prototype of a man cave?' Jack suggested. 'Keep
some beers cold below, fix up a dartboard, just hang on in there
a couple of centuries for satellite TV to be invented, then kick
back to enjoy the Giants beating the Jets at football.'

'It's kind of odd.'

'Looks like something was here though,' Jack said, bending
down and running his hands over the ground where there was a
deep indentation along the floor. Amelia came across and
looked over his shoulder. Another slightly shorter line lay at a
right angle at one end.

'Could have been a rectangular box, with something that
was weighted down at one side.'

'Yeah,' he agreed, 'very possibly.'

Amelia wondered if it had contained whatever treasure was
alleged to be hidden.

'Maybe this tower was a hiding place for Jacobites,' he continued. 'There's room for at least a couple of them to stretch out, get food delivered, stay in hiding until the coast was clear.'

Amelia walked over to where they'd come up and could see there were hinges on the stone slabs but whatever had been attached was long gone. Most probably a hatch-type door.

'So, who do you think would come up here now?' Amelia said, walking round the perimeter again.

'Local kids?'

Amelia shook her head. 'They'd have left cigarette butts, beer cans, goodness knows what else.'

'Litter-aware local kids?'

'With a neat freak complex? I don't think so. I've seen the lights up here twice already so let's assume it has been the same person who has returned. There isn't anything here unless they were removing items, that would explain the imprint of a storage box or something like that?'

'It couldn't be huge as it wouldn't be able to fit through the entrance gap.'

'But it could be heavy, hence the return visit, and, of course, whoever it was could have returned a dozen times...'

'Maybe we'll never know.'

'Maybe.'

Jack grinned at her. 'But it is kind of cool.'

'Yeah, and mysterious.' She grinned back at him. 'I have my own secret tower in my back garden. Not many can say that.'

With possibly a few more secret passages hidden away in the house, too, Amelia thought to herself as they retraced their steps back down into the underground tunnel. Jack led the way and they were almost at the entrance when Amelia's boot kicked against something. She shone her torch down and saw a little wooden box. She picked it up and slipped it in her pocket and carried on towards the hidden folly entrance.

She and Jack walked back towards the house, each lost in their own thoughts, with Amelia turning the little wooden box over in her pocket, keen to look at it when she was on her own.

'We're having a party,' Amelia said as she got to the back door, kicking off the mud from her boots against the boot scraper.

'A party? Lovely. When?'

'A week on Saturday.'

He smiled. 'I'll make sure I stay out your way.'

'What? No, I want you to come!'

'Oh.' He smiled. 'Okay. What's it in honour of?'

'Hallowe'en. It's fancy dress.'

'Is there a theme?'

'Uh, I don't know. I don't think so.'

'You don't think so?'

'I'm not really organising it; Gideon and Sally are.'

'Hey, you now have people!' He winked almost imperceptibly.

'It's not like that!'

'I'm just teasing.' He grinned. 'I'd love to come. So, are you going to let me know if you see any more lights up here?'

'So you can talk me out of investigating them?' Amelia asked.

'Maybe I don't want you to have all the fun to yourself,' he said as he walked away. After a few steps he turned round. 'And you still owe me that nightcap, remember.'

'I remember.' Amelia let herself into the kitchen, her stomach jumping about from the excitement which she put down to finding the way into the folly.

She was stopped in her tracks when she saw the state of devastation the kitchen had been left in. Mugs and juice cups lay half empty with egg yolk and bacon fat congealing on the plates.

Toby was maybe an excellent cook but he still had a lot to learn as a washer upper.

21

Amelia checked her watch. 2200 hours. She had a good two and a half hours before anyone else returned from the pub, possibly longer if the rumours of the lock-in came to fruition.

She'd managed to slip away relatively unnoticed. As was now becoming the habit, after another one of Toby's fabulous meals, they all wandered along to the Whistling Haggis. Often it was just for one drink, but tonight Amelia had bought plenty of rounds in to get them started on a night of drinking to keep them out the way. Last she saw, after an hour of arguing over the best Cary Grant film with Toby, Gideon was getting wellied into a bottle of wine and Sally was getting wellied into Mike. Having stuck to Diet Coke, Amelia had watched as the others descended into deeper layers of tipsiness, biding her time until she could escape.

Her new clothing certainly allowed Amelia to get around much quicker than a pair of heels, and she made it back to the house in no time.

Tonight she was determined to find that hidden passage.

She put on a beanie hat and gloves – no matter how excited

she was about unveiling the secrets of her house, her adventure at the folly had taught her she didn't much like having cobwebs all over her face and hands, although she'd never admit that to Jack.

Her gaze fell upon the little wooden trinket box she'd found that afternoon in the folly passageway. She lifted it up, tracing her fingers over the top of it. It was beautifully hand carved in the shape of a love heart with an intricate swirling design inlaid into the wood. It was disappointingly empty, but there was an intriguing little inscription; 'Love is forever', then the initials F.A.M.

Amelia had wracked her brains thinking who was F.A.M., possibly Flora Mirchie? She doubted it was that old, though, to still be in such good condition. Also, Flora hadn't mentioned taking up wood whittling in any of her diary entries and with the amount of dull facts she put in, Amelia doubted she'd have omitted something as scintillating as taking up a new hobby.

Amelia popped the trinket box back down and stared for a moment at the pile of books beside it. She could have sworn her Denholm Armitage was on top earlier, but now the Agatha Christie was at the top of the pile. Had the ghost of Dotty floated into her room to demand she read *Murder on the Orient Express* instead? Of all the things for a spectral Dotty to do, influencing her reading material did seem quite likely, but not so likely was the possibility her ghostly godmother had also trawled through her underwear drawer and rifled through her wardrobe. It wasn't that Amelia was overly fussy about ordering her clothes but she always kept her underwear in very neat piles in her drawer and although her bras hadn't exactly been strewn about with gay abandon, they just weren't how Amelia usually placed them. The same with the wardrobe, all her clothes had been pushed to one side.

It made Amelia feel slightly uneasy but for now she had to

put all thoughts of a bedroom prowler out of her head as she had a secret passage to find.

First up was Mike's room. She let herself in and swept the torch around. Wow! She'd seen some untidy rooms in her time but this took it to an entirely different level. All his belongings were dumped on the floor with his wardrobe and drawers sitting empty. She wondered briefly if his bedroom had had a going-over too; if it was spooks at work, it must have been by an extremely messy poltergeist. If this was just how he lived it was a wonder he ever found anything, she thought as she carefully stepped over his camera equipment and discarded pieces of underwear. She didn't think Beniamino would be too pleased to see all the expensive equipment scattered about so carelessly. Amelia got to the fireplace and after removing the cold mugs of coffee and packet of condoms felt optimistic when she saw just how ornate the wooden carvings were; ideal for hidden levers or buttons. But this soon turned to frustration as no amount of pushing and pulling revealed anything other than a dead earwig and a cotton bud. She carefully placed the mugs along with the condoms back to where they'd been.

Next room along was the bathroom he and Ross shared. She pushed the door open against a wet towel lying on the floor. It was pretty unremarkable apart from more piles of underwear lying by the bath and layers of stubble shavings in the sink. Amelia quickly exited.

Ross's room was next. Opening the door she found it to be the complete opposite of Mike's, with everything neat and tidied away. On the bedside table sat a travel alarm clock and a deodorant and there was a zipped-up toilet bag lying on another table. Even the bed was made. Apart from a really creaky floorboard near the window there was nothing remarkable about his room. There wasn't even a mantlepiece, just a fire grate. She left, disappointed.

Sally's room was next. She'd left the light on and it was tidy, which was very unusual for Sally. There was an assortment of candles placed around the room, waiting to be lit upon her return, clearly assuming she wasn't going to be alone. Mike didn't stand a chance.

Amelia started to feel along the mantlepiece and fire surround. She just touched the panel on the top right when there was a clicking noise and a panel of wood stood slightly proud of the others. Amelia gave a squeal of excitement.

'Thank you, Flora,' she whispered before pulling the panel back slightly.

It was quite a tight space and once inside there wasn't a huge amount of height. Her torch allowed her to see further in. The space got narrower but did lead somewhere. Before she moved off Amelia made sure she could see the inside handle that would allow her to get back out. It was just about head height. She pulled the door closed and tried it out. It clicked back open. Feeling a little more confident, she closed it over once again and turned to follow the passage. Shining her torch in front of her she could see the passage went for another few feet, then it seemed to fall away. Steps! Using her hand to balance against the wall, Amelia gingerly made her way down the narrow stone stairs. She tried to work out where she'd end up, but another couple of turns made her lose her sense of direction. She got to the floor below. Now what, she wondered. There was a small archway but it looked as if it had been boarded up from the other side. She gave it a tentative push but nothing budged. She took a step closer to really put her shoulder against it and as she did, her foot pushed down onto the wide flagstone and she felt it depress slightly under her weight. Instinctively she pushed at the wooden panels at the same time and they swung outwards. On walking through the archway Amelia found herself in a cluttered room full of rusted gardening equipment and planters.

It was the cellar! She'd found the way that Flora had helped Gemmell escape. She looked behind her and saw the secret entrance she'd just walked through was disguised as a shelving unit which had pots of paint and gardening accessories lying on them. She was about to close it over when she stopped. She looked around for a way that would open the door up from the cellar but couldn't see anything obvious. It looked as though the passage only worked the one way. She walked over to the outside door and tried to open it but the new lock was already fitted, doing its job.

Jack said it was people trying to steal equipment. That was a possibility but what if it was someone looking for the secret passage? If they came in from the cellar they wouldn't get any further but what if they were in the house and needed to get out and the only way was to break down the cellar door?

The cellar was down a flight of steps and wasn't that noticeable from the back of the house if you were just walking past. The broken lock could have been like that for weeks, months even. Or just a couple of days.

Amelia slipped back through the secret door and pulled the shelves tight against the archway, hearing it click as the flagstone lifted up to its original position. She gave it a quick push to ensure it was sealed tight, then walked back up to Sally's room and pulled the secret door back over. She was just about to open the door into the corridor when she heard voices, recognising Sally's Cornish lilt. She looked around in panic for a place to hide. With no time to get to the secret passageway again, her options were the bathroom or bed. Diving under Sally's bed, Amelia managed to slide out of view just as the door opened. Amelia lay flat on her stomach, her heart going into overtime as she tried not to breathe loudly. Why had she decided to hide? She could have just said she was checking for towels or something like that. But now she'd hidden she couldn't very well roll out from under the bed and say she was auditing loose bed springs! If it was Sally on her own it would have been different but not if she was with Mike.

'Oh God, you've got amazing baps!'

Amelia lifted her head in surprise, banging the back of her head against the bed slats. That wasn't Mike's voice. It was...

'Oh, Lawrence! Ravish me here!'

What on earth was she doing with Lawrence? It was Mike she fancied and Mike she'd been flirting with.

There was an awful lot of grunting and wet sounds with some moaning and Amelia realised she was going to have to listen to them having sex. Then the mattress above her suddenly bowed in the middle and almost touched her head despite her lying as flat against the floor as she could, looking out the side of the bed.

She really hoped they wouldn't be having bouncy, acrobatic sex.

A pair of scruffy Nike trainers and a pair of jeans landed on the floor just a few inches from Amelia's head. Then a Ramones tour T-shirt. She waited for the socks, but they didn't appear.

Amelia grimaced under the bed as the mattress started bouncing up and down.

'Wait, wait, wait, I've candles.'

'Fuck the candles, come and fuck me.'

'But it will be more romantic.'

Amelia heard Lawrence laugh. He certainly wasn't in it for the romance if he hadn't even taken his socks off!

There was some more gasping, panting noises and Amelia wished she could stick her fingers in her ears and sing 'la-la-laaaa' at the top of her voice, but she was terrified to move in case it alerted them to her being there.

The mattress suddenly moved up from almost brushing

Amelia's head and Sally's feet landed squarely on top of the rumpled jeans.

'Let's have a bath together. I have jasmine-scented bubble bath.'

'You trying to say I need a wash?' Lawrence laughed.

His lanky hair certainly could, Amelia thought.

'Of course not, I just thought it would be nice.'

'You know what would be nice? You sucking my cock.'

Under the bed, Amelia made a face at the crudeness. The one thing that *did* suck was his line in foreplay.

'Let's go into the bathroom, I'll run us a bath. It'll be romantic.'

He laughed. 'I'm not exactly here for any Mills and Boon stuff, you know. Sharing baths, not my thing and anyway, we'd never both fit, love, not with your thunder thighs.'

Amelia jerked her head up. What? Had he really just said that? She had to stop herself from getting out from under the bed and punching Lawrence in the face. Sally was gorgeous. Yes, she was more Rubenesque than stick thin, but she was absolutely beautiful.

'Sorry, I know I'm on the big side but just think of it as more to hold on to.'

What on earth was Sally doing? She shouldn't be apologising for her size! She should be giving Lawrence his marching orders. Even worse, Amelia thought she could detect a faint tremor in Sally's voice.

'Those are certainly large love handles.'

Sally laughed, but Amelia could tell it was forced. Here she was, about to have sex and this idiot was making fun of her body? Lawrence did not deserve someone as beautiful and lovely as Sally.

Suddenly Sally's legs disappeared from view as the bed dipped dangerously close to Amelia's head again.

'We don't need a warm bath to get you wet. That's the beauty about fat chicks, you're always up for it.'

Amelia waited for the slap sound, where Sally gave Lawrence a colossal clip around the ears, then sent him packing... but no sound like that materialised. Instead, Amelia could hear Lawrence start to moan a lot louder and there was a squeaking noise from Sally. The bed began to move up and down at a ferociously fast rhythm.

'Yeah. Yeah. Yeah, yeah, yeahyeahyeahyeah. YEAH!' Lawrence shouted out triumphantly.

The springs abruptly stopped their workout.

Amelia, with her hand now covering her mouth in horror at the sorry-sounding sex, winced as Lawrence clearly rolled off Sally.

'Welcome to Scotland!' He laughed. 'You think your mate would be up for a threesome?'

'No.'

He grunted something unintelligible. Seconds later Amelia could hear him snoring. A few seconds after that she thought she could hear Sally snuffling softly. She desperately wanted to go and comfort her best friend but she had no idea how she could talk her way out of her situation. Sally always seemed such a confident and vibrant force of nature Amelia couldn't believe she let Lawrence speak to her like that. Was she that insecure about her figure? She never acted like she was.

A few moments later the bed springs moved again and Sally hopped off the bed and went into the bathroom. Seizing the opportunity, Amelia rolled out from under the bed and bolted for the door. She looked back at Lawrence, lying on his back, one arm flung above his head, the other resting over his pale, sparsely-haired paunch. He wasn't exactly an oil painting himself and therefore in no position to pass judgement on a beautiful woman who was *clearly* way out of his league but was just too insecure to realise.

And he still had his socks on.

Amelia slipped out the door quietly, all excitement about discovering the secret hideaway now forgotten.

Amelia paced the floor of her bedroom, furious with Lawrence. And with Sally for letting that idiot undermine her confidence like that. She threw her beanie hat onto the bed and yanked her gloves off. Despite all her light-hearted talk of one-night stands, maybe Sally hankered after romance. The candles and lure of jasmine-scented baths would seem to suggest that her friend was more into romance and the possibility of a relationship rather than just a quick bonk. Amelia changed into her warm, fleecy toothpaste-striped pyjamas. As she buttoned them up, she thought how much Jonathan would have hated her wearing them, they weren't silky enough, sheer enough or impractical enough for him. She paused her buttoning. She wasn't sure, but she didn't think she'd given Jonathan a moment's thought for a couple of days. With her phone still luxuriating most of its day in a reception black spot, Amelia had no way of knowing if Jonathan had been trying to get in touch. As she padded into her en suite she realised she didn't actually care! Between Jonathan and Lawrence, Amelia wondered if all the men she knew were assholes.

22

'And again!' Beniamino called up to Amelia as she made her way down the stairs. 'Gideon got into your shot.'

'Pardon me!' Gideon remarked coolly as he passed Amelia on the stairs. He was wearing pyjama bottoms, a large Fair Isle jumper with his dressing gown over the top. 'Fancy a coffee, poppet?' he asked Amelia as he passed her.

'Yes, please.'

Gideon sailed past the crew; Mike filming at the front, Ross just a little way behind holding the big furry microphone, with Lawrence holding up a fancy gadget that occasionally beeped. Beniamino stood further back still with a clipboard and walkie-talkie. Considering that everyone that needed to be there was within a five-foot radius of him, Amelia felt the walkie-talkie was perhaps a little redundant. She got to the top step and waited for Beniamino's signal before starting down them again, talking as she went.

'So far, Tom the plumber has started on the ground floor and the team of electricians are working on lights and rewiring. We're in desperate need of a new fuse box as I'm running low on batteries for the torches and our wax candle stock is sorely depleted. We're getting some posh, fancy pillar lights for the driveway as each time any of us walk the stretch in the dark we start thinking about the ghostly headless horseman story and get freaked out and run.' Amelia paused at the bottom step and grinned at the camera, then turned to walk into the kitchen to where Gideon was making coffee.

'Morning, gorgeous!' he said, turning to her and the camera with a full-wattage smile as if they hadn't just bumped into each other moments before on the stairs. 'Coffee?'

'Mmmm, lovely!'

'For breakfast we can do the continental.' He held up a Twix. 'A cooked.' He fished out a packet of chicken flavour Supernoodles from his dressing-gown pocket. 'Or,' he swanned over to the fridge, 'the hair-of-the-dog special.' He held up a bottle of vodka and a carton of tomato juice.

'Or we could ask Toby, my gorgeous brother, to cook us one of his spectacular meals,' Amelia said as Toby wandered in wearing neon lime-green cycling shorts and a Micky Mouse vest-style T-shirt. They were lucky he was wearing that as he had a habit of wandering around in just his tight-fitting briefs and Beniamino kept having to cut the scene and get him to put more clothes on.

'Eggs Benedict?' he asked to thumbs ups of approval.

'So, it's a big day, Amelia?' Beniamino asked off camera.

Amelia plucked the Twix from Gideon's hand and nodded. 'Yes, especially as we've got the Hallowe'en costumes arriving for us to pick from later on too.'

'Any hints as to what they are?'

Gideon swanned over with the mugs of coffee, handing one of them to Amelia. 'They're all going to be a surprise until the night. No hints at all.'

'What about the decorations?'

Amelia shrugged and blew on her coffee. 'I've been told it's all in hand and not to interfere.' It was actually driving her mad as she'd frequently come across Sally and Gideon giggling like naughty schoolkids, huddled together over the kitchen table with a big pad of lists but as soon as they saw Amelia, they'd shut the pads over and not even let her have a peek.

'And here is my partner in crime!' Gideon said as Sally wandered in. She gave an awkward wave at the camera and hurried over to the kettle, head down. Amelia clocked she hadn't made eye contact with either Mike or Lawrence. Amelia couldn't look at Lawrence without wanting to throttle him either.

'Cut!' Beniamino said and Mike lowered his camera. Amelia noticed he didn't look at Sally either. 'Let's go and get some footage of the workmen. Tom's always good value for an anecdote or two.'

Tom the plumber seemed to now be a permanent fixture in the house, Amelia thought as she watched the documentary crew leave. She hadn't worked out if he was just a very conscientious tradesman or fancied a career in reality television.

'Are you really making eggs Benedict?' Amelia asked Toby.

'I certainly am,' Toby said as he started cutting muffins in half. 'There's also yogurt and honey and smoothies.'

'I think I'll just stick to fruit this morning,' Sally said, looking forlornly on as Toby began to prepare the hollandaise sauce.

'You sure?' Amelia said.

'Yeah, all this lovely food is great but not so good for the old physique,' she said, patting her tummy. 'I really could do with losing a few pounds.'

Amelia mentally swore at Lawrence.

Amelia didn't want to tell her best friend *not* to lose weight if she really wanted to do it for herself as that wouldn't be supportive, but she didn't want Sally to feel she had to change her body shape to please some insensitive idiot.

'What's brought this on?' Amelia asked her lightly.

'Oh, just thinking I don't want to look podgy in front of the cameras, they add at least ten pounds on. It's very different when you work behind it, then switch to being in front of it.' Sally had already been asked to do a couple of pieces to camera by Beniamino.

'You will always look gorgeous whatever size you are.'

Sally gave a wan smile but then her chin started to wobble slightly.

'Hey, remember the costumes are arriving today,' Amelia said, trying to cheer her up.

Sally pulled a face. 'I may just cover myself up with a huge wool poncho and go as Demis Roussos.' Sally's face crumpled. 'I've made a bit of a mess of things. I slept with Lawrence.'

Amelia feigned surprise. 'But I thought you and Mike...'

'So did I. We were drunk, he went to the bar and ended up chatting to this pretty woman and I got a bit jealous so I started chatting up Lawrence. Rather than get jealous and come claim me as his woman, Mike backed right off and went home with the other woman, then I was left with Leering Lawrence.'

'Oh, and did Lawrence say something to upset you?'

'He said I was fat.'

'He's a dick. I hope you told him to do one.'

Sally shook her head miserably. 'That's the awful thing. I didn't. We shagged.'

'He's not worthy of you. He's no great catch himself if he can't even take his socks off.'

'How did you know?' Sally's eyes widened.

'Ah! Well, I just guessed. I know his type.' Amelia hoped she'd covered her gaffe in time.

'It was really awful. I feel like hell.'

Gideon, who'd been leaning against the countertop, moved over to them. 'Have a drink then, it always makes me feel better.'

'I didn't think you were listening,' Sally said.

'Don't worry, I'm not going to say anything. Put it down to experience and move on.'

'Gideon's right,' Amelia said.

'Oh sod it,' Sally said, lifting up a half muffin and taking a bite out of it. 'I wonder who else is single around these parts.'

'You wanted me to be what?' Amelia asked just to be certain she'd heard Sally correctly.

They were sitting on the bed in Amelia's room not long after the DPD delivery of a whole host of costumes arrived. The party was still a few days away but Sally had wanted to have everyone's outfit prepared well in advance. Her professionalism had well and truly kicked in with her already having sketched out the make-up for many of the people she was dressing. Gideon was unzipping the costume protectors and giggling over each discovery.

'Don't worry, we chickened out at the last minute,' Sally said soothingly.

'Thank God for that!' Amelia had nearly had a fit when Sally said she'd originally thought Amelia could go as Princess Leia, dressed in the gold lamé bikini. Apart from the modesty issue, she'd have frozen to death!

'What else is there?' Sally called over her shoulder.

'Apart from the main ones I specifically requested for us, I just asked for a selection of interesting costumes the others can take their pick from and boy, have they come up trumps! They've even sent a Cyberman costume.' Gideon pointed over to a gigantic box by the window where a silver plastic foot was protruding from the packaging.

'What are you guys going as?' Amelia asked, not for the first time.

'We're not saying.' Sally smiled enigmatically.

'It's a surprise.' Gideon blew her a kiss.

'That's so unfair,' Amelia grumbled.

'We're the ones organising this,' Sally pointed out, 'let us keep a little mystery to ourselves. Consider it like the bride's wedding dress. No one sees that until the big day.'

'Do you want to show Amelia what we thought would be good for her?' Sally said.

'Found it!' Gideon called as he started to pull something out of a costume protector.

All Amelia could see was sheaths of diaphanous white fabric as he brought it over.

'Ta-daaaaa! It's a replica costume of the bride of Frankenstein, complete with conical wig with lightning bolts running up the sides! And there's a pair of massive high-heeled thigh-high gladiator-style sandal boots which you could wear with it.'

'Wow! That's amazing!' Amelia held it up to her. It puddled on the ground at her feet.

'I could always take it up?' Sally offered.

'And in,' Gideon added. 'It looks as if it was made for a six-foot shot-put champion.'

He was right. It was huge.

'Let me work my magic on it,' Sally said, gently taking it away from Amelia.

'Are you sure?' Amelia asked, not wanting to put Sally to any trouble but also loving the look of it, along with the boots. She missed wearing her heels.

'Leave it with me.' Sally grinned. 'You *shall* go to the ball!'

'Look at this!' Gideon held up a werewolf costume. 'How about for Lawrence? He's so quiet and reserved I'd wager he's harbouring a secret identity. And all that fur would make him uncomfortable which serves him right for being such a shit to you, Sally.'

'Oh, and that would be ideal for Ross!' Sally pointed to a Fred Astaire-style top-hat-and-tails outfit, complete with cane and tap shoes. 'He's definitely got the swagger and charm to pull that off.'

'Oh?' Amelia said leadingly.

But Sally shook her head. 'Nah, he's not for me. We've gotten pissed together countless times but he's just not interested no matter how much I flaunt myself! I've never gotten any signal from him.'

'Gay?' Amelia hazarded.

'No, I really don't think so. To be honest, I hardly know him. We chat a lot but it's all surface nonsense, like work, films, music. He's a great laugh with an anecdote for every occasion but I don't know anything personal about him apart from the fact he rarely drinks anything stronger than a lemonade apart from when he's on flaming sambuca shots.' She laughed. 'Now, *that* was a wild time in the Whistling Haggis!'

'I don't remember,' Gideon said.

'Exactly! You were asleep in the corner.'

'I don't remember it either,' Amelia admitted.

'That's because you weren't there! You hardly come out with us.' Sally rolled her eyes. 'You're always making lists of things you need to do, or reading your book or drinking coffee. Please, tonight, come out to the pub with us.'

'Yes, come on, Amelia. I sometimes feel like you're our mum and we're the naughty children. You can be such a sensible-head at times,' Gideon chastised.

Amelia looked at them. They just didn't get it. To them, this was another fun shoot, full of 'what-happens-on-location-stays-on-location' frivolity. They didn't understand this was going to be her livelihood. Or that she didn't fit in with their crazy drinking and hijinks. She wasn't part of their world. But still, she did fancy a night off from list-making and diary-reading. She wasn't even enjoying her Denholm Armitage book as much as his other ones – she hoped it was just her not being in the right mood for the book rather than him going off the boil.

'Okay, I'll come, I'm heading out for a bit first though.' She checked her watch. She had something to do first and she needed to go and check it was okay to borrow Toby's car. Something slightly less conspicuous than a red Ferrari would have suited Amelia better but the only other vehicle she knew of was the van Beniamino used and she didn't want to have to explain to anyone where she was going.

Luckily, Sally and Gideon were far too wrapped up in the costumes to question her further.

'How about this for Beniamino?' Gideon laughed as he continued to look through the costumes. He held up an army major's costume.

'Don't be mean!' Sally said. 'Just because he calls you up on tardiness! He's a professional.'

'He's a dictator jobsworth! And he insists on draping those cashmere jumpers over his shoulders as if he's wandering around Rome,' Gideon bitched as Amelia slipped out the door.

Once Amelia had stopped being terrified at driving a Ferrari she settled into it and found she quite liked the sensation of sitting low to the ground in the leather bucket seats, feeling the throaty engine reverberating through her body. Insane acceleration coupled with instant braking meant the car bunny-hopped the first half of the journey into Ullapool to the little museum and library.

Amelia was originally going to get the Wee Happy Bus but after looking at the timetable and seeing the infrequency of the service and that it would be almost three hours for the round trip, she hoped Toby would lend her his scarlet supercar. He was happy to, not being in the slightest overprotective of that part of his inheritance. He still seemed bemused to own such an upmarket ride when the only other car he'd ever owned was a lime-green rusted Nissan Micra with its bumper half hanging off.

Amelia parked on the road outside the little stone-fronted building and there was immediate interest from a group of schoolkids sitting in the bus shelter opposite, eating chips.

Okay, she did rather like the attention driving such a beast of a car got her, she thought as she pressed the key fob and it trilled back at her to indicate it was now locked.

Inside, Amelia went up to the desk to where a young woman stood logging a large pile of books onto a computer. She looked up with an enquiring smile.

'Hi,' Amelia said. 'I was hoping to look through some archives to get information on plans of a house.'

'Sure, how far back do you need to go?'

'Early 1700s up to about 1890.'

The girl grimaced. 'We've only got post 1900 data on computer. Anything before that is still on microfiche. We are in the process of updating it but it'll take years to get through it all.'

'That's fine. I'm also looking for newspaper articles from the 1800s.'

'Is it for something specific?'

'Yes, I've got names and dates.'

'That'll help, come on through to the records room.' She led the way through the main library to a little annexe where there were a couple of chunky-looking computers with magnifying glass trays underneath. There were filing cabinets beside them.

'There's an index to the filing cabinets on the side. Just take the sheet you want and pop it on the lens and turn the knob to scroll across.'

'Thanks.' It seemed very labour intensive for someone used to Google search.

The woman, whose name badge said she was called Jenny, wished her luck and was in the process of closing the door when she asked, 'What's the house you're looking for?'

'Stone Manor, in Glencarlach. I've just moved into it.'

Jenny's forehead wrinkled. 'That name sounds really familiar.'

'Oh? There are lots of rumours about the house involving secret passages. I'm looking for anything to do with the house and the family that lived there.'

Jenny was still frowning. 'I'm sure I've seen something with that name recently. Leave it with me.'

Amelia slung her coat over the back of the chair and got out her pad where she'd dotted down the dates Montgomery Campbell was out of the country, from the *Herald* article Dotty had left for her, and started to look for the information she needed.

She found a fair amount of information straight off when searching for Montgomery in conjunction with Egypt. A predecessor of Carnarvon and Carter, Montgomery Campbell's finds weren't as newsworthy as Tutankhamun's but he had managed to discover many of the minor burial sites in the Valley of the Kings. The more Amelia read, the more uneasy she felt. These British adventurers dropped into the country with their wealth and egotistical belief of their superiority, then pillaged ancient sites they had no connection with in order to line their pockets with gold and jewels. Fair enough, a lot of the finds stayed in Egypt but it was definitely seen as a way of getting rich.

There was also a lot of information about the alleged treasures Campbell had discovered. Along with the usual gold there seemed to be a lot of jewels. Amelia almost stopped breathing when she found a reference to Amor Rubra; one of the largest rubies in the world! It was believed to have gone home with Montgomery Campbell but had never surfaced again.

This was what Archibald believed to be hidden in Stone Manor!

Amelia could have a huge ruby right under her nose and not know it!

This was exciting! But a ruby, albeit a huge one, could be absolutely anywhere in that huge house and grounds.

A bit more searching unearthed information about Stone Manor but it was only with the occasional reference in parish records. There were some mentions of it being built and in the various stages of extension but frustratingly, nothing about secret passages or detailed floor plans.

Amelia had been searching for almost three hours, was starving hungry and suffering caffeine withdrawals, when there was a soft knock on the door and Jenny poked her head round.

'How are you getting on?'

'I vow never to complain about slow broadband connection again!' Amelia laughed, almost cross-eyed from searching the microfiche records.

'I found something you may find helpful,' Jenny said, holding up a few sheets of photocopies. 'I found these with a Post-it note saying "Stone Manor – to pick up." I knew the name was familiar.'

'Can I see them?' Amelia asked.

'Sure. You can make another copy. It'll save you searching it out for yourself. Someone else must have been in and asked my colleague Fiona for them.'

'Does she remember who it was?' Amelia asked, interest piqued.

'She's off on holiday at the moment but is back in a couple of days. Leave your name and number and I'll ask her when she gets back.' She handed the papers to Amelia. 'We close in half an hour.'

'Thanks.' There were only a few sheets and Amelia settled down to read them.

The first was a newspaper article from 1958 about the disappearance of Charles Campbell. His brother, James Campbell, had alerted the authorities after a couple of weeks of not having heard from him. He frequently travelled through to Edinburgh but no one had seen him for a couple of weeks. There had been no definitive last sighting of Charles and the police could only speculate on his movements. There was another copy of a birth certificate for a Helen McCallum in July 1947. The mother was listed as Evelyn McCallum, resident of Glencarlach, father unknown. Amelia was sure that was the name on the inside of Flora's diary on the family tree. She dug it out of her bag and checked. The names matched although there was a question mark at both their names. There was also a copy of the notification of Dorothea's death, which Amelia found herself rereading even though she'd been the one to write it and knew it off by heart. There was also a copy of the death announcement of Charles Campbell from 1959. One year after his disappearance he was pronounced dead even though there was no body. Pieces of his boat and some of his belongings had been found floating in Glencarlach harbour and a verdict of accidental death was issued.

Amelia collected her belongings and handed the photocopies back to Jenny along with her name and number.

Despite her house being a phone blackspot, Amelia was still able to access her messages whenever she wandered into an area of reception.

Amelia drove back home, looking forward to the Thai feast Toby had promised everyone followed by an evening spent in the Whistling Haggis, but all the time there was a little voice nagging at her, wondering who else could be digging up the information on the Campbell family. And why.

23

Their tummies full of spicy, creamy coconut curry, Amelia, along with Sally, Gideon and Toby, ambled happily along to the Whistling Haggis. As they neared the gatehouse, wonderful rich aromas of woodsmoke hung heavy in the cold air and on getting level with the charming whitewashed cottage they saw Jack cutting logs of wood with an axe. He'd taken off his jumper and tied the arms around his waist, revealing a torso-hugging long-sleeved jersey top.

'I do believe I've stumbled upon my fantasy,' Toby said with a throaty chuckle.

'Mine too,' Sally added.

'Evening,' Toby shouted over cheerily.

'Hey.' Jack put down his axe and wiped the sweat from his brow when he saw them.

'You must be Jack?' Toby said.

'Guilty as charged.'

'I'm Toby and this is Sally.'

'Come on, let's go!' Gideon said, trying to hurry them along.

'What my friend means to say is, we're heading to the pub and would you like to join us?' Toby said.

'I've got things I need to be doing here...'

'He's not interested,' Gideon said, as he continued walking.

Toby looked at Gideon, then back at Jack. 'Sorry, Gideon doesn't mean to be insulting.'

'Gideon can speak for himself and Gideon *does* mean to be insulting!' Gideon called out behind him.

Jack tightened his jumper around his waist. 'Well, how could I say no to such a warm reception?' he said with a grin. 'You don't mind if I tag along?' He addressed Amelia.

'Of course not, just try not to get us arrested by the police or insult us—'

'Where's the fun in that?' Jack said with a grin.

It was just after nine and the Whistling Haggis was absolutely heaving. Amelia could see Big Davey grinning like the Cheshire cat as he served pints. Since Mike had taken up semi-permanent residence at the bar most evenings, filming the regulars for a bit of 'extra substance and local character' there were more and more 'regulars' for Big Davey to serve and Mike received free pints for drawing them in. Amelia looked around the room. It definitely seemed the Glencarlach villagers were fine about being on film. Like Andy Warhol said, everyone craved their fifteen minutes of fame. A table of young girls, of barely legal drinking age and in full make-up sat nudging each other and giggling behind their hands when they clocked Gideon.

'Ahh, my adoring public awaits,' he said as they sat at a table and Sally went to get some drinks.

'Careful,' Amelia warned. 'A couple of them don't look old enough to do anything, let alone drink.'

'Thank you, Mother, but you needn't worry, the only date I have in mind for tonight is with a bottle of vodka.'

Gideon, clearly in a sulk because Jack had joined them, sat with his arms folded, studiously ignoring the others.

Toby gave Amelia a look and raised his eyebrows.

The silence became too awkward for Amelia and she blurted out, 'I've been meaning to ask you, Jack, where in America do you come from?' Toby shook his head, hiding a smile at her pathetic attempts to make small talk.

'New York.'

'Oh, you don't sound like you come from New York, isn't it a bit more Noooo Yawk?' she said, exaggerating the vowel sounds.

'That's more a Brooklyn accent you've got. No, I'm Upper East Side.'

'Upper East Side, where's that? I mean obviously it's to the east and then up a bit.'

'UES is in Manhattan, near Central Park.'

'What he means to say is he's from the expensive bit,' Gideon chimed in, arms still folded.

'Are you?' Amelia didn't mean to sound so surprised.

'Well, yeah,' Jack said, looking a little uncomfortable.

'I don't mean to offend you, *either* of you,' Gideon chimed in, 'but doesn't it seem far more probable that someone would move *from* Glencarlach *to* Manhattan rather than the other way around?'

'What can I say, the grass is always greener.' Jack shrugged.

'Then one must ask the question, what was so green about here?' Gideon queried.

'I'm just travelling.'

'To travel, as in the verb, would suggest a constant movement, yet you seem to be somewhat stationary. Unless you've been travelling *through* this little village. If so, you've been terribly thorough and surely you've exhausted all Glencarlach has to offer by now.'

'Maybe not all,' Jack said, lounging back in his chair. 'You'd be surprised at the constant delights it keeps offering up,' he added, still smiling broadly at Gideon.

'And what are you doing bothering with manual labour?'

'I like it.'

'Do you have other skills?'

'Plenty.'

'Oh, are you being altruistic? Giving something back to the people.'

'Nope, I'm being paid for it so it's hardly out of the goodness of my heart.'

'Well, it must be paying you well if you live in an expensive part of New York,' Gideon fired back with a raised eyebrow as he made to stand up. 'I'm going for a pee.' He turned to Amelia. 'Darling, could you possibly add something to your staggeringly efficient to-do list?'

'Uh, yes,' Amelia said, thankful for a change of topic and a cool down from the simmering testosterone.

'Get Sky television installed, otherwise we may all be forced to talk to one another like this every evening.'

'There's a Monopoly board game and Scrabble in one of the cupboards in the drawing room,' Jack said, but Gideon was already a few feet away from the table.

There was a moment's awkward silence until Toby cleared his throat and said to Jack, 'I have to say, that's some jumper you've got on!'

Amelia turned to look. He wasn't wrong. It was a very long, baggy chunky knit in bright-blue with a white diagonal cross over the front.

Jack looked down and stretched it out. 'Thanks! It's the Saltire flag, I thought I'd show my patriotism towards Scotland, someone local knits them for the outdoors shop in the village. You should think of getting one as I see you believe you're as impervious to the cold as your sister!'

'Yeah, the cold has been a bit of an eye-opener!' Toby agreed, looking down at his thin top and lightweight jacket.

'I'll go help with the drinks,' Jack said, acknowledging Sally waving at them and trying to balance two bottles of wine, four wine glasses and a triple vodka and Coke in her arms.

'What's with Gideon and Jack?' Toby asked, once Jack was out of earshot.

'They take great enjoyment in winding each other up. Jack can be quite abrasive and blunt and I suppose Gideon isn't really used to people being like that with him so he's very sarcastic back and then Jack winds him up even more.'

'Sounds like a real wild ride!'

Sally came back and clinked the glasses on the table, also dropping a few packets of crisps.

She flopped down beside Amelia. 'Mike seems to be in his element,' she said, nodding over to him. He was recording Archie again and had a little group standing in a semicircle, waiting for their turn to be on camera.'

'You okay?' Amelia asked Sally. They hadn't talked about Mike or Lawrence in a couple of days.

'Tickety-boo, my lovely, tickety-boo.'

'Sals! I do believe you're being eyed up,' Toby said and everyone turned to look at a man at the bar who immediately went red and turned away. From the brief glimpse Amelia got, he looked to be big, brawny and the very epitome of 'rugged'.

But Sally simply sighed and poured the wine. 'I'm off men for now. They're nothing but arseholes. Present company excepted,' she said, looking at Toby and Jack, who'd also returned carrying Gideon's vodka and a few packs of peanuts.

'Don't worry, I've been called an arsehole many times,' Jack said, opening a bag of nuts. 'So, have you been filling them in on our nocturnal adventures?' he said to Amelia with the ghost of a wink.

Toby nearly spat out his wine in surprise as Sally raised her eyebrows at Amelia.

'Not what you think!' Amelia quickly said.

'Nocturnal adventures of the spooky kind,' Jack explained. 'Tell me, is she as obsessed with ghosts and mysteries at home?' Jack continued.

Toby banged the table and laughed heartily. 'Is she? I'll say! Amelia has a vivid imagination and a conspiracy theory for everything.'

'Well, it's not all nonsense. There are secret passages in the house!' she blurted out just as Gideon returned to their table. 'Well, in the gardens.' Amelia decided not to tell them about the ones she'd found in the house as she liked just having that knowledge to herself and also, Sally could very well get freaked knowing there was a passageway which led from the back of her fireplace.

'Yeah, we found a way into the folly,' Jack said, taking a sip of wine.

'The tower in the garden,' Amelia explained.

'How very Scooby Doo of you,' Gideon said tartly as he sat down.

'It was quite exciting. Seems something had been up there but recently removed.'

'What?' Sally asked, agog, crunching down on a cheese and onion crisp.

'Don't know. But we'd noticed strange lights flickering in the tower.'

'Is it something sinister?' Toby asked. 'I mean, after the rock through the window and then the cellar being broken into.'

'Dunno.' Jack shrugged.

'I think it's all just a big coincidence,' Amelia said, hoping she sounded as if she believed it.

'It is a bit odd though,' Toby said.

'Nothing's happened since,' Amelia pointed out.

'True,' Toby said.

'Come on, guys.' Amelia laughed. 'Aren't I the one who's likely to find mystery and intrigue at any available opportunity? If I don't think it's weird, surely you shouldn't either.'

'Hmm, fair enough,' Toby said, opening up another bag of crisps.

~

'You're really not a party animal, are you?' Sally said an hour later, as Amelia tried to stifle a yawn.

'No, I think I'm going to head back.'

Sally downed the last of her wine. 'I'll join you. We'd be better off saving our energy for Saturday night's party.'

They looked over to Gideon who had now been joined by the group of girls. Gideon looked over to them and gave a little wave, clearly in his element at being fawned over.

'I'll stay and keep an eye on that one,' Toby said, nodding at Gideon.

'I could do with getting back too,' Jack said, getting up.

'Come on.' Sally wound a very long scarf round her neck a few times and shrugged on her new woollen duffle coat. 'Let's embrace the cold.'

Outside, the pavement sparkled with a light frost and the small boats and dinghies bobbed jauntily on the water. A couple of smokers standing by the doorway said goodnight to them as they turned up the lane to head to the house. The walk had already been made easier by the large wrought-iron gates being oiled for ease (and silence) of movement. Now, along each side of the driveway, large holes had been dug all ready for placing the new pillar lights. Even just the promise of extra illumination seemed to make the walk less scary. Their breath clouded in front of them from the cold as they chatted about the upcoming party.

When they got to Jack's, they said goodnight and Amelia and Sally carried on towards Stone Manor.

'If my planned costume doesn't work out for Saturday I can always make a round fuzzy green suit and go as a gooseberry,' Sally said, linking her arm with Amelia's.

'What do you mean?'

'You and him,' Sally said.

'Jack?'

'Well, I certainly didn't mean the headless horseman. Do you not fancy double-backing and ringing the bell to see if he could be your man-size hot water bottle for the night?'

'Sally...!'

'What! I'm merely stating the obvious. It's bloody freezing tonight and he's hot. In every possible way.'

'But... Sally...' Amelia didn't know where to start. Clearly, Sally had picked up the wrong end of the stick. The wrong *stick* for that matter! 'No, Sally, just no! Just because we managed to sit through an evening without him exasperating me to the point of wanting to scream does not mean we fancy each other! I suppose some people might consider him good-looking, in a big, muscly, overbearing way, although I really don't understand why you and Toby rhapsodise over him so much. He never seems to shave, and he smells of woodsmoke and grass rather than Creed aftershave. He's fine if you like that sort of outdoorsy, unkempt look.'

'Wow, I must get you to fill in an online dating profile for me. I'll be inundated with interested ladies.'

Amelia and Sally whirled round to see Jack standing behind them with a bemused expression on his face.

'Wh... I thought you'd gone in,' Amelia managed to squeak out, mortified he'd overheard her.

'I had, then remembered you were running low on firewood.' He held up a basket filled with kindling and some small logs. 'I'll even take it to the house for you and make use of my large, overbearing, muscly physique.'

Sally cleared her throat, and Amelia knew she was trying not to laugh.

'I... I didn't mean it to sound quite like that...' Amelia started.

'Really?' Jack grinned, clearly loving seeing her squirm with embarrassment.

'I...'

'My love,' Sally whispered sotto voce, 'when you're in a hole, stop digging.' She tried to take the basket from Jack but nearly dropped it.

'Shall I?' Jack said, taking it from her. 'It also means I can prolong this excruciatingly awkward situation.' He grinned.

'I think it's only fair we also add good sense of humour, healthy self-esteem and fairly thick skin to your list of attributes, don't you?' Sally said as they continued on to Stone Manor, with Amelia trying to hurry up, desperate to escape the situation.

Inside, the house was just as messy as Amelia remembered with planks of wood lifted from the floor, lying in piles at the edge of the hall and propped up against the walls along with balled-up dust sheets and abandoned tools. Dust clung to everything and floated, stagnant, in the air.

'Wow, this is some mess.' Jack whistled. 'You really think it will be cleared for Saturday?'

'That's what the workmen said.' Sally shrugged.

'I'll stick these in the drawing room, goodnight,' Jack said, going into the room, carefully stepping over the open gaps in the floor.

'Goodnight,' Amelia said, still unable to look Jack in the eye.

'Come on, let's get to bed,' Sally said, giving Amelia's arm a squeeze.

They trudged up the stairs together. Now Sally was yawning. 'I don't know how Gideon has the stamina to keep going night after night.'

'He's a medical wonder,' Amelia agreed just as they got to her door. 'Night.'

'See you in the morning,' Sally said, continuing down the corridor to her room.

Amelia flicked on her light, waiting for a split second to see if a loud bang and darkness followed. Fortunately, for tonight's game of electricity roulette, the lights stayed on. She'd be very glad when the new wiring was linked up as she couldn't imagine having a hotel where she'd have to give the guests a torch and a couple of candles on checking in. Despite a lot of people gladly paying more money for a genuine rural Scottish experience Amelia doubted they'd as readily embrace the full experience of dodgy plumbing and freezing rooms and ice on the *inside* of the windows.

She kicked off her boots and made her way across the room, pausing as she saw something on the bed.

She stared at it for a few seconds, trying to work out what she was looking at.

And when she finally did, she started to scream.

24

S he was still screaming when Sally burst into Amelia's room.
'Amelia! Are you okay, what's wrong?'

Amelia managed to stop the noise coming from her mouth and pointed mutely to the bed.

'What... Oh my God! Is that...? Come away.' Sally grabbed Amelia's shoulders, turning her around just as Jack ran into the room.

'What is it?'

'The bed,' Amelia said.

As he went to have a closer look Beniamino joined them, closely followed by Ross.

'Oh, is that a–' Ross started to say in horror.

'Dead crow,' Jack finished grimly.

'Sorry I screamed, I just got a fright,' Amelia said shakily. 'How do you think it got in?' She'd not opened her windows. She wouldn't have thought it would have fitted down the chimney. She didn't even know if the chimney was in working use.

'I think someone put it there,' Jack said. He'd lifted the bird up and beneath was a puddle of blood.

Sally turned away, then saw something that made her gasp.

Amelia and the others turned to see what she was looking at and Amelia felt her knees go a little jelly-like when she saw someone had written 'GO' on the wall in smeary red blood.

'I'll get a mop,' Sally said.

'Wait. Can you wait until we film it?'

'For Christ's sake!' Jack interjected.

'I'm sorry.' Beniamino shrugged. 'It's a horrible thing to have happened, but we can film it and use it as part of the documentary but also to show the police as I'm sure you'll want to report it.'

'Film it, I don't care,' Amelia said, looking in horror at the blood on the bedcovers. 'I don't want to sleep in here tonight anyway. Can I bunk in with you, Sally? I don't want to be on my own.'

'Of course.' Sally nodded.

'Thanks. Now, does someone else have a phone that works as I don't have any reception here,' she said numbly.

'Yeah,' Jack said. 'I'll give Ray a call, I changed my network to one that works this far north.'

'Come on,' said Sally, 'let's get you a cup of tea.'

'I'll go get Mike from the pub and track down Lawrence,' Ross said, giving Amelia's shoulder a squeeze on the way out.

'I'll be downstairs when you want my reaction shot,' Amelia said, only half joking.

In the kitchen she sat down as Sally busied about making tea and opened a packet of custard creams. She also stumbled across a bottle of whisky in the cupboard and brought that over with some glasses.

Jack joined them a couple of minutes later. 'Is it okay if Ray comes over in the morning? He's off duty and his deputy is two villages away trying to track down a runaway goat that's rampaging through gardens and eating up people's plants.' He stood for a moment before saying, 'I can't believe Beniamino is going to film it, are you sure you're okay with it?'

Amelia nodded. 'Don't be too angry with them, it's what they do, they document interesting goings-on. And for them, this is interesting.'

'It's bloody gruesome!' Sally said hotly, crunching down on a biscuit.

'You okay?' Jack asked Amelia as he sat down at the opposite side of the table.

Amelia nodded distractedly. 'Why would someone do that?'

'Because they're sick in the head,' Sally said, offering the biscuits round and taking another two for herself.

'Do you think the crow is significant or was it there purely because whoever did this just happened to catch one and it could have been any bird?'

Jack shrugged. 'Well, a crow is a symbol for–'

'Death,' Amelia finished.

Sally made a whimpering noise.

'There's more to them than that,' Jack said. 'They're connected to mystery and magic and also the sign of a trickster or mischief-maker.'

'And sick bastard!' Sally interjected. 'Why write "GO" on the wall?'

Amelia took a sip of her scalding-hot tea, realising Sally had put a tooth-buckling amount of sugar in it. First, the rock through the window with 'LEAVE' on the note wrapped around it, and now 'GO'. Someone was clearly trying to tell her something. And they wanted to make sure she knew it was her they were targeting.

'But why "GO"? Go where? And why?' Sally asked in bewilderment.

'Maybe someone doesn't like my plans for refurbishment. I don't know.'

'And even more to the point, *who* would do something like that?' Sally pressed.

'Someone who clearly doesn't want me here.'

'But *who*?' Sally repeated.

'Thing is,' Jack said, 'the house has been open for the last few days with half the village coming and going. Someone could have slipped in at any point and done that. Those big tool bags could have easily hidden the bird.'

'Yeah,' Amelia agreed, 'and all of us had been discussing our plans for this evening and it was no secret we were going to the Whistling Haggis.'

'Maybe it wasn't meant specifically for you, maybe it was just a general warning,' Sally said, trying to cheer Amelia up. 'I mean, who would want to target you? Now, Gideon, I could understand.'

'I think it's safe to assume it was directed at me.'

Sally frowned. 'You seem to be taking this very calmly. If it was me, I'd have my bags packed and be halfway to Glasgow by now.'

'I think that's how whoever is doing this wants me to react. But it really just makes me want to stay and find out who it is that's behind this and why.'

Despite her strong words, Amelia couldn't help but feel a little shaky as she said them.

25

19th May 1920

    My worst fears are being realised. Charles is becoming like his father; the restlessness is within him too. James has not been touched by the madness, but the same cannot be said for his elder brother. He paces and plans. I am in no doubt he has found out about the Amor Rubra. I do not know how he has come unto this knowledge as I thought the stories died with his father. This house holds so many secrets Charles could very well have stumbled upon something. With so many books in the library it could be possible that Montgomery left notes. Or even Archibald. I wish it could be permanently lost... or finally found, for then it could be left alone, but instead it consumes this family once more. I have tried to divert Charles with sport and outdoor pursuits but I know it is only a matter of time before he returns to drinking and gambling. James worries. He is a good boy and a scholar. He is not ignorant to his brother's disposition yet he has shown no desire to become close to him. I pray that something soon comes his way to halt this growing unrest. But I do not know what.

I t had taken an awful lot of dull diary extracts for Amelia to get to that little nugget. So, it turned out the apple didn't fall far from the tree. First Archibald, then Charles consumed by the search for the alleged treasure. No wonder Dotty had been reluctant to let Amelia know of the legend.

All thoughts of continuing with the diary were put on hold as Sally opened the bedroom door and ran in calling out 'Rise and shine!' as she dive-bombed onto the bed and started bouncing up and down. Although a few days had now passed since the dead crow incident and the bloody message on the wall had long been washed off along with the mattress and bedding being replaced, Amelia hadn't any urge to move back to her room and had simply taken all her belongings and bundled them in with Sally's. Despite having plenty of vacant rooms, Amelia felt uneasy being on her own as the incident with the crow had shaken her. Sally's room was certainly big enough to comfortably house both of them and after moving in another bed, it made Amelia reminisce fondly back to their days at boarding school when they lay awake at night gossiping, planning their future and playing Snog, Marry, Avoid.

'I hope you're feeling suitably spooktacular!' Sally said, continuing to bounce as the bedsprings creaked in protest.

Amelia groaned and pulled the duvet over her head.

Sally pulled it back down. 'Come on! You need to get into the party spirit. Gideon's making Bloody Marys downstairs for breakfast.'

Amelia sat up. 'Are we being allowed into the kitchen?'

For the past few days the house had been in complete chaos. Work had continued apace with the rewiring and plumbing and now almost every room had its floorboards ripped up. Toby was going spare having to make do, preparing the meals with a tiny makeshift gas burner and the outside kettle barbecue. There had been an endless stream of workmen carrying various tools and bits of wood and it seemed as if half the village had turned up to help out. The only rooms the workmen weren't in were the two drawing rooms, the billiard room and dining room because Sally and Gideon had commandeered them for the party on the understanding the workmen could get into them from Monday.

Sally pulled a face. 'No, the kitchen is still out of bounds but we've made up a makeshift one in the dining room as the catering folk have arrived to set everything up in there, and Gideon's taking advantage.'

Two months ago Amelia would have baulked at the idea of a Bloody Mary first thing in the morning, but today she positively embraced the idea, having a feeling she'd need alcohol to help her get through the day. At first, she'd welcomed hosting a party without having any of the stresses involved with organising it, but as time went on she found herself trying to glean information and earwig into Sally and Gideon's conversations to find out what they were planning. She still felt as if it wasn't entirely her house and she was anxious about people running riot and damaging the furniture. She was only slightly comforted to find out that a cleaning company was scheduled to appear first thing Sunday morning.

'Best just get dressed,' Sally said as she saw Amelia reaching for her dressing gown. 'Beniamino's filming everything.'

'Oh God!' Throwing her dressing gown back over the chair, Amelia went and picked out some clothes.

'Are you absolutely sure this is going to be safe for everyone coming to the party?' Amelia asked as they carefully made their way downstairs, only just ducking out the way in time to avoid being smacked over the head with a piece of plasterboard being carried up. She didn't want to be a health-and-safety killjoy but alcohol, costumes and a half-renovated house seemed a disastrous mix. She'd even wondered if she could get away with handing out a hard hat with every drink on arrival.

'Don't worry about it,' Sally said soothingly. 'The hallway is going to be completely cleared, as will access to the main rooms the party will be in. We'll just have to make sure no one decides to go off for a little nosey. We'll stick up swathes of police tape over the staircase and it'll add to the Hallowe'en decor!'

'I have a really bad feeling about this,' Amelia said.

'It'll be great. No, don't go in there,' Sally said, steering her away from the drawing room. 'That's under decoration construction.'

Between them, Sally and Gideon had pulled in every favour owed to them in the industry and, as well as the usual workmen wandering in and out, sparkly skeletons, yards of glittering black cloth and fake spiderwebs were being humped up the front steps by a couple of set designers.

More than ever, Amelia felt like a stranger in her own home.

Coming up the steps behind someone carrying a fake plastic coffin was Jack.

'Hi,' Amelia said, feeling a telltale blush creep up her neck. Amelia hadn't seen Jack since the night of the dead crow incident. She'd started to wonder if he was avoiding her, and she couldn't blame him after he'd heard the things she'd said about him. She'd exaggerated it for Sally's benefit, so as she could let Sally know she definitely wasn't interested. But maybe she'd gone too far the other way just to prove a point.

But if he was harbouring any hurt and resentment he didn't let it show. 'Wow! Things are moving fast,' Jack said with an easy smile. 'I stay out the way for a couple of days and then come back to all of this!'

'I was given two options, the first being the short, sharp shock approach where everything will be complete mayhem for as short a time as possible, the second, slightly less mayhem but drawn out for a longer.'

'I hope to hell this is the former.'

'So, Jack, have you got your costume organised for tonight?' Sally interjected.

'Ah, that. Well, I've got something although it's not very inspired. I didn't think to bring a fancy-dress costume over in my luggage.'

'Well, if you want to come and have a rummage in our costume box, I'm sure we've got something to fit your manly, outdoorsy physique!' Sally teased, clearly not at all prepared to forget Amelia's insults.

'I'll keep that in mind. You got yours sorted?'

'Oh yes! I'm all set,' Sally said just as there was a loud bang from inside the drawing room. 'Don't worry! I'll go sort it out,' she shouted over her shoulder at Amelia as she slipped in through the door, closing it tightly behind her.

'What about you?' Jack asked Amelia.

'Yes, I'm all ready,' Amelia said. Sally had worked wonders with taking in the bride of Frankenstein costume, adding in a thigh-high split to show off Amelia's legs in the high-heeled strappy sandal boots.

Sally opened the door and slipped back out carrying two Bloody Marys. 'Compliments from our cocktail waiter, which is actually just Gideon at the moment as the real cocktail waiter is on the slow train from Glasgow. Must dash back!' She thrust the glasses at them, then disappeared back into the drawing room.

'Your party is pretty much the only talk in the village.' Jack shouted to be heard above an electric drill that had started up from the other side of the door, accompanied by frenetic hammering.

'Really? Do you think many will come?' Amelia said, trying

not to think of what damage could be occurring through the wall.

Jack laughed and took a sip of his drink, which then became a cough at the eye-watering strength of it. 'I think everyone will come.'

'Oh dear, Big Davey won't be happy if he loses business on a Saturday night.'

'Don't worry about him. He's coming to the party and who do you think is supplying the alcohol?'

'Now I'm worried we'll run out, especially if Gideon is given free rein beforehand.'

'I'm sure we can commandeer a wheelbarrow for emergency-booze runs to the pub and back if need be.'

'Or possibly just check under Gideon's bed for his secret stash!'

'True.' At that point a passing workman barrelled into the back of Jack, sending half his drink flying out the glass. He shook the tomato juice mix off his hands. 'I was hoping to have a quick word but I'll catch you later at the party if that's okay?'

'Uh, sure.'

He gave her a warm smile and, setting his glass down on a nearby stack of floorboards, left.

Amelia watched him go, intrigued as to what that word was going to be.

The workmen were as good as their word and by early afternoon the hall had been returned to its previous state, with just a little layer of dust which added some authenticity to the Hallowe'en atmosphere. Despite many attempts at trying to get past Sally, Amelia still hadn't managed to sneak a peek at the decor. In the end she'd given up trying and with nothing else to do she went and ran herself a bubble bath and settled back to read another instalment of Flora's diary. She certainly wasn't a regular diarist! There were months at a time missing, then a couple of really banal ones just mentioning the weather or food.

14th June 1930

It was the most beautiful day for a wedding. The sun was out but not so warm that it would drain one's energy. The service was perfect and intimate, with James so handsome and tall and Florence Delaney his perfect bride. She is a quiet girl but I can tell there is a strength within. She will be good for him and he her. Not even Charles could ruin the day with his drinking. He scares me sometimes when he looks at me, it's as if he hates me. It's as if he knows.

Amelia sighed as she relaxed further down into the bubbles. Charles sounded a right chip off the old block from Archibald. She wondered how Flora managed to carry the secret of the nature of her husband's death. Did it eat away at her? Did she confess to anyone else? Did the gardener ever tell anyone? It was really quite frustrating to just have the one-sided diary to read. She read a few more pages about a distant relative who had died and how the gardener planned to convert the flower patches to make an Italian-inspired herb garden.

21st January 1942

My heart is racing and I am shaking. A man called on me this afternoon. He said he was a friend of Charles, but I know not what friend would try and extort money for a gambling debt. He started to talk of the Amor Rubra. He told me to give it up to him and he would release Charles from his debt. Thankfully, James appeared and gave this man short shrift but I have not stopped thinking of it since. Is this to hang forever over our family? I explained to James all that I know, which isn't much. I even confessed to my hand in covering up the truth with Archibald. He took a grim view of the events but remembered enough about his father to know what sort of man he was. And, of course, he has heard the rumours. I fear the man will return, despite James telling me not to fret. I worry for us all, especially little Dorothea.

Amelia got such a start at the mention of Dotty's name that she half sat up, but slipped on the bath and almost fully submerged herself along with the diary. Of course! Dorothea was born in 1940 so she would have been two years old. Just thinking of her at that age made Amelia feel that same dull ache in her chest. But it was also odd that the first entry Flora made about her granddaughter was just as an aside. Amelia closed the diary over and that's when she noticed the slight gapping. The spine of the book was very thick but it didn't seem to correspond with the number of pages within. She flicked back a page, where the entries went from 1930 to 1942. The book was threadbound and there was a considerable indent between the pages... which would possibly indicate that someone had ripped pages out.

Amelia's mind was racing. Who would have ripped out pages of a diary rather than take the whole thing... and why? What on earth was on these missing pages that would be of interest? Whatever it was, Amelia guessed it wouldn't be what kind of gravy the cook had chosen to go with the mutton. Clearly, the missing pages contained something of interest to someone. And it must be something quite juicy as they'd left the pages about the death of Archibald. Amelia could have understood if it had been James stumbling across it and wanting to remove any evidence of his mum having a hand in his dad's death. But then why not just burn the entire book? And she had no idea when the pages had been removed. Now Amelia's interest was really piqued.

She heard the bedroom door open – it had developed a bit of a squeak and she kept meaning to get hold of some WD40 from the workmen to sort it out. She made a mental note to add it to her to-do list.

'How's it going downstairs? Has the DJ arrived?'

No answer.

'Sally? Has the DJ arrived? What time did you tell everyone to come?'

Nothing.

'Sal?'

Then she heard the squeak and the door softly clicking closed.

Amelia suddenly felt a little cold, despite the warm bath. She had an odd feeling. Sally was definitely a door-banger, not a softly-closer. She got out the bath and wrapped a towel around her and very slowly opened the bathroom door and looked out into the room. There was no one there. She also crouched down to check under the bed as she already knew it could hide a person, but there was nothing there apart from the same dustballs and fluff which she still hadn't removed, and a balled-up hiking sock.

Still clutching the towel tightly around her chest, she carefully looked around the room. Nothing seemed to be amiss. Her eyes settled on the pile of books. Was it her imagination or had they been moved slightly?

The door opened and Amelia gave out a startled yelp.

Sally stood there looking flushed. 'Sorry, I didn't mean to scare you!'

'Were you in here just a minute ago?'

'No, I've been downstairs seeing to the last of the finishing touches. You're going to love it! We've even got a dry-ice machine to make mysterious fog.' She clapped her hands in excitement. 'Now, let's get your costume on.'

Amelia went over to the bed, where she'd laid it out, as Sally held it up.

'Oh!' she said, realising she was just holding the sleeves of the bride of Frankenstein dress. The rest of it lay on the bed, in pieces.

Someone had slashed the costume.

26

Sally dropped the sections of fabric and looked at Amelia in dismay.

'I thought I heard someone come in the room when I was in the bath.'

Sally visibly paled under her artificially bronzed glow. 'You were here when someone did this?'

Amelia suddenly felt a little shaky. They would have had scissors. Or a knife.

'This is getting out of hand. Why is someone doing this? We need to cancel the party.'

Amelia shook her head. 'No, you've done too much to–'

'Sod that! None of that matters if there's a crow-killing, costume-slashing nutter on the loose!'

'No,' Amelia said firmly. 'I'm not going to be scared away by some idiot.'

'But what about your costume?' Sally wailed.

'I'm so sorry, you worked so hard on it.'

'Don't worry about that. What else will you go as?'

'Let's have a look at the other costumes.'

And a mere ten minutes later, they'd worked out an absolutely stonking idea for one.

~

The house looked incredible.

Amelia couldn't believe the transformation when she walked down the stairs two hours later. Cobwebs had been draped all down the bannisters and over every doorway. Wall hangings of ghostly apparitions hung in place of the usual Campbell family ancestors (which Amelia thought were creepy enough anyway). Candelabras adorned every surface, giving off an eerie glow.

'Don't worry, they're state-of-the-art LED and not likely to set anyone on fire,' Sally said, pre-empting any worry. Sally, done up as a curvaceously sexy Marilyn Monroe, in a replica of the iconic white halterneck dress, pointed out more little spooky touches as they continued down the stairs.

The drawing rooms had swathes of black silk draped from ceiling to floor with strange occult symbols painted over them. Slap bang in the centre of the room was a large table dressed in purple velvet with a Ouija board in the middle. The adjoining billiard room was very similar, but had the addition of a small stage erected with a DJ setting up his equipment. The dining room, where the catering staff were laying out a buffet, was Gothically decadent. Tables and chairs were skirted with black taffeta and purple ribbon and another similar table was groaning under the weight of skull goblets and cauldron-shaped bowls, and cutlery which looked like miniature tridents and daggers. Hanging from the ceiling was a huge crystal chandelier, covered with cobwebs and alarmingly realistic spiders. In the corner the life-size, or possibly death-size, coffin was filled with ice and had bottles of champagne sticking out. A few feet away the mixologist had set up a large cauldron which was full of dark-green punch, with dry ice cascading gently from the lip.

'This looks amazing.'

'Wait until you get a look at the food. Skull vol-au-vents, can you believe?' Gideon said from behind. Amelia turned and gasped when she saw him. He was dressed as David Bowie's Ziggy Stardust. Sally had fixed his make-up authentically with a lightning flash on his forehead, completed with the bristly orange wig. Gideon's high cheekbones and sinewy frame were perfect for the costume; he looked a carbon copy of the late legend.

'And you look *stunning*!' Gideon said, taking in her appearance. 'That's no bride of Frankenstein though.'

'I changed my mind,' Amelia said, shooting Sally a warning look. She didn't want to put a dampener on the evening's events.

After the wardrobe disaster, a quick trawl through the leftover costumes showed that most of the good ones had gone, but a little bit of imagination went a long way. They'd found a pretty awful Edwardian-type red-silk bustle dress with a high-neck lace insert. A quick rip removed the lace panel and with a push-up bra underneath, Amelia's décolletage was risqué but remained on just the right side of decent. Amelia kept the bustle at the back and the full skirt underneath but ripped away the front of the skirt so it was a very short mini. With it she wore the lace-up thigh-high gladiator sandal boots. Over the top she'd put on a tweed Inverness cape, harking back to the Basil Rathbone interpretation of Sherlock Holmes. She even found a deerstalker hat but stuck a pair of driving goggles over the top. Instead of a pipe she discovered an elegant cigarette holder.

'I'm a steam-punk, feminine Sherlock Holmes.'

'Of course you are! And who knew Mr Holmes had such a penchant for dramatic kohl eyeliner with violet sparkly-eye make-up and lips to match.'

'I used artistic licence,' Amelia said as she gave Gideon and Sally a hug. 'You guys have done an amazing job! Thank you.'

'It's been great fun!' Sally hugged back, whispering, 'Are you sure you'll be okay?'

'We should go and welcome our guests,' Amelia said. Although she nodded she was okay she did feel a little nervous. She always did before a party, but this time she was aware that there was someone out there, who would even possibly be coming to the party, who meant her ill will.

'How will we know some of the locals are in costume?' Gideon drawled.

'Gideon!'

'Don't worry, I'll be on my best behaviour.' He gave a Scout salute.

As Amelia moved through the rooms to the front door she said hello to a variety of witches, vampires, zombies, cult movie figures and even a Dalek, although she couldn't see that costume staying on for much longer as whoever was wearing it was already having problems trying to get at their drink. There was even a creepy-looking V from *V for Vendetta* in full mask and black cloak standing watching everyone from the corner of the room.

Someone in the full *Scream* costume was walking towards her. Amelia had never been a fan of costumes which completely covered the face, not liking being unable to see their expressions. She had a horrible feeling the person was looking just as murderous underneath the disguise. But instead, the *Scream* costume let out a low wolf whistle.

'I love your costume,' Jack said, lifting up the mask.

'I'm a steam-punk, feminine–'

'Sherlock Holmes! I love it! I'm not very original, I'm afraid. It came with a free knife though.' He held it up and bent back the bendy rubber tip. 'I love what you've done with the place.'

'I'm thinking of keeping it.'

'It'll certainly be a point of difference for your hotel.'

'Haunted horror mansion specials. Scare the one you love,' she said with a smile. She actually did quite like that idea!

Just then Mike and Ross came over to them, Mike filming them and Ross holding out the boom. Mike was dressed as *Doctor Who* circa Tom Baker and Ross had indeed plumped for the top-hat-and-tails costume and looked good.

Beniamino was behind them with possibly the best costume of the night as far as Amelia was concerned. He was dressed as a plague doctor from the Venice carnival, the mask was black and feathered with a long silver beak, decorated in crystals. His hat had a flat wide brim in black leather and he wore an elaborately embroidered black-and-silver waistcoat over black trousers and a wide-sleeved black shirt. Over the top of it all was a long black cloak.

'Buona sera!' He smiled, lifting the mask slightly. 'Can we get a quick word on how you feel about the transformation of your house, Amelia?'

'It's spooktacularly splendid! I was just saying to Jack...' she turned towards him but he'd lowered his mask and was melting back into the crowd, '...um, that I could possibly keep the decor like this and have themed haunted mansion weekends. Excuse me, I'd better circulate.'

Still feeling unsettled, Amelia's senses were on high alert as she made her way through to the dining room to get herself a drink.

'Zombie, my darling?' Gideon sidled up beside her, thrusting a lurid orange drink at her.

Amelia took a tentative sniff and nearly fell backwards at the hit of rum she got off it.

'You okay?' she asked as Gideon stood surveying the party,

his body pulsing to the beat of the tunes coming from next door's DJ set.

'I. Am. Fucking. Awesome, poppet!' He danced backwards away from her, giving her a little wave.

She took a sip of her drink. It was actually delicious, if a little on the strong side. Just then, the person in the *V for Vendetta* costume walked by, turning to stare at Amelia as he passed.

Amelia shivered despite the house being so packed with bodies. It was the warmest it had been since she'd arrived.

She looked around for someone she could talk to. Gideon was obviously dancing in the DJ room, she could see Sally, in character, in full flirt mode, blowing kisses to a couple of young guys she didn't recognise. She couldn't see Jack anywhere after he'd been scared off by the documentary crew; he really did seem to be very camera shy as she'd noticed he avoided being in any of the film footage. Toby, she knew, was helping with the catering. She stood for a moment, drinking alone at her own party, feeling a little sorry for herself.

'Get a grip!' she told herself firmly and forced herself to go back to the hall to mingle with the partygoers. She could at least be there to welcome the people turning up. As she got there a Cruella de Vil and six-foot tall dalmatian walked in. She turned to direct them to where the food and drink was located, and as she did, out the corner of her eye, she saw the edge of a black cloak disappearing along the corridor at the top of the stairs. No one was meant to go up there as the workmen had left all their tools lying out and there were missing floorboards which could be dangerous. Leaving her glass on a side table, Amelia didn't waste another minute before following.

27

T high-high, heeled gladiator sandal boots weren't the easiest footwear to run up stairs in, but Amelia got up to the first floor as quickly as she could, heart pounding through the exertion and the excitement of following someone. On reaching the first-floor landing she could see there was no one there. She picked her way carefully along the corridor, avoiding all the half-finished building work and making sure her heels didn't get stuck in the floorboard gaps where the carpet had been lifted up. It was a lot darker up here as only the furthest away chandelier worked in the corridor she was standing in. The corridor followed round the four sides, making a square, with the bannister running round each side. Unless the person was hiding behind one of the occasional structural columns which broke up the open-plan feeling, the cloaked figure must have gone into one of the rooms. She kicked away a tarpaulin sheet covering a big pile of plasterboard panels and couldn't help but think how handy they'd be at protecting from blood splatters if someone were to be gruesomely murdered. With that comforting thought playing in her mind, she quietly moved along the corridor. All the doors had been closed over on the first few rooms. When everyone had taken their rooms they'd kept to the first and second corridors, but only half the rooms were being used. As Amelia hadn't heard a door being closed she figured whoever had come up had either closed the door very quietly or walked beyond the first corner. She looked across to the other balcony and corridor but still couldn't see anyone. She thought she'd feel really silly if it was Beniamino she'd followed up the stairs; she had only caught a glimpse of a cloak after all. She looked over the bannister below just in time to see Beniamino walking through the hall with Mike in tow. Okay, so the cloak didn't belong to Beniamino. She followed the corridor round until she came across a room with its door open and she very gently pushed the door open wider. It was almost completely empty. There was just one table in the middle of the room with a vice on it along with some offcuts of wood. The carpet was rolled up against one wall and there were new, unfinished sockets with the wires protruding from them.

Being up a floor meant the party noise was nowhere near as loud, but Amelia could still hear the deep bass thump of the music but it was much softer and the deafening chatter had mellowed to a murmur of voices. She was now on full alert in case she heard someone moving about.

Walking on the balls of her feet, aware that she, too, could be heard, she crept back out and into the next room along. This had a lot more furniture, she could see that even from just the little light that was coming in through the doorway behind her. The carpet had also been rolled back and there were some massive vintage leather storage trunks stacked against the back wall. The bed was covered with the same thick, clear plastic sheeting from the hall, with more folded-up sheets of it piled behind the door. There was a large boxed-in window seat and beside it a few smaller trunks and storage boxes. She quietly tiptoed over to the storage trunks to open the top one to see what was inside.

There was a creak on the floorboards outside, along the corridor.

Then another.

Amelia froze, hand still outstretched towards the box. Suddenly, following the person in the swishy cloak didn't seem such a good idea. What if this person was the one behind the rock through the window, the dead bird and the ripped costume? The one who badly wanted her to go.

There was another creak. Whoever was out there was walking slowly, but they were still walking. She could just imagine them, pressed against the wall, keeping to the shadows, listening for a sound. She glanced down to the large vintage trunks. Any one of them could easily hold a body. A handcuffed, gagged, unconscious body. That would certainly get her out of the way.

A shadow appeared at the door, cutting off some of the light. Amelia held her breath, feeling her insides quiver as she caught a glimpse of the *V for Vendetta* costume for a split second before the door slammed shut, leaving her in complete darkness. She heard a click.

She'd been locked in!

There was a line of light under the door with a darker shadow in the centre. She ran over to the door and pulled at the handle. The door rattled but didn't budge.

She banged on the door. 'Let me out!' she screamed, but no one answered. The shadow moved off, leaving an uninterrupted chink of light under the door. She was on her own.

She tentatively sniffed the air, aware of a strange smell, but one that she half recognised. She then covered her nose in case it was a poison her kidnapper had used. She knew cyanide was almondy but this smell wasn't of almonds. She backed away from the door just in case it was some other noxious gas.

Panic started rising in her chest as she tried the light switch beside her. No light came on.

She tried pulling at the door again, but eighteenth-century joinery was solid and unrelenting. She rested her palms against the wood, thinking what she could do. There was no space for a torch in her costume but luckily there was a clear moon and some light shining through the window. Unless she got out she could be locked in the room for hours as nobody would hear her shouting and nobody would need to come up the stairs, especially if they'd been told not to. She could wait it out... but what if whoever had locked her in was planning to return and not just to suggest a game of dooking for apples. She needed to escape. A quick look about revealed no handy axe or hammer or even a Philips head screwdriver she could break the door down with. There were, however, piles of dust sheets. She went over to the window and managed to lift up the sash casement. Looking down made her feel a bit dizzy from a sudden attack of vertigo; although she couldn't jump it, she may be able to abseil down it. Not that she'd ever abseiled before.

Luckily, the knowledge she'd gleaned for her Girl Guide knots badge had never left her and she quickly tied five of the dust sheets securely together. Now she just needed something to tie it to. The only solid stationary object was the door handle. She tied the line of dust sheets to it and then tied the other end round her waist and up over her shoulders. She stood at the window and looked down again. Fortuitously, she was beside an overflow pipe. She leant out and gave it a shake. It seemed pretty secure. She took off her boots and threw them out the window. It seemed a long drop until she heard them hit the gravel. Wiping her palms on the thick tweed of the Inverness cape, she swung one leg onto the windowsill.

'Shitshitshitshitshit...' she swore under her breath as she very gingerly edged out a little more and reached over to cling to the pipe. She stayed half in and half out for a moment or two, trying to regulate her breathing and build up the courage to push her body further away from the window. The stone facade was rough, with natural grooves where she could wedge her toes... just as long as she kept holding on to the pipe. The dust sheets were just there as another safety net, she told herself, gripping the bunched-up length of them tightly, ready to let them out bit by bit. Very slowly she inched down, feeling the cold stone graze her knees and chest as her upper body took on all her weight as she clung to the pipe. She was breaking a sweat already and her hand hurt from where she was clinging on to the pipe, but she managed to slide her foot down a bit and found a metal bracket which attached the pipe to the wall. She put a little more of her weight on it and it held. She slowly let go of the window ledge, which was now at a full arm's stretch, and let the pipe bracket take all her weight. The ridge of the metal cut deep into the soft pad of her foot but she knew she couldn't stop now. She moved her entire body over towards the pipe and gradually slithered down the cold, damp stone until her other foot made contact with the next metal bracket down. She winced as she carefully removed her first foot and slid it down the wall, all the time letting more and more of the sheets out. Looking up at the windowsill, it seemed very far away as she gripped the pipe with one hand until her other foot worked its way down and reached another bracket. She momentarily steadied herself against the wall. Part of her brain registered the pain of the sharp plastic pipe, the metal ridge and rough stone cutting into various parts of her but her survival instinct overruled any misgivings. With ragged breathing she continued her painfully slow descent. After a while she dared look down and she could have wept when she saw she was only about six feet from the ground. Even if she fell now she would be okay, she figured. Just as she had that thought her big toe slipped on the metal bracket securing the pipe to the wall. Scrabbling for the pipe, her hand clawed the wall instead and with a small gasp of fear she slid down a couple of feet before the dust sheets pulled taut and left her dangling in mid-air, in front of a window, set back from the wall. She circled round, wincing as her body slammed into the wooden frame, then swung back out again, before swinging back, pendulum-style. She flailed, trying to turn around so she could gain purchase once again. But she swung further out, dangling from her waist. Unfortunately, the sheet had pulled so tight the knot also tightened and she was unable to loosen it. She hung for a moment, trying to turn herself around so she could grab hold of the pipe again.

'Hey! What are you doing hanging around here?' A familiar American voice said nearby. She craned her neck to see Jack standing looking up at her.

'Can you help me?'

'Sure, what with?' he said obtusely.

'The frigging *Times* frigging crossword, what do you think!' Amelia retorted, still slowly spinning round in mid-air.

'If you're going to be rude about it...' He made to turn away.

'WAIT! Please help me, Jack.'

'Well, when you ask so nicely. But, just what the hell did you do?'

He'd come back over and lifted her up on his shoulder, fireman's carry-style, while he got to work untying the knots of the dust sheets.

As soon as she was free, she wriggled away from him, sliding down his chest, onto the ground.

She pulled up her top and smoothed her skirt down. 'I saw someone going upstairs and I followed them and they locked me in a room–'

'And clearly the best way out was risking your life by climbing out a window,' he cut in, sounding annoyed.

'I assessed the risk and decided it was, yes,' she said defensively. 'I didn't want to take any chances.'

She gingerly stepped over the stones to retrieve her boots.

'Hang on, what do you mean?' Jack called out after her.

'Just that I was concerned enough to need to get out of the room as quickly as possible.'

He caught up with her. 'Tell me.'

'So you can laugh at me some more? Not likely.' She went to stride forward but Jack barred her way and Amelia practically barrelled off his chest.

'I'm not going to laugh at you.'

He did look very serious, as well as concerned. She sighed. 'Someone came into my room while I was in the bath and slashed the costume I was going to wear.'

'What?'

'It freaked me out a little, especially after the dead crow incident, and the rock through the window telling me to leave.'

Jack's eyes widened. 'Asking you to what?'

Bugger, she'd forgotten she hadn't told anyone about that.

'Ah, the rock thrown through the window? There was a note attached which said "leave".'

Jack's forehead creased. 'Why didn't you tell anyone?'

'Because I didn't want people looking at me the way you are now!'

'But this is serious!'

'Maybe, but maybe not. Someone wants me scared. They clearly don't know me very well.'

'Well, bully for you for being stubborn, but you could be in danger.'

'They can go take a jump.'

'Amelia!' Jack called out but she was already storming round to the front of the house. Or storming as much as bare feet over small sharp stones would allow.

It didn't take Jack long to catch up with her again.

'Wait a minute. I'd no idea things had become so serious.'

'Why would you?'

'I like to think I know what's going on around here and I could have...' He trailed off.

'Could have what? Protected me?'

'Possibly. Or someone could.' He ran his hands through his hair which was sticking up in every direction thanks to the *Scream* mask he'd been wearing. 'Dammit, Amelia. Is it so terrible if I was trying to look out for you?'

'Thank you for helping me down,' she said, wanting to change the subject.

'Is that all you're going to say?'

'Thank you *very* much?'

'That's not what I meant.'

She ignored him as she put her sandal boots back on. She'd hoped he'd wander off but he stayed right where he was despite it taking forever for her to lace her sandal boots back up.

Seeing as he wasn't moving, she held on to his arm to steady herself as she finished putting her sandal boots back on. Not usually an expert in muscles, Amelia couldn't help notice just how impressively steel-like his arm felt through his clothes.

'I just don't want anything to happen to you,' Jack said, as she straightened up, wobbling slightly on her ridiculous heels.

'Well, that makes two of us,' Amelia retorted.

'I mean it, I...' They were standing so close, her hand still on his arm, his eyes searching hers, that for a moment Amelia thought he was going to kiss her.

She wasn't the only one, as someone let out a wolf whistle nearby.

It broke the moment as Jack took an imperceptible step away

and Amelia removed her hand from his arm and looked over to where the whistle had come from, noticing two Draculas and a Darth Maul standing at the bottom of the steps smoking cigarettes.

Amelia felt a little flustered and confused by the encounter with Jack – could it even be classed as an encounter; maybe it was more a moment... or possibly just her overactive imagination making something out of nothing...

'So, what do you remember about the guy you followed who locked you in the room?' Jack said, clearing his throat.

'Um, he was wearing a black cloak and had a *V for Vendetta* mask. He was tall, or tallish... well, taller than me. There was a funny smell?'

'Oh? Body odour, aftershave...'

'No, it was kind of familiar. Smelling it made me think of medicine but not medicine.' Judging by Jack's expression, she was not making herself clear. 'Okay, I know it sounds mad but the smell took me back to childhood, to a time when I wasn't feeling well, sort of like, like, toothache, or mouthache.' She clicked her fingers as it suddenly came to her. 'Bonjela! That's it!'

'What?'

'Bonjela, a gel for mouth ulcers.'

'So, we're looking for someone with poor dental hygiene?'

'Well, it was *like* that, but different...' Amelia trailed off, realising her recollection skills left a lot to be desired.

'Excuse me!' Amelia called out as she walked over to the smokers. 'Have you seen a guy wearing a *V for Vendetta* costume?'

'Yeah, I saw a guy dressed up like that earlier,' one of the Draculas said.

'When?'

'About an hour ago.'

'Did you see him take the mask off at any point?'

'Nah, sorry.'

'I don't think he'll be making another appearance,' Jack said. He'd walked up the steps and had stopped by one of the decorative cauldrons flanking the front door. Half stuffed inside was the *Vendetta* mask. 'It seems our guy has ditched his disguise.'

'He could still be in there.' Amelia felt quite uncomfortable at the thought of him wandering around just like any other party guest.

'Possibly, but more likely he's left and dumped that on the way out.'

'I hope you're right.' Now Amelia really wished the party would end.

'Ames!'

Amelia turned to see Toby threading through the people in the hall towards her. Dressed as a zombie in ripped clothes, his make-up, courtesy of Sally, was scarily authentic and it looked as if he had a large open bite mark in his cheek.

'Have you seen Gideon?' he asked.

'Not for a while.' Amelia realised Toby, beneath the make-up, looked concerned. 'Why?'

'He's acting odd.'

'Yeah, he seemed really drunk when I saw him earlier. In fact, I don't even know if it was all down to drink.'

'He's high as a kite.'

'Don't worry, he'll probably be dancing it out of his system.'

Toby gave her a small smile. 'Yeah, you're probably right. I'm just going to get some fresh air and make sure he's not being sick behind a hedge,' he said, walking down the steps.

'Oh, Jack, what was it you wanted to talk to me about?' Amelia asked, remembering what he'd said earlier on in the day.

'It'll keep for now. Come on,' Jack said, dragging Amelia

away by the hand, 'I love this song,' he shouted as they got nearer the DJ room. 'I want to dance.'

Okay, so Jack could dance and not in a I'm-a-bit-embarrassed-but-I'll-sway-along-to-the-beat-anyway-in-a-dad-dancing style. Jack could *actually* dance. Up until this evening, Toby was the only male Amelia knew who could dance. She knew she was making a very broad generalisation, but thought it was something only gay men excelled at. Any previous encounters she'd endured involving men and a dance floor were torturous events where her male partner shuffled uncomfortably around her on the periphery of the dance floor whilst looking longingly at the bar, or had been so drunk she'd had to stand well back while they pogoed erratically along to Chumbawamba's 'Tubthumping'. Once she and Jonathan had planned an evening meal and a night away at a secluded country hotel. Unbeknownst to them the dinner also involved entertainment; a band covering well-known easy listening classics. Amelia had tried to drag Jonathan up to 'Fly Me to the Moon', but he looked as horrified as if she'd suggested she was going to perform rectal surgery on him without an anaesthetic.

But here Amelia was dancing to the Rolling Stones' 'Sympathy for the Devil' with someone who had rhythm. By this point Jack had completely discarded his *Scream* costume and was wearing jeans and smart tan leather shoes and a dark-green shirt which brought out the green of his eyes. Something very strange was happening, and it wasn't just because she was dancing with someone who seemed to be enjoying themselves, she'd suddenly become very self-conscious of her body in relation to Jack's. The floor was so crowded they were dancing closely together and occasionally touching and there was something about it which seemed more intimate than had they been holding hands. Whatever temporary magic was happening, Amelia was glad of it because for the first time in a long time she wasn't worrying about house renovations, had stopped dwelling on Dotty and had even managed to forget there was a nutjob running loose who possibly meant her harm.

28

'Oweeee...' Amelia winced hours later as she removed her boots and rubbed her heel, already feeling a huge blister forming. It was half past midnight and she was sitting in the almost deserted drawing room in the post-party aftermath of discarded cups, food and pieces of costume. All the helpers and set designers had gone back to the Whistling Haggis, where they were staying, after Big Davey promised them a lock-in.

'Have you got dance fatigue?' Jack asked, sitting beside her, taking a swig from a bottle of beer.

'My feet certainly do.'

'I figured dancing with you was the only way I could keep you in my sights and avoid you getting into any more scrapes. You okay now?'

'Yeah, I think so.' Despite her near kidnapping experience, the evening's moment she kept playing over in her mind was the point where she and Jack were standing together outside and she thought he was going to kiss her. But more puzzling was the exhilaration she'd felt.

'Did anyone use this tonight?'

'Hmmm?' Amelia turned to see Ross standing over at the table in the drawing room.

'This,' he said, tapping the Ouija board, 'did anyone use it?' Ross asked again.

'Don't think so.' Although Amelia wouldn't really have noticed, she had been far too preoccupied in dancing with Jack.

'We should do it now!' Beniamino said, wandering in, hat and mask in hand. 'Let's film it.'

'Now?' Amelia said, thinking she'd rather be heading off to bed with a hot chocolate.

'Or are you feart?' Ross asked with a cheeky grin.

'Am I what?' Amelia asked.

'Feart. It means scared. You'll have to brush up on the Scottish lingo if you want to stay here.'

'No, I'm not *feart*. I'm just not very comfortable with it.'

'Aye, she's feart,' Ross said to Beniamino with a wink.

'Come on! Let's do it! We can maybe summon up one of the owners of this house. Maybe your godmother?' Beniamino said.

Amelia felt a surge of anger at his remark. She was damned if Beniamino was going to use her godmother as nothing more than a cheap parlour trick. It was one thing reading the letters Dotty had left for her to find, another to suggest they have a one-to-one chat.

'Or maybe you'll tap into the headless horseman,' Ross said, making a ghostly wailing noise.

'What's all this?' Gideon, still looking scarily like David Bowie, asked as he walked unsteadily into the room, swigging heartily from a bottle of champagne. For the amount Gideon drank, Amelia had never seen him completely drunk, but tonight he had a wide-eyed look about him and an unsteady gait.

'Fancy contacting the dead?' Ross asked.

'Only if they've anything interesting to say. Although I'm

starting to feel so utterly bloody awful I can't guarantee what side I'd be speaking for,' he said, palming two paracetamol into his mouth and washing them down with another swig of champagne straight from the bottle.

'Ooh, count me in,' Sally said as she padded over, carrying her white stilettos, wig slightly askew, as a big, tall man followed her who was dressed as a pirate, but now had lifted the eye patch to sit on top of his head. Amelia half recognised him as the one who'd been looking over at Sally from the bar the other night. Like every good cop in every good American cop show, Sally always got her man!

'Let's round up whoever's left,' Beniamino said.

In the end the documentary crew managed to get Amelia, Jack, Sally, Gideon, Toby, Tom the plumber, and Archie, who didn't look like he'd be going home any time soon. Sally's new pirate friend, Hamish, who it transpired was Archie's grandson, also agreed to join in. Mike stood filming them with the main camera and Ross with the smaller of the cameras so they could get split-shot angles on the action. Beniamino and Lawrence joined the others round the table.

'Let's make it more moody,' Mike said, going and flicking off the main lights and bringing clusters of the LED candles over.

Lawrence got up to check his gadget to make sure the light was okay, nodded, then sat back down in the circle.

It was dark. And creepy. Everyone had thought it a great laugh only moments before but now, with them sitting there looking at the strange board with YES and NO at the top and all the letters of the alphabet spelt out, Amelia felt a little shiver of trepidation.

'What do we do?' Hamish asked, looking very uncomfortable.

'Everyone puts their index finger on the glass and we ask questions,' Sally said. 'Well, that's what they do in the films.'

There was a rustle from the various costumes as everyone obliged.

'Now what?' Hamish asked again.

'We ask if anybody's there,' Sally said.

'Maybe Amelia should do it,' Beniamino said.

'Why?' Amelia asked in horror.

'I just thought with your connection–'

'I'm not a blood relation,' Amelia corrected him hastily. It was one thing sitting with her finger on a glass, another entirely to be the conduit between the living and the dead.

'Closest thing to it though,' Archie piped up.

There was a low murmur of conversation before Sally said, 'Don't worry, I don't mind doing it.' She cleared her throat. 'Is there anybody there?' Sally asked in her best theatrical voice. Gideon creased up with laughter beside her, resting his head on her shoulder. Hamish laughed nervously.

'Shhh,' Beniamino hushed them.

'Is there anybody there?' Sally asked again.

Gideon sighed. 'This is a colossal waste–'

The glass moved to 'yes' as a couple of people gasped.

'Is someone moving that?' Gideon asked in a shrill voice.

There was a chorus of 'no'.

'Who are you?' Sally continued.

'It's moving again!' Amelia said in morbid fascination as the glass shifted to the M, then the E.

'ME? Well, that's hardly helpful, is it!' Gideon scoffed.

'Maybe it's someone's initials?'

'Mike!' Sally shouted.

'As far as I'm aware, I'm still alive,' he retorted and everyone laughed nervously.

A couple of people began to second-guess names.

'Shhh,' Sally said, then continued with, 'Do you have a message for us?'

The glass shot to 'YES'.

'What's the message? Crank up the heating, I'm bloody freezing?' Gideon hazarded, taking another swig from the bottle, then burping loudly.

'Gideon!' Sally chastised.

'That's hardly going to scare it away.'

'What do you want to tell us?'

The glass began to move...

'I.S.A.W.Y.O.U,' everyone chanted together.

'Isa, Isaw. Oh, I saw you!' Sally gasped.

Everyone moved a little closer as the glass continued its work around the board.

'I.K.N.O.W.W.H.A.T.Y.O.U.D.I.D.' The glass stopped.

'Oh,' Sally said quietly as everyone looked at the board.

'Oh for Christ's sake!' Gideon stood up, swaying. 'This is complete and utter bollocks. Someone's clearly moving the glass.'

'Gideon!' Sally said. 'You've spoiled it, you'll have scared away whoever was trying to give us a message.'

'Gideon, sit down,' Toby said quietly.

'Shut up! Just... just shut up,' Gideon shouted at him. 'I'm fucking bored and need another drink.' He strutted off into the next room.

Amelia looked at Toby, wondering why Gideon was so angry with him, but Toby just shook his head as if to say, 'leave it'.

'Maybe we should stop,' Amelia said. She felt a little shaky, but also quite confused. Who was the message addressed to? I *know what you did*. Just *who* had done *what*? And why was it of any interest to ghosts?

'We should keep trying for a family member to see if they know where the treasure's buried,' Sally said with a nervous giggle just as Gideon staggered back in carrying a few bottles of wine which he deposited on the floor beside him. He sat back down in his chair and took another swig from the open bottle of champagne.

'I've got a game we could play,' he said.

'Who's first to get admitted to hospital for alcohol poisoning?' Jack asked lightly.

Gideon necked the remains of the champagne and put the bottle on its side in the middle of the table.

'Truth. Or. Dare,' he said, giving the bottle a spin.

There was more nervous laughter.

'Come on, how old are we?' Jack asked.

'If you're chicken, you know where the door is.' Gideon eyeballed Jack.

Amelia really didn't like where this was going now. 'I really think I should be going to bed, it's been a long day,' she said, making a move to stand up.

'Stay,' Gideon said in a low voice, his hand wrapping round her wrist in a vice-like grip.

'Um... okay.' She sat back down, very aware that the green light of Mike's camera was floating inches from her face.

Gideon gave the bottle another spin. 'I'm quite a fan of this game.'

'I suppose you have to think of something to do with all the empty bottles,' Jack said with a smile that didn't reach his eyes.

Everyone laughed and a split second later Gideon joined in, but Amelia could see the muscle in his jaw pulsing double-quick time.

'Does your reluctance to play indicate you have something to hide?' Gideon enquired pleasantly.

'My life is an open book,' Jack said, sitting back in his chair and taking another swig of beer.

'Why don't I start,' Gideon said, spinning the bottle in the middle of the table. Everyone watched and Mike continued filming, waiting to see where it landed.

Toby.

There was a collective 'ooh' from the table.

'I'll take the truth,' Toby said.

'You can't handle the truth,' Hamish fired back in a very impressive Jack Nicholson impression from *A Few Good Men*. Everyone laughed and Amelia saw Sally give his knee a squeeze under the table.

Gideon tapped his chin. 'What are you most ashamed of?'

'Straight in there with the big questions!' Mike laughed from behind the camera.

Toby slowly blew air out his cheeks while he thought. Amelia was also interested in hearing this.

'Cheating on my maths exam when I was at school.'

'Toby!' Amelia said in shock.

'I know. Sorry, sis. My mate Paul broke into the head's office and for some reason knew the safe combination and took the papers, wrote out the answers and returned them. He got chemistry and physics papers too.'

'Oh my God! I remember you got A's in maths and chemistry and I didn't know how. But you got a C in physics.'

'Yeah. I didn't really need it for my course and I didn't want it to look suspicious.' He grinned. 'My turn.' He reached out and spun the bottle. It stopped at Sally, who plastered her hands to the side of her face in mock horror.

'Dare,' she announced boldly. 'But nothing too horrible,' she warned, giggling nervously.

Toby handed her a full glass of wine.

'Drink this in less than ten seconds.'

'Oh, my love,' she said, taking the glass from him with a jaunty toss of her Marilyn Monroe wig, 'that is my speciality.'

'Fucking lame dare,' Gideon whispered under his breath so only Amelia could hear. 'Let's get to the real fun.'

Amelia felt uneasy. She didn't like Gideon in this devil-may-care mood.

She started to half-heartedly count with the others as Sally drank down the entire glass of wine. They only managed to get to six when she held the empty glass upside down over her head. She received a round of applause.

'Right, you lot, be prepared,' Sally said, spinning the bottle ferociously. Everyone watched as it began to slow down and finally stopped at Gideon.

Sally grinned.

'Truth. Just don't ask if I've ever slept with any of my leading ladies.' Gideon laughed.

The temptation was too much for Sally. 'Ha ha! That's my question. Have you ever had relations with anyone on one of your sets?'

'We-ellllll,' Gideon said ponderously, and Amelia could clearly see he was delighted that Sally had played right into his hands as it was exactly what he wanted to talk about, especially as Mike's camera was firmly settled on him. 'It depends on what you mean by "relations" and what you mean by "set".'

'Ooh, gosh, it could mean anything you want!' Sally pinked at the prospect of gossip.

'Let's see, I'll start with the most recent one, shall I? It was before we got here and it wasn't anything more than a kiss, but a lot can happen from just one kiss. Can't it, Amelia?'

29

Amelia's head snapped up to see everyone staring at her, mouths agape. Jack raised a quizzical eyebrow at her.

'Gideon!' Amelia exclaimed at his flagrancy of the truth.

'Oh, come now, Amelia, don't be so coy,' Gideon chastised. He turned to the camera. 'It happened before we got here.'

'Amelia! You never said,' Sally exclaimed.

'I–' Amelia started in her own defence but Gideon cut in over her.

'We got stuck in a lift together during a power cut. Well, you know how situations like that can bring people closer together. Anyway, we struck up a beautiful friendship, ending in a very memorable evening together.' He smiled dreamily. 'You have very kissable lips as I recall.' He leant over and brushed his thumb over her bottom lip.

Amelia was too shocked to move away in time. She gave him a warning look with her eyes.

Gideon, ignoring her silent protestations, rolled his eyes in mock exasperation. 'Oh, Amelia, don't look so horrified. You can't deny we kissed!'

Her mouth went dry. Everyone was looking at her and Mike's

camera was back in her face again. 'It wasn't–' she started to explain but Sally had started bouncing up and down in her chair with excitement.

'Oh. My. God! You're the mystery woman involved in the split between Gideon and Veronica Bliss. The photos taken at Shakedown!'

Horrified, Amelia looked at Gideon, willing him to stop this nonsense but he was just sitting, nodding sadly. 'I'm afraid it's true, darling. Veronica saw the photographs of us in the paper and that was that. I had to come clean. She dumped me.' He held up his hands.

'But you said–' Amelia tried to cut in, but Gideon talked over her.

'I couldn't lie to her about us,' he said, his mellifluous voice resonating with emotion. 'It's not that often you meet someone that you have such an instant, physical attraction to.'

Sally gasped, clutching her hand to her heart.

Gideon looked down at the table, idly spinning the bottle. 'I never told you how I felt. I didn't want to complicate your life any more than it already was. I know you were still messed up and feeling guilty because of your affair with your married boss,' he added quietly although his theatrically-trained voice projected enough to make sure everyone heard perfectly.

'But it wasn't like that!' They had to realise the kiss was instigated by Gideon and was purely for the press, and that Gideon's relationship with Veronica wasn't really a relationship but a publicity stunt to boost her career and to make him look as if he was calming down to pacify the jittery studio bosses. And she hadn't known Jonathan was married! But no one was looking at her, except Toby who was frowning. Jack was sitting, carefully picking at the label on his beer bottle.

'We never got a chance to explore what could have been with our relationship,' Gideon explained.

Amelia looked around. Could nobody see Gideon was acting? He'd never felt that way about her, she was certain of it. What the hell was he playing at?

With her reputation in more tatters than her bride of Frankenstein costume, Amelia wanted to stand up and demand people listen to her but Toby caught her eye and, almost as if he'd read her mind, he gently shook his head.

The next half hour passed agonisingly slowly as the game played out until people were yawning too much to continue. Everyone got up to go and Amelia tried to speak to Gideon but he just disappeared out the room before she could catch him, then Jack also slipped away. With everyone else leaving just Amelia and Toby remained in the room.

'Judging by your reaction I take it nothing is going on between you and Gideon?' Toby said as he teased out a latex globule of realistic brain gunk from his hair.

'No! And I need to sort this out.'

'Leave it for tonight. He's not in a good place.'

'And I am?'

'Better than him, yes. You'll get no sense from him. Speak to him in the morning and, even if he doesn't retract anything he's said, I'm sure Beniamino won't put the footage into the documentary.'

'I suppose so.' Amelia chewed her bottom lip, wondering what else she could do to stop any rumours.

'Get to bed. The cleaning crew are due here at 9am. Don't worry, I'll get up to let them in.'

'Okay.' Amelia started to head up the stairs but stopped. She still felt uneasy. She didn't know why, but she wanted Jack to know the truth, Lord knows she didn't *have* to explain anything to him but she wanted to. And she was also still curious to know what he wanted to talk to her about. There hadn't been any opportunity to speak quietly all evening, especially as they'd been dancing for most of it. She couldn't help but smile as she remembered. Amelia waited until Toby had his back turned as he switched off the lights, before slipping past the doorway and across the hall and out the front door, almost tripping over Sally who was saying goodbye to Hamish.

She hurried along the drive to the gatehouse, her blistered heels causing her to wince at every step. Luckily, she still had on her Inverness cape which kept the top half of her body slightly warm, which compensated a little for her bare legs being freezing.

Eventually she got to his house. The lights were on and she knocked on the door. No reply. The curtains had been drawn so she couldn't even peer in. She walked round the back of the house. The back door was half glass and Amelia could see into the kitchen. She knocked but there was no reply. Without really thinking, she gave the door handle a rattle. It opened. And he kept telling *her* to lock up, she thought as she pushed it open a little further.

With the door just being open a crack she got a lovely warm rush of air. She took a step inside.

'Hello!' she called out.

There was a noise, a rushing of water; Jack was taking a shower. She stood frozen in the kitchen unsure what to do. Should she wait inside, make herself at home? Should she wait outside until he'd finished his shower. Technically, she supposed this property belonged to her, but she didn't want to start acting all Lady of the Manor. She did like the look of the kitchen though. There wasn't one hint of orange Formica anywhere. It was warm and cosy with an Aga range and wood-burning stove in the corner where the heat was emanating from and there was a lovely Belfast sink and real oak cabinets and grey flagstones on the floor. Sitting in the middle of the room was a gorgeous big oak table although it was horrendously messy with papers strewn all over it. She happened to glance down and something made her look more closely. She pushed that morning's paper away to reveal house blueprints underneath. On pulling them closer to her she realised they were blueprints for Stone Manor. Her heart started beating wildly. Okay, she tried to reason, being a handyman he'd maybe need plans of the house... She looked closer and saw he'd highlighted the area of Sally's bedroom where Amelia had discovered the secret passage. There was another cross on the wall where Amelia had found Flora's diary. Another cross against the wall in one of the bedrooms Amelia hadn't searched yet. She looked underneath and found copies of many of the pieces of information she'd found at the library, detailing Montgomery Campbell's excavations and articles about the missing treasure, including a few Amelia hadn't found, on the priceless ruby.

Her mind tried to catch up on why Jack would have all this information. It went far beyond his capacity as handyman to know about it all. She felt sick. And cold, despite the wood-burning stove. She clutched the side of the table as a horrible thought washed over her; was Jack responsible for the dead crow and her costume being slashed? He'd been with her the night the rock was thrown through the window, but he could easily have paid someone to do it. But why? Just to find the treasure? Had he duped poor sick Dotty into hiring him without her realising the truth? All those cosy chats they'd had in her Chelsea flat, were they just for him to extract information about the legend? She didn't want to believe it.

She whispered the Sherlock Holmes quote to herself. 'When you have eliminated the impossible, whatever remains, however improbable, must be the truth.'

The water stopped. She didn't feel up to confronting him now as her brain was in turmoil. She needed to leave. She was quietly letting herself back out the door when she heard Jack's voice.

'Hi, yeah, I got your message.'

He was making a phone call. She slipped back outside and closed the door silently behind her. Crouching low she tried to listen in. Fortuitously, he'd walked back into the kitchen.

'Yup, no. Don't panic, I'm still on deadline to finish on time.'

Finish what on time?

'No, the research is mostly done, I just have to knuckle down and get on with the job.'

Had he been hired to find the ruby?

'Mm-hmm. Yeah. What do you mean distractions? Oh, you heard? Jesus, you have spies everywhere!' He gave a rueful laugh. 'No, nothing I can't handle. You know me, I'm a professional... Amelia? No, she doesn't have a clue... mmm... yup... You know what my plan is if she finds out. I'd rather not blow my cover, but if I need to I will. She won't talk.'

Amelia covered her mouth with her hand, feeling sick. Jack was a professional what? Hitman? And from the comment about spies was he involved in some sort of espionage too? What didn't he want her to find out? Clearly the ruby. And he had a plan for her if she did.

She hugged her knees tightly to her chest where she crouched behind the back door. She felt sick as her mind raced over the events of the evening. She felt stupid and duped. When they'd been dancing... the moment she thought they might kiss, that had all been him trying to inveigle himself into her good books so she would lower her guard and not notice he was looking for the ruby. Had he really been the one to lock her in the room and leave the dead crow on her bed? She just couldn't see it... or maybe didn't want to. But she'd heard him say he had a plan to make her not talk. Was he really going to kill her? Despite the damning evidence her gut just didn't think so. But whatever he was planning, she now knew he wasn't just a handyman. She didn't have enough to go to the police with though. She would just have to find the ruby for herself and find a way to trap Jack, unearthing his true identity.

Having eavesdropped the conversation she was now ahead of the game.

A game that was well and truly afoot.

She crept away from the back door on tiptoes until she got back onto the path, then ran home as fast as her blistered heels would let her.

By the time she got back to the house, her feet were burning. She could see Sally and Hamish were still at the front door; Sally snuggled into his chest as they talked and laughed together.

Amelia didn't want to have to speak to them so she ran round the back of the house, hoping the back door was unlocked. She nearly screamed in shock when she rounded the side of the house and saw a figure, seated cross-legged on top of the patio table, looking out towards the garden. Still in the orange wig and leather trousers, Gideon had also thrown his dressing gown on over his naked torso. As Amelia got closer she realised it was damp from the slight smir of rain in the air. He turned on her approach and she saw his make-up was slightly smudged with his face looking more gaunt than chiselled. He was smoking a cigarette.

Without acknowledging each other Amelia got up onto the table and sat beside him, pulling her Inverness cape tighter round her body. They sat in silence for a moment or two, each lost in their own thoughts as they looked out into the blackness.

Wordlessly, Gideon handed Amelia a half-finished bottle of

Grey Goose vodka. She took a small sip and shuddered as the neat spirit burned a path down to her stomach. He offered her his cigarette and she took it, despite not having touched one since she was in school. Taking a puff she immediately coughed as the smoke caught the back of her throat.

'Give it here,' he said, taking the bottle and cigarette back. 'You're useless in a drink-and-smoke-yourself-into-oblivion scenario.' He looked at her, his golden eyes bloodshot and tired. 'I know why I'm here, what's up with you?'

Amelia shook her head, still unable to do anything but wheeze from inhaling the smoke.

'I'm sorry about earlier,' he blurted out, looking away again. 'About the kiss thing. It was really shitty of me.'

'It's fine.'

'It's not. Not really. I made you out to be a relationship-wrecking floozy.'

He was right, it was really shitty. 'So, why did you do it?'

Gideon sighed. 'I don't know. I thought it would add spice to the documentary. I thought it would guarantee high viewing figures if there was a relationship angle. Everyone likes to fall in love, don't they,' he said, his voice loaded with cynicism.

'This means everything to you, doesn't it?' Amelia said. 'This documentary is going to get your career back on track.'

'It's my last hope.'

'Then it's fine.'

He turned to her sharply. 'What do you mean?'

She sighed. 'If it helps with your career we can pretend to be an item. And it *will* be pretend as we both know neither of us want a relationship with each other.'

'You are gorgeous, darling, but at the moment the only thing I seem to be able to have a deep and meaningful relationship with is a bottle of booze.'

'Why do you drink so much?'

He gave a hollow laugh. 'You're already fitting into the role of nagging girlfriend perfectly.' He took another sip of his vodka. 'It numbs me. I like the numbness,' he said after an age, resting his head on Amelia's shoulder.

They sat like that in silence for a while.

'Why are you doing this, Amelia?' Gideon eventually asked.

'I don't honestly know.' And she didn't, not really. She knew she couldn't put into words how she felt after hearing Jack on the phone. Before she'd found him she wanted to tell him there was nothing going on between her and Gideon, but now...? Now, she didn't care. In fact, if she did pretend to be with Gideon, she would be able to use it as an excuse not to go near Jack.

'Well then, let's be emotional wrecks together,' he said, passing her the bottle once again.

30

'Are you seriously telling me you and Gideon are together. As in an item?' Toby asked Amelia next morning in the kitchen, after he'd poked his head into the hall to make sure Mike wasn't lurking with the camera.

'Are you seriously telling me you're wearing that?' Amelia said, trying to change the subject. Toby had gone and bought himself a jumper just like Jack's and was now sporting an oversized, chunky knitted Saltire-flag woollen.

'Yes, it's warm and practical and my new favourite jumper. In fact, it's my only jumper so learn to love it and stop trying to change the subject. Are you and Gideon an item?'

Amelia and Gideon had decided not to tell anyone it was all a facade just in case word got out. She hated lying to Toby but it was the only way. Gideon had also asked one of the set designers to make an anonymous tip to one of the tabloids when he got back to London. Word would get out and there would be a flurry of interest for the documentary.

'Amelia! Look me in the eye and tell me you're dating him.'

She looked up at her brother... and was saved by Sally dancing into the kitchen.

'What's for breakfast? I'm starving!' She grabbed a banana from the fruit bowl Toby had placed in the middle of the kitchen table.

'Where did you get to, you dirty stop-out?' she said to Amelia. 'I was a good girl and tucked up in bed but you didn't get in until the very early hours.'

'I was with Gideon.' Amelia looked directly at Toby as she said it. It wasn't a lie. She'd sat with him in the garden until almost four in the morning, watching him smoke cigarette after cigarette as they worked out their game plan.

'Are you a couple?' Sally asked, halfway through peeling the banana.

'Yes, darling, you could say that!' Gideon said, swanning in. He stood behind Amelia, encircling her in an embrace, kissing her on the side of the neck.

Jack also chose that moment to walk into the kitchen. He did a momentary double take as he saw Amelia and Gideon. Amelia was very glad that the first time she saw Jack again was when she was surrounded by others. She still couldn't quite believe that Jack was behind the incidents to scare her off but she needed to get to the bottom of what he was doing.

Jack rubbed his palm against his jaw. 'Morning, everyone. I was hoping to have a quick word, Amelia.'

'Sure, what is it?' she said as normally as possible but not moving.

'Is it possible to see you in private?'

'It's not really a good time at the moment.'

'Uh, sure. Okay.' He looked a little taken aback. 'Later?'

'To be honest I don't think there's a good time at the moment. Sally and I are heading out to look at decor. Then–'

'Then we're having an evening together. I don't think there's room for three,' Gideon added.

Jack jammed his hands in his jeans pockets. 'Okay, well, if

you find you have a spare moment, it would be good to talk to you. I'll see you later.'

'Do you want to stay for breakfast?' Toby called out to him.

'Thanks, but no,' Jack called back.

Toby looked at Amelia. 'Why are you being so cold towards him?'

'I'm not.'

'It was positively arctic,' Sally said. 'I don't remember we talked about going to look at decor, maybe I had more to drink than I thought,' she said.

'I think you were too enamoured with Hamish to notice anything last night,' Amelia said, not letting on she'd just come up with the decor plan there and then.

Sally grinned. 'I can tell you all about it over wallpaper samples.'

Sally hadn't been joking. From the moment they got into the car – another head-turning journey in Toby's Ferrari – to the point they arrived in the large retail park, Sally hadn't stopped talking about Hamish McDonald. He was almost six foot four, was a farmer – sheep and cows, he played rugby for the local team in his spare time. Amelia knew the films he liked, and didn't, his favourite ice-cream flavour (mint choc chip), his shoe size (12), his thoughts on politics, religion and Jeremy Vine. The only area Sally didn't cover was about the sex.

'Well, we haven't!' Sally said, as virtuously as a vestal virgin, when Amelia prompted her.

Amelia wasn't sure how to respond. All of Sally's relationships or even just brief encounters started with her sleeping with the man in question.

'We're going out for a drink tonight,' Sally said and Amelia could have sworn she looked as if she was blushing slightly.

The good thing about Sally being preoccupied with shopping and a potential new love interest was that she didn't ask Amelia one question about Gideon.

'So, where are we going first?'

In the industrial estate there were flooring specialists, bedding stores, warehouse-proportioned stores selling every type of furniture and lighting style imaginable, two kitchen design units and a massive department store.

'I'm fed up looking at orange Formica and crazy wall and floor tiles. I know everyone thinks it's hilariously retro but I'd really like something that didn't induce a bad LSD trip every time I looked at it.'

'Like you've ever had LSD.' Sally snorted in amusement as they headed into the first kitchen showroom.

~

Amelia had no idea just how much there was to buying a new kitchen. All she thought she'd have to do was pick some nice cupboards, a work surface, then some tiles for the walls and the floors and possibly some lighting. The array of handles alone was dizzying and that was before she even got into the drawer configurations and recycling compartments. Traditional, modern or Shaker?

Laden down with brochures and an appointment for a kitchen designer to visit, Amelia and Sally were leaving when Amelia's phone rang. Sally took the pile of brochures as Amelia answered it.

It was Fiona from the library and museum in Ullapool.

'Jenny said you were looking at information on Stone Manor. You wanted to know who'd requested the information.'

'I just wondered if you remembered who'd asked for them,' Amelia said, although she had a horrible feeling she knew who it would be.

'I do, it was a lovely American man. Tall, good-looking with darkish-blond hair. His name's Jack. Do you know him? He's been in quite a few times now for research.'

'Yeah,' Amelia said with a sinking feeling in her chest, 'I know him. Thanks for letting me know.'

'He's such a nice man, and always so appreciative. He brings us cakes.'

Amelia didn't want to hear how lovely Jack was.

Nevertheless Amelia thanked Fiona and hung up. She didn't bother to check her phone for texts or other messages.

'You okay?' Sally asked.

'Yeah,' Amelia said hollowly.

'Great!' Sally said brightly. 'Because we've got the return journey for you to tell me just what the hell the deal is between you and Gideon.'

31

For the next couple of weeks Amelia managed to successfully avoid Jack, along with pretty much everyone else. Sally was constantly with Hamish, Toby was in talks with the kitchen designers, a job Amelia was only too pleased to hand over as soon as they started asking if she had a preference over induction or gas hobs (she did not) and what her thoughts were on 'proving drawers' (she had none).

The documentary crew were holed up editing the next lot of footage ready to send back to the bigger bosses in readiness of it being rolled out to a sample test audience. The plumbing and electrical work was now well underway throughout the entire house and Amelia was left looking through a bamboozling amount of furniture and decor catalogues along with back copies of *Ideal Home* and *House Beautiful* magazine. James Armstrong had sent through pages of information covering all the legalities of starting up a small hotel. He'd sent her a very sweet letter apologising for not sending the information sooner but the lawyers' offices had been broken into and he'd had to spend quite a while tidying up the mess, although he was quite smug that the thieves had only had a rifle through his rooms as he didn't have a computer to steal like the other lawyers had had.

Amelia knew she still had time before picking new furniture and deciding on the interior, which was just as well as she had no idea what 'theme' she wanted; did she want to be on-trend or classical? She looked at the helpful suggestions of mood boards and the proportions of 80/20 colour schemes with a growing sense of panic. She had a colour wheel for reference and the helpful bullet points reminded her she could pick sympathetic colours which were side by side or contrasting colours from opposite sides to one another on the wheel. But then she'd have to consider where the light came from as that altered the colours and she'd have to adapt accordingly. And if she just picked one colour she had to be mindful of tones and would have to rely on textures being layered playfully. How did one playfully layer a texture? Amelia wondered if everyone else in the world understood this language. Couldn't eclectic mishmash of colour and style be a valid theme?

There were now fewer places to seek refuge within the house as the workmen had spread into all the rooms and Amelia was on constant alert, expecting to be told about another secret passage being discovered. They'd already alerted her to the many mice they'd discovered which meant it was far more likely to have been rodent activity rather than Dotty's ghostly interventions which led to Amelia finding Flora's diary. Each day Amelia found herself wandering from one dust-sheeted room to another trying to seek out a place to read. She'd almost finished her Denholm Armitage book and didn't know if it was because of Jack's comments influencing her, but she'd not enjoyed the latest Inspector Grayson instalment as much as previous ones. It did seem a little pedestrian and yes, some of the characters could be a little more rounded and, okay, it was a little twee in parts, too, but she didn't know if she was more annoyed at Jack for being right or annoyed that she was feeling such disappointment in one of her favourite authors. She'd also got to the end of Flora's diary with nothing else terribly noteworthy happening. It was sad to see the handwriting of Flora get shakier as she got older and she seemed like a woman haunted by her situation; a husband and one of her sons proving to be an alcoholic bully obsessed with finding a treasure taken from an ancient historic burial site.

The weather did nothing to raise Amelia's mood either as each day brought another round of sleet, high winds and grey skies. Marching well into November it was now dark by mid-afternoon and some days it didn't seem to get light at all. The village was still as cheery as it always was and more and more Amelia sought refuge in the little café on the main street, enjoying its cake of the day (so far, her favourite was Chocolate Melting Middle Mondays) along with a latte as she watched people going about their daily business and the moored boats bobbing up and down and sometimes, when she timed it right, she could catch a glimpse of the Ullapool CalMac ferry on the horizon, sailing over to Stornoway.

Once, Jack walked past talking on his mobile and she froze, forkful of cake halfway to her mouth, but he didn't look in. She'd become constantly alert for his presence in case she had to jump into a shop on the main street to avoid him. She just had no idea what to say to him; she was finding it difficult to think he could be behind all the threats but who else could it have been? Clearly her 'psycho radar' had let her down.

And she was so angry with him.

If she was being totally honest with herself, as she sometimes was when it was four in the morning and she was in Gideon's bed while Gideon slept on the chaise longue a few feet away, part of Amelia's anger at Jack stemmed from the fact she'd started to like him. Although intensely annoying, she'd started to enjoying their bantering insults towards one another. Yes, they bickered but he made her laugh and she couldn't stop her thoughts meandering back to the night of the Hallowe'en party when she and Jack had been dancing, and she remembered how green his eyes were and how they crinkled up attractively when he laughed and that momentary feeling of exhilaration when she thought he was about to kiss her... and then she felt foolish because he was very possibly infiltrating her life to steal the alleged treasure from under her nose and possibly murder her in her bed too.

And the really amusing thing about it all was Amelia couldn't care less about finding treasure. It was exciting to think there was a mystery under her roof but she wasn't that bothered about finding the ruby in a bid to make her rich. Especially when it should no doubt be returned to the Egyptian authorities.

More and more Amelia would find herself restlessly turning in bed, trying to escape her thoughts as she listened to Gideon's booze-induced snores. She thought many times about confronting Jack but couldn't quite bring herself to. For the time being, Amelia found the best course of action was all-round avoidance.

Luckily, keeping up the charade of being with Gideon was easier to continue as not much had to change. As Gideon had expected, the story had been leaked and was doing the rumour rounds of the red tops and after a couple of days Amelia had moved her belongings from Sally's room to Gideon's and now she just had a different room-mate. One that didn't spend half the night talking about how handsome Hamish was and telling her how to differentiate between the breeds of cows and sheep.

Beniamino seemed ecstatic at the way the documentary was taking shape. Having not seen any of the footage, edited or otherwise, Amelia had no idea how they were being represented and she was now feeling more than a little apprehensive about it all. At least she knew she'd always look her best as, despite Sally's infatuation with Hamish, she was always ready to do make-up in the mornings. But with the crew holed up editing for a couple of days, Amelia didn't have to worry about being filmed for a while.

She'd just had that thought when Beniamino came into the kitchen, which Amelia had found unoccupied and had hoped for a quick coffee and ten minutes of peace.

'I just heard that initial feedback is good after the first lot of footage we sent out,' Beniamino said, grinning widely. 'If that continues, we're probably looking at a prime channel,' Beniamino said as he searched the contents of the fridge. 'For a while I was sure this project wouldn't even get off the ground.'

'Really?' Amelia didn't want to be rude, but she really fancied being left on her own for a bit, but Beniamino was in a chatty mood as he began making himself a sandwich.

'Yes, because it wasn't an idea the studio had, the funding was next to nothing. I'd already lost out on a couple of great documentaries and although this wasn't my usual style, I didn't want to miss out on this either. And then, just two days before we were due to fly up here one of my original crew was attacked in the street. A mugging that went wrong. He died.'

'Oh my God, that's awful! Did you know him well?'

'No, I hadn't worked with him before. But still... so, it was panic stations to get someone to fill in at the last minute.' Beniamino laid lettuce on bread with fastidious precision. 'It was terrible, yes. But it has all worked out well. I think it will be a hit.' He crossed his fingers. 'Everyone loves a romance, the more intriguing the better, don't you think?' He looked at her sagely.

'Yes, I'm sure they do,' Amelia said awkwardly, hating that she and Gideon were lying just to make good TV. 'I'll see you later, Beniamino, I need to, um, organise a couple of things,' Amelia said as she stood up. Picking up another couple of interior design magazines and the well-worn copy of *Murder on the Orient Express*, Amelia left Beniamino and walked through the house looking for a tiny corner in which to seek a little privacy. Eventually, she found the library was completely void of workmen. There were no dust sheets or tools strewn about or any other indications that anyone would be back imminently so Amelia sat down, cross-legged at the bay window, which looked out over the garden. In the background she could hear a multitude of drills, circular saws and hammering which echoed through the house and she tried to block it out as she flicked through one of the magazines. After a few minutes she realised it was no use, it felt as though the drilling noise was boring through her skull, and because it kept stopping and starting it kept jarring her out of her concentration as she looked at an article on elaborate bathroom makeovers.

Suddenly her phone rang. Amelia had forgotten she was sitting in what seemed like the only area of reception in the whole house.

'Hello?' she answered, not recognising the number.

'Hi, Amelia? It's Fiona from Ullapool library.'

'Oh, hi!'

'I've just remembered something you may be interested in,' Fiona said. 'When I called before about the American, Jack, looking at the information about Stone Manor I'd completely forgotten about the other man who'd been in before him.'

'Another man?'

'Yes, it was maybe seven or eight months ago, it was definitely after Jack had been in because I'd already looked out a few things for him and they were easy to lay my hands on.'

'And it was definitely for information on Stone Manor?'

'Yup, very specifically only the house and the inhabitants.'

'Do you remember his name?' Amelia's heart was beating fast.

'I'm sorry but I don't remember anything much about him,' Fiona said. 'I didn't get his name. He was pretty nondescript really. He was wearing a hat, a baseball cap, so I don't even know what colour of hair he had. He did have a beard, I remember that. He just came in the once and was in all day. Asked for a lot of things and was rather curt and didn't once say thank you.'

Although disappointed at the lack of detail, Amelia couldn't help be excited that someone else had been sniffing around about the house. It didn't explain why Jack also wanted the information but it did put another person in the frame to be the psycho crow-killer and saboteur. 'Thanks for letting me know.'

'No problem. I'll let you know if I remember anything else. Bye.'

Amelia hung up, wondering just who else would be interested in the house. Seven or eight months ago would put the time frame back at when Dotty had died.

She needed fresh air to think.

Pulling up the hood of her fleece, Amelia abandoned the magazines and slipped out the glass door and into the garden. She stopped at the patio area as she saw Toby in his ridiculously oversized Saltire jumper lugging about big bags of compost. He'd been muttering something about setting up propagators to encourage home-grown potatoes and other veg. Preferring not to speak to anyone, Amelia dodged back the other way and stayed low as she ran alongside the hedge before getting onto the grass. Looking over her shoulder she could see that Toby was far too engrossed in his gardening project to notice her.

For the first time in days the rain had stopped and a watery sun was valiantly trying to break through the clouds and with no gale-force winds present it was actually rather pleasant to be outdoors. Jamming her glove-free hands into her pockets, Amelia strode out over the grass. She toyed with going up to the folly but decided against it when she saw that the path had changed into a mudslide from all the recent rain. Instead, she followed the grass off to the left which took her into the forest. A natural path had formed, taking her on a winding route through the trees. Some of the trees had reached a phenomenal height, no doubt hundreds of years old, and the forest floor had a wonderfully rich russet-and-gold carpet from all the fallen leaves which Amelia took great delight in scuffing her feet through, kicking up huge clouds of them in front of her as she walked. Her tree recognition wasn't the best but she did spot a horse chestnut a little way in front of her, and that meant one thing: conkers.

Foraging along the ground, she felt like a kid again as she cracked open the spiky shells with the heel of her boot to reveal the beautiful shiny brown jewel nestled within and after a few minutes her pockets bulged with them. Feeling incredibly satisfied with her haul she had a last look along the ground, making sure she hadn't missed any huge conkers. She heard a branch crack a distance away and looked up, expecting to see some wildlife, but instead, about fifty yards in front of her was a hooded figure, all in black, crouching behind a fallen tree trunk with his back to her.

Amelia very slowly crouched down, careful not to make any noise. There was something rather suspicious about him as she doubted he was scavenging the forest floor for conkers. The figure stayed completely motionless and Amelia started to wonder if it *was* a person and not just an old jacket draped over the tree. But then she saw the figure move, albeit slowly, as it pulled something up from the ground.

An air rifle.

Could it be a poacher? Was he hunting rabbits? Was hunting

rabbits even allowed or was it deemed as trespassing? She had absolutely no idea.

She got out the tiny bird-watching monocular from her combat trouser pocket and looked to where the gun was pointing. She soon saw the target, adorned in the blue Saltire jumper. She immediately thought it was Toby, but realised it couldn't be her brother; Toby couldn't have overtaken her to get to the woods without her noticing, but also, this person was wearing a blue beanie hat and no matter how cold it got Toby would never wear a hat in case it flattened his hair. Amelia refocused her monocular and realised she was looking at a lesser-spotted American. Surely the man must be pointing his gun at something else and he'd soon shout at Jack to get out the way? But no, Jack was picking up pieces of wood, probably for kindling, without any idea he had a target on his back.

Amelia's heart started beating wildly, not quite believing what she was witnessing. She needed to get the gun pointing away from Jack, but preferably not making herself a target either. But what could she do? She only had her keys and pocketfuls of conkers...

Conkers!

She quickly felt in her trouser pocket. That morning the postman had handed her a bundle of letters and Beniamino's returned DVD with comments on the latest footage for the documentary all bound together with an elastic band. She'd taken the band off and jammed it into her pocket before flicking through the mail to find any letters for her. The band was still in her pocket! She quickly wound it twice round her index and middle fingers to make a slingshot, then, pulling it back and nestling a conker in the curve of the band, she pulled it back and let it go, watching the conker sail through the air. It didn't hit the figure but it was near enough to cause him to start, just at the point he fired off a shot. The crack of the rifle seemed to ricochet off the trees and was immediately followed by a frenzy of flapping wings and caw-cawing as rooks and pigeons took flight all around her. Amelia ducked back behind the tree but not before she was aware of a cry... of pain or surprise she couldn't be sure, but then there was a lot of American cursing which meant Jack was still alive. She risked poking her head out just in time to see the hooded figure running off through the trees, keeping low and holding the rifle at his side. He didn't look back.

Amelia left her hiding place and ran over to Jack, jumping over tree roots and fallen logs. He was kneeling on the ground, clutching the top of his arm.

'What the hell just happened?' he said, looking shocked.

'Someone shot you,' Amelia said, hunkering down beside him and prising his hand away from his arm to assess the damage. There was a big rent in the sleeve of his jumper, with blood already seeping through the wool. She needed to get him back to the house.

'Jesus, that hurts!' Jack said, wincing.

'Come on, can you stand?' Amelia didn't want to hang around in case whoever did it came back to finish the job.

'Yeah,' Jack slowly got to his feet.

Amelia took off her scarf and made a tourniquet around the top of his arm. 'Keep putting pressure on it.'

They hurried along the path leading back to the garden, only slowing down slightly when they were halfway across the grass, the house in their sights. Amelia's mind was in overdrive. Why was someone trying to shoot Jack? Had she stumbled in on a Robert Ludlum spy-thriller conspiracy. Or was it that Jack was also now a target of the crow-murdering, costume-slashing psycho too? Which would mean Jack wasn't the psycho himself. Not wanting to jump to any conclusions, Amelia just focused on getting to safety.

At the house Amelia led Jack into the kitchen where he gratefully sank down onto one of the chairs. He looked quite ashen and was still clutching the top of his arm where a bloody stream was running through his fingers.

'You okay?' she asked.

'Just dandy considering someone just shot me. Did you see who did it?'

'No, he had his back to me. I didn't see his face. I didn't even know what he was doing until I saw the gun and realised he was pointing it at you, so I caused a diversion and then he ran off.'

'You caused a diversion? Thank you. What did you do?'

'I catapulted a conker at him.'

'You what?'

Amelia took out the elastic band and a conker and gave Jack a demonstration.

He started to laugh. 'Thank you for saving my life in possibly the most amusing way I've ever heard.'

'My pleasure.'

'And making me appear the least macho I've ever felt in my life.'

'Also my pleasure.'

Amelia untied her scarf and helped get his jumper off to assess the damage. He gritted his teeth as he straightened out his arm.

Amelia washed her hands and fetched some tissues and a bowl of water and began to mop up the excess blood. There was a large gash at the top of his arm and the skin around it was already turning an angry purple but it looked as if the pellet had glanced across the skin and not embedded itself in his flesh.

'Hang on a sec,' she said as she went to the fridge and got out Gideon's bottle of vodka. She came back and poured a little over the wound.

'JESUS!' Jack nearly leapt up out his seat, but Amelia

restrained him with her hand on the shoulder of his uninjured arm. 'You could have warned me!'

'Surprise is better.'

'For whom?' He took the bottle off her and took a swig. 'I don't think your boyfriend will be too enamoured that we're using his vodka for first-aid purposes.'

'Tough.' Amelia went out to the boot room where the first-aid kit was kept. Her eyes glanced to the shelf below where they'd stored a big box of lost property left over from the party. She took an item from the top and tucked it into her pocket. She returned to the room with the first-aid kit under her arm. The bleeding had stopped and she had a bit of a prod about the wound.

'There's definitely nothing lodged in there. We should go to the hospital and see if you need stitches.'

'What, you mean you're not going to whip out a darning needle and some yarn and do it yourself?'

'I'm tempted. And I'll sew up your mouth, too, if you give me any more cheek!'

Jack took another swig of vodka and looked down at his arm.

'I don't think it needs stitches. And I don't think my masculinity could take it. Isn't it meant to be the other way around, that I'm meant to be the one rescuing damsels in distress?'

'Is this really the time and place you want to discuss gender stereotyping? Especially as we should be discussing why someone wanted to shoot you?'

'I have no idea. Maybe I've offended someone.'

'Enough to shoot you?'

'I often rub people up the wrong way.' He reached out for the bottle of vodka again.

'Especially if you're being disingenuous,' Amelia said lightly.

He paused the bottle halfway to his lips, his green eyes scanning hers.

Amelia took a breath. In for a penny... She suddenly lunged, and, removing the red furry devil-costume handcuffs someone had left from the party, deftly secured the wrist of Jack's good arm to the bar on the back of his chair.

'What the...?' He tugged uselessly at the handcuffs.

'Why do you have papers showing all the floor plans of this house along with information on the treasure? It's interesting that you've just been shot at because I suspected you were the one behind all the threats.'

'What?' Jack looked startled.

'The crow, the costume slash, locking me in the room at Hallowe'en? You would have needed someone's help with the rock-throwing as you were standing next to me when it happened. Maybe your partner in all this? Although it looks like they don't fancy sharing potential spoils anymore.'

'Amelia! No!' He looked shocked. 'Okay, yes, I do have all the plans for this house and articles about the treasure.' He carefully lowered the bottle of vodka onto the table. 'But I'm not behind those threats. Please trust me on that. I know I've kept some things from you and we need to talk. I've been trying to for the past few–'

'I heard your phone call.'

He looked more confused.

'After the party. You need to finish your job on a deadline? You're working with a spy? Amelia doesn't have a clue but if she blows your cover, you'll make sure she doesn't talk? Ring any bells?'

Realisation began to dawn on Jack's face. He began to shake his head.

'Amelia... no! It's not...'

'What the hell's happened here?' Toby said in horror as he

walked into the kitchen, taking in the bloodied balls of tissues scattered over the table.

'Hey!' Jack tried to raise his good arm in greeting but the handcuff stopped him.

Toby raised an eyebrow.

Jack nodded to Toby's identical jumper, now covered in soil. 'We need to co-ordinate our wardrobes more, otherwise we're gonna look like two members of a nineties boy band.'

'Jack got shot,' Amelia said, frustrated by her brother's interruption.

'What?'

'Don't worry, it was an air rifle, not like an AK-47,' Amelia qualified.

'I don't care if it's a fucking Luger Parabellum. Jack's been shot! We need to call the police,' Toby blustered.

'I don't think it was on purpose,' Jack said smoothly. 'I think it was kids out shooting rabbits.'

'I don't care if they were aiming for elephants, kids should not be out there with weapons if they can't tell the difference between a six-foot-something man and a long-eared, furry pest. A word?' Toby jerked his head towards the hall and Amelia reluctantly followed him out. Toby closed the door behind her.

'What the fuck is going on?' he hissed.

'Jack got–'

'No.' He shook his head. 'Long before this incident there's been stuff going on here. The creeping about, the brick through the window, the dead crow, the buried treasure and this ridiculous farce that you and Gideon are an item.'

Judging from her brother's reaction it was probably just as well she hadn't told him about the guy in the *V for Vendetta* mask and the slashed costume.

But Amelia didn't really care about those incidents at the moment, she wanted to get back and question Jack. Unless he was an even better actor than Gideon, he'd seemed genuinely shocked and surprised that she'd accused him of being the saboteur psycho.

'I need to speak to Jack–' She tried to dodge past her brother but he held the kitchen door closed fast.

'Nope, not until you tell me one truth. You and Gideon are not an item, I know that. There is no way you can fool me, Ames. You may be able to pull the wool over Ben and the other guys' eyes, hell, they probably realise it's all fabricated, too, but don't care because it will make good viewing figures. I just don't see what you can be getting out of all of this.'

'Please, Toby, I promise I will tell you all about it later but for the next few minutes I really need to be able to go and speak to Jack.'

With a despairing sigh, Toby stood back and opened the door for Amelia.

But when the door was opened, the kitchen was empty. Jack, and the chair he was handcuffed to, were gone.

32

There was no sign of Jack at the gatekeeper's house. All the doors were locked and a quick look through the kitchen window showed all the papers from the kitchen table had gone too.

Amelia walked round to the Whistling Haggis just in case he'd gone there. He'd seemed very keen to talk to her so she couldn't understand why he'd run off at the last minute. She was determined to finish their conversation.

On the main street she bumped into Sally and Hamish walking hand in hand as they stopped to look in the gift shop window. Although preoccupied with finding Jack, Amelia realised she'd never seen Sally so happy. Normally when Sally started seeing someone and was in the first heady, lust-filled days there was always drama, an air of temporary fragility about the relationship, but these days Sally looked contented and settled. Amelia didn't know if it could all be accredited to Hamish; Glencarlach had a habit of creeping into your very being with its laid-back charm and welcoming people. Despite her extremities being the coldest they'd ever been, Amelia's soul had never been warmer.

'Hi, have you two seen Jack?' Amelia asked, breaking into their conversation.

Both of them shook their heads.

'If you see him can you tell him I really need to speak to him?'

'Sure. Fancy joining us for a late lunch?'

'Sorry, can't stop!' Amelia waved and jogged along to the Whistling Haggis, keeping her eyes open for Jack.

Inside the pub, a quick glance showed that Jack wasn't there either, it was very quiet from the post-lunch lull with just Archie sitting at the bar chatting to Big Davey as he poured a pint of Guinness for another customer. Ross, sitting at a nearby table reading the paper, gave her a friendly wave.

'Hi, have any of you seen Jack today?'

Ross shook his head with an apologetic shrug before burying it back into the sports section.

'No, he's not been in for a few days,' Davey said as he took the pint over to one of the other regulars.

'No, me neither, I'm glad I caught you though,' Archie said, reaching into the inside pocket of his shooting jacket. 'I thought you might like this.' He handed her a thick A5 envelope. 'It's just a few bits and pieces I've collected over the years, just some old photos of the house and some historical articles about the local area. I thought you might like to have a browse through them, just whenever you've got time. They're just some silly old memories.' He smiled, his bright eyes disappearing into the network of creases and weathered folds of his face.

Amelia was touched by the gesture. 'Thank you, that's very kind. I'll look forward to doing that.'

'Can I get you a drink?'

'Thank you but I really need to find Jack. Will you let him know I'm looking for him if you see him?'

'Of course, hen, and we'll do that drink another time.' He winked.

'You can get me one though, Granddad,' Hamish joked, coming up to them and leaning against the bar.

'Ach, but you're nowhere near as bonnie!' Archie laughed.

Clutching the envelope to her chest Amelia thanked Archie again and darted back out the pub, looking up and down the main street in the hope she'd see Jack. Had he possibly decided to get himself to hospital to get his arm checked out? She was just wondering where else he could be when she heard the throaty engine of a car. Amelia turned to see Toby pull up beside her in the Ferrari.

He leant over to the passenger side as the window slid down.

'You need to get back to the house pronto, Amelia. Your ex has turned up and he's just challenged Gideon to a duel.'

Someone had had the sense to get the workmen out the house and for the first time in weeks there was silence when Amelia walked in through the front door. In fact, the silence was a little too eerie.

'Where are they?'

'They were right here, in the hall, when I left.'

'Shh.' Amelia held up her hand to silence Toby as she heard a shout coming from the back of the house.

'The billiard room!' Toby shouted, and they both ran through the main hall to the back of the house and along the smaller hall.

They burst through the door to see Gideon and Jonathan at either side of the long room with Mike filming everything. Tom the plumber was sitting on one of the chesterfields, eating a packet of crisps, thoroughly engrossed in the floor show.

Amelia was acutely aware that with her entrance all eyes turned to her.

'Amelia!' Jonathan shouted over to her and she could tell straight away from his slurring that he was completely pissed. Rather surprisingly, Gideon seemed relatively sober and was standing, smacking the shaft of a billiard cue into the palm of his hand.

'It would seem that I have a rival for your love,' Gideon said with a haughty flick of his head. 'I can't believe this pathetic specimen was the arsehole who made you so miserable.'

'We were fine until you poked your nose into our business,' Jonathan shouted.

'Fine? You were married to another woman and leading poor innocent Amelia on.'

'Stop it! Both of you!' Amelia shouted angrily, smarting from Gideon's rather patronising description of her.

'Amelia,' Jonathan said beseechingly to her, 'I love you. I want to be with you. I read all about you in the papers. About this house, about you now being an item with him. I want you back. I miss you. Let's start again.'

'You mean you miss someone picking up your dry cleaning?' she said wearily.

He vehemently shook his head and for a moment he nearly wobbled over, but he righted himself. 'No, no, no. I love you. But what did happen to my suit, it was Italian, my most expensive one...' He hiccuped.

'Seriously, sis? You were having an affair with him?' Toby whispered in her ear.

Amelia looked dispassionately on as Jonathan stood swaying on the spot and she wondered what on earth she'd seen in him. She'd thought him lean and elegant and sophisticated, but now he looked wispily thin and rather weedy. His boyish looks no longer held any appeal, in fact she was rather turned off at his clean-shaven, insipidly juvenile face. And Amelia knew beyond any doubt she was completely and utterly over Jonathan.

Looking at the two men before her, it hit her like a blow to the solar plexus that it wasn't so much that she was horrified by the thought of being duelled over, it was just that they were the wrong men to be doing it. She didn't care two hoots if they wanted to fight over her. She wasn't theirs to win.

She suddenly wondered how she'd feel if one of them was Jack... The thought of it made her a little light-headed.

Oh shit! *Now* she was having an epiphany of the heart?

Beniamino came running up to them from behind, holding his laptop open.

'Okay, I've found the duelling rules.'

'You're surely not condoning this?' Amelia said in horror.

'Our job here is to record and assist and document.' The Italian shrugged.

'I don't believe this,' Amelia said to Toby who looked equally horrified.

'Okay, okay.' Beniamino held up his hand. 'The code duello states that at any point there can be an apology and the duel will stop.'

'No chance,' Jonathan slurred.

'Never apologise, never explain,' Gideon said, slicing the cue dramatically through the air with a Zorro-like motion.

'Oh, hang on, we need a doctor present,' Beniamino said.

'I know first aid,' Tom said, wiping his hands on his overalls and standing up.

'Fine by me,' Gideon said.

'Yup,' Jonathan agreed.

'Okay,' Beniamino continued, 'the duellists must remain dignified at all times.'

'Too late for that,' Toby said drily.

'Now, we've checked and we don't have pistols–'

'Oh dear God!' Amelia said.

'–so you'll have to pick other weapons.'

Gideon brandished the cue as Jonathan went to the stand to choose one and proceeded to knock them all to the floor. Swaying exaggeratedly, he bent and picked one up.

'Take your places at either end of the room and when I say go, the duel commences,' Beniamino said. Mike gave him a thumbs up to indicate he was ready.

'This is for you, Amelia,' Jonathan said.

'Go!' Beniamino shouted.

Gideon took a couple of steps forward as Jonathan launched himself forth at a full run. Jonathan managed to get three paces before tripping over the edge of the rug and, pitching dramatically forward with his arms flailing wildly, the billiard cue flew out his hand and sailed through the air. Jonathan gave out a yell of surprise which was abruptly cut short when he knocked himself out on the side of the billiard table. Amelia watched as the cue continued its javelin-like slice through the air and caught Gideon square in his side.

Gideon fell to the floor with an agonised scream.

'He got me! That bastard ran me through.'

'Oh shit!' Toby said, running over to Gideon who had slumped to the floor, hand clutching his side.

'How deep is it?' Gideon whispered as he reached out his other hand to beckon Amelia.

Amelia strode over to him, stepping over Jonathan who lay sprawled on the floor, out cold. She hunkered down beside Gideon.

'Is it bad?' he asked, his eyes fluttering closed.

'If you're referring to your acting, yes, it's terminal,' Amelia said, none-too-gently pulling Gideon's hand away and lifting up his shirt. The skin wasn't even pink from the contact.

She stood up, distracted by a movement by the doorway.

Looking over, she saw Jack standing there staring at the scene before him. A whole host of emotions hit Amelia when she saw him. Aware of everyone's eyes on her, waiting for her to take charge over the incident between Jonathan and Gideon, Amelia felt the walls closing in on her, despite the billiard room's vastness.

'I need to get out of this madhouse,' Amelia said to no one in particular, hurrying past Jack and heading towards the kitchen, only breaking into a half run once she was out the back door, not stopping until she was around the side of the house and sitting on a low wall out of sight.

Amelia closed her eyes and concentrated on breathing to try and quell the rising panic.

Her eyes flew open when she heard gravel crunching underfoot as someone walked towards her.

Jack.

'Wow, I can't believe you went out with that asshole,' he said, plonking himself beside her.

Amelia closed her eyes again and swallowed, she was confused enough without Jack sitting beside her with his thigh gently pressing against hers. He smelt of woodsmoke and outdoors, which she realised was far more alluring than any expensive aftershave Jonathan had ever worn. Now, sitting so close to him Amelia was very aware of the heat emanating from his body, which wasn't just down to his double-knit yarn. Was it just her, though, or was he aware of the chemistry crackling around them too?

'I didn't know he was married when we started an affair at work,' she said, picking at a loose thread on her trousers to give her something to do that didn't involve looking up at Jack. 'I stupidly thought he wanted to keep us quiet because we worked together.'

Jack sucked in air. 'He's bad enough, but to then follow him up with Gideon, jeez. I'm gonna come right out and say it, you have lousy taste in men. I wonder what the collective noun of assholes would be?'

Amelia snuck a sideways glance at him. 'A butt?'

'A butt of assholes, I like it.' He laughed.

They sat for a moment in silence, the only noise being the birds in the trees. Dozens of questions formed in Amelia's mind to ask Jack but she didn't know where to begin.

'How's your arm?' Amelia eventually asked.

'A bit painful but I'll live.'

'I looked for you after you disappeared from the kitchen.'

He nodded. 'Yeah, I heard. I needed to get something.'

Amelia sat up straight and looked at Jack.

'Tell me what's going on.'

He sighed and took something out of his back pocket.

'I haven't been honest with you, but before I go into any more detail you need to read this first. This is what I was getting when you were looking for me.'

He handed her an envelope. It was addressed to Amelia in Dotty's handwriting.

'But how...?'

Jack stood up. 'Read it first. I'll be waiting at the gatehouse and we can talk more then.'

33

My darling Amelia

I had planned on writing a couple more letters but I fear I don't have a lot of time left and I think this will be the last. If there is any possible way, I will write another one, think of it rather like a band coming back onstage for an unexpected encore, but I more than suspect this will be my fat lady singing moment. Dr Khan wants me to go into one of those hospices but I'm determined to stay at home. It will be interesting to see who wins this battle.

So, let's assume this will be my last letter to you. I desperately wish I could go on writing to you forever. I think I believed as long as I kept writing these I'd stay alive. I realise how ridiculous this is, but I seem to have turned into a silly old woman who is clinging to any slight superstitious notion. It's difficult thinking of death as a finality and I keep having to remind myself I won't be here to see you find these. I know those God-botherers talk about the afterlife and the start of another journey, but I've always had my doubts. Don't get me wrong, I'll gladly and optimistically pack my passport just in case, but I have a sneaky feeling this is my final destination. Oh darling, I'm sorry, I don't want to get maudlin, but it's so difficult to talk of anything without this shadow hanging over me, tapping me

*on the shoulder at every turn to remind me of its presence. All I want
to do is scream and beat my fists at it to go away and leave me alone.
Selfishly, I don't want it to be my time yet.*

*You may have guessed I've had help with the letters, Jack Temple
has been my cohort and partner in crime. I hope you get to meet him.
I think you'd like him. He's also very attractive...*

Amelia laughed. Dotty was another one of his fans! Everyone
loved Jack.

*...In fact, even if you don't get to meet him, please look him up, James
Armstrong has his details and I'm sure you'd have a lot to talk about.*

*Mr Temple is due to stay on at Stone Manor until January but I
hope you've checked out your house long before then. I'm afraid I've
been a bit naughty and asked Jack to look out for you if you did
arrive while he was there. Don't get your hackles up as I know you're
more than capable of looking out for yourself, but sometimes it's nice
knowing there's someone else who also has your back. Wouldn't it be
lovely if, when I'm dead, I get a guardian angel assignment for you
and Toby? I could protect you both from high up on my cloud. But in
case that doesn't happen, Jack will have your back until he leaves. I
also asked Jack to keep a few things from you. Don't be angry with
him, I know he'll tell you what you need to know when you need to
know it. He's posing as a handyman – oh how we chuckled over that
as he didn't even know the first thing about wiring a plug when I
'hired' him.*

Amelia read the last part again. If Jack was just posing as a
handyman, what was he really doing there? She read on...

*Okay, I have some straight-talking to do now, and everyone knows
you can't deny a dying woman her last wishes:*

One. Leave those hellish office jobs behind you. You have a creative mind, my darling, you need to set it free. I have nothing against office admin jobs but you do seem to go out your way to pick ones where they don't even remember your name! If I thought your heart lay in administration and filing and photocopying and answering the phone in a polite fashion, I'd be all for you sticking at them but it doesn't. Be more like Toby; he'd never settle for doing something he didn't love. I know you fret over him, but he'll work out what he wants to do for himself in his own time and if it's being a cage dancer in a San Francisco gay club, so be it, and you can guarantee he'd strive to be the best cage dancer the club has ever seen. He probably doesn't realise he's ambitious, but he is.

Two. Don't waste a moment. Oh, I know everyone says, 'live for today' and 'seize the moment', and all the other usual psychobabble, but it's so true, my darling. But contrary to popular trends I don't believe in 'bucket lists'. I don't have a list of far-flung destinations to visit or dangerous sports to partake in, my last while on earth is far more humdrum than that. It's the simple pleasures that I now want, like sitting in my little patch of garden in the sunshine and eating a slice of terribly good cheesecake; smelling snow in the air; going to an art gallery and appreciating the perfection of a Rembrandt. Please always try and appreciate what you're doing, grasp every bit of life out of every situation you are in and enjoy yourself. Don't rush to get to the 'big things'. There is beauty in everything if you know where to look.

Three. I have absolutely no regrets about my life but when I look back at those moments when I faced a choice and I was scared, I really wish I hadn't let fear guide me. Live without fear. I know it sounds so simple but it is harder to do than you realise.

Four. Fall in love. At least once. Look for it, seek it out and when you find it let it consume you. You can't love by half measure or restraint. I know this from experience. Yes, you did read correctly. I never told you about this period in my life. He was called Francis and I met him when I came back to Glencarlach for my year's recuperation. It was wrong on many levels, not least because he was engaged to a local girl. We were from different worlds and maybe that's what we wanted. It was never going to be forever, some love isn't destined to be. Tennyson said it far more eloquently, 'Tis better to have loved and lost than never to have loved at all.' We had such a passion and it truly felt as if we were the first people to discover love. We would meet in the folly (yes, there is a way in and you'll have fun finding it!). We would spend hours there. It was our secret place. As the years passed, whenever I returned to Stone Manor I went to the folly, as he did, too, as over the years we would leave letters and little keepsakes for each other in a wooden box. He was my one great love...

Sometimes it seems so far away it happened to someone else. But I still have my keepsakes and my memories. I've dreamt a lot about him lately, I think my mind is retreating back to my happiest times. In my dreams I still see him so clearly. He was good-looking, oh, such a looker! I know he'll be an old man now but I still remember his jet-black hair and strong outdoor hands, the turn of his head, the way he squinted into the sun, the twinkle in his eyes when he teased me, the way he said my name... these little things never leave you.

Amelia wiped away a tear on the sleeve of her top. She'd had no idea Dotty had loved anyone like that. She'd always just assumed her aunt had no time for such frivolities. The little wooden heart she'd found in the passage to the folly was F.A.M. It must have been Francis. The groove in the earth in the folly could have been from a bigger box which housed all their letters and keepsakes. Could it have been Francis returning to take away the mementos of his love?

She folded the letter against her chest, saddened and frustrated that she'd never be able to get answers to these questions. She composed herself before carrying on with the letter.

...Five. Question everything. The world needs more questioning minds. You may not always like the answer but it is far better than staying ignorant. Too many people accept quietly and go on their way. Stand up for what you believe in. Hold up a banner and protest against unfairness. And always shout loud enough to be heard.

And six. Have a signature cocktail. It may not be as important as my first five points, but I've always believed you know where you are in life when you have a go-to drink.*

All my love, forever

Dotty

* As long as it isn't a Fluffy Duck. You will lose all credibility asking for that in a bar, and advocaat is the work of the devil.

Amelia sat touching her fingers over the paper for a few moments, keenly feeling the loss of her godmother all over again. Wiping away the last of her tears, she took a deep breath; now she had to go and see Jack, and she had no idea what he was going to tell her.

~

A melia found Jack in his kitchen, bent down stocking up the log burner. He'd changed into a long-sleeved T-shirt and she could see the bulge at the top of his arm where he'd obviously bandaged up his wound.

She gently knocked on the open kitchen door, feeling a flutter of nervousness as well as a kick of attraction as he stood up and looked at her with a tentative smile.

'Hi,' she said, aware that she must look a wreck, with puffy eyes and black tear-tracks from her non-waterproof mascara.

'Hey. You okay?'

Amelia gave a non-committal shrug, aware she may start crying again if she went into any detail.

'So...' He ran his hand through his hair, looking at the floor for a moment, as if waiting for inspiration. He eventually looked up. 'I haven't been entirely honest about who I am and why I'm here.'

Jack didn't say anything else for a few moments and all Amelia was aware of was the shallow breathing in her chest as the second hand of the kitchen clock audibly ticked on.

'Okay, I'd rehearsed me saying that to you but nothing else after that,' Jack said with a nervous laugh. 'D'you want a drink, a tea, coffee, something stronger...?' He made to move towards the kettle but Amelia caught his arm and shook her head.

'No, I want the truth.'

'Okay.' He took a deep breath and exhaled it slowly. 'Me being here has nothing to do with travelling and being a handyman or anything else like that.'

'So I gather.'

'Dorothea knew my backstory and knew exactly why I wanted to come here. As does James Armstrong the lawyer so you can double-check everything I tell you with him. Let me start at the beginning. A couple of years ago I got in touch with Dorothea, I was doing some research on some lesser-known Egyptian excavations that took place in the early 1800s. Everyone knows about Lord Carnarvon and Carter and Tutankhamun but there were many other Egyptologists making discoveries all the time and there were links with curses and stolen jewels aplenty. I'd looked into Montgomery Campbell and realised there was definitely a link to some missing treasure from the tombs he'd excavated.'

'You're a treasure hunter?'

He smiled. 'Nothing so exciting or intrepid, I'm afraid. I got in touch with Dorothea to see if I could interview her and she kindly agreed to see me. We met and she told me what she knew and she was the one who suggested I come and stay here while I worked. She also thought it best if I didn't broadcast what I was doing, hence the "handyman" persona.'

'Your hands,' Amelia blurted out.

'My hands?'

'I knew there was something off but didn't know what, but of course; they're too smooth and callous-free to be used to outdoor work.'

He looked at his hands, turning them over, smiling to himself before carrying on. 'By this time she knew about the cancer and she told me about Toby and you, her amazing god-daughter, who'd be inheriting the house and how you loved mysteries. She was torn between wanting you to know about the treasure and wanting to keep you safe from it, too, because it seemed to curse those who looked for it. That's why she got me to leave the letters for you as a clue. She thought by not telling you directly it meant it was in the hands of fate.'

'You're the one who filled in her dates in the family tree,' Amelia said.

'Yeah. She asked me to do that, to keep everything accurate and she made me swear I wouldn't tell you any of this, unless I had to, but I figure this is the time. She also asked me to keep a lookout for you, to make sure you were okay,' he added with a wry smile.

'Yeah, how's that going for you?' Amelia asked, nodding at his arm.

'It's worth saying I won't be moving into the bodyguard industry after this.'

'What were you researching all this for? And were you not worried you'd succumb to the curse too?'

'I figured I'd be immune as I wasn't searching to find the treasure, just the story behind it.'

'Why?'

'I was researching my new book. I'm a writer. I'd been

suffering hellish writer's block as I'd fallen out of love with everything I'd ever written and I wanted a change of direction and wanted to explore this.'

'Oh.' Amelia hadn't expected that. 'What do you write?'

'I *did* write twee crime fiction set in a one-dimensional town with stereotypical characters.'

'That's what you said abou–'

Jack nodded, looking sheepish.

'But... Denholm Armitage is quintessentially English! ... You're American,' Amelia said.

'You noticed.'

'But...'

'It started as a laugh. I'd had a little success with my first novel but nothing after that. As a joke I started to pen a new novel that ticked all the boxes of the crime novels which were never out the top ten fiction lists. It got picked up by an agent. I made up the persona of Denholm Armitage and people lapped it up. Don't get me wrong, I loved writing the first few but then I felt hemmed in by my characters. Any time I tried to write differently I was told to keep the same style as before as that's what people liked and expected. I started to hate Inspector Grayson and his crew. Financially I didn't need them anymore so I began to form another story, one that involved a family torn apart by cursed treasure from an Egyptian tomb. Turns out I was rusty and the more I tried to write something different, the harder it became. It was only when I came here to Glencarlach I started being able to write again.'

Amelia just looked at him. All that vitriol towards Denholm Armitage. Amelia felt she had to stand up for the little English gentleman writer when in fact he'd been insulting himself and his own creation.

'I'm sorry I wasn't honest with you,' Jack said.

'Did you research the house?'

'Yeah, I got a load of information from the little museum and library in Ullapool.'

'Including floor plans?'

He nodded. 'Yup. Your house is some place, with all the little hidden cabinets and passageways.'

'I saw you had the plans the night of the party. I came here and let myself in and saw them all on the kitchen table.'

'And that's why you thought I was behind all those awful incidents. The phone call you heard me make was to my agent. She'd been worried I wasn't going to be able to get the first draft to her in time.'

'That was your deadline?'

He nodded. 'The job I had to get on with. Somehow she knew about the documentary crew, so I jokingly said she must have spies everywhere. At that moment, you didn't have a clue about my true identity, and if you did start to guess, I knew what I'd do... I would come clean and confess all. In fact, I'd already decided to tell you. I tried to just before the party.'

Amelia felt all the anxiety leave her body.

'So, the big question is, did you find the treasure?'

Jack smiled and shook his head.

'Do you think it is somewhere here?'

'I honestly don't know. It could be, but if it is it's hidden very well. Did Dorothea shed any light on it in her last letter?'

'No, just some very valuable life lessons. So, have you any other admissions you need to make?'

'Uh, I hate pickles and I cry whenever I watch *Titanic*?'

'I was meaning more about your double life.'

'Ah, that! No.'

'You're not married or anything like that,' Amelia asked lightly. 'Just that the last time someone decided to fudge the truth a little it was about that.'

'No, I'm definitely not married. Or seeing anyone.'

Amelia moved slightly closer to him.

'Me neither.'

'What about Gideon?' he said, smiling, also moving closer so that there was barely a centimetre between their bodies.

'That's all just for the cameras. We're not interested in each other like that, never have been.'

'Good to know.'

'Is it?' Amelia could feel her chest tightening.

'It is, yeah,' Jack said, 'otherwise I'd feel a bit bad doing this...' He tipped her chin up to his and kissed her, Amelia's stomach fizzing into life as his mouth sought out hers. *Fall in love. At least once*, the words Dotty had written to her ran through her mind as Jack pulled her closer and continued to kiss her.

He was a good kisser, Amelia was delighted to discover as his mouth explored hers assuredly and sensuously, creating delicious sensations throughout her body. She slid her hands up the inside of his top, feeling the smooth, hard muscles of his chest and arms, so sexy under the tightness of his fabric. Amelia's hands glanced over the makeshift bandage and Jack pulled away slightly.

'You may have to be gentle with me,' he whispered, lifting his head from kissing her neck, 'I've lost a lot of blood.'

'Or you could just man up and deal with it.' Amelia laughed as she pulled his head back to hers again.

Hours later Amelia lay in Jack's bed, luxuriating in the delicious post-sex, leg-shaking exhaustion she felt as she snuggled into him, his arms wrapped around her. Somehow, it had become completely dark without them realising but neither of them had made a move to turn on the light.

'Who'd have thought we'd have ended up here after the first

time we met,' Amelia murmured contentedly as she lazily trailed a finger down his well-defined abs. 'You were so rude!'

He lightly kissed her shoulder and laughed. 'You completely threw me. I was fully expecting Amelia Adams turning up but I thought she'd be a little old lady in twinset and pearls with a grey perm. Instead, you appeared, all cute and sexy with your big eyes and pixie hair and stilettos, so I did what every grown man does when met with someone he's instantly attracted to, I was incredibly rude and insulting and tried to get you arrested.'

Amelia laughed. 'You thought I was cute?'

'And sexy. Then I tried to look out for you and keep things hidden from you and all I really wanted to do was this.' He kissed her.

'Mmmm, I wish you had, that was nice.' She wriggled closer into him. 'So, who do you think is behind all these warnings?'

'I'm not sure. I thought it was Gideon for a while.'

'Gideon!' Amelia laughed. 'Definitely not! Why him?'

'It just seemed terribly convenient the way he met you and wormed his way into your life and then organised your travel up here and then he turned up too. With a documentary crew!'

Amelia chuckled. 'Ah, yes, the filming, which you always seem to avoid.'

'Yeah, I didn't want to appear on film in case someone recognised me and I was no longer incognito.'

'Ah, so you're not just camera shy then.' Amelia chuckled. 'Hmm, I suppose it does all look a bit suspicious with Gideon until you realise Gideon was doing it all purely for himself. Well, mainly for himself. I genuinely think he also wanted to help me. He's not a bad person, a little misunderstood perhaps, but he's okay. I've got a list of suspects although I've not got terribly far with it as all the renovations and decision-making with the house has taken over. The librarian in Ullapool told me that as well as you going to request information someone else has been there, too, but they couldn't remember anything about him except he wore a hat and he had a beard.'

'Hmm, sounds like we need to compare our lists.'

'I'll show you mine, if you show me yours?' she said teasingly.

'That sounds like a plan.'

'But it involves leaving here. I don't want to leave here.'

'Tempting as it is to stay, don't you think we should check in back at the house?' Jack said.

'Gideon will still be milking his duelling injury.'

'And what about your ex's concussion?'

'Shit!' Amelia sat up in bed.

'He may still need to be packed off home again if he hasn't got the message by now,' Jack said as Amelia jumped out of bed and started gathering up the clothes she'd hastily discarded on their way to the bedroom.

'I'd totally forgotten about him! Does that make me a bad person?' she said, calling through from the hall where she located her bra.

'I'd have been more upset if you *had* been thinking of him,' Jack called back, appearing in the doorway, pulling on his jeans.

She looked at Jack in his sexily dishevelled state, feeling a kick of lust in her stomach. 'Bugger him.' Amelia said, running at Jack, catapulting him backwards and pinning him onto the bed as he laughed encouragingly. 'If he's still there waiting after all this time, he can wait a bit longer,' she said.

34

Amelia and Jack walked hand in hand back to the house. It was slow progress as both of them seemed to want to draw out their time together for as long as possible. They were currently in a little bubble but as soon as they walked through the doors of Stone Manor they knew reality would kick in. Letting themselves into the house, they could hear voices coming from the main drawing room. Amelia opened the door to find all the house residents there, including Hamish who was standing awkwardly next to Sally at the fireplace. Unusually, Mike wasn't filming anything but his camera was by his side, poised for action. Jonathan was in the centre, sitting in one of the wing-backed chairs looking hellish. Normally so pristinely turned out, his suit was rumpled, his hair flattened from the discarded bag of frozen peas he'd been pressing against his head, and he looked an unbecoming shade of hungover ashen.

'Darling.' Gideon waved over at her. 'For once it isn't *me* with the banging hangover from hell.'

'How's your head?' Amelia addressed Jonathan stiffly.

'Agony, evidently,' Gideon chipped in before Jonathan could answer. 'But it's not as sore as our heads, as we've had to endure the endless complaints and rants for the past few hours after you disappeared.' Gideon's eyes were glittering strangely. He looked like a highly strung racehorse about to bolt.

'I drove him to the hospital and he got the all-clear. We're not long back, actually,' Toby said, his eyes darting questioningly between her and Jack.

'Amelia, can we talk? Without your entourage,' Jonathan said, standing up shakily, looking sorry for himself.

'Say whatever you want to say here.'

'I...' He looked as if he wanted to argue but a quick look around the hostile room convinced him not to push the point. He took a deep breath. 'I've really missed you. This time apart has made me realise I want to be with you.'

'What about your wife?'

'I've split up with my wife.'

Amelia looked on dispassionately as he stood there looking quite pathetic. She doubted Jonathan would ever have the gumption to make such a bold move himself. 'Did you leave her or did she leave you?'

His eyes shifted to the side as he licked his dry lips.

'I can phone and check,' she said. She was completely bluffing as she had no idea what his wife's phone number was, but it did the trick as his grey pallor started to turn slightly red.

'Okay, she asked me to leave, but I realise now it was the best thing that could have happened to me.'

'Do your children agree?'

'Ouch!' Gideon sucked in his breath.

'Are you really telling me you'd rather be with *him*, than me?' Jonathan said, turning to glower at Gideon. 'Okay, Amelia, I completely admit I fucked up, big time. But I love you and I came up here to try and win you back any way I can. I could move in here with you while we get to know each other properly... and your family.' He smiled at Toby who stared stonily back at him. 'I'm willing to forget about you starting up with... him.' He gestured to Gideon.

'What about your job?'

'Some things are more important than jobs.'

'He got fired,' Gideon said cheerfully. 'I did a little bit of detective work while he was in Accident and Emergency. Misappropriation of funds, allegedly.'

'That is all a misunderstanding!' Jonathan blustered.

'You may also be interested to note he's got a few suitcases with him in his car. I think he expects you to take him back,' Gideon added.

'Wait, I can explain about all–'

'No, Jonathan!' Amelia cut him off. 'I'm sorry things aren't going well for you and that you came up here to try and get back together with me, because you've wasted your time. We're finished.'

'I know it must be a surprise, me turning up like this–'

'More a nasty shock,' Gideon added as he walked over to the drinks cabinet.

'I think you should go along to the Whistling Haggis and see if they can find a room for you for tonight, then first thing tomorrow get home and try to repair the damage to your marriage, at least for the sake of your children.'

He looked as if she'd slapped him.

'But I came up here to be with you.'

'You've had a wasted journey.'

'So you two are going to set up home here, together?' Jonathan cast a disapproving look at Gideon. 'Please! What are you going to do up here? Live off your love?' he said scathingly.

'Your concern is touching but I have a job here,' Amelia said coolly.

'Doing what?' he scoffed. 'Tending sheep and cows.'

'There's nothing wrong with that!' Sally said hotly, linking her arm through Hamish's.

'I do have a lot of land here and one day I may start a smallholding, but for the time being I'm channelling all my energy into being a hotelier.'

'What?'

'That's right,' Toby said, getting up from the chair arm and walking over to stand with Amelia. 'My very clever and talented sister is venturing into the hospitality business. And she's going to be bloody good at it.'

Jonathan tried to square up to Toby, but tripped over the edge of the rug. He looked livid when Sally giggled.

'I think it's time you were on your way,' Jack said quietly, but forcefully, from beside Amelia.

'For once I agree with that man!' Gideon said, gesturing to Jack with a crystal tumbler before pouring a hearty measure of Glenfarclas into it.

'And just who the hell are you?' Jonathan said to Jack.

'I'm the man who will become your worst nightmare if you don't do as Amelia says,' Jack said smoothly.

'Let's all hear it for Captain America!' Gideon laughed, a touch hysterically, as he downed the malt in one.

Looking round and not seeing a single friendly face, Jonathan picked up his suit jacket and stormed past them all. Amelia and Jack followed him into the hall and watched as he let himself out the front door, slamming it closed behind him.

Amelia turned to Jack. 'The man who will become your worst nightmare?' she said, unable to keep from laughing.

'I've always wanted to say that line. Hey! It did the trick, didn't it?'

She smiled. Then she turned and looked back into the drawing room and saw Gideon standing by the bridge table, watching her.

'I need to go and see Gideon for a minute.'

'Want me to come with you?' he said, his green eyes scanning hers.

'No, I think it best you stay well away.' She walked him to the front door.

'I'll come get you in a bit, okay?'

'Sure.' She touched his hand, their fingers momentarily lacing together and Amelia felt her heart quicken at the thought of when she would see him again.

He leant down and kissed her, not a peck on the cheek but a full-on, X-rated teaser trailer for what was on the cards for later.

'Now go.' She shooed him out the door, laughing, feeling light-headed. How could she not have seen just how damn sexy and attractive he was from the start? she wondered, as she watched him walk away, lingering over the way his muscular thighs and bum looked so good in his jeans. He turned and on seeing her check him out, cockily blew her a kiss.

'You look very cosy together,' Gideon remarked as she returned to the drawing room, still with a grin on her face. It was just the two of them, and she saw he'd topped up his glass with another hefty measure of whisky.

Amelia took a deep breath. 'Gideon, I don't want us to pretend we're an item anymore.'

'Ah,' he said as he stood looking down at the pack of cards he'd fanned out over the table. 'I see. Should we say it's irreconcilable differences? We've grown apart? You cheated on me?' He looked up at her pointedly.

'I don't mind. I just don't want to be living a lie.'

He gave a hollow laugh. 'Oh, the irony,' he said before taking a swig of his drink.

'Don't worry, Gideon, I'm sure that the footage the guys have will be more than enough to catapult you back into the hearts of the public again. You don't need to rely on us being an item to get your career back on track.'

He closed his eyes briefly. 'Oh shit, you really don't have a fucking clue, do you?'

'Gideon–'

'No, poppet, it's fine. You're right. It's unfair of me to ask this of you.' He smiled bravely and downed the rest of his drink. 'I'll get someone suitably connected to start the hints tomorrow, and I'll tweet something in a couple of days.'

'Say I'm with someone else, because, well Jack and I...' She trailed off, not knowing quite what she and Jack were yet.

'I guessed as much. You both had a very obvious post-coital glow about you.'

Amelia felt as guilty as if she *had* been cheating on him. 'Will you be okay?'

'Oh, darling, don't you know by now, I'm always perfectly okay. Absolutely fucking perfect.'

Now Amelia was really concerned, there was something slightly unhinged about Gideon tonight.

'Fucking whisky!' he said, going to pour more but finding the bottle empty. He walked past her, leaving her standing in the middle of the room feeling wretched.

She went to follow him but bumped into Sally coming down the stairs with Hamish carrying a heavy-looking holdall.

'I'm so glad you saw sense with Jonathan,' Sally said, giving Amelia a hug, 'what a complete arsehole! I'm sorry to love you and leave you but I'm heading on out, we're going to see a band in Ullapool and I'll stay over at Hamish's. It's an early start on a farm.'

Sally, who never willingly surfaced before mid-morning unless there was the promise of a bacon sandwich and caramel latte, looked so happy she positively glowed.

'Think he's a keeper?' Amelia said, glancing over at Hamish who was studying something intently on the hall table.

Sally nodded happily just as Hamish turned around holding the little carved wooden love-heart box with the initials F.A.M. As far as Amelia knew, Hamish was the first person to notice it since she'd left it in the hall a few days earlier in the hope someone would recognise the initials or the workmanship.

'This is lovely,' he said, turning it over in his hands.

'Isn't it. I don't suppose you know who in the village would have those initials.'

He nodded. 'Aye, I do.'

Amelia nearly stopped breathing. 'You do?'

'Aye, and very well too. He's always been good with his hands and making carvings.'

'Who is it?' Amelia asked.

'My granddad.'

'But... that's Archie.' No matter what potentially strange Gaelic spelling, Amelia was pretty sure Archie never started with 'F'.

Hamish nodded. 'His proper name is Francis Archibald McDonald but he always hated Francis. His dad was also called Archie and when he died, Archie, my granddad, started calling himself that.'

Amelia tried to get her head round the information. *Archie* was the love of her aunt's life? Nice, old, weather-beaten, twinkly-eyed Archie? Dotty did say in her letter that he had a mischievous twinkle in his eye and she supposed as a young man he could very well have been good-looking...

'Where did you get it?' Hamish asked.

'It was Dotty's.'

'Oh.' Hamish looked a little taken aback as he replaced the box.

'Come on!' Sally said. 'We don't want to miss the support act.

I'll see you tomorrow,' she called out to Amelia as she dragged Hamish out the door behind her.

Suddenly Amelia remembered about the big envelope Archie had given her that lunchtime which he said was full of old photos of the house and his memories. She wondered what else was there. She'd left it in the car. She needed to find Toby to get the keys.

Walking into the kitchen, Amelia almost bumped into Toby as he was coming out.

'I need your–'

'What did you say to Gideon?' Toby interrupted, looking anxious.

'What's wrong?'

'He just came through here going on about how everything was ruined and then he muttered something about it all being over, grabbed a bottle of whisky, then bolted out the door.'

'I, uh, I said I didn't want to keep up the pretence of us going out.'

'So it *was* all an act?'

'Yes, I'm sorry I lied.'

'I knew it! Why on earth did you go through... oh, it doesn't matter now. Oh shit,' Toby bit his bottom lip and looked towards the kitchen again. 'We're going to have to find him.'

'What's wrong?' Amelia asked, not really understanding why Toby was so concerned or why it had all become such a big deal.

'I'm really worried he's going to do something silly.'

'Like what?' Amelia started to feel panic rising at how worried Toby looked.

'With him, who knows?' He shrugged his shoulders helplessly.

Amelia went to the back door and opened it wide, looking out into the blackness.

She called out his name...

...No answer.

What was he up to? Was he just being his usual overdramatic self or was he about to do something monumentally stupid?

Flicking on her torch, Amelia ran out after him.

35

Amelia ran out onto the grass blindly. With no idea of what direction Gideon would take, she just ran forward, along the grass for as far as she could, chest burning with the exertion. A couple of minutes later she caught a glimpse of his white shirt in the distance like a ghostly apparition, beckoning her to follow. Amelia managed to keep him in her sights as he led her towards the very edge of the grounds, and as far as she'd ever walked in this direction. She was aware that she was now running slightly downhill and into another cluster of trees.

She caught up with him in a small clearing. A three-quarter full moon allowed her to see he was standing on top of a thick branch of a fallen tree which protruded out over the edge of a drop. Fresh bottle of whisky in one hand, he held out his other to the side, aiding his balance.

A quick sweep of her torch ascertained he was balancing over a high gorge, so high she couldn't see the bottom. She could also hear the sound of running water below.

She guessed this was Hangman's Gorge.

Amelia bent over double, trying to catch her breath, leaning against another tree for support.

'Gideon, what are you doing?' she said between gulps of air.

'Be a love and bugger off, darling,' he said, staring straight ahead, his shirt flapping against his torso in the wind.

Amelia winced as the cold air hit her lungs. 'Gideon, what's going on? Is something really wrong or is this for the benefit of the documentary crew? If it is, I'll push you off that log myself,' she tried to joke, then gasped, heart in mouth, as he teetered slightly.

He slowly righted himself.

'Gideon, what was all that about back at the house? What don't I understand? Is this about us not pretending to be together anymore? Is it that big a deal?'

'Please, leave me alone, Amelia,' he shouted, his voice raw with emotion.

'No.'

He turned round to look at her, annoyance sweeping across his face, then he gave a half laugh, but suddenly lost his footing.

They both let out a cry at the same time, but Gideon managed to stop himself falling by grasping hold of the overhanging branch of another tree, his right leg sweeping out over the drop.

Amelia didn't breathe until he'd slowly returned to an upright position again. He still clutched his whisky.

'Gideon, what's going on?' Amelia asked again, tears threatening, no idea how to persuade Gideon to come back off the log.

He turned and flashed her his professional, full-wattage, scene-stealing smile. 'I rather think I've got myself into a bit of a pickle, angel.' His smile wavered slightly as he shivered beneath the thin fabric of his shirt.

'Please come back here and we'll talk about it.'

'I don't think talking will solve an awful lot in the long term.'

'It'll at least give the hypothermia a fighting chance to finish you off first,' she tried to joke.

'You're such a comfort.' He laughed, then stopped abruptly. 'Why did it have to get into such a fucking mess?' he said, peering down into the gulf.

'Whatever mess you're referring to can be talked over and maybe won't look so bad in the morning,' Amelia said as she took a couple of steps near him. She also didn't think a whole shedload of whisky was going to help clarify his thought process. 'Why not come back to the house, I'll stick the kettle on and Toby can rustle up some biscuits or something.'

'Death by Horlicks, a rich tea, and the bearing of my soul? Sounds almost as bad as nosediving off this.'

Heart nearly jumping out her chest, Amelia stepped onto the tree trunk. She could see his legs shaking through his trousers.

'I'm not scared of dying, you know,' he challenged.

'Well, I am,' Amelia said, tears now spilling over, hot on her cold cheeks. 'I don't want you to die. The whole reason I'm here is because Dotty died and it's not cool and it's not romantic. It's cruel and hateful and makes your insides feel raw and I don't want to go through all that again.'

He didn't move.

'Fine!' Amelia shouted, wiping her nose on her sleeve. 'If you're bloody well going to do this, at least have the decency to tell me what it's all about before you leap off into the abyss.'

'I'm gay.'

The words momentarily hung in the air before being caught on the wind and whipped away into the night.

He turned to look at her and Amelia stared at his pinched face, unsure what to say, unsure what he wanted her to say. She was taken aback at the admission, yes, but it wasn't earth-shatteringly shocking and it didn't change how she saw him, yet she didn't know how to get this across without belittling it and saying that obviously it was fine and it shouldn't be a big deal because she knew if that was the case, he wouldn't have gone to such pains to keep it hidden. In her experience Toby had never really 'come out' in the sense that he'd had to make a big announcement. It had just always *been*, as far back as Amelia could remember, been understood that Toby didn't like the girls at the school but harboured crushes on the cool group of sixth-form guys who smoked and were arty and snuck out to concerts. Toby always fancied boy bands and rocker hunks, having no opinion on pop princesses but then again Toby hadn't had to live his life in front of the press in an image-conscious profession.

'You know that it makes no difference to me and to all the people who care about you.'

Gideon laughed hollowly. 'And just who are those people, Amelia, just who are these caring individuals? All these people queuing up to be my friend, eh?' He swept his arm around dramatically as if talking to an invisible audience. 'I don't know if you've noticed, Amelia, but I don't have many friends. A few hangers-on and sycophants and contacts I've gone out on the piss with but nobody else that really gives any kind of flying fuck.'

'What the hell about me then!' Amelia shouted.

'I've managed to take advantage of your good nature, darling. You're too good for me. You need to forget about me.'

'I don't know if you've noticed, Gideon, but I don't respond that well to people telling me what to do anymore. I'm old enough to make up my own mind about people and as far as I'm concerned we're friends. You're a drama-loving, complete arsehole of a lush at times but I still want you to be in my life. And it's not because I'm a soft touch. And if you must know, I'm bloody choosy about who I consider my friend, but like it or not, you've made the cut and I don't want to go and have to drag your cold, lifeless body up out of this gorge because you're too pissed to think straight and too engrossed in your pity party–' She stopped abruptly, fearing she may have gone too far and possibly pushed him over the edge, and not just figuratively.

He looked away again and she could see his shoulders shaking. Oh God, she'd made him cry. Some friend she was, shouting at him and insulting him to the point he was visibly weeping. But then he threw back his head and she realised he was laughing. Huge guffaws of laughter.

'Darling, I love how you manage to keep it all real!' He reached out his hand for her and she grabbed it, pulling him back towards her and they fell back, together, onto the safety of the ground. Just to be sure, Amelia bum-shuffled them back another couple of feet away from the edge.

He sat, elbows resting on his knees, the bottle of whisky dangling between his feet. Amelia grabbed it off him and took a swig; if ever there was a time for strong drink...

Wiping the whisky from her mouth, she turned and hit him on the shoulder. Hard.

'NEVER scare me like that again. If you do, I will no longer be your friend!'

They sat together in silence for a few minutes, passing the whisky between them, both shivering in the cold but not getting up to leave.

'I thought you would have guessed. I think a part of me wanted you to guess. I mean you're gorgeous, you've spent every night in my room and I've never laid a finger on you. Never tried it on. I wasn't just being chivalrous, you know.'

'But there's never been so much as a rumour, you've gone out with actresses...'

'All publicity. My agent would speak to some up-and-coming actress's agent and we'd be photographed together. A mutually beneficial situation for both parties. No relationship ever lasted but it was part of the act, my hard drinking, my love-them-and-leave-them attitude.'

'But is being gay really that big a deal now?'

'It would be the end of my career,' he said flatly.

'But plenty of actors have come out as gay.'

'My career would be over,' he repeated, slower, so it would sink in.

'But Rupert Everett, Ian McKellen, Russell Tovey, they're all–'

'Yes, but they're all ac-tors. World of difference. I know I'm not Oscar material, I'm hired because I do sexy and brooding. I play the romantic rogue. The audience buys into me being like that in real life. I get the girl. No one wants to watch me in a film when they know I'd prefer the cute wingman. My shelf life is short enough as it is, coming out would kill it off completely.'

'But if there was never any hint of a rumour, why bother to go to all the trouble of pretending to go out with me now?'

He rocked back and forth slightly. 'The night of the Hallowe'en party.' He screwed up his face at the memory. 'I was careless, one of the guys who'd come up from London to help with the set designs brought some gear. I did a line.'

'Of cocaine?'

'Well, I don't mean as in dance! Yes, coke. I was completely off my head and I ended up kissing a guy. I normally wouldn't be as stupid but I was high and this gorgeous guy was right there and I'd fancied him for ages and... then the Ouija board had that horrible message: *I saw you, I know what you did.*'

'You think it was a ghostly message?'

Gideon looked at her witheringly. 'I may be emotionally wrought at the moment, but I'm not simple, Amelia. I know it wasn't the ghost of Dorothea Campbell-Delaney who'd popped down for a bit of voyeurism. I realised someone at the party had clocked me and was sending me a cryptic message and I was terrified they were going to blackmail me.'

'Who would have seen you?'

'Who knows, caution was not top of my priorities that night.' He gave a rueful smile.

'What about who you were kissing, would he have told someone?'

Gideon looked at her. 'I doubt it, darling, as your brother strikes me as one of the good guys.'

'You snogged Toby!' No wonder her brother hadn't believed her when she'd adamantly held on to the story that she and Gideon were going out. Yet he hadn't once let slip Gideon's secret. She grinned and shoulder-nudged Gideon. 'So, you like Toby, you've fancied him for ages! I never knew.'

'I like to think I normally manage to keep my emotions in check.'

'So who else knows?' Amelia wondered aloud after a few moments of silence.

'If I knew that do you think I'd be up here about to end it all?'

'Clearly it was someone at the seance who then doctored it to make it look as if the glass moved.'

'At the end of the day it doesn't matter who. I fucked it all up. I really wasn't thinking straight,' he paused as he laughed at his pun, 'and I thought it would solve everything if I roped you into my sorry life and got you to lie for me.'

'Wow, you made me your beard.'

'Yes I did and for that I'm sorry. And I'm sorry about your brother. I've not been able to look him in the eye since. He must think I'm hateful.'

'He doesn't. He was worried about you.'

'Ugh!' He buried his head in his hands. 'Even worse, he pities me.'

'Dear God, you're determined to play the martyr card aren't you!'

'Excuse me,' he said, sitting bold upright again, 'but I was suicidal a few minutes ago.'

'Oh, shut up!' she said and swiped the bottle off him again for another swig. 'So did you hear anything else from a potential blackmailer?'

Gideon shook his head.

'You can't keep pretending you're straight.'

'I don't see why not.' He looked at her and sighed, his shoulders slumping in defeat. 'I know. Just give me one last moment of denial.'

'Anything has to be better than lying if it's messing you up like this.'

'You think?'

'You drink too much.'

'Alcoholics usually do.' He turned and looked at her again. 'I'm not really that much in denial, Amelia. I'm not a fool, although I do sometimes choose to act like one. I know I need to sort myself out, it's just that it all seems so bloody overwhelming at times.'

'Why don't you try and cut down to start with?'

'Because I'm scared I can't.' He gave a sniffle and wiped his hand across his cheek. 'Just some dust,' he said as way of explanation.

Amelia fished about in her pocket and handed him a tissue. She waited until he'd blown his nose. 'Maybe if you were open about being gay you wouldn't feel the need to drink as much.'

'Very probably, but even contemplating that makes me dive for the bottle.'

'But with your friends beside you, it might not be as bad as you fear.'

He reached out and squeezed her hand again. 'I do love you,

Amelia. If it hadn't been for you these past few weeks I may very well have jumped for real tonight.'

'Judging by his reaction I think Toby would be a bit distraught at that too.'

'Oh please, I burned any chance of a relationship with Toby long ago.'

'I wouldn't be too sure of that. But I'd definitely suggest having a shower and a good sleep first before you have any deep and meaningful chats with him.'

'I think that may be a good idea, darling.'

'Here,' she handed him another tissue, 'just in case there's any more dust.'

They stood up and, arm in arm, walked back to the house.

36

Toby and Jack were in the kitchen when Amelia and Gideon returned to the house, shivering and completely drenched thanks to the impromptu hail shower that had caught them on their way back.

For all its retro psychedelic craziness, Amelia was delighted to be back in the painfully bright-orange kitchen, it was at least warming and cocooning, she thought, sitting down at the table opposite Jack who mouthed 'You okay?' to her. She nodded.

'Well, there's nothing quite like a near-death experience and being pelted by large stones of ice to sober one up,' Gideon joked feebly as he also sat down at the table.

Toby threw them each a towel and then brought over a cup of tea for them both before sitting down, arms folded.

'Thank you,' Gideon said meekly.

Amelia offered Gideon the whisky but he shook his head.

'I'm afraid I've been a colossal twat,' he said, taking a sip of his tea, his golden-brown tiger-eyes darting from face to face, as if testing the room for friendliness. 'I've been on a spiral of self-destruction and hell-bent on taking others with me it seems. I'm sorry.' He spread his hands out in a helpless manner. 'I've so much to say but I'm too tired to even know where to begin. Can this wait until the morning?'

Everyone nodded.

'Feel free to fill in the blanks, darling,' he said, giving Amelia's shoulder a squeeze, before taking his mug of tea and going on up to bed.

And Amelia told them the story, punctuated by mouthfuls of chocolate digestive and strong, hot tea.

They all sat in silence for a moment, taking it in.

'So, it looks like he really likes you,' Amelia said to Toby.

'After all that disclosure and you're still trying to matchmake?' Her brother rolled his eyes, shaking his head in mock despair. 'Gideon has so much baggage he needs his own valet.'

'But you like him too?'

Toby chuckled slightly. 'Yeah, despite him being quite often completely insufferable, I do. But there's no way I'd get involved with him until he sorts himself out. If we were to get involved, and I'm saying *if*, Ames, he'd need to be in a better place, otherwise he'd use me as a crutch instead of his drinking and then if we were to split up, or have an argument he would be tempted to go back to his self-destructive ways. He'd just perpetually swap one reliance for another unless he broke the cycle to start with.'

'When did you get so wise?' Amelia asked, quite impressed by his insight.

'Probably around the time you got some self-confidence and a backbone and started believing in yourself,' he retorted, sticking his tongue out at her.

Amelia looked between Jack and Toby. 'Do you think whoever is behind the sabotage and the warnings was also trying to scare Gideon, because that means they would have been at the Ouija board part of the evening?'

'It's very possible,' Jack agreed.

'If it is, we need to focus on that small group of people.' Amelia's lined notebook with her to-do lists was sitting at the end of the table and she pulled it over.

'Shit! You do actually have a suspect list!' Jack said, in wonder.

Toby sniggered and Amelia flipped her brother her middle finger.

'Present in the room were... Amelia, Archie, Beniamino, Gideon, Hamish, Jack, Lawrence, Mike, Ross, Sally, Toby and Tom,' Amelia read aloud.

'Oh my God, you've even put them in alphabetical order,' Toby said, getting up and looking at the list over her shoulder.

Ignoring him, Amelia circled Mike and Ross. 'They were in the room, but filming, so didn't have a chance to manipulate the glass.' She sighed, looking at the names. 'There was something odd with that whole night, between my costume being destroyed...' Amelia looked up to see Toby frowning at her. 'Yeah, sorry, I didn't bother mentioning that before. But there was also the *V for Vendetta* guy that was acting suspiciously and locked me in the room.' She looked at Toby. 'I was fine!'

Jack sat back in his chair, looking thoughtful. 'There is one thing that sets these incidents on this night apart from the others.'

'There is!' Amelia said, realisation dawning.

'There is?' Toby asked, reaching for a biscuit.

'Yes, everything was being documented by Beniamino that night,' Amelia said. 'I know he wasn't the *V for Vendetta* guy because when I was upstairs following the *Vendetta* person, I looked down and saw Beniamino and Mike walking through the hall.'

'It doesn't rule out more than one person being behind this,' Jack pointed out.

'True, but we've got to start somewhere. Wait there!' Amelia went out into the hall and returned a moment later with a padded envelope. 'This was delivered for Beniamino earlier, it's the latest sample of edited footage being returned, which includes the Hallowe'en party. I know it would be better to have the original but I don't know how to work any of the equipment in their editing room.'

'Hey, this is a start.'

Toby brought his laptop over and they inserted the disc and began to watch.

It was easy to forget what they were watching it for as they all got engrossed in the documentary. Although living through it all on a daily, hourly basis, the filmed version of events put together by the crew made everything seem far more glamorous and together. The tedium of getting the plumbing sorted was turned into a soap opera of amusing anecdotes thanks to Tom and his band of workers. Amelia was left helpless with laughter when they watched footage of Gideon making coffee one morning, oblivious to being filmed as he sang along to 'Bohemian Rhapsody' on the radio. He was terribly out of tune but threw everything into it especially when he started head-banging along to the guitar solo but misjudged it as he went to get milk which resulted in him head-butting the fridge door. There were some lovely scenes of Sally working on the Hallowe'en costumes, unselfconsciously chatting to the camera. Amelia got a lump in her throat when she watched her best friend say to camera how she'd stopped liking her job so much, that flitting from one country to another with no roots being laid down had once been so exciting but now felt lonely, and how she was so glad to visit Amelia and be able to just stop for a while to take stock.

There were shots of Amelia, sitting in the peace of the library, reading Flora's diary, and many of Toby talking to the camera as he prepared dinner.

There was also the time in the Whistling Haggis when Amelia fell into Jack and ended up with a pint over her head. Toby laughed uproariously as they watched the beer dripping down Amelia's face and Gideon drape over a scarf to cover her modesty. Then as Amelia and Gideon walked off, the camera hovered over Jack watching them go, a small smile playing on his lips.

'Oh my God, you're checking out my sister!' Toby said, laughing.

'What can I say, guilty as charged.' Jack laughed along. 'Hey, I told you I thought you were cute from the start,' Jack added to Amelia.

Toby cleared his throat and pointed at the screen to where the footage cut to the Hallowe'en party and again it was Jack and Amelia talking to one another.

'Look!' Amelia said. There in the background was a guy in a long black cloak but when they turned around they saw it was Darth Vader.

'Is that–?' Toby squinted.

'Nope,' Amelia said, peering at the screen. 'Oh, it's Hamish, in his pirate cape.'

'This may be fruitless, I hadn't realised just how many costumes involved long black cloaks. Oh look, there's me!' Right enough, Toby was standing, expertly making cocktails, spinning the cocktail shaker and throwing it up in the air.

'Show off,' Amelia said witheringly.

Then Gideon wandered into shot, looking spookily like the late David Bowie as Ziggy Stardust. Sitting like a barfly, watching Toby make drinks, they laughed and chatted together. There were some more general party shots spliced together, then, very clearly, the *V for Vendetta* costume floated past, pausing to look at the camera for a second before looking away.

They all peered closer to the screen and could see, beyond where Mike was filming, the *Vendetta* costume was now standing in the corner of the far room, motionless.

'Creepy,' Toby murmured.

They continued watching but nothing else came to light.

'Hey, it was always a long shot,' Jack said.

'Ooh, here's the Ouija board.'

They watched as everyone clustered around the table and sat down. The crew had done a great job of splicing the footage together to make it tense and spooky.

'*Maybe Amelia should do it,*' they heard Beniamino say.

Amelia laughed at the expression of herself on screen. 'I was horrified at the thought!'

'*I just thought with your connection–*'

'*I'm not a blood relation.*'

'*Closest thing to it though.*' The camera cut to Archie.

Then very audibly someone was heard saying 'bitch'.

'What the–' Toby said.

'Rewind that bit again,' Jack said as the footage moved on to Sally hamming it up as she asked if anyone was there.

They watched the scene again.

'Someone definitely says "bitch",' Jack said, 'at the very bit where Archie says you're the closest thing to a blood relation.'

'It's no coincidence,' Toby said quietly.

'Well, that's not creepy!' Amelia tried to make a joke of it.

'Can we tell who says it?' Toby asked.

More viewings didn't help.

'It's too whispery, you can't even tell if it's male or female, old, young, anything,' Jack said, frowning. 'And seeing this makes more sense as to why someone shot at me.'

'Really? It isn't just your winning way with people?' Amelia suggested.

Jack looked at the list of the people present before her. 'I think someone thinks they have the right to the inheritance over you.'

'Someone is targeting you to leave...' Toby agreed.

'...to have free rein to search for the treasure...' Amelia finished hollowly.

'Or if you're *completely* out of the way, maybe access to the inheritance if they think they're somehow related,' Toby added. 'But why shoot you?' he asked Jack. 'Wouldn't I be the more logical choice?'

'Yes, you would be as you'd inherit everything from me,' Amelia said.

'You *were* the intended target,' Jack said quietly. 'You were wearing the same jumper as I was.'

'Shit, yeah! I'd been wearing it all morning because I was working outdoors. But we don't look anything alike.' Toby pointed to his hair.

'I was wearing a hat. From a distance the height difference wouldn't be that obvious. You hadn't shaved for a couple of days...'

'Oh shit.'

'Hang on.' Amelia dug out Flora's diary and turned to the front page with the family tree.

'Of course, Archibald Campbell was a complete bastard but there weren't any hints that he'd fathered illegitimate children. But Charles...' she pointed at his name, 'beside him is the name Evelyn McCallum and a question mark.'

'And Helen McCallum,' Toby said, pointing to the other name.

'So it could be that Charles and this Evelyn had a child.'

'Or this Evelyn claims it's Charles's but there's no real evidence, hence the question mark hanging over it.'

'But someone is possibly trying to find evidence,' Jack said.

'It does all make a strange kind of twisted sense if you were a psycho!' Toby said, studying the family tree.

'Evelyn died in 2003, but Helen could still be very much alive. She'd be early seventies,' Amelia mused.

'I bet Archie would remember her.'

Amelia's hand flew to her mouth. Archie! The envelope!

'Toby! I left something important in your car, can I have your keys?'

'Sorry, sis, I gave the car to Sally and Hamish for the evening to go to their concert.'

Amelia sat back, frustrated. Tomorrow wasn't that far away, she'd be able to wait another few hours.

37

A melia was brought out of a deep sleep by the house's equivalent of the dawn chorus; workmen whistling along to the radio. She opened her eyes, momentarily surprised at where she was before remembering she and Jack had gone to the room Amelia had originally stayed in before the dead crow and blood-on-the-wall incident.

'Morning, sleepy.'

Amelia rolled over to see Jack smiling at her.

'Oh, you're still here?' she said in surprise.

'Mm-hmm, where did you think I'd go?' he asked in amusement, before realisation dawned. 'Ah, I guess your ex-asshole never stayed the night, did he?'

He sat up in bed, his hair even more tousled than ever.

'Amelia, I want to be completely open with you, especially after keeping so much a secret already. I'm not into playing games and all that nonsense about waiting so many days to text or to call for a second date. I like you and considering the things we got up to last night, I'd like to think you like me too.' He grinned. 'I want to spend time with you and hang out with you and do that unfashionable thing of being girlfriend and boyfriend. And hold hands and make mix tapes and–'

'I'd like that too,' Amelia said quickly, laughing as he kissed her. She did like Jack. Very much. And it felt liberating not to have that jumpy feeling she always had with Jonathan, wondering when he'd call... even *if* he'd call. To be having an actual relationship rather than a series of snatched moments made her stomach flip-flop with excitement.

'Although saying that, I am going to pop back to mine to grab a shower and a change of clothes and brush my teeth before we do any more hanging out together.'

'That sounds like a plan.'

She got out of bed and stood looking out the window at the garden as Jack got dressed. He came up behind her, circling his arms around her waist and resting his chin on her head.

'You've got a great view of the folly from here.'

'I know, I'm just imagining Dotty looking out the window, thinking about her love. I still can't believe it's Archie. I wonder if they had a signal, like a candle in the window or something like that, to arrange an encounter.' Amelia had told Jack all about Dotty's last letter and how Archie was Francis. She had so many questions she wanted to ask Archie and she was still keen to get hold of the envelope from Toby's car.

'And how are you feeling this morning after watching the footage from the Hallowe'en party?'

'Okay.' She was still a little freaked out after watching the Ouija board footage but now more determined than ever to find out who was behind all the threats.

'I think Toby was a bit unsettled when he realised he was more than likely the intended air rifle target.'

At that moment a workman knocked on the door saying they'd need access soon.

'I'm going to jump in the shower. And I should check on Gideon too.'

'Cool, I'll see you later on, how about lunch in the Whistling Haggis?' Jack said as he left the room.

'Sounds perfect.'

For once Toby wasn't bustling about the stove but sitting at the table with Gideon, their heads close together and deep in conversation. They jumped apart slightly when Amelia came into the kitchen.

'Morning!' Amelia said as she went to make a coffee.

'No Jack?' Toby asked.

'He's heading back to his for a bit.'

Gideon nodded and took a deep breath. 'I need to apologise about yesterday. And, well, all the other days before yesterday too.' He looked tired and a little drawn but there was also an air of calm about him.

'You really don't,' Amelia said, boiling the kettle.

Gideon looked down at the table, studying it for a long moment before looking back up. 'No, I really do. I've a lot of ground to make up and I need to start today. In fact, there is no time like the present,' he added with a flash of his usual spirit as he stood up just as Beniamino and Mike came in. 'Excuse me, but I've got a hair shirt to put on.'

'Is he okay?' Amelia asked as Toby got up from the table and came over to her.

'Do you know, I do believe he is.' Toby glanced back over at Gideon who was looking very serious as he talked to Beniamino. He turned back to Amelia with a grin. 'And how are you, you debauched wench?'

'I'm okay too,' she said, unable to keep the smile from her face.

'Stop looking so smug that you've had a shag.'

Amelia laughed and lobbed the wet dishcloth at him.

'I wonder what's going on?' Amelia said to Toby quietly as she looked back over at Gideon who was working out where to sit at the table as Mike set up his camera.

'Gideon's doing a piece to camera,' Toby whispered.

'What's he saying?'

'I think he's planning on coming out,' Toby whispered back.

'But last night he was distraught at the thought of anyone finding out! It's a bit of a quick turnaround to bare all to a camera.'

Toby laughed softly. 'Do you really think he could have done it any other way?'

'Shhhh! Guys!' Beniamino said. 'A little quiet so we can film this?'

Amelia had to hand it to Gideon, he knew how to speak to a camera. She and Toby watched his interview where he spoke honestly and candidly about his struggle with his sexuality. Amelia and Toby barely moved a muscle as they stood at the other end of the kitchen watching the interview take place, and at many points Amelia got a lump in her throat as Gideon very eloquently put across his feelings and broached the subject of his drinking. After an initial couple of questions, Beniamino just sat back and let Gideon talk.

'Wow, powerful stuff,' Toby said to Amelia as the interview wound up.

Gideon stood up and hurried out the door and Amelia could tell Toby was torn between letting him go and going after him.

'I'll give him a few minutes, then see if he wants a cup of tea,' he said, his eyes clouded with worry.

'He will be all right, you know,' Amelia said.

'I know. It's just not the same without his barbed comments and outrageously rude behaviour.'

'Don't worry, he'll be back to being insufferable in no time.'

Mike wandered over to them both.

'I'd absolutely no idea about Gideon. He's very brave being so honest. I hope anyone who was even thinking of blackmailing him about it will go and do one now. And I don't want to be crass about this, but that interview we did is absolute television gold. We'll be looking at TV awards for this. Don't you think, Ben?' he said to Beniamino who was looking at the playback on the camera.

'Um, yeah, gold,' he said a little distractedly. 'I'm just going to get this backed up and saved,' he said. Picking up his notes and taking the camera with him, he hurried off out the kitchen.

'I'd better go give him a hand,' Mike said and followed Beniamino.

Seconds later there was a slight rap on the door. Amelia turned to see Archie standing in the doorway.

'Archie! Hello! I was about to come and look for–' She stopped when she saw the look on his face. 'Is everything all right?'

'I just wondered if you'd seen Hamish and Sally. He wasn't at the farm this morning, which is really unlike him as he's never missed work. I've not been able to reach him on his phone either. I've a horrible feeling something's happened.'

'Okay, let's not panic, I'll go up and see if Sally came back here last night,' Toby said, leaving the kitchen.

'Maybe they both came back here and slept in?' Amelia hazarded, but not quite believing they'd have slept through all the drilling and hammering that had started up.

Archie nodded and stood, wringing his hands together as he politely declined Amelia's offers of tea and coffee. Although desperate to ask about his relationship with Dotty, Amelia knew now wasn't the time to bring it up. A couple of minutes later Toby returned, out of breath from running and shaking his head. 'The bed's not been slept in.'

Amelia took out her phone and silently cursed as she saw 'no signal' on her facia. Toby got his from out his pocket.

'I changed the network provider so I've better coverage,' he said, pressing a few buttons. 'Voicemail,' he said, before leaving a message for Sally to get in touch.

'Do you know whereabouts they were going?' Toby asked.

'Sally just said Ullapool, to see a band. She wasn't any more specific than that, then she said they were going back to Hamish's and she made a comment about having to get up early.'

'They're no there at Hamish's,' Archie said, rubbing his rough chin with his hand.

'They'd borrowed my car, was that there? Could they have gone for a walk and lost track of time?'

Archie shook his head. 'Your car wasnae there either, just Hamish's old jalopy.'

'Were they meeting up with anyone else to see the band with?' Toby asked.

'I don't know!' Amelia said, starting to worry.

'Okay,' Toby said, pressing more keys on his phone. 'I'm just going to give Ray a call, just in case...'

'In case they've been in an accident.' Archie nodded solemnly.

Archie and Amelia stood silently watching Toby as he spoke to the policeman.

'Right,' he said, hanging up. 'Good news is there hasn't been an accident reported. Ray is going to get in touch with the road traffic crew and they'll do a more thorough sweep of the stretch of road, paying close attention to any bends where there's a chance a car could swerve off. It's pretty much a single road from here to Ullapool and he's fairly optimistic any bright-red car will be easily spotted, especially at this time of year when there isn't much foliage.'

'Aye, and the big galoot could have run out of petrol or anything and he's so loved up he's probably no charged his phone properly. Love can make an eejit out of us all.'

'Grab a seat, Archie, I'll stick the kettle on,' Amelia said, taking Toby by the hand and leading him out to the boot room on the pretence of him getting more teabags down from a tall shelf.

'Maybe I'm being completely paranoid here, and I really hope I am, but... do you think this has anything to do with the recent threats? What if someone has done something to the car thinking you were driving it? Or was it because of the envelope? If Archie put information in it that has to do with the treasure...'

Toby peered back at Archie to make sure he wasn't listening. 'I honestly don't know. It could be I was the target but it could also be they've blown a tyre and are waiting for the AA in a local garage. Or... or they could have had an accident. Shit! I should never have let them take the car.'

'This isn't your fault!'

'But I let them take it. You don't drive a Ferrari because it's a safe ride and economical on petrol! And that's without taking anything else into consideration.' He shook his head. 'Oh God, maybe we are getting overly paranoid.'

Amelia nodded. 'But whatever happens, this is not your fault. We don't even know what "this" is yet!' Amelia whispered. 'I'm going to ask Archie what was in that envelope.'

'Wait!' Toby hissed, pulling Amelia back. 'We don't actually know much about Hamish, do we? What if he's behind all this?

He's local. He knows about the treasure. He could be Charles's illegitimate relation. He was at the party wearing a cloak and could easily have put a *Vendetta* mask over the top.'

'But then Sally...' Amelia trailed off, feeling sick at the thought her friend could be in danger.

She looked through the crack in the door to Archie.

'Unless he is a top-notch actor, I don't think he'd be in on it. Look at him, he's worried sick!' Then a thought struck her. 'Last night, just before they left, Hamish found the little trinket box, the one that Archie carved for Dorothea. He looked surprised that she'd had it.'

Toby's phone beeping made them both jump.

'It's Sally!' he said, his voice breaking with relief.

They both walked back into the kitchen and Archie stood up, looking at them expectantly.

'Sally sent a text, it says, *"Sorry guys but Hamish and I have gone AWOL for a couple of days. Don't be angry but we just want some time together. I'll see you soon".*'

'That's no like him.' Archie shook his head. 'I canny believe he'd be so thoughtless with the farm. I'm gonna kill him when I get hold of him. I need to go round and get to work and tell the lads what he's done,' Archie said, heading off.

Toby was already trying to call Sally back. 'It's just gone straight on to voicemail again,' he said to Amelia.

'There is something very odd about this,' Amelia said. 'Sally would never just go off with your car like this.'

'I know, but what if they have just decided to act completely immature and go off together. I mean, they could be heading off to get married for all we know!'

Just then Toby's phone rang.

'Sally?' Amelia asked expectantly.

Toby shook his head and answered and Amelia gathered it was Ray.

A few seconds later he hung up.

'I told him we'd had a text and because of that they're not treating it as a suspicious missing person. I can report the car as stolen and then the police would be on the lookout, but I don't really want them to get arrested over this if they have just taken off together.'

'This doesn't sit well with me,' Amelia said.

'Nor me,' Toby agreed, 'but at the moment, until we find out any more information there's not a lot we can do.'

38

When Amelia met up with Jack in the Whistling Haggis he also agreed it was strange behaviour from Sally and Hamish.

'Just with everything else that's happened lately, I don't like this either. Does anyone else know about them going missing?' Jack asked her.

'I don't think so.'

'Keep it like that. I'm going to head to Ullapool and have a proper look about and ask if they made it to the venue last night.'

'How will you get there?'

'Big Davey lets me borrow his van now and again. Stay around here and I'll phone the pub landline when I've had a chance to ask around.'

'Okay. Be safe.'

'Always.' He leant over and kissed Amelia before stealing a chip from her plate and heading up to the bar to talk to Davey.

Amelia very quickly and quietly whispered over to Toby to let him know what was going on.

'How are you?' She turned to Gideon.

'On sparkling form as usual, darling,' he said, flashing her a Hollywood smile. 'But it seems everyone else is despairingly boring without the veil of alcohol.'

Despite swearing off alcohol, Gideon had insisted he join everyone in the Whistling Haggis, saying he'd be even more depressed if he was to be sober all alone in the house. 'I'd be doing a hell of a lot better if you and your brother loosened up slightly. I don't know what's going on but you're acting like startled rabbits. I do hope you don't think I'm about to jump over the bar and attach my mouth to the gin optics,' Gideon chastised lightly. Amelia and Toby had decided not to let Gideon catch wind of anything that had happened with Sally and Hamish but clearly he was picking up on the tense atmosphere.

'We might as well tell him,' Toby said with a sigh as Gideon started to drum his fingers on the table.

'Ooh, tell me what?' Gideon immediately perked up at the sniff of gossip.

'You do it, I'll go get another round,' Amelia said, standing up. 'Want some crisps?'

'Yes please, surprise me with the flavour,' Gideon said, looking at Toby expectantly.

Amelia walked up to the bar and sat on one of the bar stools, waiting until Big Davey had finished serving another customer.

'Same again and can I have an Old-Fashioned, please?'

'Don't get many calls for them around here,' Davey said as he went off to get the drinks.

Archie came up and sat beside her at the bar.

'Hi. Any word?' Amelia asked.

Archie shook his head. 'Nothing, his phone has either been turned off or he's run out of battery.'

'Please try not to worry.'

Archie patted the back of her hand. 'Aye, they'll be grand, wait and see.'

Davey came back with a tumbler and put it down in front of Amelia. 'One Old-Fashioned,' he said, popping a cocktail cherry into the glass with a flourish.

'An Old-Fashioned!' Archie chuckled. 'That's what Dorothea used to drink.'

'I know, she recommended I find a signature cocktail. I thought I'd toast her with her favourite and then steadily work my way through a cocktail book and find my own.'

Big Davey chuckled and slapped his hand on his head. 'Hang on a minute, that reminds me. The last time she was in here, Dorothea gave me something, it was a cocktail book and she asked me to hang on to it. I'd totally forgotten about it until now. Now, what was it she said about it.' He scowled down at the bar as he tried to remember. 'Aye, something like I could use it, but only for a reference as long as I always kept it here until one day when I'd know what to do with it.' He looked up at Amelia. 'I guess now's as good a day as any to give it to you, if you're looking for a cocktail, wouldn't you say?'

Amelia did nothing but nod her head, having no idea what she was about to be given. It wouldn't surprise her if it was a treasure map of the estate with a big X written on it and 'find ruby here' written beside it.

'I'll away get it,' Davey said.

'That sounds just like Dorothea.' Archie chuckled. 'She loved her mysteries.'

'I know about you and my godmother,' Amelia said, taking a sip of the drink.

The older man nodded. 'Aye, I guessed you would.'

'I only found out a couple of days ago. She told me in a letter she'd left me.'

He gave a little chuckle. 'She was one for her letters, was

Dotty. We left little notes and suchlike for each other over the years, in a box.'

'In the folly.'

'Aye, you found a way in then!'

'Yes, and I found the little heart-shaped box, had you been in to remove it all?'

He nodded. 'There had been a few odd things going on at the house and I didn't want someone else, other than you, to stumble across the private keepsakes. I realised I'd dropped the little box when I got home, I went back over the grounds and the folly again but couldn't find it.'

'I must have picked it up by that point. So, what kind of odd things had been going on at the house?'

Archie puffed his cheeks out. 'Lights at night, which I knew wasn't down to Jack. I even came across someone trying to get in a window and scared them off.'

'Did you get a look at them?'

'No. It was dark and they had their hood up.'

'Archie, last night, just before Hamish and Sally drove off, Hamish found the little carved box and told me it was you who'd carved it and I said it had belonged to Dotty.'

'Oh!'

'I'm guessing he didn't know about you and Dotty.'

'No, he didn't.'

'I'm sorry to ask this, but do you think there's any way Hamish could be involved in any of the strange goings-on up here? Possibly looking for the treasure?'

'My grandson?' Archie looked completely taken aback. 'No chance. He'll no doubt give me a right roasting over my dalliance with your godmother when I see him. I mean, once I married his grandmother, I never once strayed, it was purely platonic correspondence with Dotty. Hamish is a good lad. A very good lad. It's what makes this disappearance all so strange.

Girl or no girl, he has his head screwed on the right way. And anyway, Hamish wouldn't be looking for any buried treasure as he's more than all right for money. His clothes are all worn and he doesn't drive a flash car but don't let that fool you. My son, his father, married money so Hamish has grown up with the finer things in life but he chooses to farm and he makes a good living at that too. He's not materialistic in the slightest.

'But equally, he's no some romantic dreamer either who'd go running off with a bonnie lassie and forget about his responsibilities. That's why this business doesn't sit right with me.'

That's what Amelia's gut said too.

'Archie, do you remember a Helen McCallum? She was born in 1947 to Evelyn McCallum. There was a possibility Helen's father was Charles Campbell.'

Archie shook his head. 'The names don't ring any bells with me, I'm afraid. There aren't any McCallums around here that I know of.'

'Don't worry, Archie, we're going to get to the bottom of it. You know the envelope you gave me? That was in the car along with Sally and Hamish. I didn't have a chance to look at it, what was in it?'

'Love letters, photographs, some papers and little notes, nothing of any great value, apart from sentimental.'

Just then Davey returned with an old navy-and-silver cloth-bound book.

'Here you go!'

Excited at what lay inside, Amelia turned the heavy book in her hands. Entitled 'Cocktails and how to mix them', it was an all-encompassing retro guide to 1950s soirees as it had extra chapters on accompanying canapés and advice on how to host the perfect party. Amelia flicked through the book, half expecting a letter addressed to her in Dotty's handwriting to flutter to the floor, but there was nothing loose caught between the pages.

'Was there anything that came with it?' Amelia asked in disappointment.

Davey shook his head. 'Not that I can remember. I've never even looked through it as we don't get much call for cocktails here, although we do seem to be expanding our clientele,' he said, nodding over at Gideon, who was now holding court to a group of young women much to Toby's bemusement.

'I'll catch up with you later,' Archie said, finishing his pint and shrugging his jacket back on before leaving. Davey went off to serve someone else.

Amelia sat for a moment, unable to believe there wasn't anything within the book's pages. She flicked through it once more in case she'd missed something. For Dotty to be so specific about finding a signature cocktail and to have left a cocktail book aside for 'the right moment' was too much of a coincidence. As a last hope Amelia turned to the page with the recipe for an Old-Fashioned to see if there was anything there, but frustratingly, there was just a recipe for an Old-Fashioned.

Then Amelia had a flash of inspiration. She looked up the index to see if 'Fluffy Duck' was there. It was. With shaking hands Amelia turned to the page with that cocktail on it.

And there! In the margin, in very faint pencil was the sentence, '*Never judge a book by its cover.*'

The cover! She opened the book once again and there, where the paper was sealed against the hard cover on the inside, Amelia could feel it was slightly raised. She got out her Swiss army penknife and began to work at the sealed-down edge, now convinced it had been lifted and re-stuck after concealing something.

Finally, Amelia managed to peel back enough of the inside cover page to reveal there was indeed something tucked inside.

She pulled out some folded-up pages, instantly recognising the rather shaky writings of Flora.

26th February 1948

I have given in and paid off Evelyn McCallum, that sly, deceitful girl. She showed me the child, a girl, just four months old. It bears no resemblance to Charles, or Archibald or me, or anyone else in this family, but I have to take her word for it as she has told me she could make trouble for me if I didn't pay her money. I gave her a large amount, far more than she deserves, and I told her that it was a one-off payment. I made precautions that she does not come back for more money as I drew up a lawyer's letter and made her sign it. She is of no great intelligence and I believe she was scared by such a formal response. Part of her payment involved her leaving this village. I know not where she is going and I care less. I tried to look on her child with love but felt nothing apart from pity that it has been born into her greedy arms. I have no doubt Charles lay with her but from what the locals say about Evelyn McCallum, he is not the only one. Working out the dates of a possible conception do not add up as Charles was away for a large part of the time when she became with child, but I do not wish any closer inspection paid to me or my family.

And there, clipped to the back of the diary entry was a tiny little cut-out piece from the paper. Dated June 1967 was a marriage announcement of Helen McCallum, aged nineteen, (daughter of Evelyn McCallum) marrying a Robert Blair, aged twenty-two.

She quickly folded up the pieces of paper and slipped them into her pocket as she closed over the book.

'Ready to try another cocktail?' Davey said, coming back over.

'Possibly a Singapore Sling later.'

'I might be needing that book back then.' He said through a laugh. He then leant a little closer to her over the bar. 'Just thought I'd let you know, your, er, friend hasn't checked out yet. He's staying another night and he's just sat down at a table,' Big Davey said, nodding to one of the back alcoves of the bar.

Amelia glanced around the corner and saw Jonathan slouched over a table, reading the paper. He looked up and Amelia cursed under her breath as he immediately stood up and headed over.

39

'Amelia!' Jonathan said, smoothing down his shirt and tie and giving her a winning smile as he leant nonchalantly against the bar. In his fitted shirt and Savile Row suit Jonathan looked woefully out of place in the Whistling Haggis.

'I thought you were leaving,' Amelia said, barely able to hide her annoyance.

'Faint heart never won fair maid,' he said in a smug way that set Amelia's teeth on edge. Had she really ever been taken in by him? Was he always this smarmy?

'I'm not some maid to be won, Jonathan. The sooner you understand we are completely and utterly over the better.'

'But if you'd just listen to me for ten minutes, I–'

'So you could try and bully me into taking you back? I'm not interested, Jonathan. I am not being coy. I am not stringing you along so that when I think I have made you suffer enough I can turn round and say let's give it another go. We will never be together.'

'But, Amelia–'

'I don't like you!' Amelia said slowly in the hope it would sink in.

At that moment Ross came over to her. Amelia hadn't noticed the documentary crew come into the pub.

'Is he annoying you?' Ross asked her quietly. 'Want me to keep him out your hair?'

Amelia must have looked grateful as Ross patted her on the shoulder as he loudly said,

'Jonathan, mate, let me buy you a drink. Come on over and sit with me.'

Jonathan, grateful for a friendly audience, dutifully followed as Ross winked at her over his shoulder.

Mike and Lawrence sat down with Toby and Gideon, as Beniamino came up to the bar beside Amelia, waiting to be served.

'Amelia, how is Gideon?' the Italian said, looking agitated.

'Um, he's okay. I think.'

Beniamino rubbed his hand over his face. 'I worry he's putting on the brave front, you know?'

'Don't worry about him.' Amelia doubted Gideon would ever do this as he revelled in the drama and attention of feeling torturous.

But Beniamino didn't look pacified. 'I fear I have done something very bad and very unprofessional.'

Amelia stood still, her imagination leaping in all directions as she wondered what Beniamino could be talking about. He leant closer.

'May I speak with you frankly?'

'Of course.'

'Gideon has just given me absolute television gold. He's come out as gay and wants it included in the documentary. He speaks movingly to camera, it's very beautiful.'

'You should be pleased, surely.'

'I am, but I feel very guilty as this has all come about from my own meddling.'

'What have you done?'

'The night of the Hallowe'en party, when we decided to do the Ouija board. I was the one who moved the glass to spell out the words. The words that triggered Gideon's upset and depression.'

'You'd seen Gideon with Toby? Why would you want to scare him like that?' Amelia was surprised as Beniamino didn't seem like the blackmailing type.

'No!' Beniamino shook his head vehemently. 'I just thought it would add a little spice if I put something cryptic. My thinking was that surely *someone* would be hiding something in a roomful of people. I thought I'd get an amusing reaction but I hadn't realised it would be quite such a *big* reaction. And it could have had a very different outcome if Gideon had well... you know...'

'You weren't to know,' Amelia said but she did think it was bloody stupid of him.

'But it was wrong of me to try and manipulate a documentary. It's not as if we needed anything else as the footage we have is great. I think I may have got carried away with the evening's entertainment.'

'I'm guessing you haven't told Gideon this?'

'No, I don't know how he'll take it.'

Amelia couldn't shed any light on that either. Gideon could choose to take it as a positive, and look on it as the trigger for turning his life around or he could possibly retreat back into the closet and carry on drinking.

'I know I must tell him so he knows no one wishes to blackmail him. I will get some Dutch courage, then let him know.'

Not really knowing what else to say to Beniamino, Amelia took her Old-Fashioned, the other drinks and some crisps back to the table and sat back down next to Toby and Gideon who were deep in conversation now that Gideon's fan club had moved away.

The next couple of hours passed by incredibly slowly for Amelia as she couldn't help but clock-watch, wondering how Jack was getting on tracking Hamish and Sally in Ullapool. Eventually, Amelia went up to the bar to ask Davey to double-check the phone was working properly. It was.

Ross had done a good job of keeping Jonathan out of her way but her ex was now very drunk and kept looking over at her, trying to catch her eye, and Amelia knew it wouldn't be long before he came over to talk to her.

'You okay?' Toby asked her.

'I just wish I could go back to the house but I can't until Jack calls me, and then there's Gideon...' She trailed off as she looked over to where Gideon and Beniamino were talking. After a couple of stiff drinks the director had clearly decided to come clean about the Ouija board incident.

'Here,' Toby slid his phone across the table to her, 'take this with you and I'll call you on it as soon as Jack calls here, okay? And don't worry about Gideon, I'll deal with any fallout.'

'Okay, that would be brilliant,' she said with a grateful smile, and grabbing her jacket, hurried out of the pub.

Back at the house Amelia sat at the kitchen table and opened Toby's laptop. She unfolded the diary entry and newspaper cutting and did a search for the name Helen Blair along with her birth date. There were a lot of hits. She made herself a coffee and settled down for a long night.

~

Toby's phone ringing jolted her awake only an hour later.

Feeling slightly disorientated from falling asleep, she answered.

'They've found Sally and Hamish. They're going to be okay!' Toby said, his relief apparent. 'Jack found my car parked behind the concert venue and he started asking around. Someone remembered seeing them, both really drunk. There were a couple of empty shop units nearby. Jack called the police and they searched them and found Hamish and Sally. They'd been tied up and gagged. They're shaken up but they'll be okay.'

Amelia felt sick at the thought of Sally and Hamish going through that ordeal as they must have been terrified. For Sally's sake, Amelia was also relieved Hamish had nothing to do with it.

'Did they say who it was, who did it?'

'The police got Jack to stay outside and he couldn't get to them. But he did look through the car window. The envelope was gone.'

'Oh shit, so they were taken because of this stupid bloody treasure.'

'We don't know for sure, but it looks possible. It obviously wasn't a car theft as they left it there. Jack phoned me from the car and he's on his way back now.'

'What about Sally and Hamish?'

'They're being taken to the local hospital. Looks like they'd been drugged rather than them being drunk. We can phone in a couple of hours to see how they are. Apart from a touch of dehydration, they're physically fine, but the police need to speak to them first.'

'Okay, thanks, Toby.'

She hung up and poured away her cold coffee.

Settling back in front of the computer screen to carry on her searches she discovered the laptop's battery had run out. Growling in annoyance, Amelia looked about for the charger. So far she hadn't found anything of relevance pertaining to any of the Helen McCallums or Blairs she'd looked at but she had to start somewhere and now, more than ever, she wanted to track down who was behind Sally and Hamish's abduction.

A quick look around the kitchen counters didn't reveal the laptop's charger. If it was in Toby's room she'd possibly never find it as he took messy to a whole new level.

The documentary crew's equipment bags were piled up on the floor and Amelia figured there was bound to be a charger amongst them. She pulled up the top rucksack but all she found in it was some confusing-looking film equipment, a notebook and a lot of broken biros. She hauled up a much chunkier-looking leather bag and a quick look inside revealed a jumble of extension cables and chargers. Amelia began untangling the most likely-looking one and as she did so, her eyes fell upon the front of the leather bag. There was a little brass plate engraved with initials. She looked at it for a moment or two, letting it sink in. '*R. B.*'

Ross... Amelia realised she had no clue what Ross's surname was. Her heart started beating wildly in her chest, her nerves jittery. Just because it began with a B didn't automatically mean it was Blair, she told herself. She tried to think if there had ever been a time when he'd talked about himself. Apart from knowing he was from Glasgow, Amelia didn't know anything else about him.

Beniamino would know! She went to pick up Toby's phone to call the Whistling Haggis but remembered Ross was there and she didn't want him to get suspicious. Checking Beniamino's room was a better idea in case he had any correspondence or information on the others.

With her mind turning over the possibility of Ross being behind all the incidents, Amelia walked out into the hall.

Standing, swaying just a couple of feet from her, was Jonathan.

40

Jonathan looked rough, his wide-stanced drunken sway so exaggerated he looked like an extra from *The Walking Dead*.

He lifted his hand slowly in what Amelia took to be a greeting.

'Come on, let's sit you down,' she said. She turned him round and guided him towards the drawing room, pulling back slightly from the harsh boozy smell that seemed to be seeping from his pores. There was something horribly familiar about the smell, a smell she instantly associated with a bad feeling; the same odd smell she remembered from Hallowe'en when she'd been locked in the room.

It was spirity and...

'Jonathan, what have you been drinking?'

'Ssshambuca sots. Shotsh. Shotz.'

'Sambuca?' Of course! Aniseed. That's why it reminded her of Bonjela. She remembered Sally saying Ross had been downing sambuca shots one night at the Whistling Haggis. The evidence seemed to be stacking up against him.

'Jonathan, where's Ross?'

'In the pub, I shaid I was going to bed, and he went back to see your brother and the other filmers but then I shneak, sne... snucked out to see you.'

'Lucky me. Why don't you sit down here,' she led him to one of the wing-backed chairs and gently pushed him into it, 'and when I come back we can have a nice chat.'

'Yeah. You need to listen to me...' He closed his eyes and within seconds was snoring.

Thankfully, Ross was still at the Whistling Haggis but Amelia didn't know how long she'd have so she needed to be as quick as possible.

She bounded up the stairs and into Beniamino's room. Luckily, he was a fastidiously organised man and she found a leather document binder laid out on his dressing table inside of which was a series of emails he'd printed out in date order. Amelia flicked through them. Part of her still hoped she was wrong and, despite the mounting evidence, Ross was innocent. She felt unsettled to think someone with such a horrible agenda had sat with her at dinner, chatted to her on walks back from the pub, even slept under the same roof as her.

Amelia turned to the back of the emails, starting with the oldest. There was some toing and froing about time schedules and budgets and Beniamino airing his concerns about working with Gideon. Then there was a host of correspondence over the mugging and death of the guy that was meant to work with them. Then another email about the replacement: Ross. Beniamino had scribbled at the bottom 'CV – appendix A'. Amelia quickly flicked to the back of the papers and there, under 'appendix A' was the CV for Ross Blair, replacement sound technician and editor. And at the very top was his photo, in which he had a beard.

Just like the man who'd gone into Ullapool library to ask for the information on Stone Manor.

Amelia felt sick. She tidied up the papers and slotted them back into the document folder.

She let herself out of Beniamino's room and as she did so she glanced across to Ross's room. Slowly, she walked towards it. She didn't know what, if anything, she was likely to find in it but she was going to have a look.

Hands shaking with nerves, she turned the handle and the door swung open. She flicked on the light and looked around; it was still as neat and tidy as the first time she'd been in it when she'd been looking for the secret passageway. In fact, the room was remarkable by just how unremarkable it was. Just as she remembered from before, there was nothing amiss, apart from the squeaky floorboard. She was about to close the door over when a thought struck her. A floorboard tended to squeak when walked over a lot or if it didn't fit properly. The placement of the squeaky floorboard wouldn't have a lot of footfall. The house was solidly built and had been well maintained over the years, so why would there be one squeaky floorboard? Unless it had been lifted up...

Amelia walked over to it and as soon as her foot landed on the board she could feel it soft and springy beneath her weight. She went to the edge of the room and began to roll the rug back to expose the boards. There was no nail holding the squeaky one in place. Amelia knelt down and lifted the board. There, nestled under the floor was rolled-up papers of house plans, newspaper articles and the brown envelope Archie had given her that had been in Toby's car. She lifted it up and tipped the contents out. There were photos and letters, she recognised Dotty's handwriting and what looked to be letters to Dotty from Archie, but there, in the middle of all the mementos were the missing pages of Flora's diary. Quickly scanning the subject matter of them gave Amelia no clue as to why they'd been ripped out and kept, but at the top of these pages were random words and locations, like 'cellar, exit only, no entry to house'. It was a list of all the secret passages and possible locations of the treasure! Clearly, Flora had scribbled them down randomly throughout her diary as little addendums. Dotty must have removed them all and kept them hidden in the folly. Obviously, none of them had led to the ruby otherwise Dotty would have found them but she didn't want them turning up in just anybody's hands to reveal the secrets of the house.

Finding the envelope was proof beyond doubt that Ross was behind the abduction of Sally and Hamish.

She needed to call the police. And get word to Toby to warn him. Amelia checked her pocket for Toby's phone. It wasn't there. Damn, she realised she'd left it on the kitchen table.

Stuffing the contents back into the envelope and taking it with her, Amelia ran out of Ross's room and bolted down the stairs. She'd just reached the bottom of them when she heard the front door slam closed. She turned, hoping to see Jack or Toby but, instead, Ross stood looking at her.

'Oh hi!' she said, hoping to sound as normal as possible, inconspicuously moving the envelope behind her back. She couldn't let Ross think she was onto him.

'Thanks for looking after Jonathan. He still managed to find his way here though.' She laughed slightly, hating that it sounded terribly forced. 'I was just about to walk him back to the pub.'

Ross took a step forward and looked into the drawing room where Jonathan was still snoring loudly.

'I don't think he'll be going anywhere in a hurry. I think it would be best if he slept it off. Good evening?'

'Yup. Quiet. Just needed a bit of thinking time. All the decor stuff needs decisions, you know.'

'Oh, I know what you mean! It's hard to think at times with all the noise going on with the workmen.'

'Mmmm.' Amelia tried to smile but her mouth was so dry from nerves her top lip stuck to her teeth and she realised she was probably grimacing at him.

'Oh! Did you hear that Sally and Hamish were found?'

Amelia hesitated, not sure how she should react. 'Really?'

There was a beat before Ross laughed and shook his head. 'See, that's what gave you away, Amelia. Not so clever after all. Trying to play the long game, judge my reaction before committing yourself to yours?'

'What–'

'You see, I know you know. I heard Toby call you at the bar. Which means I don't have an awful lot of time left because we all know what a blabbermouth that Sally can be and how she'll soon be shooting her mouth off about her ordeal and then you might put two and two together and work it all out. I should have killed them and dumped their bodies and let everyone think they'd eloped together. But you see, I'd only really wanted a couple of deaths on my conscience. In fact, I'd started all this off not wanting any, but I soon realised it wasn't going to work out that way.' He shook his head sadly. 'But I still want to keep it to just the ones that matter. Yours and your brother's. But now, there's going to be a little more collateral damage to work out.' He looked off towards Jonathan. 'Although I'll actually enjoy killing him as he really is a complete wanker.'

Amelia, who had been frozen, took the chance of Ross looking away to turn and race down the corridor, but Ross was fast and Amelia had just reached the kitchen door when he caught up with her and slammed her head into the wall.

She reeled back from the impact and fell to the floor, pain searing through her head.

'That was silly.' Ross tsk-tsked as he pulled her back up by the hair.

And then, for a split second, behind the kitchen door,

Amelia caught sight of Gideon, crouched down, eyes wide with terror as he looked out at her through the crack. But then Ross yanked Amelia away, dragging her back to the drawing room.

Ross roughly shoved her into the chair next to Jonathan's. Still dazed from the bang on the head, Amelia tried to get back up again but Ross hit her hard across the face.

She tasted blood.

This was not good. She needed to stall for time in the hope Gideon would run and get help or find Toby's phone and call.

'What are you going to do?' she asked, her lip feeling swollen and strange.

'I'm going to kill you,' he said matter-of-factly, looking down at her.

'But why?'

'Because you have swanned in here to take ownership of something that should be mine. You and your brother have stolen this from me. You have no right!'

'Dotty left it to me,' Amelia said slowly as it was painful to talk. She touched the back of her hand to her mouth and it came away with a smear of blood. 'Do you think it's yours just because you might be Charles's illegitimate grandson?'

'Shut up!' Ross screamed, bearing down on her, his eyes bulging and the veins on his forehead standing out.

Amelia recoiled in terror, but then Ross began to pace, composing himself.

She knew her only hope was to keep him talking for as long as possible.

'How did you find out about Charles?' Amelia asked.

Ross stopped pacing to look at her. 'My grandmother would talk about this place like it was some magical kingdom, like it was fucking Brigadoon.' He looked around. 'She loved the place, despite being made to feel like a dirty whore for getting pregnant. You know, it wouldn't surprise me if she'd been raped by that bastard Charles. Folk like him always take without asking.

'She would always tell me about the treasure that should be mine, all the gold and the artefacts stored up in the house. They were my bedtime stories every night. They were mine for the taking, that's what she'd say. She was going to turn up and claim them for us. My mother wanted nothing to do with it, figured it was all romantic nonsense. After my gran died, I gradually forgot about the stories but then I read about Dorothea Campbell-Delaney dying and it all came back. There was this massive house and estate and all the treasure just waiting for its rightful owner to turn up. And then I heard the old bitch had left it to some non-blood relation. I came up to do a recce and it wasn't long before I heard about the legend of the lost treasure. I went to the local library to do some research and that's when I discovered all about the hidden rooms and passageways, it was a puzzle waiting to be solved. But I couldn't get close to the house; between Jack and that old interfering man, someone was always sniffing about. I'd been camping out nearby but had to keep moving on in case I got caught. And then, like a sign, I heard about the documentary.'

'So are you a sound engineer or is that just a lie?' Amelia asked.

'Oh, that's my trade all right.'

'But you had to make sure you were picked for the job. You mugged the original guy, didn't you?'

'I was presented with the opportunity to render him unemployable.'

'He died.'

Ross shrugged. 'Collateral damage.'

'So you changed your appearance by shaving off your beard and came back up to Stone Manor to kill me and get the treasure?'

'You know, I didn't start off wanting to kill you. I just wanted you to leave, to fuck off out my way so I could find the treasure, but you're bloody stubborn. You wouldn't go,' he shouted in exasperation and started to pace the floor again.

'You were the one to start with the headless horseman stories.' Amelia remembered back to the night they were all walking home and he'd started the talk of ghosts and hauntings.

'Yeah, although I knew that wouldn't be enough to send someone running scared.'

'The brick with the note?'

'Yes, that was quite exhilarating.'

Amelia gave a half laugh as she realised how he'd done it. 'You were upstairs. If you knew about the secret passageways you could have slipped through to Sally's room, gone down the back stairs, out through the false wall into the cellar, break the padlock to get out, run round, throw the brick, and then you just had enough time to get back inside and up to Sally's room before slipping back into yours again, then come down the stairs.'

'Yes, I timed it so I'd be seen coming down the stairs.'

'You already knew about some of the secret passages but you didn't go for the obvious and take Sally's room but the one next to it.'

'Naturally. I didn't want it to look too obvious, just in case you found the passageway. But then I realised you just weren't going to leave. And I had no idea where the treasure could be buried. That's when I realised it would be better if you were out the way permanently, because that would give me much more time to find the treasure. But then I had a brainwave. If I could also find Charles's body I could get DNA proof that all this belonged to me! I would be the rightful heir. Then your brother and your friend turned up. I stupidly hadn't realised you had any relations as Dorothea left this only to you. Poor sod couldn't have been as much of a favourite.'

'You broke into the lawyers' offices, didn't you?'

'I did. I wanted to see if you had a will drawn up. As I suspected, everything went to your brother but I also wanted to check there weren't any other siblings waiting in the wings to inherit this from you.'

'You shot Jack, thinking it was Toby.'

'Yes, I did, not one of my finest moments as I missed and got the wrong guy, but yes, that was me.'

Amelia sat taking it all in for a second before asking, 'The night of the party. Were you planning on killing me?'

'When I locked you into the room?' He paused to think. 'I'm not sure, but possibly yes. I had originally planned to search the house some more for the treasure. Despite living in the house, there had been surprisingly few opportunities to search the rooms and I figured a party would be the perfect distraction as everyone would be busy elsewhere. But I didn't figure on you doing a Nancy Drew and following me. You really are a meddling little bitch.'

'The cloak?'

'Oh, that was flimsy enough to pack into the pocket of my costume, I could take it on and off at will and kept the mask in my inside pocket too.'

Now the ringing in Amelia's ears had lessened slightly and she strained to hear if she could make out sirens in the distance but it was worryingly quiet. She realised she was in a lot of danger; Ross was completely insane.

'You're not going to get away with this.'

He made a pained expression. 'You disappoint me with such a lame response. Of course I'll get away with it. I didn't show Sally or Hamish my face. I drugged their drinks and by the time I caught up with them after the concert I was wearing a mask.'

Amelia realised Ross was completely deluded as he really did believe he could get rid of her and then move into Stone Manor and find the treasure and live happily ever after. Dotty had been right, the Amor Rubra was cursed.

'How did you know about the envelope?'

'I saw Archie give it to you in the Whistling Haggis. The beauty of editing all the film footage was that I was able to piece things together. I knew you had a diary and that you'd found letters.'

'You went through my things looking for it.'

'Yes, although you always carried them with you. Even when you took a bath.'

Amelia felt sick.

'But now, I've been presented with the perfect set-up.' He nudged Jonathan's leg with his boot. 'Angry, jealous ex-lover gets paralytically drunk, gives his buddy the slip by saying he's going to bed but actually comes here. He played right into my hands as I was feeding him the lines, telling him how he shouldn't believe your rejection and how he should come here and try and talk to you. And look! He decided to bring the antique pistol from the Whistling Haggis.' Out from the waistband of his jeans Ross produced an old-fashioned firearm. 'Oh, and it does work, I primed Jonathan to ask Davey lots of questions about it tonight, each time he went up to get another round in, which will make him look even more guilty. Obviously, there's going to be a tussle. You've already been hit by him a couple of times.' He gestured to her face. 'Isn't domestic abuse shocking? Oh, I know he hasn't actually hit you but I'll be able to create a scene which will tick the DNA boxes, it's great the knowledge you pick up when you film forensic science documentaries.'

'Shame you haven't filmed anything about living with psychosis.' Amelia knew she was playing a dangerous game by goading someone who had completely lost touch with sanity but she needed to keep him talking. Surely Gideon would have managed to get to the pub and be back at the house by now?

'I'm just unsure of the final act, whether I have Jonathan wake up to see you in a pool of your own blood, which he's also covered in. He'll feel so guilty he'd probably just confess it all, or possibly kill himself too. Or do I not take the risk and finish him off here, too, in a murder suicide, like a modern-day, Scottish version of Romeo and Juliet. Or maybe you could inflict a fatally defensive blow as you take your dying breath...' He gave a little giggle.

By now, Amelia's head had stopped throbbing enough for her to be able to look around to see if there was any possible weapon to hand. The fire poker was too far away to reach in time, as was the candlestick on top of the mantlepiece. Then Amelia remembered one of Gideon's less savoury housekeeping habits of leaving his empties lying about instead of recycling them. She was constantly retrieving them from under chairs and sofas, and his bed.

She knew she only had one chance for this to work. She really hoped Gideon's epiphany into sobriety hadn't gone hand in hand with tidiness.

She clutched her head and gave a groan, tipping forward. Bingo! She could see the neck of a whisky bottle under her chair. She slumped forward just a little bit more, ending up on her hands and knees on the floor.

'Come on, sit up, we've barely started yet,' Ross said as he marched over to her and gave her a swift kick in the ribs. Quick as she could, Amelia turned and hugged his legs, just below the knees and pulled him off balance. Reaching under the chair for the bottle, she yanked it out just as Ross started to sit up, swearing at her. With all her might Amelia brought the glass bottle smashing down on Ross's head. He fell back against the carpet, motionless.

41

Amelia jumped over Ross's sprawled legs and ran to the hall, nearly careering into Gideon, who was waiting with one of Toby's cast-iron Le Creuset frying pans in his hands, ready to strike.

His cry of rage turned to relief when he saw it was Amelia and he dropped the pan with a heavy clunk, to the floor.

'Why didn't you get out!' Amelia said.

'I wasn't about to leave you here with that psycho, darling! I couldn't believe it when I heard him talking. I'd been making tea but hid so he wouldn't think I was here in the hope I could overpower him and help you.'

'Did you call for help?'

'I tried. But the Whistling Haggis line was engaged. I tried the police but the phone died before I could tell them the story.'

Amelia suddenly felt very alone knowing there wasn't a string of cars with flashing blue lights heading towards them.

'Come on, we need to get out of here.'

They ran to the front door but it was locked. 'Shit, he must still have the key on him,' Amelia said, pulling at the door frantically.

'The back door,' Gideon said, and they started to run towards it.

They were almost at the kitchen when a shot fired out.

Amelia screamed, covering her head with her hands as part of the chandelier shattered and rained glass down on her.

'STOP!'

Amelia and Gideon skidded to a stop and turned to see Ross standing pointing the gun at them, blood pouring down the side of his head.

'Told you it worked,' he said, grinning cockily. 'I see we have another addition to the party. This makes it trickier, but not impossible. Clearly Jonathan didn't know about your great coming-out announcement, Gideon, and still sees you as a threat to him rekindling his love with Amelia and very sadly you will get caught up in the crossfire. Now, who do I kill first? Eeny meeny miny moe... Oh dear. Night, night, Amelia.'

Ross swung the gun slightly round to the right, aiming it at Amelia, and pulled the trigger. Amelia just had time to let out a startled scream before Gideon pushed her out the way and they both landed on the floor together.

'Shit, darling, I may have just done my first selfless act,' Gideon said with a laugh as Amelia disentangled herself from him. 'Bloody ironic it's probably my last,' he said, looking down at his stomach to where a large circle of blood was spreading across his shirt.

'Gideon!' Amelia whimpered as Gideon gave a cough and fell back against the floor, eyes wide with panic.

'Oh shit, Gideon...'

'Run, Amelia, get the hell out of here,' he said through gritted teeth.

Amelia looked over at Ross. Something had clearly gone wrong with the gun as he was shaking it and pulling the trigger but nothing was happening.

'Looks like it's just you and me, one on one, babe,' Ross said, throwing the gun away.

'My pleasure,' Amelia said, picking up a loose piece of floorboard and running at him.

Taken by surprise, Ross didn't move out of the way in time and although he ducked, Amelia managed to smash the wood off his shoulder and back. Ross stumbled slightly but grabbed hold of the end of the floorboard and jabbed it into Amelia's stomach, sending her flying back, towards the stairs. Ross slowly stood up, blocking her escape.

The only way was up.

She turned and ran up the stairs, going two at a time, using her hands to propel herself forward when her leg muscles screamed in protest. She knew running upstairs was the downfall of any heroine in a horror movie but there was nowhere else for her to go.

She realised she was crying as she ran; she was no medical expert but Amelia had watched enough episodes of *Casualty* to know a gunshot wound to the abdomen wasn't good. On the first-floor landing Amelia hesitated for a split second before bolting down the corridor towards Sally's room. She quickly glanced down over the balcony and saw Gideon motionless on the floor, a large pool of blood spreading out from under him. With a sob she barged into Sally's room, and ran to the fireplace and the secret entrance.

She pulled at the secret lever but it didn't budge. She tried it again. It was stuck. Then she looked down and could see there was a clear plastic seal around it and she could smell adhesive. It had been glued closed. Most likely an overzealous workman had noticed it was a bit loose and had sealed it closed.

'I'm coming to find you... ready or not!' Ross called out in a sing-songy voice. It sounded like he was at the top of the stairs, clearly not thinking he had to hurry. Amelia didn't have much time. She looked around for anything that could be used as a weapon but apart from some lip gloss, scented candles and a vented hairbrush there was nothing that could be used in self-defence.

Unless...

On the mantlepiece, next to a large cluster of candles was a disposable lighter. Amelia snatched it up, then ran into the bathroom to search the shelf. Thankful that Sally had never adhered to the more environmentally friendly pump dispenser, Amelia grabbed a large aerosol can of extra-hold hairspray before racing back through to the bedroom. At the door she paused for a second to catch her breath and calm down slightly as her hands were shaking so much she'd never be able to ignite the lighter.

She could hear Ross getting nearer as he called out to her.

'One... two...' Amelia whispered to herself, hoping to time it right. As she mentally got to 'three' she ran out through Sally's doorway, screaming like a banshee. As she hoped, Ross was taken aback for a second, and that second was all Amelia needed as she flicked down the lighter, pointed the hairspray at him, then sprayed the flame.

With a soft 'woomph' a stream of fire lit up the air. Amelia almost immediately dropped the lighter from the sudden burst of heat. But that second was all she'd needed as the ball of flame caught Ross in the chest, setting alight his clothes.

He screamed, arms windmilling around him as he staggered backwards, trying to put out the flame. Amelia watched as he backed into the balcony, but instead of stopping he momentarily looked surprised before toppling over the top.

There was a brief moment of silence before a colossal thud and the sound of splintering wood.

Amelia stood, paralysed, unable to look over the bannister at the floor below.

Suddenly there was a commotion at the front door and Amelia heard Toby and Jack shouting out to her. Dazed, she walked to the top of the stairs just as Ray, along with a dozen other police officers ran in. Jack looked up and saw her and came bounding up the stairs.

'She's okay, Toby! She's up here!' he shouted out as he reached her and engulfed Amelia in a hug.

'It's okay, you're going to be okay,' he whispered into her hair, holding her tightly as Amelia buried her face in the scratchy wool of his jumper which smelt of fresh air, woodsmoke and comfort.

She could feel Jack's heart racing, or maybe it was her own, she wasn't sure. Downstairs, people were shouting and she could hear the static crackle of police radios.

'Gideon!' she said, breaking away from Jack. 'I need to see Gideon!'

Amelia ran back down the stairs, with Jack close behind her. She hesitated for a brief moment at the police officers clustered round the smouldering mass at the bottom of the stairs, but she shouldered past them to get to Gideon. Toby was lying beside him, cradling his head.

'Is he...?' Amelia said, starting to cry.

One of Gideon's eyes fluttered open. 'Still here, poppet,' he said faintly with the ghost of a smile.

'He stopped the bullet meant for me,' Amelia said, bending over and stroking Gideon's hair. His forehead felt cold and sweaty. 'Thank you for saving me. Please hold on, the ambulance will be here any minute, just please hold on,' she begged, unable to hold back the tears.

'It is a far, far better thing that I do now for mankind than... um... oh bugger, what's the Dickens' line? Oh well, you'll have to excuse the ad-libbing, but you... get... the gist,' Gideon said. 'Maybe... maybe...' he grimaced in pain, '...I could get a part in one of his televised books. The Beeb always do something over Christmas, don't they?'

Just then, the paramedics ran over and Amelia, Jack and Toby had to stand back to let them get to Gideon.

'Whoa, come here,' Jack said to Amelia, pulling her towards him, just as she felt her legs start to shake uncontrollably.

'He can't die, he can't...'

'They're going to do their best to make sure that doesn't happen.'

Amelia watched as another team of paramedics came running in and over to Ross. 'Is he dead?'

'Doesn't look like it.'

'How did you know to come here?' Amelia asked Jack as she rested her head on his chest.

'Sally kicked up such a fuss in the ambulance. At first, they were going to give her a sedative but she demanded to speak to the police then and there and they had to pull over at the side of the road, just a few miles from here. She'd recognised Ross as being the one who'd tied them up. She'd not been as drugged as he thought and played possum so she could get a look at her abductor. I'd been following the ambulance and stopped when they pulled in to make sure everything was okay. She was shouting at me from the ambulance to come back here and find you because you were in danger. But then I couldn't get hold of Toby or the Whistling Haggis as it was engaged.'

'Wee Davey's got a girlfriend and spends hours on the pub landline to not run up huge mobile costs. Big Davey's furious with him,' Toby said, trying to smile as he cast an anxious look back to Gideon and the paramedics who were now attaching him to all sorts of wires and machines.

'I called the police and got to the Whistling Haggis but found out you'd gone, so Toby and I raced round here and arrived at the same time as the police.'

Ray came over to them. 'The paramedics will need to have a look at you,' he said gently to Amelia.

'I'm fine,' Amelia said, trying hard not to show how much she was shaking and that her head had started to throb again.

'Honey, you've got a bit of bruising,' Jack said, concern clouding his eyes.

Amelia touched her face and could feel her mouth was swollen.

'And we'll need your statement, love,' Ray added. 'We can do it tomorrow if you'd rather.'

The paramedics wheeled Gideon past them.

'Go with them,' she said to Toby.

'No, I'll stay with you, make sure you're okay.'

'I'm fine, Jack's here, so I'm not on my own. Go! Let us know what's going on?'

'Of course.' Toby gave her a hug, then bolted after the paramedics.

Someone shouted, 'There's another one in here!'

Jack looked at her curiously.

'Jonathan, although he's probably just needing to sleep it off.'

Still standing, leaning against Jack with his arms wrapped around her, Amelia watched as the paramedics also carted Ross out the door.

'Quite fitting that he fell in the same way Archibald did over a hundred years before him,' Amelia said, 'although he's completely ruined the bannister. That was part of the listed building we weren't meant to touch. I hope we can repair it.' She looked at the beautiful, intricately carved bannister which was now smashed where Ross had crashed down onto it. The carved wooden pineapple which had sat on top of the pillar had been completely knocked off.

Amelia looked round the floor for it.

'We can clear up later,' Jack said.

'I know, but I just want to find it in case it's... oh, there it is!'

Amelia saw it near the back wall, it had obviously rolled away after being knocked off under the impact of Ross landing on it. Amelia went to pick it up, feeling slightly woozy as she bent down.

'Wow, this is heavy!' she said, picking it up. 'Oh no, it's ruined,' she said, running her finger down the massive crack that ran along the length of it, suddenly feeling inexplicably tearful over the wooden carving.

'Come on, I think you're probably a little in shock.'

'Yes, I think I might need to sit dow–' Amelia stopped as she turned the wood over in her hand, noticing a sliver of something glinting through the crack. She lifted it up and bashed it against the wall.

'Well, it's even more ruined now,' Jack said.

'I need a knife!' Amelia said, taking it through to the kitchen. Grabbing one of Toby's new chef's knives, Amelia wedged the point into the crack and levered it open. With a loud crack a large splinter of wood flew off.

Nestled beneath was a very large, very red and very priceless ruby.

'It's the Amor Rubra,' Amelia said. 'And the irony is, Ross was the one to find it,' she added, sinking down into a chair.

42

'Can I get a few words to the camera?'

'Now?' Amelia asked, peering at Beniamino from behind the large potted fern she was hurrying through to place in the vestibule.

'Yes, so we can get a notion of the excitement and nerves of the moment.'

'And the sheer panic because we're hideously behind and the guests are heading up the driveway as we speak?'

'Yup, that sounds about right.' Mike chuckled from behind the camera.

'Don't worry! You're camera-ready, darling,' Sally said, swooping in and taking the plant from Amelia.

'Okay,' Amelia acquiesced, smoothing down the front of her deep-plum, raw-silk, fifties-inspired evening dress. Despite swearing she'd never let a documentary crew back into Stone Manor, Amelia had found herself agreeing to a follow-up documentary, focusing on the first few weeks of trading as a luxury boutique hotel and wedding venue. It had been hard to say no after the runaway success of the first series of *Stone*

Manor. Ratings had gone through the roof, with viewers tuning in each week to revel in the high drama, especially knowing the real-life events that had overtaken the filming. Glencarlach Village had never been busier, with tourists flocking to see the location of the documentary and taking the guided walks up to the folly and Hangman's Gorge. But it wasn't just the mystery and the ghoulish macabre events that attracted the high viewing figures; the nation had become hooked on the growing love stories which the film footage had caught. Archie, especially, had a huge fan base on the back of his brief and passionate, but ultimately doomed, love affair with Dorothea. Although it was fair to say his long-suffering and slightly formidable wife wasn't as enamoured with history being dragged back up again. But whatever the reason, the network and fans of *Stone Manor* couldn't get enough.

Toby appeared over Amelia's shoulder, looking very dapper in his tuxedo. Amelia was delighted his ridiculous peroxide mohawk was gone, never to return, and his dark-brown hair had been smoothed over in a smart fifties James Dean style. Toby made a funny face for the camera before heading back into the kitchen. Amelia watched him go. Her brother looked very relaxed and was smiling at everyone but Amelia wondered if he was putting on a brave face.

'How's Toby coping?' Beniamino asked.

'Well, I think he's okay, but tonight is going to be hard for him... although he still hasn't really opened up to me about how he feels,' Amelia added with another worried glance back towards the kitchen where Toby stood supervising the trays of canapés.

'Amelia!' Sally squealed from the front door, indicating the first of the guests were arriving, all in black tie for the charity bash.

A reporter from the *Wester Ross Chronicle* came over to Amelia.

'Are you going to say a few words?'

Amelia started to shake her head but Toby came up behind her and nudged her forward.

'Yes, she is!'

Feeling flutterings of nerves before addressing such a large group, Amelia walked up a couple of stairs as all the guests filed in. She looked at the spot where Ross had smashed into the floor dispassionately. The staircase had managed to survive, and had been repaired and restored, and to the naked eye appeared exactly as the original. Ross, too, had survived, despite the burns and the fall and was currently serving a very long sentence at Her Majesty's pleasure.

Amelia cleared her throat as the grand hall became silent. 'First of all, I'd like to thank you all for coming to tonight's event at Stone Manor. We've had an eventful year,' she paused as a few people laughed, 'but finally, after quite literally a lot of blood, sweat and tears, and streams of workers and interior designers and helpers and volunteers, Stone Manor is up and running.' People applauded and one or two cheered. 'And,' Amelia added, 'if any of you like what you see, feel free to make a reservation, for dinner or afternoon tea or a lovely little relaxing weekend break.

'But for tonight,' Amelia continued, 'we're holding a very special one-off, murder-mystery hunt. The sordid, scandalous story is penned by the very talented Jack Temple.' She grinned over at him as he stood, leaning against the wall, glass of champagne in hand, unshaven, with his hair, impervious to brush or comb, as messy as ever. Amelia could feel her chest tightening with the rush of emotion at how much she loved him as he grinned back and raised his glass to her.

'You forgot to say handsome!' he shouted out, with a wink.

'Your very talented and *handsome* stud of a boyfriend, Jack Temple.'

There was another cheer and a couple of whoops of agreement.

'So, ladies and gentlemen,' Amelia said as everyone calmed down, 'please take a glass and some tasty canapés and start to work out the clues from the backstory provided. There will be an assortment of actors along the way to help with the atmosphere and to add a little more intrigue and excitement to your evening. And remember, all the proceeds from tonight's event will be going to the local cancer charity, which I'm sure Dorothea Campbell-Delaney would have wished.'

There was a round of applause as the guests were handed out paper and pencils and the backstory for the murder-mystery evening.

As all the guests spilled back out the front door to follow the clue to the first location, Jack bounded over, sweeping Amelia off her feet in a spinning hug.

'Right, you can relax now and have a drink, the hard work is over! Everyone's in place.'

As if on cue, Toby came over and handed her a Singapore Sling cocktail.

'You okay?' she asked her brother.

He nodded. 'It won't be the same without Gideon, will it?' he said quietly, biting his lip.

Amelia shook her head. 'No, and I'll bloody well kill him if he doesn't turn up soon. Not only won't it be the same without him, it'll be ruined without him! He's got the integral part at the end! He knew he had to be here on time!'

'He must have been held up in the village. He swore he wouldn't be long.'

'That's no—'

'Darling! I'm so sorry!' Gideon gushed as he ran in through

from the kitchen. 'I got mobbed in the outdoors shop, another group of *Stone Manor* fans had just arrived.'

'I don't see why you had to leave it to the last minute,' Amelia said tetchily.

Gideon held up a pair of thermal gloves. 'If I'm having to hang around outside for my role I'm not bloody going to get hospitalised with hypothermia. I've spent enough of my time there! Anyway, my bit isn't until the end.'

Beniamino and Mike came back over as Toby handed Gideon an orange juice and kissed him.

'Not tempted to have champagne, Gideon?' Beniamino asked.

'It's funny, but when a bullet lodges itself just a few inches away from one's liver, one realises how much one likes having the major organ intact. I don't plan on fucking it up again any time soon,' Gideon said and raised a toast towards Mike, who was filming it all.

'I'll go check on the food,' Toby said.

Amelia pulled his arm back. 'Are you sure you're up for this? I know how difficult it must be to be in charge of all this catering tonight when you're being reminded of... well, of...'

'Oh dear God! Will you tell her the truth?' Gideon said in exasperation.

'What truth?' Amelia asked as Toby ducked his head in embarrassment and Gideon explained.

'You've been so anxious that Toby is distraught at not getting into his fancy foody cheffy school. Well, he did, but then he told them where to stuff it.'

'Why on earth did you do that?' Amelia said, frowning at her brother.

'Thanks, blabbermouth,' Toby said wryly.

Gideon downed his orange juice and blew them all a kiss.

'Right, my public awaits, so excuse me while I go and freeze my ass off.'

'Why didn't you tell me?' Amelia said, appalled that her brother had turned down the opportunity to attend one of the most prestigious chef programmes in the world. It was so bloody typical of him!

'Uh-oh, you're in trouble now!' Jack said with a grin.

'I knew you'd be annoyed,' Toby said calmly. 'I know it's a real honour to be accepted but, without blowing my own trumpet, I'm pretty good at what I do. I'm not saying I know everything because I obviously don't, but I kind of have everything I want right here for now and I'd much rather learn on the job.'

Amelia was slightly taken aback. 'You want to stay here? You mean in Scotland?'

'I mean at Stone Manor. I really like being the head chef.'

'Wow! You wanna work for this tyrant?' Jack joked as Amelia swiped at his arm, surprised and delighted at Toby's decision.

'I've got so many ideas for this place, I'd really love to continue here and aim for a Michelin star. Means you'll have to put up with me for a while longer.'

Amelia felt close to tears, very happy tears as she'd loved the time spent with her brother who seemed an entirely different person from the rudderless, lackadaisical dreamer who'd gone off round the world to find himself just a couple of years ago.

'I'd like to get a permanent base here too.' Toby laughed. 'Don't worry, I'm not going to intrude on your gatehouse love nest! Where would I sleep for a start?'

Toby was right. The gatehouse was cosy and perfect for Amelia and Jack but it was very compact. It was also in the ideal position as Amelia was still close to Stone Manor without having to live inside it.

'Gideon and I have been talking about a permanent base

here for months and we've put in an offer for our very own love nest in the village.'

Amelia hugged her brother. She adored having him close. And Gideon who, after so dramatically 'coming out' had been amazed to find he'd not lost out on any jobs but rather had a far greater variety of scripts sent his way now he wasn't interested in the stereotypical love interest role. He'd also stopped trying to make it in America and was happier doing home-grown projects and because he'd become far more choosy, he was able to spend a lot of time between film shoots with Toby in Glencarlach.

A group of guests ran past them, giggling, as they headed towards the billiard's room.

'Are they meant to be going that way?' Amelia asked Jack.

'Nope, they've clearly fallen for the red herring I put in place,' Jack said in delight.

Toby headed back into the kitchen whilst muttering about making sure his quails weren't burning and Jack took hold of Amelia's hand as they walked towards the front door.

'Hey, well done for tonight.'

'I couldn't have done it without you.'

'Yes you could, you can do anything you put your mind to. That's one of the many reasons I love you.'

He kissed her and Amelia felt her stomach dip with desire.

'Do you know something?' Amelia said as they broke apart. 'I think Dotty would have approved of this.'

'Without a doubt. Her house being used for murder-mystery evenings is perfect. We should make it a regular thing.'

'You wouldn't mind?'

'Nope, I'd love to, some light relief between novels.'

Amelia looked out to the front of the house where a fountain had been constructed, in bright colourful mosaic. At the top, shining brightly, sat a replica of the Amor Rubra. Obviously, a replica as the first thing Amelia had done on finding the original was to ship it back to Egypt where it was on permanent exhibition at the Cairo Museum.

Amelia had no idea if the stone had been cursed or not, but looking around at the hotel she'd helped create alongside those she loved dearly, in the village she was proud to call home, Amelia Adams felt a very lucky woman indeed.

THE END

ACKNOWLEDGEMENTS

I would like to thank a few key people who have helped with the journey of getting *The Murderous Affair at Stone Manor* into print. Betsy for believing in the book. Ian for his superb editing – I will always try and reference Doctor Who. Also, Tara for being so patient when I panic over my lack of tech know-how. And with everyone else at the amazing Bloodhound Books, the gang I'm so proud to be a part of.

To my husband, Pete. Thank you for your good-humoured patience and not minding me running ideas past you about people I assume you know because they're lodged in my imagination. Thank you for having faith in me and buying that bottle of champagne all those years ago to be drunk when I published my first novel. Let's get it chilling!

My gorgeous girls, Thalia, Adeline and Oriana – for adding your own stamp of crazy and unique insight to every day. Never change. But tidying your rooms a bit more would be nice.

To all the other writers I've met along the way, from the creative writing evening classes all those years ago, and Elizabeth for being a total inspiration. And to the Novel Writing

Group where many an enjoyable evening was spent critiquing, talking and drinking red wine.

The cats and their uncanny knack of sitting on a crucial Post-it note. And Harlan, your golden-retriever devotion is humbling, however, I would also appreciate if you didn't roll in unmentionable smelly things before sitting adoringly at my feet whilst I write.

Katherine for being the first person I ever entrusted to read this – I wouldn't want to be standing in a forest at midnight in Iceland with anyone other than you.

And to Lindsey, for being my best friend.

A NOTE FROM THE PUBLISHER

Thank you for reading this book. If you enjoyed it please do consider leaving a review on Amazon to help others find it too.

We hate typos. All of our books have been rigorously edited and proofread, but sometimes mistakes do slip through. If you have spotted a typo, please do let us know and we can get it amended within hours.

info@bloodhoundbooks.com